The
TAVERN
on
MAPLE STREET

Also by Sharon Owens

The Tea House on Mulberry Street
The Ballroom on Magnolia Street

The

TAVERN

on

MAPLE STREET

SHARON OWENS

**Doubleday Large Print
Home Library Edition**

G. P. PUTNAM'S SONS
New York

This Large Print Edition, prepared especially for Double-day Large Print Home Library, contains the complete, unabridged text of the original Publisher's Edition.

ⅢP

G. P. PUTNAM'S SONS
Publishers Since 1838
Published by the Penguin Group
Penguin Group (USA) Inc., 375 Hudson Street, New York, New York 10014, USA • Penguin Group (Canada), 90 Eglinton Avenue East, Suite 700, Toronto, Ontario M4P 2Y3, Canada (a division of Pearson Penguin Canada Inc.) • Penguin Books Ltd, 80 Strand, London WC2R 0RL, England • Penguin Ireland, 25 St Stephen's Green, Dublin 2, Ireland (a division of Penguin Books Ltd) • Penguin Group (Australia), 250 Camberwell Road, Camberwell, Victoria 3124, Australia (a division of Pearson Australia Group Pty Ltd) • Penguin Books India Pvt Ltd, 11 Community Centre, Panchsheel Park, New Delhi–110 017, India • Penguin Group (NZ), Cnr Airborne and Rosedale Roads, Albany, Auckland 1310, New Zealand (a division of Pearson New Zealand Ltd) • Penguin Books (South Africa) (Pty) Ltd, 24 Sturdee Avenue, Rosebank, Johannesburg 2196, South Africa

Penguin Books Ltd, Registered Offices:
80 Strand, London WC2R 0RL, England

ISBN 0-7394-6467-1

Printed in the United States of America

ACKNOWLEDGMENTS

Many thanks to everyone at Poolbeg, especially Paula Campbell and Gaye Shortland; and to all the team at Penguin, including Aimee Taub, Clare Forster, and Clare Ledingham. To my agents, Ros Edwards and Helenka Fuglewicz, and all the lovely people in the media around the world who have supported me, a major thank-you.

To my husband, Dermot, and daughter, Alice, who are always there for me, thank you. I love you both. And to the readers who bought my first two books and sent me such kind letters, thank you. I hope you enjoy this story.

For Dermot

The
TAVERN
on
MAPLE STREET

1

THE TAVERN

THE ORIGINAL NAME of the tavern on Maple Street had been lost to memory for many years. It was simply called Beaumont's Tavern. The owners were Jack Beaumont and his hauntingly beautiful wife, Lily, and they had lived there happily for nearly twenty years.

The tavern was situated right in the heart of the city of Belfast, down at the end of a narrow, cobbled alley off Royal Avenue. This particular alley was closed to traffic because it was a dead end and there was not enough room to turn even a small car around. The buildings on either side were four stories high, and all the windows were caked in speckled black and gray dust. But that didn't matter, because they were only the sides of big department stores anyway. Nothing much for the shoppers to see except the backs of clothes rails within and rows of large metal bins without.

There were no trees of any kind on Maple Street. It was far too dark and shadowy for anything but weeds to have a chance of growing. Few people ever paused to wonder why a street could be named after a maple tree when there were none at all in evidence. And if they did wonder, they declared it a mystery.

The tavern was a small bar by city center standards. It was long and rectangular in shape, with a row of eight mahogany booths down the right-hand side, the bar counter all along the left, and a cluster of small round tables and chairs in the middle. The low ceilings and broad wooden beams overhead suggested that the bar had been built at least two centuries earlier. And it was true: a weather-beaten carving above the door said 1804, but the founder's name was now im-

possible to decipher. The thick stone v
and heavy brocade curtains on the ....
amber-colored windows, kept out the noise
of the traffic on Royal Avenue. Rush hour
would come and go without a single car horn
being heard inside the tavern's smoky
depths.

There was a solid grandfather clock with a
cracked yellow face standing just inside the
entrance, by the coatracks. It hadn't worked
for years and that was the way people liked
it. Time literally stood still in Beaumont's.
There was no sense of urgency there. It was
a quiet place, untouched by the modern
world.

It was popular with students, and retired
gentlemen with time on their hands. This
was due mainly to the bar prices, which
were the lowest in the city. And also because
Jack and Lily didn't mind if some customers
sat on the ladder-back chairs all day long,
idling over a couple of pints of stout.

Lily Beaumont poured a glass of golden
brandy and a cup of fresh orange juice over
the small mountain of dried fruit in the
saucepan. She set the cast-iron pan gently
on top of the old Victorian stove. Within minutes, the little kitchen was filled with the

heady aroma of boiling alcohol. She dropped a sticky handful of chopped figs and dates into the mixture and gave it a thoughtful stir with a wooden spoon, which was worn down to a flat edge after many years of faithful service. She smiled a gentle smile and sighed happily. Only six weeks to go until Christmas. The countdown to the big day had finally arrived. There was a sense of mystery in the dark afternoons and the chilly air, a hint of Santa Claus and wonderful surprises to come. And she remembered that long-ago Christmas when her husband had inherited the tavern, just when their circumstances were looking so bleak.

Jack had been out of work then, and feeling very shaken after his close shave with the explosion. Lily had dropped out of college and was so poor she couldn't even afford a new winter coat. They were desperate to rent a little place of their own so they could live together as a real couple. The passion between them had ignited like a forest fire, despite its plain beginnings. They'd met in the lunchtime queue for cut-price groceries at a market stall on Royal Avenue in the summer of 1984, and by teatime they were kissing passionately on a wrought-iron bench beside the Lagan River. She thought she would die of frustration if they didn't sleep together, but they both still lived at home with their parents and there was never a moment when either house was empty of younger brothers and sisters, and neighbors calling in for a cup of tea and a gossip.

When they had known each other for six weeks, Lily knew that Jack was the man she wanted to marry. Her cheeks were red and flushed with all their romancing in the open air. She missed so many classes to be with Jack (she told him her classes had been cut) that she was suspended from her college course, and never went back to finish her degree. Her parents stopped speaking to her for months, over all the fuss and up-heaval of dropping out. She could still re-member her father's final words on the subject and what he had called Jack.

"The government gave free schooling to your generation. And what did you do with it, madam? You threw it back in their faces, to mess about with a jobless waster. What's wrong with him anyway? He's too quiet by half. There's no chat in him at all. I'm ashamed of you both, and that's the truth."

It was a cruel thing to say when every

other young man in the city was also out of work in those days. The big factories were all closing down. It was the era of Thatcherism, and profit before community. She had never forgiven her father for his lack of generosity toward Jack. It wasn't Jack's fault she had left college, and he had tried hard to convince her to go back, but Lily said she was going to look for work instead, and that painting and drawing full-time was a luxury she couldn't afford anymore. She got a few shifts cleaning in a nursing home for the terminally ill, but soon left that place to work in a shirt factory. Jack got a temporary stint as a garbageman. Both jobs made them miserable. They rented a basement room together with damp running down the walls, and a family of rats in the garden. It wasn't the most romantic of places to set up home. And it certainly wasn't a suitable setting for Lily and Jack to begin exploring each other's bodies. They decided to wait a little bit longer, and they slept side by side on the lumpy bed each night, wearing warm cardigans over their pajamas.

And then, all their prayers were answered at once when kindly bachelor Ernest Pottinger went peacefully to his eternal reward, and left his beloved pub to his favorite sister's eldest grandson, Jack. There was terrific jealousy on all sides when the will was read out two days after the funeral by the family solicitor, but Jack moved into the pub right away and took Lily with him. They declined to answer the door to well-wishers hoping for a night of free drinks, and they refused to hand out jobs to all their unemployed cousins and acquaintances. It was hard, but they knew they would go bankrupt if they ran the pub in a sentimental way. There simply wasn't enough trade to support an entourage, and the frostiness between Lily and Jack and their many relations only deepened.

When they suddenly ran away to Scotland to get married without a grand wedding reception, the final nail was hammered into the coffin. The family members on both sides said what else would you expect from a gray-haired garbageman and a college dropout? And they never spoke to Lily and Jack again.

But Lily and Jack didn't care. They were so in love that the rest of the world had ceased to exist for them. They saw each other in brilliant color, and everyone else in black-and-white. When they finally made love for the first time, on the huge brass bed that came with the tavern, Lily was glad they had waited. They were perfect together. As a lover, Jack was nothing like his usual quiet and reserved self. Lily was amazed by her new husband's passion in the bedroom. He was tender, strong, erotic, gentle, romantic, generous. He was everything that lonely or unhappy women everywhere dream about. He kept his arms around her afterward, and slept with his nose buried in the back of her neck, smelling her perfume and breathing warm air onto her bare shoulders.

Of course, since she was a sensitive woman, Lily's happiness was tinged with fear that something might happen to split them up. Secretly, Jack felt the same way. And so the tavern became like a refuge for them, where they could hide themselves away from Belfast and the world. They decided not to hire staff or try to increase trade in any way. As soon as they became successful, the paramilitaries would come looking for a share of it, they decided. So they kept a low profile, and life went on.

The young couple spent Christmas Eve of that first year cleaning and polishing their new home, and celebrating their good fortune, and decorating a small Christmas tree in the sitting room. Lily made some paper angels out of silver card and gold paper, and Jack found a Christmas star in the attic. With their first week's profits, Jack bought Lily a beautiful wool coat, and she still wore it when the weather was freezing. Winter was a lucky time of the year for Lily and Jack.

Lily moved the pan of steaming fruit to the draining board to infuse for a few minutes, and dropped a soft stick of unsalted butter into a large ceramic mixing bowl. The dark brown sugar and sieved plain flour were all ready in their little glass bowls, as was the tiny measure of Christmas spice and the four large eggs. It was great fun, setting all the ingredients out like this beforehand, she thought. She could almost pretend she was cooking on a television program. The noisy hand whisk made short work of the mixing and then she stirred in the brandy-soaked fruit. All too soon, it was time to spoon the glossy weight of the cake ingredients into a greased and lined baking tin. She made a wish as she opened the door of the oven with a thick towel and slid the heavy tin onto the hot shelf. The smell of melting butter was delicious. She could hardly wait until Christmas Eve to ice the cake, when she was going to try out a new design of peaked white icing and oven-dried oranges. She even had a length of orange organza ribbon, ready for tying around the edge.

The Christmas cake was a central part of the holiday festivities for the Beaumonts. Jack and Lily always walked hand in hand to Midnight Mass and lit a candle for Ernest, before sleeping late on Christmas morning. When they awoke, they would drink two huge mugs of tea with a generous slice of cake each for breakfast. After that, they would exchange gifts, and watch old movies on the VCR, snuggled under the blankets until the turkey was ready. *It's a Wonderful Life* with James Stewart, for starters. Halfway through *Miracle on 34th Street,* Lily would nip out of bed to place a dish of vegetables into the oven to roast. If there was time they might watch a modern film, too. Something funny like *Trapped in Paradise.* Or they would make love, slowly and peacefully, luxuriating in the stillness and peacefulness of the day. Then and only then would they ease themselves out of bed and get dressed. It was usually after five in the evening by the time they sat at the little pine table in the warm kitchen for their festive feast. It was Lily's favorite moment of the entire year. They would drink sparkling white wine, and take photographs of each other and dance around the apartment to the Christmas edition of Top of the Pops.

"I wish that Jack and I can stay in our cosy little home forever," Lily whispered softly as she took a last look at the uncooked cake. Then she closed the door with its familiar echoing rattle and began to tidy up.

Downstairs, behind the bar, Jack had heard the whirr of the whisk, and he felt a warm glow of pleasure. When Lily was baking her cakes, all seemed well with the world. Lily worked as a freelance illustrator occasionally, designing whimsical Christmas cards on the kitchen table with her big box of pastel chalks. And then posting the artwork off to Germany to be printed and sold by an avant-garde design company there. The pay was good enough for all the time it took her, but the best thing about running the tavern was that the two of them could be together all the time. Lily served in the bar alongside her husband, helping with the sandwiches and the lunchtime pints, and chatting to the regulars. The couple had not been blessed with children, and they had few very close friends, but they didn't mind about any of that. In fact, they preferred it that way. They lived for each other. Not a single day had gone by in their twenty-year marriage where Jack and Lily hadn't said *I love you* to each other. And they'd meant it sincerely, every time.

Jack was only thirty-nine but his hair had been pure gray since the age of nineteen, when it lost its rich black color overnight. Nobody knew why this had happened. Some people said it was because he was standing up against a drystone wall in December 1984, when a huge bomb exploded on the other side, and the shock made all the color in his crowning glory fade away.

He'd been waiting for a bus and the blast made him fall into the road but he wasn't even scratched. He was partially deaf for a month afterward but apart from that, he was fine. Stress counseling hadn't been invented in those days, and the police told him how lucky he was, and to take himself straight home and forget all about it. Lily almost died of shock herself when she heard the bomb go off, because she knew her beloved Jack was in the affected area. She came running into the town to find him, and in the middle of the dust and panic, they vowed to let nothing come between them ever again. That was the moment when Jack decided to ask Lily to marry him, even though they had only been dating for six months, and they were both very young.

Not many women can boast they received a proposal of marriage beside a bomb crater, and Lily said yes straightaway. But anyway, Jack's hair was gray from that day onward, and in a city where nicknames were commonplace, it was inevitable that he would go by the title of Badger Beaumont. Of course, Lily never called him Badger, but everyone else did. It would be a good name for a pub landlord, they said, and by a strange twist of fate, Jack inherited the tavern a couple of weeks later.

Nowadays Jack kept his head shaved to disguise a receding hairline so the nickname was barely relevant, but it persisted among the city center neighborhoods and among the licensing trade in general. Despite his gray hair Jack was considered a handsome man. He was tall and well built, with serious-looking eyes so dark brown, and skin so naturally tanned, he could easily pass for an Italian. He had wide Slavic cheekbones and long black eyelashes. He had a neat square chin, and he wore denim shirts and faded blue jeans seven days a week. His eyes were usually half-closed against the smoke from the fire and the smoke from the cigarettes and pipes of the drinkers, and this made him look older than his actual age. But still he was very good-looking. He wasn't a larger-than-life or even an interesting character, the sort of jovial landlord who could tell outrageous jokes and outlandish stories, or sing cheery songs at Christmastime. He was the original quiet man. He kept himself to himself, as the locals put it. And that was the exact reason why Lily loved him so much. She found his introverted nature very erotic and mysterious. He never raised his voice to her, and she knew things about him that nobody else knew. And because he was devoted to her, she didn't have to share him with a wide circle of friends and acquaintances.

Jack looked at his watch. It was ten o'clock, and time to light the fire. Every morning, Jack would sweep out the ashes from the huge brick fireplace at the back of the room, and lay some bright-white fire lighters and small dry sticks in the grate. Then he would ignite the kindling with a long match and watch the flames take hold, carefully adding several clods of dark brown turf from an old wicker basket. The turf he bought weekly from a businessman in the county of Fermanagh, by the name of Arnold Smith. The smell of the smoldering turf gave the tavern its soul, Jack often said. Without the bright red heart of the fire and its occasional crackles and sparks, the tavern would have been nothing more than a dark and dreary little cave filled with dusty old junk. But there was a wonderful warm atmosphere when the flames were dancing merrily against the soot-black bricks, making the horse-brasses sparkle on the walls. Lily's collection of multi-colored glass bottles glowed with a million pinpricks of light when the fire was lit. The tavern seemed to come alive then, and shimmer with the secrets of centuries.

Jack lit that fire every single day of his life, even when the summer sun was threatening to dry up the water reservoirs in the Silent Valley. Even when the bar was closed on Sunday evenings, they would sit by the hearth and talk about people and places they had known, and events in the past and things that might happen in the future. During the twenty years that he had been landlord there, Jack couldn't remember a time when the fireplace had been empty and cold.

Harry Frew, a rep from the brewery who looked uncannily like Henry VIII, once said that Jack and Lily should be making a fortune, sitting as they were in their own little gold mine. A public house of such a great age should be making them many thousands of pounds a year. They should market the tavern better. That was his advice. Attract busloads of wealthy foreign tourists, triple the bar prices and start serving gourmet food. The money some city-center bars were charging for a small rustic pottery dish full of shepherd's pie was nothing short of criminal. They should hire some pretty waitresses, and dress them in tight white blouses and short black skirts. That would get plenty of young men into the place and the young women would soon follow, in perpetual search of love and romance. He said that Jack should look into the history of the place and find out exactly who built it, and if there was anything interesting there that could be exploited. They could have a new sign made and showcase the tavern on the Internet. Maybe some producer would like to film folk groups playing in the corner beside the fire, for local television? For heaven's sake, some film director might offer a fortune to shoot movie scenes in it. Johnny Depp in a top hat! The possibilities were endless.

But Jack said he had no time for the Internet, folk music nights or anything else that might take away from the peaceful atmosphere that his loyal customers were used to. Other bars might be offering football matches on wide-screen television, live music at the weekends and all kinds of hot and cold snacks throughout the day. But his tavern was unique because he was offering nothing at all except silence. And in 2004, silence and stillness were precious commodities in the Western world. The brewery man shook his head sadly. Some people wouldn't know how to make money if their lives depended on it, he sighed. How could Belfast ever stand shoulder to shoulder with the great cities of Europe, with this kind of small-town attitude lingering on into the new millennium?

Many times Jack had been asked to name his price and sell the bar as a going concern but he only smiled and said the big decisions were up to Lily. And Lily wanted to stay where she was. The brewery man could understand that much, at least. If he had a wife like Lily, he would do what he was told, too. Lily was a very desirable woman. She had a small pale heart-shaped face and big velvety blue-green eyes, perfectly arched eyebrows and skin so smooth she didn't need to wear any makeup, even though she was thirty-eight. She had dark red lips, and long dark hair, which she wore in a shining plait down her back. She was intuitive and sensitive by nature, with a graceful walk and long, thin fingers. She was often asked if she exhibited her artwork, or if she made any money out of it. And was her degree in graphic design or fine art? Some people in Belfast had curiosity in their veins instead of blood.

"No, I don't exhibit very often," Lily would say casually, not wanting to reveal that she had missed her degree because of her all-consuming desire for Jack. Or that she had thrown away the chance of a good career to spend some wonderful afternoons walking with him along the River Lagan. She just liked to design Christmas cards, she would explain, if pressed.

Lily wore long flowing coats. And scarves made of unusual fabrics, decorated with intricate embroidery and feathery fringes. She had a lavender-colored felt hat with a big purple moonstone brooch on it. She carried a small tapestry bag with leather handles that must have been an antique, and her hands were heavy with cheap glass rings and silver-colored bracelets from India. She had an umbrella with a carved wooden handle in the shape of a horse's head, and she wore strong spicy perfume that could be detected in the air long after she had left the room. She looked like a lady in a Victorian painting, and Jack adored her. That was obvious to anyone. He watched her as she moved around the bar, saying hello to the customers, and setting out clean plates at the sandwich counter. More than once, Jack and Lily had been caught in a passionate embrace when they thought the bar was empty, with Jack's hands underneath Lily's blouse and with her ring-encrusted hands caressing his shaved head. They were very happy together.

They lived above the saloon in a high-ceilinged apartment that had once been an elegant dining room in the days when the tavern provided hot meals for its coach-traveling patrons. There was an ancient iron stove in the kitchen with a rail along the front for drying cloths, and Lily loved cooking on it. She often said it was the one thing she was most fond of, after Jack, of course. The stove burned turf and wood, and the smoky aroma of it was glorious on a winter's day. Sometimes they left the little door open and sat daydreaming beside the fiery furnace, but they couldn't do that very often because of the danger of sparks catching the woodwork.

Occasionally, Jack fretted that the Fermanagh bog where he bought his turf would come under some kind of protection order. God knows they must have burned hundreds of bags of peat in the tavern over the years. From time to time he asked his supplier about the bog's status. But Arnold Smith was always pretty touchy on the subject of legalities.

Some other countries were starting to look after their natural resources and it was only a matter of time before it would happen here in Ireland, too. The Troubles had kept all that kind of thing at bay. But nowadays hardly a week went by without a hue and cry about some aspect of the environment.

Governments seemed to care more about butterflies and orchids than they did about human beings. At any rate, he was confident that nothing would ever happen to affect the little haven he and Lily had created for themselves.

So Jack was completely stunned when a bunch of smartly dressed town planners came into the tavern at lunchtime that bleak day in November, and told him that a big developer from Dublin wanted to demolish the entire block and build a shopping mall on the site. The tavern was a beautiful building and it would be a shame to see it close, they all admitted that. But couldn't it be taken down, stone by stone, and moved somewhere else?

The spicy smell of Christmas cake had drawn them in, they said, and they were all weak with hunger. At that moment, Lily came down the stairs with a tray of sandwiches and immediately sensed that Jack was worried about something. There was a crease of concern in the middle of his forehead. She looked toward the new arrivals, and almost before she had time to formulate the thought in her mind, she knew they brought bad news.

"These gentlemen seem to think we are about to be flattened by the bulldozers," said Jack to his wife, and he attempted a chuckle of amusement. Such a concept was unthinkable to Jack, given that the tavern had survived intact for over two hundred years. The eager faces of the men were flushed with excitement, as they nodded a greeting to Lily, and the other drinkers sitting in the shadows. They rested their expensive briefcases on the bar counter and asked loudly for the lunch menu, hoping that roast turkey and ham with all the trimmings was top of the list. They were very disappointed indeed to discover that they could have cheddar cheese sandwiches, or bacon and tomato sandwiches, or nothing at all. They ordered shots of whiskey instead by way of consolation, then produced their trendy mobile phones and arranged to eat in a Thai restaurant on Botanic Avenue. They checked their text messages as they waited impatiently for Jack's reaction.

"Well? What do you make of that, now? Eh? What do you think?" they said.

"Nice one, lads," Jack stammered. "You had me going there. I admit, you had me going for a minute."

"It's as true as I'm standing here," said one of the men. "No joke. No, sir-ee."

"Yes, indeed. The whole city is being rejuvenated," said another. "The phoenix rising from the ashes, if you like. About time, too."

"Oh, yes. We've a lot of catching up to do and this is a prime retail location," said the first planner, downing the last of his whiskey and winking crookedly at Lily. Lily ignored him, and reached for a clean cloth and some wet glasses from the draining board. She didn't want to believe a word they said. All businessmen fancied themselves as comedians, she knew from her experience behind the bar. Given half a chance, they would tell her their awful jokes for hours on end, until her face was cramped with smiling. They were just having a bit of fun at Jack's expense, she decided.

But Jack had a sinking feeling in the pit of his stomach that told him what the men said was true. He recalled seeing a couple of engineers in luminous jackets, taking measurements in the street several months earlier.

"Perhaps there will be a new mall somewhere around here but not on this actual site?" he said quietly.

"Definitely, it's Maple Street." They were very sure about that.

"There must be some mistake, some misunderstanding? You see, this entire block is Victorian-Gothic," explained Jack in a husky voice. "It's part of our national heritage. And the tavern itself is a listed building. We've changed nothing here, ever."

"We're not jesting, Mr. Beaumont," they replied, with great enthusiasm. "We've seen the proposal with our own eyes. A big, glass mall with six floors of offices above it and fountains everywhere you look, and a basement carpark for eight hundred vehicles. Yes, indeed. Like something out of California."

The color drained from Jack's face.

"What's the name of this developer?" he managed to croak. Not that it mattered. If there were large sums of money on offer, would he and Lily be the only ones to refuse to sell? Would they be held responsible for the whole project being canceled if they did say no? What would happen when the other business owners on Maple Street found out that the Beaumonts had ruined their early-retirement prospects? And even if they did manage to stay where they were, would the developer go ahead and build some kind of mall anyway? Could these overbearing town planners really allow the genteel character of the area to be destroyed with a modern glass and steel monstrosity? With a sigh, he realized that they could.

"His name? Oh, that's a big secret, for the moment. Can't say who the guy is, I'm afraid. But all the small businesses hereabouts will be offered generous sums to relocate. I can tell you that much. If I were you, I'd bargain the price up by about twenty thousand quid and then give in gracefully. You'll make a fortune!"

Lily dropped the glass she was polishing, and it shattered on the stone floor. They all stopped talking and stared at her.

"The tavern is not for sale," she said slowly. "Not now. Not ever."

In bed that night she clung to Jack and wept bitterly over the proposed new plans. Even with the soft glow of the pink bedside lamps and a row of tea lights flickering in violet-colored glasses on the windowsill, the bedroom seemed cold and frightening. Jack dug out the red fairy lights from the blanket box in the hall and strung them over the headboard in an attempt to cheer his wife up a little bit. He even played a Tori Amos CD she loved (one he usually found too bleak to listen to), but it was no use. All the little things that Lily usually loved only made her more emotional tonight.

"The nerve of some people," she railed. "Greedy grasping fat cats. The whole world will be covered in concrete and chrome, soon. Maple Street is our home."

"I wonder what the other traders are doing? If we're the only ones to turn down a good offer we won't be very popular around here." Jack's heart was in his mouth. How would they cope with living in the real world? They'd been very cosy in their little tavern. Too cosy, perhaps? Their lives had been like a fairy tale for twenty years. The prince and the princess, living happily in their miniature sandstone castle. And now this property developer was coming like the wicked fairy, to take it all away from them.

"We'll refuse to talk to him. We'll ignore the letters when they come," Lily vowed, as she rested her head on Jack's firm chest. He traced a line across her delicate shoulders with his right thumb. Lily's bare skin glowed in the flickering candlelight. He unraveled her hair from its tight braid and spread it out over her slender back.

"Let's just wait and see."

"I don't care what the other traders do. We'll brazen it out, Jack. We should sue that man for the distress he's caused us today."

"Lily, pet. We've got to be careful," said Jack. "Builders like this are very powerful. They have connections and contacts in high places. No doubt, the council will take his side. They love all the fuss and fanfare of a new project coming to the city."

"Yes, Jack. But despite all that, they can't force us to leave. Can they?"

"I honestly don't know, my love. I'll have to ask an expert. I wonder what sort of consultation fee would they charge someone in our situation?"

"But what will we do? Where will we go? They can't get away with this. It's not fair." She began to cry again.

"They've done it before, sweetheart. And even if we do manage to stay on, assuming the design of the mall can be altered in some way, the rates will be sky-high. Once the area is full of famous high-street names the rates will quadruple. Not to mention the upheaval while the building work is going on. We might have power cuts. There might be no running water. Constant disruption for months, definitely. I'll speak to a solicitor, of course, and find out what the other businesses are doing. But I'm afraid we must prepare ourselves for the worst."

"Oh, to hell with the lot of them," Lily sobbed. "Why can't they just go away and build their stupid mall somewhere else? Why do these development people always want to build everything in the same place? Squeezing in more and more shops, and ruining the place with traffic? There are lots of sites all over Belfast, with nothing at all on them but weeds and litter. But they just want to tear down our dear little home and build some ugly great brute of a thing instead. And fill it full of boring clothes shops. Oh, I hate them."

"Hush, my darling," said Jack gently. "As long as we have each other, we'll be all right. Isn't that true? Isn't that the main thing? Remember when we had nothing, in the early days? Not enough money to buy a warm coat for you? At least this time we'll have a bit of cash to start again."

"Yes, you're right," she agreed. "That's true. But you know we haven't much hope of finding new jobs. No qualifications to speak of. And I don't want to be stuck in some noisy factory all day long. Or behind a shop counter. I'm not just being snobbish about it. It's not that. I'll miss you so much, Jack. And as for the way house prices are going through the roof. Pardon the pun. We haven't a prayer of getting anything nice, close to the city center."

"Does it have to be close to town?"

"Yes. Jack, honestly. You know we don't drive."

"That's true," he said quietly. "But we can learn to drive. We'll survive. Maybe we can afford to buy some old cottage on the out- skirts and fix it up? And work in a bar or restaurant close by?"

"Maybe." She dried her eyes with a tissue. "I suppose that's what we'll have to do? Trundling along on two bicycles to work in someone else's bar. That will be you and I, this time next year. I never thought I'd see the day when I'd be leaving Maple Street."

"That's my girl," he soothed. "We'll be fine. Something will turn up."

"Make love to me," Lily said then, with a trace of tragedy in her voice. Whenever something unfortunate happened, her first instinct was to be close to her husband. As if by making love she could avoid the worst of the bad luck. And because he could never resist her, even in the middle of a crisis like this, he began to kiss her perfect shoulders and she sighed with happiness and closed her eyes. Waiting for him to make everything better. The brass bedstead glimmered dully in the dimly lit room as he slipped off her pajamas. Jack wondered if they would be able to dismantle the bed and take it to their new home. He just couldn't bear to leave it behind. So many happy memories of loving nights spent there with Lily.

And that wasn't all: the kitchen stove, the antique furniture. The beautiful china plates, and the gleaming pewter cutlery. All gifted to them by the late, great Ernest Pottinger. What would become of them and all their lovely things? Oh God, he pleaded to the ceiling beams high above them, as Lily wrapped herself around him under the handstitched eiderdown. What on earth are we going to do?

2

THE DRINKERS

 RETIRED PAINTERS AND DECORATORS Bernard Cunningham (Barney), Joseph Fontaine (Joey) and Francis Maclean (Francy Mac) sat in their usual booth in Beaumont's Tavern and pondered the information that had destroyed their peace of mind the previous day. The news was all over the morning papers and on four local radio stations. A big developer man from Dublin was offering to demolish the entire block and build a multimillion-pound office complex with retail units on the ground floor, and parking underneath. It was true. Vincent Halloran was his

name. It was rumored he was so wealthy he had a Rolls-Royce and even his own helicopter. The town planners had been only one day ahead of the media with their big news story.

Already the leading lights of the Belfast Heritage Committee were up in arms. They gave a series of interviews to reporters while standing on Maple Street with their collars turned up against the biting winter winds. The carvings on the department-store fronts were hand-done, they said. It was outrageous to even think of demolishing the historic buildings. And the traffic congestion would be a nightmare. And what about the ancient cobbles on Maple Street? There were only half a dozen such streets left in the entire country. The whole idea was sheer madness.

As expected, the council members responded by calmly (and rather smugly) saying that the city would benefit hugely from the proposed new investment. There was hardly anything else they could say, having recently voted to close down three loss-making leisure centers in the poorer districts of Belfast. Yes, there were buildings of historical value on the site, but some of the architectural details could be salvaged and used elsewhere. And the new project would bring jobs to Belfast. Low-paid jobs in the retail sector. Fair enough. But gainful employment, nonetheless. And lots of white-collar potential, too, in the offices above.

And Vincent Halloran was no fly-by-night, either, they said. He had already built modern penthouse apartments beside the river in Belfast, and two suspension bridges, and a world-beating conference hall. He was a genius, they declared on the radio. He could get past any red tape, any planning restrictions. Any objections by the heritage people. He could lay a six-lane motorway right through the middle of Washington and build a tollbooth in the Oval Office, if he took the notion. That's what one woman said when she was interviewed on Downtown Radio by gravel-voiced presenter Eddie West.

"This guy builds over everything in his path," she warned. "Graveyards, battle sites, primary schools, everything."

Barney, Joey and Francy Mac didn't like the sound of that. They listened to the radio show as they waited for their first pint of the day.

"Multimillion this, and multimillion that," complained Barney, as he took a tin of loose tobacco out of his jacket pocket and laid his tweed cap on the bench beside him. "What would they do if the phrase 'multimillion' had never been invented? Tell me that."

"They'd have to call it a wild price of a building," said Joey, after a minute's thought. "That's what they used to say in my day. A wild price."

"A cruel expense?" suggested Francy Mac. "My mother, God rest her soul, used to say that new shoes were a cruel expense. There were thirteen of us so she said those words constantly. It was like a prayer to her." And they all laughed at the thought of those upper-class BBC TV announcers in their pink jackets and designer hand-painted ties, saying that anything was a wild price or a cruel expense. They thought, too, of Francy Mac's twelve brothers and sisters, all dead and buried now. The earthly struggle for new shoes merely a distant memory.

"If you ask me, it will come to nothing," said Barney. "By the time this Halloran fellow counts the cost of buying out the current owners, and a few court battles with the objectors and another mint to the architects, he won't have enough left for the building materials." Barney filled his pipe with slightly

trembling fingers and lit it, then reverently replaced the cap on his head. It was a kind of
ritual with Barney, to light the pipe with his
cap off. "I mean, what will they be selling in
this so-called mall? T-shirts and televisions,
no doubt?"

"Let me get this round," said Joey, as Jack
carried three pint glasses of black stout over
to their table. "Put your money away, boys."
And they all laughed again because it was
Joey's round anyway.

"Is it really true?" Francy Mac asked Jack,
setting the drinks down on the worn table-
top. "Will you sell the pub, do you think?"

"I've had no official offer as yet," Jack said
sadly. "But I heard this morning that seven of
the other independent traders are willing to
go. They can barely compete with the big
chain stores as it is. So it doesn't look good
for Lily and me."

"I'll be very sorry indeed to see Beaumont's closing down," said Joey, with a sigh
that went all the way down to his shiny
leather boots. "I'm heartily fond of the old
place all right."

They were all very fond of the tavern.
Long-term widowers in their eighties, it was
a second home for them. They got to sit be-

side the fire all day for the price of a few drinks. Sometimes they would talk for hours and sometimes they would just sit quietly together, watching the smoke from Barney's pipe drift up to the rafters. Their favorite booth, the first one on the right-hand side of the fireplace, was practically reserved for them, as Jack kept it blocked off with the basket of turf until they arrived each lunchtime. It would be hard to find another peaceful pub like Beaumont's. One that hadn't been destroyed by the relentless beeping of gaming machines and loud music and snooker tables.

"We're not giving up without a struggle," said Jack. "That's what Lily maintains," he added. "I'm not convinced there's any real hope, but she's determined to go down fighting."

"Ho, ho," cried Barney. "Good for her. Don't make it too easy for them, Jack."

"Lily is right," said Francy Mac. "They call it progress but they're very misguided. I mean, where will all this progress get us? Someday we'll be living in glass cubes and eating nothing but vitamin tablets and communicating by telepathy. Is that progress?" They all laughed again because they knew he was

exaggerating but there was a kind of sadness in their laughter. It was even harder to
accept change when you were an old man,
thought Jack.

"Any news with you boys?" he asked, anxious to change the subject.

"Not a bit. Not a bit of news," Barney said,
and lifted his ice-cold glass to his lips. The
other two reached for their glasses also.

"No news is good news," said Joey wisely.

"Cheers," added Francy Mac.

Later that afternoon, Liam Bradley came
into the bar and chose a small table beside
the fire, near to the booth where the old men
always sat. Liam was a writer, and Mr.
Bradley was his preferred title, but people in
the international publishing trade called him
Limo Bradley, on account of his expensive
tastes. It was a standing joke among the
booksellers of Ireland. Liam Bradley always
arranged for a stretch limousine to take him
to his book signings, even if they were being
held in out-of-town shopping centers or in
small villages in the countryside. He wore
dark glasses all the time and gave the im-
pression that he was a man familiar with
danger. He dropped heavy hints about being
able to handle lethal weapons, and kickbox

to a level where he was obliged by law to inform any possible opponents of his deadly skills. Lightly built, he wore tailor-made charcoal-colored suits. And there were suspicions his jet-black hair was dyed.

He'd had a book published four years before. A crime caper. Full of smart answers and stupid women. The usual thing: a maverick detective, divorced from his overeducated wife. (Merely a device to prove he wasn't gay.) The hero in Liam's novel was called Slinger Magee. (Slinger was short for gunslinger.) Slinger's favorite saying was "I didn't get where I am today by warming my backside on a radiator." Liam had overheard a real policeman saying that once in a smart hotel in Coleraine. This fictitious hothead detective was somehow able to crash three cars, burn down an entire street and shoot five criminals dead, without losing his job. Not to mention his effortless seduction of a very attractive forensic scientist called Claudia. They had a roll in the heather on top of Cave Hill one stormy night, when they were supposed to be searching for a missing murder weapon. Slinger was drunk on vodka and Coke, and Claudia had a tattoo of a love heart on her left breast. Ridiculous non-

sense, the critics said. But the male members of the reading public lapped it up. It was
the kind of life most men dreamed of living
as they sat in five-mile-long traffic jams on
their way to the office.

Twenty-seven countries stocked Liam's
novel on their bookshelves. The cover design featured a matte smoking gun on a
glossy black background, surrounded by flu-
orescent blue fingerprints. There was a
photo of Liam on the back, looking cool and
disheveled in a vintage leather jacket.
There'd been an extensive publicity tour in
2000, lasting three months. Liam's ego rock-
eted into outer space on that publicity tour
and never came back down. He went a bit
crazy: drinking too much and getting into arguments with other writers and even journalists. But that was okay, his agent Perry
Shaw, of Shaw Stories Literary Agency, London, assured him. All writers were a bit odd,
Perry said. They were unpredictable and
temperamental creatures. It was proof that
Liam was a born writer and not just in it for
the money. Which was very wrong of Perry,
because that's exactly what Liam was in the
writing game for. Money, and plenty of it.

Not long after one particularly drunken

book launch in Paris (where Liam was
thrown out of the bookshop by two irate fem-
inists and then punched in the face by one of
them), a national TV channel in the UK
asked him to adapt his book into a six-part
miniseries. Liam's photograph was still
posted on billboards and train stations
everywhere. And Perry had been kept very
busy ever since. During the last four years,
Liam's novel, *Bang, Bang,* had been published several times in several different languages. There were thousands of black
Bang, Bang jackets and baseball hats for
sale, in various student union shops around
the Western world. It was incredible how
much money Liam had made from it all.

So incredible, that Perry was now desperate for the second book. But Liam had
chronic writer's block. He hadn't written anything of worth since his first book went off to
the printers. He'd deluded himself that he
was biding his time and storing up all his
ideas in the subconscious. And that when he
was finally inspired he would rattle off a
best-seller that would shake the international publishing world to its foundations.
The *Bang, Bang* royalty checks came
through his letter box so regularly that he ex-

pected they always would. Now, however, the gut-wrenching realization was dawning on Liam that he had nothing left to say, and that his first book had been nothing more than a lucky accident.

Perry warned him that interest was waning slightly among the publishers and that unless there was a sequel in the pipeline they were both in trouble. Liam didn't know whether Perry was telling the truth or trying to scare his number-one writer into doing a bit of work. But Liam simply couldn't dream up an original plot for his second book. He'd spent many sleepless nights drinking coffee from the fancy machine in his bespoke kitchen while making notes on loose-leaf pages, which he then balled up and threw in the bin. He'd pulled his own hair out over the sheer frustration of trying to come up with a story that hadn't been done before. But there was nothing fresh or exciting about his ideas. High-risk kidnapping and chaotic car chases had been done already. Complicated double-crossing drug rackets and dressing up as a woman to go undercover: nothing original there. Impossible explosions in fireworks factories where the hero escapes with two seconds to spare: that had been done, too. Ridiculous brawls

that went on for twenty minutes without anybody sustaining a serious injury: yawn. All
those things had been done to death.

Perry telephoned Liam at his home on
Marlborough Avenue every few weeks. He
had offers sitting on the table gathering dust,
Perry purred down the phone from London.
He had pots of cash on offer and no book to
sell. He had mountains of scripts in his
basement from decent-enough writers desperate for a publishing deal, but all the buy-
ers wanted was the follow-up to *Bang, Bang*
and hopefully enough material for another
miniseries.

"How hard can it be?" Perry soothed.
"Come on, Liam. Just throw some kind of
daft heist together for me. Yes? A beautiful
girl, wearing a shirt that's far too small for
her. A few of those big, massive explosions?
Slinger gets his leg over and all the bad guys
end up in handcuffs. Bob's your uncle. It's no
problem to you, Limo. I mean, Liam. Just
give me one hundred pages and we'll ex-
pand it together. I don't want to worry you but
we need to strike while the iron is hot."

But, hot iron or no hot iron, Liam couldn't
write fifty pages if his life depended on it.
The sheer pressure of all those blank

checks was stifling his creative power. And he needed more cash badly. He'd spent most of the money he'd already made on a luxury home on Marlborough Avenue, a black sports car with a soft top and a state-of-the-art hair transplant in a top-secret Los Angeles clinic. Liam dreaded the sound of the phone ringing now, afraid that it would be Perry calling to nag him into action.

And Betsy was sharp with him a lot recently, too. His wife had been restless, unhappy and irritable for several weeks. She'd been in a gin-and-shopping daze since his first book deal but Liam felt she might now be having a crisis of some kind.

They enjoyed an open marriage but didn't usually discuss their affairs or one-off encounters with each other. Liam loved the thrill of imagining his wife with other men. It made him feel dark and dangerous to think that he and Betsy were two damaged souls in a conflict-torn province. Or a couple of dirty beings, as one of their neighbors called them.

He was sure Betsy managed more conquests than he did because she had so much more free time but he didn't want actual confirmation of the numbers involved.

The situation had arisen slowly after many hints were dropped by Liam about spicing things up a little with consenting adults. She met her lovers in hotel bars and department stores, and he met his at book fairs and in back-street pubs. Betsy tolerated Liam's secretive personality and his various affectations because of the pots of money he made. And in the early days of their marriage he'd been very attracted to Betsy's plainness and bawdy sense of humor. But now she bored him a little bit. It wasn't exactly a fairy-tale marriage. He was beginning to wish he'd married someone sophisticated and softly spoken like Lily Beaumont. A woman who could keep him intrigued and interested. A woman who wouldn't show him up at literary dinner parties. He might not be faithful to Lily, either, if she was his wife. There were no guarantees on that score. But he would definitely try a little harder to behave himself when he was out and about.

They practically lived separate lives in their ultra-modern townhouse in South Belfast but Liam couldn't divorce Betsy because she had three brothers and they were all top lawyers. He'd met her in a shoe shop but she didn't work there anymore. Instead he gave her a generous allowance every month and she blew the lot on expensive beauty treatments and long liquid lunches in various hotels. She kept out of his way when he was trying to write, and never refused his lustful advances. That was why he didn't make more of an effort to ditch Betsy and find an upmarket replacement for her. They had breathless and desperate intercourse a couple of times a week. Casual encounters over the heavy glass desk in his study or in the shower room with hot water gushing out of several body jets. And she didn't need a lot of conversation, either. Liam didn't have to endure boring hours of pillow talking and dreams of a rosy retirement together. Just the way Liam (and Slinger) preferred it.

But Betsy was not her usual submissive self these days. Only yesterday he'd crept up behind her, slapped her smartly on the backside and suggested they try it standing up in the walk-in wardrobe. She was wearing a new skirt, in a shiny fabric that had suddenly, and surprisingly, turned him on. But she'd pushed him away and sulked all evening. It was the first time she had rejected him in ten years of marriage. They were both quite shocked by the incident.

"I've got other things on my mind," she informed him at bedtime, as they brushed their teeth at the twin sinks in the main bathroom. "You take me for granted, you know. And I draw the line at debasing myself in a closet full of dry-cleaning bags. Are you nuts, or what?"

"Sorry," said Liam. But he didn't mean it. "I don't know what I was thinking."

Betsy was not impressed by Liam's apology. She peered at his hair in the mirror above the bathroom counter. That shade did look very artificial, she thought sadly.

"Yes, well, never mind that now," she muttered. "Have you thought any more about my suggestion?"

Betsy was thinking of selling their lovely home, just off the Malone Road in Belfast, and moving to the chic neighborhood of Malahide in Dublin. There was a tennis club there she could join, she said. She wanted to make some new friends in similar high-income brackets. It was hard to find wealthy women of leisure in Belfast. And Liam could avoid the taxman into the bargain, she wisely pointed out. Writers living in the Republic of Ireland were spared the indignity of a good going-over by the Inland Revenue.

Land of Saints and Scholars, they said on the RTE news. And now that the Saints were in short supply, they had to look after the Scholars.

Betsy was bored with Belfast. There weren't enough glamorous parties or glittering fashion shows. Or upmarket nail and beauty parlors, either. Or private dentists offering American-style teeth whitening. And as for members-only restaurants! It was pathetic, really. Belfast was just too far behind Dublin for Betsy's liking. Betsy had taken to reading *VIP* celebrity magazine every week and drooling over the glossy pictures therein. Poor Betsy, who was reared in a tenement block on the Falls Road, thought she was the equal of the sons and daughters of the old-money elite of Dublin. Betsy Trotter that was: who swore nonstop, smoked forty cigarettes a day and drank milk straight from the carton, actually believed she would be welcomed with open arms by world-famous icons of music, theater and fashion. Liam didn't even take her to book signings anymore, ever since the time she'd disgraced him in front of a buyer for Waterstone's bookstores by claiming she'd never heard of W. B. Yeats.

They'd gone to bed without kissing each other goodnight, and this morning things were no better. Betsy boiled an egg for herself, and Liam had to fix his own breakfast. He decided to spend a few days sitting around in public houses, avoiding Betsy's faltering libido and listening out for examples of colorful use of language and comedy-Belfast phrases. He was always quick to borrow material from the man in the street. As he was leaving the house, the phone rang. It was dear old Perry. Still hopeful of the second book but letting Liam know that he was now having to consider manuscripts by other budding crime writers.

After Perry's phone call, Liam had been in a foul mood and he had nobody to take it out on except his wife. He'd told her that with an accent like hers, as rough as a vulture's arse, she wouldn't get in the back door of the Clarence Hotel or the Four Seasons or anywhere else on the A list. So she needn't be counting the days till Liam wrote another book and could afford the extortionate Dublin property prices.

He recalled the conversation now, as he waited for Jack Beaumont to take his order.

*   *   *

"WE'RE AS COMMON as muck, Betsy. As common as hell, we are. You'll just have to get used to it."

"That would be true if you were anything else but a writer," she said patiently. That was one good thing about Betsy: she could handle tough criticism.

"Author," he corrected. "I'm an author."

"Whatever. You know what I mean, Liam. When you're an author, a singer or a painter, being working class is an asset. Some might say it's an absolute necessity. How can you write about suffering if you've never suffered?"

"I'm mightily impressed, Betsy my little armchair philosopher. And whoever taught you how to use words like 'necessity'?"

"A real estate agent, if you must know."

"Richard Allen, was it? Still dallying with that lizard? Isn't he a bit old for you? What age is he, anyway? Fifty?" Betsy was an immature thirty-two and Liam was an even more immature forty.

"I have no idea what age he is," she snapped furiously. "And I am not dallying with him. I simply invite him to value my townhouse from time to time, that's all."

"What a quaint way to put it," he laughed

uproariously. Betsy had seen quite a lot of Richard Allen over the years but Liam wasn't jealous in the slightest. Betsy was entitled to amuse herself in the afternoons in whatever way she could. And it was cheaper than paying those eye-watering gym-membership fees.

"Anyway, it's true," she said. "There's nothing wrong with being working class. It's only stubbornness staying on here when we could be living in comfort beside the sea. It might even help our marriage, Limo." He flinched at the hated nickname. "I mean, Liam. It would be a fresh start for both of us? Just you and me, no complications, no third parties?" She adjusted her new breast implants and lit another cigarette with a disposable lighter from Portugal.

He reminded her that they could never leave Belfast because that was his USP, or unique selling point. Dublin was full of James Joyce wannabes. You couldn't throw a stone in Dublin without hitting an aspiring author on the forehead. But Liam Bradley was special because he was one of the few Ulstermen who hadn't deserted the old sod when he made it big. Betsy told her husband that he was impossible and that she would continue to buy *VIP* magazine, and check house prices in Malahide on the Internet.

LIAM DRIFTED BACK to the present, nodded hello to Jack and ordered a pint of lager and a cheese sandwich.

"Any chance of a bit of Roquefort, Jack?" he joked.

"You'll have Coleraine Cheddar and like it," replied Jack, with a twinkle in his eye. "I bet if we wrapped Coleraine Cheddar up in fancy paper and sold it to the French, they'd be over the moon. They'd be desperate for it."

"Worth a try," said Liam, laughing. "God loves a tryer."

Liam looked around the bar for Jack's delectable wife, Lily, but she wasn't on duty that morning. Pity. He liked to admire her in her long swirling skirts and dainty black button-boots. It was a pleasant distraction for Liam, trying to catch a tantalizing glimpse of Lily's slender ankles, or the suggestion of a lacy brassiere beneath her linen blouses. Such a change from Betsy's slashed denim mini-skirts and barely-there T-shirts. That was the main problem with Betsy: when sex was so clearly on offer, Liam didn't want it nearly as much as when it wasn't. And with her new white and pink highlights, and tattooed-on lip liner, his own wife reminded him of a stripper. Strippers were fine for one-night stands but Liam didn't want to be married to one.

Of course, he hadn't a snowball in hell's chance of a fleeting fling with Lily Beaumont. He knew that. Lily's passionate feelings for Jack were obvious even to a sham merchant and sexist fool like himself. But it was always nice to dream. Someday he'd be really famous and he wouldn't need to do any more PR ever again. He might even get a movie deal if Perry Shaw pulled his socks up. Forget the move to Dublin if that happened. He'd give up writing, drop Betsy like a hot potato and move to a little wooden house in the Bahamas. If only he could get an idea or even the beginnings of an idea, Liam knew he would overcome this dry spell and get back to work.

He listened to the conversation of the three old-timers in the first booth as he waited for his sandwich. They were discussing the tavern's possible closure and speaking with great nostalgia of their days in the painting trade, when they would call in for a glass of cold beer on the way home from work. And of how they used to go calling from house to house in the early days of their apprenticeships, with tins of gloss paint and brushes at the ready, offering to redo the skirting boards of the big houses in the Malone district. Hard days, hungry nights and begging for odd jobs from the gentry. No big story in this lot, thought Liam. But he kept his ears peeled anyway.

Then, his heart missed a beat as Lily came downstairs and he noticed that her eyes were red with crying. Her lavender hat was pulled well down around her ears and the purple moonstone brooch caught the light and shone darkly. She had her tapestry bag over one arm, and the unusual umbrella with the horse's head carved out of wood. But even though she looked very upset, she still paused to kiss her husband tenderly, as she always did before popping out to the shops. Liam wondered if Betsy, or any woman, would ever love him enough to kiss him like that. He doubted it. He leaned back in his chair and gazed into the heart of the fire. Lily's perfume drifted across to him as she went out.

She was probably upset about the proposed new mall, Liam decided. He hoped they would not move too far away from

Maple Street when it was all over. He
wouldn't like to lose touch with Lily.

He wished he had so much money he
could buy the entire block and give it to her
as a gift. Would she be grateful enough to
spend the night with him? he speculated.
What would he give to see Lily Beaumont
naked? Answer: millions. Or even to see her
with her hair out of that tight braid for once?
Stop lusting after the lady of the house and
come up with a plot, he scolded himself.
Think about all those royalty checks, he
thought. And then, don't think about them,
he decided. Do not think about them at all.
They put me under too much pressure. So!
Analysis time. What is wrong with current
drama?

Most of the serious crime dramas he had
watched on television in recent years were
set in dismal carparks or in dirty alleyways
full of rubbish. And usually there was some
poor, bedraggled streetwalker who met with
a very unpleasant fate indeed. Red stilettos
lying abandoned in the ditch during the
opening credits. Perverted, that's all it was.
Liam liked his titillation to be harmless, soft-
focus and fun.

Wouldn't it be a nice change if he set his

story in an old bar like this? he thought suddenly. He felt a fizzy rushing feeling start up
in his chest. Yes. Some ludicrous mystery set
in a nineteenth-century pub like this one?
Maybe some impulsive murder committed
on the premises two centuries ago? A sub-
sequent cover-up by the local community
because the victim was hated by all of
them? The terrible secret is handed down
through the generations. . . .

Then the bones turn up in the present day
when a gas company starts digging in the
yard, and Slinger Magee is called in. Slinger
starts asking questions, aggravating people
and throwing punches. He finds old letters
and documents in the cellar. He discovers a
list of possible suspects and several very
good motives. All of the main suspects are
long dead, of course, but maybe there's one
or two of their descendants still hobbling
around on the fringes? The emotional side
of things didn't really matter to Liam or to his
readers. It was all about the plot. Liam pulled
a small notebook out of his pocket and began to make notes.

He wrote:

"The setting: an ancient tavern. Down at
the end of a dark and deserted alleyway.

There is no rubbish on the ground. No hookers hanging around, either. None of the usual jazz-blues background stuff. A soft Irish jig is drifting out of the bar instead. Long shadows in the moonlight at closing time. Next day, bones are discovered when a gas company digs up the yard. Work is halted for a time. The street is cordoned off. Bones are shown gleaming white against the compacted mud. Would the bones have survived for two centuries? Never mind, they will in my novel!"

This is a very good start, he told himself.

"Slinger Magee is called in. Introduce the current owners of the tavern at this point: a happily married couple. They don't have much fun in the bedroom department, though. Slinger notices twin beds in the bedroom during his investigation. Why? Research medical problems. Slinger quickly identifies the long-dead victim from a distinctive piece of jewelry. A ring or belt buckle?"

I like it, Liam thought.

"Subplot: an embarrassing encounter with Claudia, the forensic scientist at the mortuary. Ice maiden turned stalker. She cuts some of Slinger's belt-keepers with a scalpel and his trousers fall down? He has to leg it out of the morgue in his Y-fronts. She wants to see him again but he has taken a fancy to the landlady of the tavern and can't be bothered with Claudia anymore. Claudia takes rejection badly and starts making nuisance calls to Slinger in the middle of the night. Contrast Claudia's pure white bob and white medical coat with landlady's colorful vintage clothes."

The tavern landlady would be the most beautiful woman in this story, totally surpassing the pretty scientist in the looks department. She would look exactly like Lily Beaumont. Liam took a long sip of his pint and kept writing.

"The beautiful woman character this time round is the landlady of the tavern. She is dark-haired, pale-skinned, wide-eyed and watchful. Wearing full-length skirts and tight lace blouses. A buttoned-up and repressed beauty, just ripe for Slinger's manly attentions."

There would be a theme night or a fancy-dress party in the second book, with this Lily look-alike in a very low-cut peasant blouse. Liam's hand was shaking with excitement. He could hardly get the words down on the page in a straight line.

"Research: peasant blouses and corsets 1850–1890 for the fancy-dress night."

Liam ordered another pint and almost frightened himself with how happy he was feeling. It was such an almighty buzz when he was creating.

There would be another murder not long after Slinger turned up. There was always another murder or two when Slinger was close to the truth. Possibly the second murder could be carried out with an antique pistol or sword displayed on the wall of the pub. Hooray!

"The second murder is committed to avenge the one that happened two centuries earlier. Research: period weapons. There is a battle for the ownership of the pub among the surviving relatives in the present day. Slinger establishes the rightful owner of the tavern in a lengthy and emotional court case. The current owners get to keep it and the beautiful landlady is very grateful to him. Very grateful indeed."

Bingo! Slinger would solve both murders and seduce the landlady. And crack many jokes about antique undergarments, all the way through the book. Things were looking up at last. He would make the novel very visual so that TV producers wouldn't have to try too hard to imagine it on the small screen. The actors who would play the parts in the miniseries could also play their own ancestors in the flashbacks. He would include a smattering of background information on the history of the time, as well. Just to impress the critics.

"Hunger, anger and death. A people obsessed with land ownership. Note, nothing has changed, except maybe the hunger."

"Wonderful stuff," he said out loud. The entire plot was almost resolved, and all in one morning. Who said hanging around in pubs was the road to nowhere? Liam was so pleased with himself he almost did a power-grab.

He had a setting, a story and a beautiful woman. All he needed now was the original crime circa 1804 and he was back in business. And that would be easy. Say, two rival brothers fighting over the newly built tavern because their father has died intestate? "Two brothers fight over the pub. Maybe they are twins but they don't know which one was born first so the rule of primogeniture does not apply? A spectacular punch-up ensues with many broken beer bottles and chairs.

One brother drowns the other in a barrel of ale in the cellar? He is desperate for a livelihood because his wife is pregnant and they are about to be made homeless. And then he buries his brother in the yard and tells everyone the dead man has emigrated. What he doesn't know is that the victim has already fathered a son with the local strumpet, and the strumpet has an intuition that her lover has been dispatched. And their child will grow up to bitterly resent his rich uncle. . . ."

Okay, the two brothers could have shared the tavern, Liam thought, but hey, this is literature. Yes! Crime-caper number two could begin to take shape. Liam could barely wait to get home and rip the dustcover off his computer.

He decided to do a little research on Beaumont's Tavern at the Public Records library on the way home to Marlborough Avenue. He might unearth something for his new novel. Some legal jargon of the time, at least. Holy smoke, Liam thought. He actually felt like doing some research. He must be a real writer, after all. He went to the Gents and checked that it was empty before punching the air several times with sheer happiness. He would phone Perry Shaw that evening and tell him that he was beginning the second book right away. A quick visit to the urinal and he was back in his seat. He ordered a third pint, drank it in one go and jotted down a brief description of the tavern in his notebook.

"Worn floorboards underfoot, exposed brick chimney (huge), turf fire (good for atmosphere), very low doorways (potential there for some interesting head injuries), many glass bottles on the windowsills (could be knocked over and smashed in a fight scene), flickering gas lamps on the walls (good possible source of explosion?)."

And then he came up with some sexy images, just for fun. Inspired by Lily Beaumont, naturally.

"Woman's heaving cleavage in flimsy costume, dotted with beads of perspiration, as she begs Slinger (with her eyes) to take her to bed. The woman's husband is obviously not able to satisfy her. Slinger tries to resist for about ten seconds! Then, our hero does what he does best, trousers round his ankles. Again! Landlady falls in love with Slinger but cannot leave her sick husband. They have another few romantic moments as the loose ends of the case are tied up. But soon, Slinger must take the pieces of his broken heart (and his burned-out car, courtesy of Claudia) and stagger on toward the next crime scene."

"Phew," Liam whispered to himself. "Christmas TV special, here we come!" A sudden surge of nervy adrenaline shot through him. He might even grant Betsy's wish to move house if the new book turned out well for him. It would be nice for Betsy to make some new friends in Malahide before he abandoned her forever for the bright sun and waving palm trees of the Bahamas. He would tell her this afternoon that he was prepared to think about relocating. If she would agree to move out of the master bedroom for a while and go and sleep in the guest bedroom on the second floor. Just for a few weeks to give him peace to write the new book. Those tattooed lips of Betsy's were a slightly disturbing sight, first thing in the morning.

3

THE BARMAIDS

JACK HELD THE LETTER in his hand. It was ten in the morning on Saturday the twentieth of November. He'd been setting the fire in the grate, when, with a small flutter, a single brown envelope landed on the doormat. Lily had just come into the bar with two cups of tea and a plate of buttered pancakes on a tray. She set the tray down on the counter and looked at Jack with fear in her eyes.

"This is it, Lily," he said simply. She nodded. He collected the letter gently and they sat down beside the fireplace. Jack opened the slim, buff envelope slowly as if that would somehow lessen the impact of its contents. The letter explained that an exciting new project was being planned for the area. It would greatly enhance the entire city center and also bring many much-needed jobs to the retail sector.

"What about our jobs?" asked Lily in a trembling voice. Her hands went up to her face.

"Now, don't cry, pet," said Jack quietly, scanning through the pages. "This is only the pitch, remember? It's not an eviction notice. It says that most of the new jobs will be highly paid professional positions. It's good news for the economy, the usual thing. Software companies, IT, banking."

"Well, big deal. It's far from software companies we were reared, as Francy Mac would say. What else?"

"Let's see. This bit cuts straight to the chase. It explains how we can accept or reject an offer from the developers. Here's the name and address of their solicitors."

"How much are they offering?" she asked.

"We have to arrange an appointment to find out, it seems. They'll only tell us the amount in person." Jack double-checked the pages for a quote but there wasn't one.

"How condescending! Well, they can stuff their appointment where the sun don't shine. I'm not taking a morning off work to go bowing and scraping to that shower of sharks."

"Lily, look. Here's the news we were hoping for. It says that because the bar is a listed building, we can block the demolition on the grounds of heritage preservation. But that, given the high level of commercial interest here, the council has given us special permission to sell. And they'll bring in experts from England to assess the tavern for possible relocation."

"What does that mean, Jack?"

"It means that we could stop the bulldozers. But if everybody else wants to take the money and run, we'll be branded spoilsports. It's emotional blackmail."

"The dirty rotten sneaks! I say we ask our neighbors what they're doing. Face-to-face. I want to hear it from them, personally. This Halloran guy may be bluffing us?"

"That's not all, Lily. The letter also says that only you and I are registered as working here. Just two people. They have plans for a

huge delicatessen and coffee bar, employ-
ing forty-five staff. We could end up being
portrayed as two selfish has-beens, just running a hobby bar."

"So, that's their angle? Not enough staff?
Right."

"I'll tell you what, we'll have to toughen up
to get through this, Lily, my love."

She watched him in silence as he lit the
fire. They sipped their tea in a halfhearted
way, imagining all the other traders on the
block lining up to collect their closure
checks.

"We've got about three months left, as
landlord and landlady," Jack said as he finished his breakfast. "It seems the tide is
against us. And if this thing goes ahead with
some altered design, the atmosphere of
Maple Street will be destroyed forever.
Would we be happy then, living in the
shadow of some Brave New World edifice?"

"Shush, Jack. I'm thinking," Lily whispered.

They didn't speak for nearly twenty minutes, each one contemplating where they
would be spending the following Christmas
and all the ones after that. Lily wondered if
their all-consuming passion for each other
would be eroded by the ceaseless demands

of living in the real world. Compared to thousands of other married couples, they hadn't had to face many tough challenges together. Jack was thinking he should learn to drive right away so he could at least run a taxi service or drive a bus maybe, or a lorry. Lily was remembering her few backbreaking weeks in the shirt factory, where she had to ask for permission to use the bathroom during working hours. But they didn't talk about it any further. Today was simply for digesting this awful news.

"What are you going to do now?" he asked, as Lily stood up and dusted the pancake crumbs off her skirt.

"I'm going to bake a cake. It always helps me to think clearly when I'm working in the kitchen. I thought a nice Madeira sponge?"

"That sounds lovely," he said gently. "You do that."

She went up to the little kitchen and collected a small mixing bowl from the shelf above the sink, and packets of self-rising flour and sugar, and some eggs and butter from the fridge. She usually came up with a solution to whatever problem was vexing her when she was pottering in her beloved kitchen, with its red gingham curtains and neat rows of glass storage jars. All she had to do, she told herself, was stay calm and keep her mind open to fresh ideas. Jack seemed to have given up already, which irritated her a little bit. But then, she told herself, that was why she loved him so desperately, because he was always calm and rational. No, she would not beseech her husband to do something radical when she hadn't a clue what he could do. She would think of some kind of survival plan on her own.

Jack straightened up the chairs in the bar and gave the windows a quick rub with a faded duster. He doubted that the demolition of an entire block of shops could be halted with one of Lily's sponge cakes but he loved his wife far too much to criticize her efforts. He would simply have to investigate if there was any property for sale that they could afford to buy with the money on offer. He might even be able to persuade Lily to go along to the solicitor with him so they would know what they might have to live on. Then, they'd look for bar or shop work in their new neighborhood. It was a grim enough plan but it was the best he could come up with. Maybe they could ask for jobs in this fancy new diner? Or would that be too painful for them?

Best to move right away and start again, he decided.

Upstairs, Lily traced a finger around the edge of the bowl and licked it thoughtfully. The cake mix was almost as lovely at this stage as when it was cooked. It was a comforting taste and it gave her a reassuring feeling. She wanted to run screaming into the street, crying and complaining about the injustice of everything. Typical woman that she was. But Lily knew she had to start thinking like a man. Practical solutions were required now, not just useless emotions.

"Staff, the letter mentioned. A distinct lack of," she told the red curtains, which were tied back with pretty woven ribbons. Well, she could certainly hire more staff. They could raise the profile of the tavern about the city. Attract lots more customers through the doors and ask them to sign a petition against the mall. They still had until the end of February to give their final answer. Maybe they could still convince the other store owners not to sell. At the very least, they should try to make as much money as possible before the keys were taken away from them. Thousands of pounds every week. That's what the brewery guy, Harry Frew, always said they could achieve if they put their minds to it.

Lily and Jack had never been the material types. As long as they made enough to pay the bills and keep going, they were happy. They had no staffing worries, and filling out the books for the accountant each year was a doss. But now everything had to change, and change immediately. They had no time at all to spare. Not one single minute should be wasted. She slammed the cake tin into the oven and went running down the stairs in her flour-covered apron.

"Jack, it's going to be all right! I'll tell you what we'll do. We'll hire more staff. We'll make pots of money! We'll have those folk nights that Harry suggested. And proper food, too. Hot comfort food that will draw in the crowds."

"Steady," he said softly, catching her around the waist and giving her a kiss. "You're only delaying the inevitable, my love. And you'll wear yourself out with the catering. Isn't that why we haven't bothered before?"

"I won't wear myself out, Jack. I'm going to hire some girls, first thing on Monday morning. They can help me."

"Girls? No barmen?"

"No. Girls will be much handier in the kitchen. And better-looking behind the bar. I know that's a sexist thing to say but we can't afford a chef."

"It won't work," Jack sighed. "There isn't enough time. And where are you going to get a bunch of good-looking girls from, in a hurry?"

"Look, my darling. Listen to me. We've kept a low profile for twenty years, and that's worked well for us. We've had time for each other and no real stress. Now, it's time to change tactics. We'll shout our name from the rooftops. We'll become a legend. You'll see."

Jack smiled. He loved to see Lily so animated and excited, but he feared she was not being realistic.

"I don't want you to get your hopes up too much, that's all."

"But we can't lose, Jack. We'll take some girls on, on casual pay conditions. I'll make a few pies in the stove each morning and we'll sell them by the slice, with a handful of salad leaves on the side. And soup, too. I can have a big pot of soup simmering on the top plate. Three pounds fifty a bowl we'll charge. We can rent the dishes from our supplier. Oh, please, Jack?"

"If it makes you happy, sweetheart, then go ahead. Just don't overdo it. Promise me?"

"I promise," she said. "Besides, you admitted yourself, we need all the money we can get with house prices the way they are. We'll need to buy outright, too. If we end up slaving for minimum wage, we'll never get a mortgage."

"That's true enough, sweetheart. You just tell me what you want me to do, and I'll do it."

"I love you," she said softly.

"I love you, too."

And then she dashed back up to the kitchen table to make a very long list of catering ingredients, addresses of good suppliers and various novel ways to make money. She almost forgot to keep an eye on the Madeira, she was so absorbed in her thoughts. And when she finally rushed to the stove and yanked open the door of the oven, the cake was slightly overdone.

Lily phoned the employment agency on Monday morning and told them to send over some potential bar personnel immediately. She would interview any males, she decided, just to play along with the current equality legislation. But she would only hire females. Pretty females, to be exact. However, she needn't have worried about breaking the law. There were no unemployed barmen in the city that day. The young clerk who answered the phone said he knew four terrific girls who would be perfect for the tavern. He would call them on their mobiles, and surely to goodness, Lily would have her staff by the end of the day. Their names were Daisy Hardcastle, Bridget O'Malley, Marie Smith and Trudy Valentine. That young man was extremely nice and courteous to me, I must say, thought Lily as she replaced the receiver. He couldn't have been more enthusiastic.

Within sixty minutes, there were four hopeful applicants standing on the doorstep. Daisy was over six feet tall with back-combed red hair. Bridget was tiny with platinum-blond ringlets. Trudy was kind of Spanish-looking although very heavily made up. And Marie, the last one to arrive, had a lovely smile and a head of tumbling brown curls. Lily thought they looked very suitable and nicely turned out, apart from Daisy's punk hairstyle. But that could be toned down easily enough. Lily thanked her lucky stars they were all extremely attractive. She would hire them certainly but she knew she still had to go through with the formalities. She informed the girls she would interview them, one at a time, in the end booth beside the grandfather clock. She would fetch them all a cup of tea first, she told them, and begin interviewing right away. They nodded nervously and sat down on stools at the bar to wait. If Jack was surprised that Lily had begun recruiting so soon, he didn't show it. He just went on polishing the bar counter and slicing lemons with a sharp knife.

The black-haired girl with the big brown eyes turned away from him when the tangy smell of the bright yellow lemons drifted across the serving space toward her. Jack thought she'd said her name was Trudy Valentine but he couldn't remember. The girl's eyebrows had been removed somehow and she had drawn on two high curves in their place. She looked permanently surprised, Jack thought. Trudy was also wearing very heavy makeup and her hair was an elaborate confection of clips, combs and colored extensions. She looked like a pop star, not a waitress, he thought. Jack sighed softly to himself. He didn't really want to have to work with other people behind the bar. He was feeling under pressure already and it wasn't even lunchtime yet.

Meanwhile, Lily had served the tea and was doing her best to conduct her first-ever interview.

"My name is Daisy Hardcastle," said the six-feet-tall girl with the fire-engine-red hair and the witch's-stripe tights. "But I always tell boys I'm called Daisy Chain. You'd be amazed how many of them call me that for months before they cotton on!"

"I can well believe it," said Lily, noting how Daisy's long legs seemed to go on forever. "You're very, um, striking-looking, Daisy."

"Thanks a lot. I use other names, too, sometimes. Rose Garden, Gaye Couple, Honey Comb and Penny Farthing to name but a few. I like to wind the lads up a little bit but don't worry, they enjoy it." They both laughed. Lily thought that Daisy was very amusing but she was anxious to get on with her plans.

"That's all very interesting, Daisy, but have you worked in a bar before?" asked Lily. "It's not as easy as you might think. Some customers can be difficult to handle when they're tanked up."

"Well, I'm only nineteen, you see, so I don't have a lot of work experience. I'm a full-time art student at the moment. Did I mention that? But I have worked in a bar. In Donegal last summer, it was. So I know my way round the optics and pumps. I'm not terrific with cocktails, mind you."

"We don't serve many of those, as it happens. But that's all about to change. You seem competent enough to me. There's just one thing, Daisy. Does your nose ring come out?"

"Oh, please, Mrs. B! That's one of my best features. Boys love it."

"Do they really?" asked Lily, wondering how she could ask Daisy not to call her Mrs. B in public.

"Yeah. It's a great conversation piece. They pretend they think it's outrageous, but really, they wish they had the courage to get one, too. I practically have my own fan club in the Art College. They call me Crazy Daisy, there."

"In that case, you have the job." Lily smiled at her new member of staff.

"Wow." Daisy was amazed. "Thanks."

"I like your positive attitude. We're trying to cheer the whole place up for Christmas and we need some staff with a sense of humor.

Just jot down your details, Daisy, and the hours you'll be available to work. And I'll be in touch." Lily smiled. "Send in the next girl on your way out, would you?"

"Sure thing, Mrs. B."

Daisy skipped out into the weak November sunshine, absolutely delighted with herself. She hurried down Royal Avenue toward the college, barely pausing to peer into the shop windows and only stopping once to buy some sherbet wands at the newsagent's on York Street. She'd enjoy telling her friends in the college that she had just managed to nab herself a flexible-hours job in a cosy little pub on Maple Street. She wasn't intending to work up much of a sweat in Beaumont's Tavern, however. The place is on its knees, by the looks of it, she thought happily. They had hardly any customers when I was there. It'll be a total breeze! Money for nothing, and no mistake!

The pub was full of antique stone jars and pretty glass bottles, too. And there were three tweedy old pensioners slouched in the corner. She'd get some terrific sketches in her notebook while she was sitting behind the bar. Not a bad achievement for the girl they all called Crazy Daisy.

Back at the tavern, the second interviewee, Bridget O'Malley, aged twenty-five, was busy telling Lily that she was a very experienced barmaid and that she had won several prizes in the hotel business in America for her Irish coffees. She'd spent a couple of years serving drinks in an Irish bar in Atlantic City and she'd learned a lot of very useful things during her time there. She could prepare any cocktail under the sun in record time and she could also pull the perfect pint. Lily was delighted to hear that.

She was also delighted that Bridget's hair was an angelic halo of natural white-blond ringlets and that her waist was barely eighteen inches in circumference. Bridget's feet were the smallest Lily had ever seen. She guessed they must be about a size two. Which wasn't surprising, really, because Bridget was barely five feet, two inches tall herself. She was wearing dainty silver high-heeled shoes and a neat white lacy dress and jacket. She looked like a Christmas angel who had lost her wings. Lily always did have a soft spot for images of angels and all things heavenly, and she was convinced that Bridget had been sent to her by a higher power. Lily wasn't proud of her observations.

It felt a trifle lecherous to be sizing up the candidates in this way but times were truly desperate. The tavern was like a little honey-pot in the center of the city and every honey-pot needed worker bees. Attractive barmaids would bring in the customers. That's what Harry Frew always maintained. And Lily planned to send all the barmaids safely home at night in a taxi so she wouldn't be worrying about them being pounced on by lovelorn customers.

Bridget told Lily that she had just left her current job in a posh hotel after a silly falling-out with her supervisor. At this point, Bridget bit her lip and looked as if she was fighting back tears.

"It's okay," said Lily. "Just tell me, basically, what happened."

"It was over the smallest little thing, Mrs. Beaumont. A mere misunderstanding, you know. This poor woman, my supervisor, she was a bit paranoid. I suppose it was the medication she was on for depression, or maybe she was starting to go soft in the head. But anyway, she accused me of making personal telephone calls from the office. The bill was sky-high but it wasn't my fault. I told her it was a ridiculous accusation and totally baseless.

There was barely time to draw breath in that hotel, never mind conduct a personal life."

"So, who made the calls? Did you ever find out?"

"Now, I don't like to tell tales but it was the owners' teenage daughter. Tara was her name."

"But surely the bill was itemized?"

"Yes, it was. Mostly to psychic chat lines, though. I couldn't prove it wasn't me and I didn't like to say anything about Tara. She's a lovely girl, is Tara. An only child, you see. I felt sorry for her. She was like a little sister to me. I couldn't get her in trouble with her parents. They were a right pair of bullies." Bridget looked devastated and Lily duly clucked her sympathy.

"That's okay, Bridget. These things happen. And besides, their loss is our gain," Lily finished brightly. "I hope you'll accept a full-time position here?"

"I'd be delighted to, Mrs. Beaumont. Thank you very much indeed."

"Excellent. So, let's talk money?"

"Money? Well, I'm looking for somewhere to live at the moment, as my boyfriend and I have just split up and we lived together in his apartment. So I'll need a fairly decent wage,

I'm afraid. Hopefully enough to rent a little bolt-hole of my own?"

Lily was jolted out of her happy mood for a moment when she heard that. She'd been hoping to get away with paying the girls the absolute minimum but she hadn't been thinking of them as real people with real lives. Poor Bridget was homeless and job-less, and loveless, and still she was cheerful and chatty. And wearing full makeup and high heels. What an inspiration she was to wronged women everywhere. Lily was full of admiration for her. Then Bridget dropped her accommodation bombshell.

"I don't suppose there's a room going here?" she asked hopefully. She rubbed her arms gently and shivered a little.

"No, I'm afraid there isn't," said Lily sadly, wishing with all her might that there was a cutesy comfy spare room she could offer the little waif. She had visions of herself buying a patchwork quilt in Henry's department store for Bridget, and a pair of velvet slippers to keep her fairy feet warm at night.

"How many bedrooms upstairs?" asked Bridget casually. "Just out of interest? It looks big enough to have several bedrooms."

"Just the one, I'm afraid. Up on the second floor. Which used to be the storeroom, in the old days. My husband and I live above the pub so we use it as a bedroom now. There's a very large sitting room on the first floor that used to be the dining room, but that's no use to you."

"Never mind. I'll get a bed-sit in the student quarter," Bridget said, with infinite sadness in her big blue eyes. She hated living in student digs. It was always impossible to dry laundry in the cold, damp rooms of period properties. But modern apartments in the professional district cost several hundred pounds a month to rent. Bridget looked at her watch as if considering other important appointments.

"So, Bridget," said Lily gently. "Full-time hours? Starting right away? Tomorrow, if that's okay?" She named a salary.

"That's great, Mrs. Beaumont," Bridget sighed softly. "I suppose it will keep body and soul together."

"Good. Now, there's just one more point we need to discuss. I'm planning to serve hot food and I thought you could help me? Can you cook?"

"I don't do food," said Bridget quickly, gathering up her coat and handbag. "I find some publicans take advantage where the catering is concerned."

If only you knew, thought Lily, with a sensation she identified as guilt welling up in her chest. She was planning a sixteen-hours-a-day regime for all of them.

"In my last place, you see, even before the phone-calls incident, I was rushed off my feet," explained Bridget quickly. "Frying chips, making fancy open sandwiches, pulling pints and clearing tables all at the same time. And we got no lunch break, either, if the part-timers didn't turn up. So, you'll understand if I don't want to get caught like that again." Besides, the steam from the fryer had played havoc with her ringlets.

"That's okay," said Lily, in an artificially light voice. She was slightly put out by Bridget's sudden personality change. But she didn't want to lose the chance of hiring a skilled barmaid. "It's agreed, then. There'll be no kitchen duty for you, Bridget. Please show in the next girl, and leave your details with me before you go."

"Will do." Bridget got up to leave. "Pity about the room. It's nice here. Cosy and warm."

"Can you not go back to your family for a

while until you find something more permanent? I'm sure they'd be thrilled to have you
home for Christmas." Bridget sat down again.

"Mum and me don't really get along, Mrs.
Beaumont, to be brutally frank. My mother
looks down on me, I'm afraid, because I'm
only a humble barmaid. And Daddy always
takes her side. That's the God's honest
truth." Bridget lowered her gaze to the floor,
suddenly consumed with shame and embarrassment.

"I see," said Lily, sympathetically. Her own
mother had almost driven them all insane
with her constant complaining when Lily lost
her precious place at the Art College. She
just hadn't understood that Lily was so
deeply in love, her education hadn't mattered to her anymore.

"Does your mother have a fabulous career, herself?" Lily couldn't help asking.

"Yes, she does," said Bridget, in an awe-
filled whisper. "She's a shop assistant in
Marks and Spencer's food hall. She's got her
very own monogrammed body-warmer." Lily
tried to turn her laughter into a cough. She
forgot all about Bridget's reluctance to get
her hands dirty in the kitchen.

"Do you know, I've just had a brain wave,"

said Lily. "How would you feel about renting a room here in the tavern? On the condition that you work all Friday and Saturday nights over the holiday period?"

"But you said there was no spare room."

"I'm going to convert the sitting room into a bedroom. I've just thought of it. You'll have a lovely big sofa and a brand-new TV set all to yourself. How does that sound?"

"Keep talking, Mrs. Beaumont. I think I've died and gone to heaven. All my stuff is in carrier bags in the boot of my car and it'll be ruined with damp if I don't get a place soon."

"Would seventy-five pounds a week rent be reasonable? Electricity included. Phone calls extra. Bathroom, you share with us. And of course, you'll have to do your own laundry."

"You're a saint, Mrs. Beaumont. An absolute saint. I'll take it."

"But you're welcome to share our meals and have as much coffee and toast as you like, naturally." Lily felt this would not be a dangerous offer to make. Bridget looked as if she ate less food than a sparrow.

"Agreed. Oh, this is sheer bliss." Bridget wiped a tear of happiness and relief from her eyes.

"Welcome, then, to our little ship." Lily was feeling very charitable. It was a terrific feeling to share your good fortune with other people. She wondered why they hadn't hired staff years before.

"When can I move in?"

"Right away, Bridget. You fetch your stuff and I'll send my husband out to buy a new bed."

"A brand-new bed for me? Oh, joy! Can this day get any better?"

Lily gave her new full-timer a spare key to the front door and shook her hand warmly. Bridget swept out of the tavern on a cloud of happiness.

"Let Gerry Madden take a run and jump now," she laughed, as she hurried past the metal bins on Maple Street. "Him and his perfect crew cut and his fancy BMW. And his moldy old mattress that he claims is a French antique. He'll be waiting for me to come crawling back to him tonight, begging him to let me into his so-called prestige apartment. And I'll be sitting pretty in Beaumont's in a brand-new bed." She rooted for the shiny key of Gerry's apartment in her handbag, kissed it goodbye and threw it up in the air. It turned over three times, flashing in the sunlight. When it came down again, it landed on a drain cover, wobbled for a moment and then plopped through the grille into the dark water beneath.

"It's a sign," she trilled. "A sign from above. It's a new beginning for me. A new job, a new home, a new bed! All I need now is a new man."

Back in the tavern, Jack was trying to take in what Lily was telling him. They were standing beside the grandfather clock, talking in whispers so the two remaining girls could not hear them. Jack was to go at once to the big furniture store at Sprucefield and purchase a single bed with a storage drawer underneath. Lily would buy some fashionable new sheets to go with it later on that evening.

"What on earth would I want to do that for?" he gasped. "We've got a bed already. A lovely big double bed."

"I'm renting out the sitting room to Bridget. I've given her a key already."

"What? Bridget who?"

Lily consulted her notes. "Bridget O'Malley."

"You didn't even remember her name,

Lily!" he exclaimed. "And you've given her a key to our home? What were you thinking of? She could have a criminal record."

"Will you keep your voice down? She's an experienced barmaid, Jack. She looks like an angel and she's so brave and she's been through hell recently. It's all arranged. The poor love was homeless and we're only a month away from Christmas Day. It would be cruel not to help her out."

"That's not our problem, Lily. She should go to the Housing Bureau Office if she needs a home. There's no point taking her in here when we could be moving out, ourselves."

"Jack, have you no compassion? It's only for a few weeks."

"She's a stranger, Lily. I don't want to share my home with a stranger for any length of time. This is all getting out of control." He sighed deeply and scratched his head.

"She's lovely, Jack. Just wait till you get to know her."

"I don't want to sound like a wet blanket, but we'd be far better off enjoying what might be our last few weeks here in peace and quiet. In fact, maybe we should close the tavern down altogether and just rest up for when we move?"

"Look, sweetheart, I've got it all worked out. If we beat the developers, we'll let the staff go and give Bridget notice to move out. Things will be just the same as they were before. If we lose, then at least we'll have made some extra money. Seventy-five a week rent, for maybe ten or twelve weeks? We can't lose."

"We know nothing whatsoever about this girl. If she's so wonderful, then why is she destitute? And where are we going to relax in the evenings?"

"We aren't going to relax, Jack. We're going to work our socks off. Right up to the bitter end."

"Oh, Lily."

"Now, off you go and get the bed. I've still got to interview Marie Smith and Trudy Valentine."

Jack reluctantly set off to hail a taxi outside the City Hall and felt as mean as Scrooge, as the cheerful driver leaped out of his vehicle and opened the door of the cab for him. All around the city Christmas decorations were going up and the crowds were increasing steadily every day, scouring the shops for gifts and bargains. And here he was, grumbling about helping some poor girl who had nobody in the world to look after her. But he couldn't help thinking that their lives were about to become a lot more complicated.

He'd thought it was too good to be true when four pretty girls appeared on the doorstep so promptly that day. Now, he knew it was because they were going to be trouble. The first one was a punk, for heaven's sake. With seven earrings in each ear, as well as the nose ring. And this Bridget was far too glamorous to be a hard worker, no matter what she claimed to have learned in America. And as for Marie and Trudy, it was only a matter of time before they discovered what was wrong with the pair of them. Probably on the run from the police, if Jack was any judge. He was halfway to Sprucefield before he realized he should have telephoned first to check if the bed could be delivered that day. He made a quick inquiry on his mobile and was told it would take at least three weeks. He bit his lip with frustration.

"I've changed my mind," he told the driver. "There's a small furniture store on the Lower Ormeau Road. That'll do me, instead."

"Righto," said the driver, and indicated that he was going to make a turn.

Twenty minutes later, Jack got out and tipped the driver. He felt like going straight home and telling Lily to forget about her ambitious plans to make a success of the pub. Jack wasn't sure he wanted to have a high public profile. Most of the men and women he knew who were successful had stomach ulcers and suffered from insomnia. He knew he should take charge of the situation and tell Lily they were going to concentrate their efforts on negotiating a good price for the business. But then, he felt a wave of loss for the tavern. He loved the pub as much as Lily did. It was like a child to them and it was their duty to take care of it. He loved lighting the fire in the mornings and watching the sun shining in through the glass bottles on the windowsills. And he liked being the owner, too. He was proud to see his name on the sign above the bar. It was a good feeling to know that he was a man of property, even if it was only a creaky, dusty, back-street pub with three retired decorators in near-permanent residence.

He'd go along with whatever Lily wanted, no matter how ridiculous it seemed. It was just for a little while, anyway. A few short weeks, he told himself. He could survive a few weeks' upheaval when the last twenty years of his life had been so peaceful and fulfilling. He went into the furniture shop. The bored young man sitting inside, beside a portable gas heater, was so pleased to get some business that he offered to load up the new bed into his van and give Jack a lift home with it, there and then.

That evening, Lily poured herself a cup of scalding hot tea and cut a slice off the over-done Madeira. Jack was downstairs in the bar, tending to the evening drinkers. Bridget was helping him and learning the layout of the bar. The new bed was stacked against the wall in the sitting room, still wrapped in its plastic sheet. In a few minutes, Lily would push the sofa and the coffee table closer to the window, and fit the bed in that shady cor-ner by the door. She'd dust the room and take all the framed photographs of Jack and her-self off the mantelpiece. She would miss dec-orating a freshly cut Christmas tree in the room this year, but she told herself that un-less her plans worked out, they wouldn't be dressing the tree there ever again. Lily hoped Bridget had been telling the truth about being good with cocktails because she had been on the phone to various colleges all afternoon, trying to secure a few student Christmas parties. She'd also arranged for some ladies from a community center on the Ormeau Road, and some more from a reading group in Bangor, to come to the tavern on Saturday for a Christmas card–making session. It was something she'd been meaning to do for ages but she hadn't been able to summon up enough courage. Now, the fear of becoming homeless was greater than the fear she would make a fool of herself.

After she finished her supper and prepared the room for Bridget, she took a big box of art materials down from the top of the wardrobe. She picked out some clean sheets of colored tissue paper, fresh white drawing paper and metallic card for the craft classes. She had a fancy biscuit tin full of pens and sharp scissors and her beloved wooden box of pastel chalks as well. She'd buy some glue sticks in the post office before the ladies arrived. She sat up until one o'clock in the morning, making a few sample cards to show the women. A fat snowman made of white tissue paper balls, a delicately drawn angel with gold-card wings, and a tall Santa with long thin legs. The cards looked very professional when they were standing in a row on the table. The women would have a great time, Lily decided. If any decided to turn up, that is. She prayed for at least ten pupils. Anything less would be slightly embarrassing. Yawning, she turned out the kitchen lights and trailed up to her attic bedroom. The door to Bridget's room was firmly closed. It was a bittersweet feeling for Lily. She had lost her beautiful sitting room for a while, but hopefully, the sacrifice would pay off.

Trudy and Marie were due to begin work behind the bar on Tuesday evening but Lily hadn't told Jack yet that Trudy seemed oversensitive to criticism, was allergic to lemons and had an acute button phobia. She was a student, in the final year of a geography degree, she'd said at the interview. And she'd be grateful for some part-time work. Lily thought Trudy seemed kind and polite and she did have excellent references. She was twenty-three with long black hair and wise, thoughtful eyes. And she was more than willing to help with the baking, too. These facts compensated for Trudy's overdone makeup, the multicolored hair extensions and the rather bizarre eyebrows. Or maybe I'm just out of touch with youth culture, Lily reminded herself. This must be the kind of thing the boys go for these days, she thought, as she frowned at her own clear skin and old-fashioned hairstyle in the bathroom mirror. On the other hand, Lily was rather pleased with herself for achieving her objective. She'd set out to hire four pretty girls and that is exactly what she had done.

Marie, the fourth new barmaid, was so quietly spoken that it was often hard to hear what she was saying. But that was her only apparent flaw. In all other aspects, she was perfect. Also twenty-three years old, she was a natural brown-haired blue-eyed beauty who never stopped smiling. She could even read sign language and speak French and Italian. And even though such talents were unlikely to be called for in the tavern, it was nice to know they were there. She had just completed her European languages course, she told Lily, and she needed a part-time job while she decided what to do with the rest of her life.

Lily was exhausted by the time she slipped into bed and molded herself along the back of Jack's lovely warm body. She fell asleep at once, imagining how she would greet her craft class on Saturday.

4

GERRY MADDEN AND THE MIDNIGHT OIL

 IT WAS THREE O'CLOCK in the morning. A light but persistent drizzle drifted down from the clouds above the city and washed all the smoke and soot in the air into narrow trails down the front of the buildings. Inside the tavern, Lily and Jack lay in a deep sleep with their arms wrapped around each other. In the corner of the bedroom were two large cardboard boxes. One containing some personal effects from the sitting room and the other full of paper, feathers, sequins and all kinds of lovely

things destined to become colorful greeting cards at the weekend.

Downstairs on the first floor, Bridget O'-Malley was sitting up in bed, wide awake and enjoying her luxurious surroundings. She could never sleep during her first night in a new place. She had to get used to the colors and textures of a room before she could relax properly. She thanked her lucky blue pebble (from a New Age shop in California) that the acting lessons in America hadn't been wasted. Nobody on earth was better than Bridget at appearing forlorn and dejected in front of an audience. And look at her now. Wasn't she on the pig's back? All her problems solved with one stroke. A little phone call from the unemployment office and she was saved from the gutter yet again.

She wasn't sure she liked the layout of the furniture in this room, though. She might change it on her next day off. Although she was only twenty-five, she'd moved house eighteen times since leaving her parents' two-bed terrace in the Markets district of the city. She could still remember the agony of having to share a room with three younger sisters who kept borrowing her clothes and makeup. However, this new setup was very different from the shabby room of her childhood. She lay back and studied her new bedroom. The walls and ceiling were painted a delicate dusty blue and there was a pretty, distressed-effect iron chandelier hanging from a beam in the ceiling. The carpet was a pale lilac shade and felt deliciously soft under her bare feet. The windows were dressed with purple crushed-silk drapes. Lily Beaumont had even made her own tiebacks by threading glass beads onto fine wire. There was a beautiful oil painting of an angel hanging above the fireplace that Lily said she had painted when she was nineteen years old. It was of great sentimental value, she'd said. She'd painted that picture to celebrate her marriage to Jack.

"See there," Lily had pointed out, when she was showing the room to Bridget earlier that afternoon. "The angel has two wedding rings in her hand."

Yes, the room was very satisfactory indeed. Bridget thought she would definitely enjoy living here. There were plans to demolish the tavern and build a mall on the site, but somehow Bridget wasn't worried about that. The final date for the decision was three months away. And three months was a very long time in the life of Bridget O'Malley.

The bed was only a single but she wasn't too worried. A double would have been nicer but it was early days as far as her love life was concerned. And maybe it wasn't the kind of house where she could entertain a young man overnight? Lily and Jack Beaumont might be a little uptight about things like that? Once Bridget was more settled she might find a new lover and ask Lily if he could stay over occasionally. In the meantime, it was all very comfortable. Lily Beaumont ran a spotless house. There was no doubt about that. There wasn't a speck of dust anywhere. Not even on top of the picture rails.

She thought of her own mother and father and sighed softly. Bridget hadn't been telling the truth about her mother working in an upmarket department store. Both her parents were fond of the drink and they hadn't worked in years. They rarely bothered with the housework, either. Bridget couldn't remember one time during her childhood when her mother had cleaned the house. Usually one of the neighbors did it as a favor to the children. And the real reason Bridget didn't get on with her parents was because she didn't ever drink alcohol and they felt she was looking down on them. Bridget's three sisters had left Ireland to work in London a few years before and didn't intend returning to the Emerald Isle. It was sad to see the family so scattered but then lots of Irish families had to bear the same cross for many different reasons. Bridget thought of her sisters now and missed them so much that she felt a stab of pain in her heart. If only they could be children together again. They would understand how important it was to savor every day they were together and not spend whole weeks fighting over borrowed clothes and broken lipsticks. She decided to send them each a nice Christmas card and sign it, "Lots of love from your big sister Bridget."

She took a deep breath and tried to think of happier things. Like the tavern on Maple Street. Lily's home was absolutely gorgeous. Bridget was very impressed by Lily's perfect decor. She'd never have had the good taste to decorate a home of her own like this. Every nook and cranny had something artistic in it. There was a pottery angel halfway up the stairs, an antique candlestick beside the telephone and a tasseled lamp with a heavy bronze base beside the armchair. And there were little fabric sachets of dried lavender hanging on every doorknob. Even the bathroom had a chunky block of olive-scented soap sitting on a frosted glass dish, and five tiny hearts made of twigs in a row on the windowsill. There was a pile of bright-white hand towels in a wicker basket, and a modern canvas hamper for the laundry. Bridget had to remind herself not to dump her own washing into it although she would have loved to. And as a final note of luxury, there was a big glass bottle of scent by Chanel sitting on a tiny shelf above the roll-top bath. Bridget sprayed some on her wrists every time she went to the bathroom. It was like living in a five-star hotel. Someday she hoped she'd have a lovely home like this. Maybe she'd meet a rich man in the tavern and he'd ask her to marry him and they'd live in a mansion in the best part of town. She'd remember these lovely things and try to recreate the same sense of faded grandeur in her own place.

In the meantime things were looking up. Bridget had four fat pillows to lie on and a

warm red woolen blanket on top of the duvet. She had a silver-colored TV set, which
she'd wheeled over to the end of the bed,
and a great slithering pile of Lily's glossy
magazines to pass the time. There was a
well-stocked fridge in the rustic kitchen and
she wouldn't even have to cook her own
meals. Bridget had a huge appetite, which
she kept satisfied with several snacks a day.
And Lily Beaumont had said she wouldn't
miss an occasional chicken leg or a nice
thick slice of Cheddar. Thinking about the
cheese made Bridget peckish now so she
listened out for any signs of life and, hearing
none, put on her robe and tiptoed to the
kitchen. As quietly as she could, she prepared a stack of sandwiches as thick as
doorsteps and a pot of tea to go with them.
She used up all the remaining bread but she
was sure Lily wouldn't mind. There was
bound to be an early-morning delivery from
the bakery.

She had a rummage in the kitchen cup-
boards and found a Madeira cake, so she
had a generous slice of that as well. Then,
she carried her early-morning feast back to
her room on a small tin tray and tucked herself up under the blankets. What sheer de-

light it was to munch her way through a small mountain of butter-laden carbohydrates, and flick through the stylish magazines, and dream of the day when she would be rich. When that day came, she'd have red toile wallpaper in the bedroom. She'd have a sunken bath, and chrome radiators in the bathroom. And a massive glass coffee table in the lounge with huge chocolate-scented candles on it that cost twenty pounds each and had three wicks.

She finished the last of the crumbs, slipped the plate under the bed and switched off the bedside lamp. It was just after four and Maple Street was as silent as the grave.

And that's when the phone began to ring in the hall, the shrill tone making Bridget jump and knock Lily's best china teapot off the rickety bedside table. The spout broke clean away as it crashed against the wall and the stewed contents splattered far and wide across the immaculate lilac carpet. Bridget swore and reached for the light switch. She swore again when she saw nearly half a pint of dark brown tea soaking into the soft pile. At first she ignored the telephone ringing and tried to dab off most of the tea stains with one of Lily's best towels. She hoped whoever it was would just hang up but the sound persisted. After a couple of minutes she heard Lily come out of her room on the top floor and yawn.

"Who on earth can be ringing at this hour of the night? I hope to God nobody's died, Jack. I'm too scared to answer it." And then the sound of Jack saying, "It'll be a wrong number, I'll get it. You go back to bed." Then Lily, reminding him to wear his robe, now that they had a lodger. Bridget held her breath as Jack came creaking down the stairs from the attic. She had a tiny hunch it might be Gerry Madden but she hadn't told him where she was living. Bridget dived under the red blanket, as there was a gentle knock on her door.

"Come in," she squeaked. But the door remained firmly closed.

"It's for you, Bridget," said Jack. "Someone called Dr. Gerry Madden, claiming to be your boyfriend."

"I'm very sorry, Mr. Beaumont. He's my ex-boyfriend. I can't think how he got this number. Please tell him I don't want to talk to him," replied Bridget in a shaky voice.

"I don't really want to get involved, if you don't mind," said Jack, his head leaning on the door with tiredness. Lily had said she wanted to attract lots of males to the tavern. Her wish was surely starting to come true tonight.

"Okay. I'm on my way," said Bridget. "Hang on!" She tugged on her threadbare robe and her old holiday espadrilles and hurried across the room, absolutely fuming with her ex-lover. Bridget gingerly stepped into the hall and caught sight of Jack's muscular calves disappearing back up the stairs toward his own bedroom. The handpiece of the telephone lay waiting on the half-moon hall table. She picked it up with her heart banging.

"Do you realize what time it is, Gerry Madden? How did you know I was living here?" she hissed.

"They told me at the employment office." He sounded very calm. Too calm, actually.

"I'll sue those hatchet-faced old goats," she said through gritted teeth. "They had no right to give out confidential information to a stranger. You're not even a relative."

"I'm a doctor, Bridget. People trust me."

"More fool them." She'd thought Gerry wouldn't find her for months. He never went to Beaumont's. He said it was far too quiet. It was an old man's pub, according to Gerry.

"Bridget, stop playing games with me and just come home. You know you won't last a week without me. Or my wallet."

"You cheeky brute. Have you forgotten why I left you in the first place? You're the limit, Gerry Madden. You roared at me in the middle of a party. In front of all the other guests."

"I did not roar at you, Bridget. You hit me on the arm with a solid-pine CD rack, for pity's sake. I only gave a playful shout in self-defense."

"Liar."

"Drama queen. My arm is still bruised. It's all purple and green blotches."

"I'm hanging up, Gerry. You cheated on me and we're finished. Most men have the decency to wait until after they're married before they start looking at other women."

"Bridget, it was nothing. It was an affectionate kiss on the cheek. She was an old flame."

"You were both a disgrace."

"We were both hammered, Bridget. I was being friendly, that's all. You were the one who went berserk and ruined a perfectly good party. Look, will you come home now? You've made your point."

"No way." Bridget was far too comfortable in Beaumont's Tavern, and who knew what might happen when she met the male customers. She would get to know the most promising ones and then take her pick. That was why Bridget was a barmaid, after all. It was the best way in the world to meet men.

"We should talk about this jealousy problem of yours, Bridget. Do you want me to come over there and collect you?" Gerry's voice was slightly slurred. Bridget knew he had been drinking, and also that he thought nothing of driving his very powerful car while under the influence of alcohol. She began to panic that Jack and Lily would label her a troublemaker and throw her out.

"Don't you dare make a show of me at my place of work. Do you hear me? I'll call the police, so I will. I'll have you arrested for drunk driving and harassment."

"I'm on my way, darling. Pack your bags." He hung up.

"Gerry? Gerry, are you there? Answer me. Good grief." She craned her neck to see up the narrow stairs. The door to Lily and

Jack's room was closed again and there was no sign of a light on. Bridget quickly dialed Gerry's number. After a minute, he picked up.

"Now, Gerry, listen to me. You're drunk out of your head. I want you to go to bed and sleep it off. We're finished and there's nothing more to be said. I can't trust you and that's the end of it. Can't you be a decent man and leave me alone?"

"Oh, Bridget. My lovely wee Bridget. With all those mad ringlets in her hair. I love you so much. Don't break my heart. I need you to make sense of this dreary world."

"Gerry. Shut up. You're only raving when you get like this."

"I'm going to sing you a song, Bridget. It's one of your favorite love songs of all time. How does it start again? Wait. I'm trying to remember the words."

"Gerry, there is nothing on earth you could do that would make me come back. I'm moving on and I suggest you do the same."

"There's a star in the sky and there's no reason why," he sang tunelessly, and fell heavily off the sofa onto the laminate floor. "Ouch! My sore bloody arm! *There's a star in the sky.*"

"Gerry, that's not even a real song. You're making it up as you go along."

"I know, and it gets better, I promise."

Four hours later, Bridget was still on the phone, begging Gerry not to throw himself off a cliff. In fact, she only said goodbye when she heard an alarm clock ringing in Lily and Jack's room. She fled across the hall and closed the door behind her with only seconds to spare before they came down for breakfast.

LILY WAS DISMAYED that Tuesday morning, when she discovered that Bridget had used the last of the milk the night before. Lily couldn't think clearly without her morning cuppa. She poured some black tea into a mug and sipped it cautiously. It tasted awfully bitter.

"It's only a cup of tea, remember that," she told herself, and then she opened the bread bin and found it was empty, too. "Someone's had a midnight feast, Jack," she sighed as he joined her in the kitchen. "I'm sure there was half a loaf here last night."

"Oh dear," he said, and then opened a packet of oat and raisin biscuits. "Will these do, instead?" They would simply have to remember to buy more groceries over the coming weeks, they decided. It wasn't Bridget's fault that she'd been hungry in the middle of the night. Still, the girl must have a bigger appetite than an elephant. There was a large block of cheese missing from the fridge and the cake was almost gone, too. Lily decided not to ask Bridget about Gerry's late-night phone call even though she was dying to know if they were getting back together.

Gerry rang again on Wednesday morning and on Thursday, Friday *and* Saturday. By then, Lily had to bite her lip to stop herself from screaming. What the hell does he want? She was desperate to know. What on earth do they talk about? Why does he always call at four? Is he a night-shift worker or just plain mad? But there wasn't really enough time to discuss matters of the heart. Daisy, Trudy and Marie were working hard and the tavern was much busier than before. Word was beginning to spread among the drinkers of Belfast that strange things were happening in Beaumont's. They had hired new staff and there was much better food. And it was interesting to read about the ongoing arguments between Vincent Halloran and the heritage committee, in the local papers. It was far more interesting than the sectarian politics that had them all nearly deranged with boredom.

Bridget was rather bossy toward the part-timers, Lily noticed. She seemed to think that keeping them on their toes was part of the job description. It was quite amusing to see her squaring up to the towering Daisy behind the bar, and telling Marie her hair was too long, and chasing Trudy around the room with half a lemon until she begged for mercy. Jack was unhappy with the way things were going but he couldn't deny that profits were definitely up in a big way. And so, they settled down into a kind of routine. Lily placed some advertisements in the local papers, informing the citizens of Belfast that she was fighting the demolition of Maple Street. Lots of people called in to wish her well and support the cause. They were always glad to hear a David and Goliath story.

"Would you mind cleaning up a little in the bar?" Lily asked Bridget, when her bossy Christmas angel came traipsing into the kitchen on Saturday morning. "Just a quick mop and polish? Jack and I do it ourselves, usually, and I wouldn't ask you when you've just started but I'm expecting half a dozen ladies here at ten o'clock for a craft lesson and we're still getting things ready."

"Have a heart, Mrs. Beaumont. I've been talking to Gerry since four."

"What? Were you chatting to him again? Were you really on the phone all night?"

"Gerry was suicidal this time. He's missing me a lot and I haven't the heart to hang up on him." Gerry was suicidal every night but Lily Beaumont didn't have to know that. Of course Bridget didn't like other people to know her business but anything was better than cleaning the pub.

"Is he okay now?" Lily couldn't help herself from asking.

"Sure he is. Things always look better when the sun comes up, isn't that the truth? He was plastered drunk, the poor eejit. He's always down when he's drunk. And he's nearly always, well, drunk."

"That's terrible, Bridget. The poor man must be in an awful state. Maybe he should see someone? Can you not persuade him to get help? A psychiatrist, even?"

"Gerry is a psychiatrist."

"Is he really?" Lily was astounded. You often heard that people in the medical profes-

sion didn't look after their own health very
well, but she'd never believed it until now.
"Well, in that case, he probably knows he
should have some therapy. Surely someone
in his practice must have noticed, if he's in
such a bad way?"

"He's had therapy. Years and years of it:
and it did no good. It's a commitment thing.
He falls in love all the time but he gets terrified
of making a commitment. So he sabotages
the relationship by having an affair. And then
he goes on the drink to avoid having to deal
with the fallout. You see, it all began when he
was seventeen." Bridget took a deep breath
to continue, but Lily interrupted her.

"Look, Bridget, this is fascinating stuff but
I really need a hand with the cleaning. Time
is getting away from us." Any talk of alcoholism always made Lily nervous. Especially
nowadays when she was trying to sell more
alcohol than ever. She tried to convince herself it was not her responsibility to control
the intake of her customers but still it was a
worry to her. She didn't want to take money
away from the mouths of hungry children. Or
from people with mental health problems, either. Although she had never met Gerry
Madden, Lily found herself feeling very sorry

for him. Imagine having the intelligence to qualify as a psychiatrist and then having the bad luck to become an alcoholic.

"Actually, I don't do cleaning," said Bridget, breaking into Lily's thoughts. "Did I not mention that at the interview?"

"You said no catering."

"That's right, and no cleaning, either. I'm a barmaid, not a cleaner. Tell you what, though. I'll be standing behind that bar at two this afternoon, ready to serve till closing time. I'll not even take my minimum legal tea breaks. Okay?" And she smiled apologetically, withdrew into Lily's gorgeous sitting room and closed the door behind her. Lily wanted to cry with frustration but she hurried into the shower after sending Jack out to buy some more groceries. And ten glue sticks. Lily decided she'd have to have a gentle talk with Bridget in the near future, about cooperation and helping other people out in times of need, but first she had a class to teach.

At ten precisely, Jack opened the front door of the tavern and was stunned to see at least fifty middle-aged women waiting there. They were all standing very still, facing the door and waiting for him to speak. It was like something out of a science fiction film. Some of the women seemed to have just come from the hairdresser's, and wore expensive coats and shoes. The rest looked more approachable and friendly in their sensible warm anoraks and windswept perms. Their faces were full of expectation.

"Just one moment," he said, and he half-closed the door.

"How many Picasso wannabes are you expecting?" he asked Lily in a whisper.

"About half a dozen maybe? Ten if I'm lucky." Lily was setting out small wicker baskets on the tables, containing paper squares and pastel chalks. "It's very short notice, but the secretaries I spoke to on the phone said they would put the word out for me. Plus, it's ten pounds each, which might be too much for a lot of people."

"I don't think the price has put them off one bit, Lily. Brace yourself," he said. And he opened the door wide and waved them all in.

Lily thought she was hallucinating when she saw the seemingly endless procession of chattering ladies file in and stand around the walls of the tavern, waiting patiently to be seated. She counted them. There were sixty-five would-be card designers. They were all looking respectfully at her. She decided she'd better get the class started.

"Okay, ladies. Welcome to the craft class. And thank you for coming here today at such short notice. I wasn't expecting quite so many but I think we'll fit in, although it might be a bit of a squeeze. Now! If you form a line here, we'll get the names and fees out of the way, and then everyone can just take a seat and we'll get started?" Lily held her breath for fear someone might object to the price she was asking, but it was going to be okay. The women were fumbling in their handbags for purses, and pointing out desirable tables to their friends, and Jack was smiling at his wife as he quietly lit the fire. He'd already offered to make the tea and offer round the sponge cakes that Lily had baked the night before. Thank goodness she'd hidden them in a tin behind the bar, otherwise Bridget might have scoffed the lot. Lily wanted to kiss Jack, but first she had to earn six hundred and fifty pounds. Wow, she thought, I did expect I'd be a nervous wreck this morning but this is going to be fun!

After much good-natured shuffling around of tables and chairs, hanging up of raincoats and anoraks and sharing out of paper and pencils, the women were finally ready to receive instruction. Lily smiled at them all and took a deep breath.

"Now, has anyone here ever drawn a stylized angel on textured paper, using pastel chalks?" she asked. And the room exploded with laughter.

The class was a resounding success. After an initial period of silent concentration, a gentle babble of happy chatter started up and continued throughout the morning. Soon, the women were rolling neat tissue-paper balls, and scoring delicate feathers onto card wings like bona fide experts. The ladies told Lily they were delighted to be doing something so enjoyable in the run-up to Christmas, as well as the usual drudgery of shopping and cooking. They also thought the class was terrific value for money, as they would have six handmade cards each to take home that would have cost them at least twenty pounds in the shops. They learned how to draw angels and fairies and plum puddings and snowmen, and they glued paper to card, and glitter to paper, and even mastered the art of making envelopes. They asked Lily if they could come back the following week and learn something else, and Lily said she'd be only too happy to show them how to weave a Christmas wreath.

When Jack served the tea and cakes at lunchtime there was a deafening round of applause, and one of the women said that the sight of such a handsome man, with a tray of cups and saucers in his hand, was the sweetest thing she'd seen in years. All too soon it was over, and with huge reluctance the women gathered up their precious creations and filed out of the tavern. Some exchanged phone numbers and arranged to meet up for lunch during the week. As the last stragglers were leaving, Barney, Joey and Francy Mac arrived. They were very relieved to see their beloved booth was still available for them even if the table was covered in glitter and glue.

"I thought I'd come to the wrong pub for a minute," said Barney. "I've never seen so many women in the same place."

"Aye. Let's have a wee nip of the hard stuff to get over the shock," said Joey. "My shout."

"Cheers," said Francy Mac.

5

THE DEVANEY BROTHERS

LILY WAS ON A HIGH Sunday morning as she cracked some eggs into a glass dish and began to beat them with a fork. To celebrate the success of her craft class she was making a cheese and mushroom omelette. She'd have preferred a huge fry-up of bacon and sausages but thanks to Bridget and her outrageous appetite, they were reduced to eating leftovers. Jack set knives and forks on the table and poured orange juice into three pretty glasses. Just then, Bridget came padding into the kitchen, covering her yawn with a well-thumbed copy of *Vogue* magazine.

"Tired?" asked Lily. And she poured the beaten eggs into a large pan full of butter-fried mushrooms.

"Frazzled," Bridget moaned, reaching for a glass of juice.

"Well, I'm not surprised. We did quite well last night in the bar. There were a couple of hundred customers at the very least." Lily gathered up the remains of several different blocks of cheese and sprinkled them on top of the eggs.

"Yeah. Since word got out about the closure, more people have been coming in for a farewell drink," Jack added. He felt uncomfortable when Bridget was eating with them and he was embarrassed by the fact that she was still wearing her too-short robe. He wished she'd get dressed before breakfast. The perfect angel the customers saw downstairs in the bar was nothing like the bedraggled starving creature he and Lily had to put up with every morning. Bridget then spent hours in the bathroom, transforming herself, and they suspected she was using Lily's perfume as well. Lily and Jack had wasted thirty minutes already today debating whether to take the bottle out of the bathroom altogether, and take the risk of offending Bridget.

"It wasn't the bar work. It was Gerry. He rang again last night."

"I never heard the phone," exclaimed Lily. "What time did he ring?"

"Four, as usual. I took the phone into my room at midnight. Just in case he woke you again," Bridget said helpfully, and drank her juice in one go. She'd decided it was much more comfortable holding lengthy conversations with Gerry when she was nice and snug under the blankets.

"How considerate of you," muttered Lily. And then she felt mean, so she asked politely how Gerry was getting on.

"He's going to America for two weeks, leaving today." Bridget eyed the omelette sizzling in the pan and checked to see if there was a place set for her at the table. She was delighted to count three plates. "Some training thing, but he said he wants to keep in touch with me while he's over there. He's missing me like crazy but he'll get over it eventually. That smells fabulous, Mrs. Beaumont."

"I see," said Lily, her face turning pink with worry. "As long as he's paying for the calls." There was an awkward silence.

Bridget yawned again. "Is a bit of that dee-lish omelette coming my way?" she asked brightly, as Lily expertly flicked her creation over with a large spatula.

"Surely there is," said Lily. "Why don't you go back to bed and I'll bring yours in to you on a tray? Tea and toast as well? Do you like marmalade? If you've been consoling poor Gerry half the night, you deserve a treat."

"Thanks very much, Mrs. Beaumont. Aren't you an absolute pet? I think I'll take you up on that very generous offer," murmured Bridget, and she drifted out of the room under a cloud of tousled white curls. "Don't bother with the marmalade, though. I don't care for it much," she called back as the sitting room door closed behind her.

"Jack, is that girl for real? I was only joking about the room service," whispered Lily, almost ready to follow Bridget into her delphinium blue boudoir and confront her about the missing drops of Chanel. "How can someone so tiny be so completely self-centered?"

"Maybe that's how she's survived this long in the big bad world? By looking out for number one? At least she's gone back to bed. Thanks, baby," Jack whispered. "She puts me off my food. What a mess! She had mascara on her chin."

"So you don't fancy her, then?" Lily asked, pretending to be jealous.

"No way. She frightens the life out of me, if you must know. I bet she has a vicious temper when she's crossed. Plus, she's half my age."

"That wouldn't deter some men."

"I only want you, Lily. You know that." She smiled at him. She did know.

"Bridget's probably a lot tougher than she looks. Now I understand why poor Gerry needed so much therapy. But she must still care for him, to chat for half the night." Jack put his arms around his wife as they waited for the eggs to finish cooking, and Lily shivered at the thought of Gerry and Bridget's doomed relationship.

"Why can't they just sort it out, for heaven's sake? Life is far too short to waste it playing mind games," she said thoughtfully.

"Hey, look on the positive side," Jack said brightly. "Bridget doesn't like marmalade and we've got three pots of the stuff here in the cupboard. At least we'll not starve this

Christmas. We can have marmalade soup, with roast breast of marmalade for mains, and then marmalade pudding for afters." They both managed to laugh although there was a tinge of worry about it. Neither one of them had brought up the subject of Christmas Day itself. Would they be sharing their wonderful romantic celebrations with Bridget this year? She hadn't said anything about going home to her parents or to Gerry's apartment for the big day. And then Lily felt guilty again for wanting her lodger out of the house at Christmas. If Bridget had nowhere else to go, then she could stay with them and they'd make the best of it. Very few women were as fortunate as she was, or as loved and cherished. She must try to be less selfish.

"I'm so lucky to have you for a husband," Lily whispered, and Jack planted another gentle kiss on the back of her neck.

"Are those eggs ready yet? I'm fading away, here."

She turned the omelette out onto a warm plate and felt almost happy. Once Jack had cheered her up, Lily couldn't be gloomy for long. She counted her blessings as she served Bridget breakfast in bed. And she tried very hard to remain in a jovial mood when she spied the broken teapot sitting on top of the television.

"Sorry about that," said Bridget, as she shoveled a huge lump of food into her tiny little mouth. "I didn't mean to do it." As if that would somehow absolve her from any sense of responsibility, thought Lily. Or from having to pay for another one.

"That's all right," said Lily patiently. "These things happen."

"Everything will be fine," she told Jack, as they enjoyed their breakfast in welcome privacy. "If Bridget doesn't eat us out of house and home, and break everything of value in the property and put our phone bill through the roof, everything will be fine." Lily hadn't seen the stains on the carpet yet because Bridget had covered them up with her suitcases and several large carrier bags.

"You know what?" said Jack. "I never liked that teapot."

"Well, I did. At least we're still ahead financially thanks to the Christmas cards." Lily had made a fortune from her craft class and there was going to be another one the following Saturday. Upon reflection, she realized that buying materials for the Christmas wreaths was going to prove very expensive. She'd have to have enough circles of florist's foam, wire, wire cutters, holly branches, fir branches, red ribbons and roses for sixty-five people. She'd have to see if she could get some of the materials in a discount store. But it was so enjoyable teaching the class that Lily didn't mind a sizable reduction in profit next time. She was just so relieved to have made it through the morning without her nerves deserting her.

"This is great," Jack said, clearing his plate. "What will we do this morning? Have we enough time for a quick stroll round the park before opening? I could do with some fresh air. The only problem with having extra customers is having lots of extra cigarette smoke as well."

"No, my love. Sorry. I want to make some adjustments to the furniture downstairs and then I'm interviewing the Devaney brothers."

"Who?"

"Our potential new in-house folk-and-blues band."

"Don't tell me, a bunch of crazy old men playing fiddles and flutes and drinking all our best whiskey?"

"No, sweetheart. They're very good-looking

twin brothers called David and Michael. A couple of twenty-four-year-old stunners in leather jeans actually. And they play acoustic guitars and they're very sexy. I saw them yesterday when I was coming back from the bank. They were busking outside Donegal Arcade. They were terrific, Jack."

"Bring it on, then. What have we got to lose?" He smiled.

"Now," she said, setting her plate in the sink, "I'm going to shift a couple of tables away from the left-hand side of the fire to make room for them to play. And then I'm going to word another few ads for the newspapers to promote the folk nights."

"It's going to be that easy to get more customers?"

"Yes it is," she said firmly.

"Won't there be sectarian riots at closing time? These folk nights can attract a certain type of customer, if you know what I mean. Hothead patriots with barely repressed violent urges. All of them thinking they're in the movies. Tearing up the paving slabs to throw at the police?"

"Not a bit of it. Honestly, you're paranoid! And you told me to look to the future. That's all over and done with, Jack."

"I'll believe it when I see it. Can't you just ask the Devaneys to sing some rock and pop? Lloyd Cole and the Commotions, maybe? Fairground Attraction, that kind of thing? Keep everyone happy?"

"I don't know if they sing pop songs. And those groups were well before their time anyway."

"Lily, tell them it's pop or nothing. They're getting a regular gig and a cosy fireside stage to go with it. I don't want the pub wrecked."

"All right." She smiled. "You're the boss."

"That's right," he laughed. "And don't you forget it!"

WHEN THE DEVANEY BROTHERS showed up at lunchtime, Lily had created a little area for them to perform in. David was very flirtatious and charming with short spiky hair and one gold earring, while Michael was shy and softly spoken with a head of Leo Sayer–style shoulder-length curls. David said the tavern looked very nice indeed and he tried out the performance area for size. Michael simply nodded at Lily and Jack politely. Both brothers had sexy, angular faces and terrific muscular thighs, an attribute not wasted in their tight leather trousers.

"Where's my sunglasses?" whispered Jack as the brothers bent over their guitar cases and Lily had to stifle a giggle as the lights above them were reflected on the brothers' firm behinds. "Where did they get those trousers? Singing for change must pay better than we think."

Daisy, Trudy and Marie were hanging up their coats behind the bar, having just arrived for work themselves. The three girls were delighted that they were in time to witness a musical audition. Barney, Joey and Francy Mac were safely installed in their booth with full pints of stout and the Sunday newspapers. The Devaneys introduced themselves to Lily and Jack and everyone shook hands. They accepted a cup of tea before donning their instruments and David asked if anyone had any unusual requests. He began to tune his guitar and Michael tried not to blush when he spotted Marie smiling shyly at him.

"I've got an unusual request," whispered Bridget to Daisy. She had just come downstairs to see what all the fuss was about. "But I don't know if David's that kind of man."

"Hands off," said Daisy in a low voice. "I saw him first."

"All's fair in love and war, my dear," replied Bridget firmly. "You get on with unloading the dishwasher. And those tea towels could do with a hot iron, Marie."

"Man-eater," said Daisy under her breath, but Bridget wasn't listening.

"I do love tight leather trousers," Bridget sighed. "There'll be no surprises for his wife on the honeymoon."

"Aren't you seeing a doctor? I mean, romantically?" Daisy wanted to know. "Mrs. B said you were never off the phone to a doctor called Gerry Madden."

"Was seeing, actually. We finished over a week ago." Bridget checked her hair in the little mirror behind the optics. She was delighted to note that it was looking great. Her ringlets were supple and bouncing, like David Devaney's thighs.

"Is that all? One week! Blimey! You don't hang about." Daisy rattled the glasses noisily in their wire trays, annoyed by Bridget's assumption that she was entitled to first pickings of any male talent on the premises.

"What do you mean by that?" snapped

Bridget, still tired from her late-night heart-to-heart with Gerry.

"Now, now. Let's not fight," soothed Marie in a tiny voice. "A lady should be dignified at all times."

"What did you say?" the other three asked in unison. Marie blushed and turned away, reaching for a duster to shine the beer pumps.

"No offense, Bridget, but I think your image is a little mainstream for David." Daisy patted one of her bright red hair knots. "Look at his spiky hair. I mean, he's obviously very cool."

"Listen to me, Daisy. You're young and immature so I'll do you a favor. My ex-boyfriend, Gerry Madden, told me for a fact that young people with way-out hairstyles and freaky clothes are extremely insecure, and desperate for attention. And he's a shrink and he knows about these things. Now, I'm not saying for one second that diagnosis applies to you. I don't know if you're insecure or not. But you might like to rethink the Halloween hair?" Two pink spots of rage appeared in the middle of Daisy's pale cheeks.

"Young and immature, you say? I'm only

six years younger than you are, for God's sake! And what does this Gerry of yours have to say about skimpy tight clothing?" Daisy looked pointedly at Bridget's short fitted dress. "What does Gerry say about women who go about the place half-naked? Huh? Advertising their wobbly bits? Why don't you just wear a sign around your neck that tells the boys when you're ovulating?"

Bridget's eyes were cold with anger but she managed to squeeze out a rather brittle little laugh. It was high time Daisy Hardcastle was put in her place, once and for all. She jabbed a finger at Daisy's baggy jumper and red velvet trousers with pink love hearts all down one side.

"All those pretty pink hearts on your slacks!" she accused. "Love me! Love me! Love me! That's what I'm hearing. Every one a cry for help."

"They are not cries for help. They are motifs. Just because you dated a shrink doesn't make you one as well, you know," snarled Daisy through gritted teeth, wondering how she was going to continue working with this miniature madwoman. That was the trouble with most jobs. They usually involved having to cooperate with other people.

By this time the Devaney brothers had begun to sing and play a selection of lively pop tunes but Daisy and Bridget were oblivious to the entertainment. Daisy had endured a week of Bridget's incredibly annoying manager-antics and she was spoiling for an argument.

"Were you ever young, Bridget O'Malley?" she asked. "Or were you born middle-aged? I feel sorry for you, to be honest. Unless you're bossing other people about, you don't feel very important. Do you?"

"Oh! Is that right? Well! Thank you for your assessment but I thought we were talking about you, Daisy? Did you run up those trousers, yourself?" Bridget gasped, sensing she was losing the fight. "I've not seen the like of them in any shops around here."

"Yes, I did make them, as a matter of fact. And I didn't run them up, as you put it. What a strange expression! Actually, I designed and created these wide-leg pants. It's called high fashion, you pint-sized little bitch. A one-off piece like this would cost thousands in a London boutique but you wouldn't understand such a concept."

"Why don't you go and clean some tables, and take your designer togs with you?" Bridget sighed, pretending to be bored.

"I will indeed. I'll be happy to clean some tables, Bridget. Because I'm only working as a barmaid while I'm a student. I won't still be a scrubber when I'm twenty-five. Like some people I could mention." And with that Daisy flounced off to set clean ashtrays on the tables. Bridget stood shaking with bad temper behind the bar and wondered if she had the power to fire the part-timers. Really, that Daisy had a serious problem with authority figures.

When the brothers had finished their audition set, Bridget had calmed down enough to toss her white curls and bat her innocent blue eyes at David Devaney.

"Do you know 'Angel' by Robbie Williams?" she purred. "Such a beautiful song." Bridget had obviously cottoned on to the fact that she was very pretty in a heavenly sort of way, Lily knew at once.

"I do. Sure, don't you look like an angel yourself?" David smiled.

Daisy rolled her eyes and even Lily and Jack were embarrassed.

"Maybe next time?" David smiled. "If we get the gig."

"You sounded good enough to me," said Lily quickly. "You're hired."

"Cool," said David. And Michael blushed

again, underneath his long fringe of chestnut brown curls.

"Will you stay for lunch, boys?" asked Jack
suddenly, to the amazement of his wife. "I'm
badly outnumbered here with all these
women." And then Lily understood his out-of-
character request. It must be hard for Jack to
have to share his beloved bar with four new
females, and to be fair to him he was coping
magnificently. The Devaneys accepted Jack's
impulsive invitation and the three men sat
down to discuss the play list. Even though
Jack was nearly twice their age they had a lot
of favorite groups in common. They all agreed
that the Beatles were nothing more than a
vastly overrated show band, and that David
Bowie was the real genius of popular music.
Also, they all admired Johnny Cash, Elvis
Costello and Elvis Presley. Lily was pleased
for Jack. She'd forgotten how shy he was.

"I'll fetch the soup, then," she said, and
hurried upstairs.

Barney, listening in to the morning's de-
velopments, slowly reached out a liver-
spotted hand and silently closed the door to
their booth.

"Did you see the cut of the clothes on
them two young fellows?" he whispered as

he puffed deeply on his pipe. "They can fairly sing, I'll grant them that. But the X-rated trousers! They're braver men than I am. That's for sure."

"Indeed. Leather should only be used for making shoes and schoolbags, in my humble opinion," said Joey. "I'd rather face a rabid dog than have to wear something like that up the street in broad daylight."

"I'd rather face two rabid dogs than have to witness you doing such a thing," added Francy Mac. "Your round, Joey. Cheers."

By mid-afternoon the charged atmosphere had settled down again. Daisy and Bridget had been persuaded by Lily to apologize to each other and make friends. Although Bridget was secretly determined to flirt like mad with David, just to make Daisy jealous. No part-time barmaid was going to call her a bitch and get away with it. And also, Bridget wasn't about to lose any man to a freak like Daisy Hardcastle with her awful red hair.

The Devaney brothers had gone home, presumably to give the leather trousers and their sex appeal a good rest. The fire was burning merrily in the grate and Lily had warmed them all up with another big bowl each of parsnip soup. Even Barney and his gang had tasted some and said it was very fancy. It was a new recipe Lily was trying out and they all thought the added curry paste and coriander leaves were a great idea.

"There's no lemon juice in this soup, is there?" asked Trudy suddenly.

"Just a drop," said Lily. "Why?"

"I'm allergic to lemons," wailed Trudy. "I told you at the interview!" She began to gasp for air and her neck and face turned red with worry. Her penciled eyebrows moved up on her forehead by another half inch.

"Oh sweet God! I clean forgot. I'm so sorry. What will happen to you?" Lily was stricken. She held Jack's hand for reassurance. "Trudy, I'm really sorry. Have I got your next of kin's contact details just in case you pass out or anything?"

"Oh, mercy!" wept Trudy. She stood up quickly, shook her hands in front of her face with pure fear, and then sat down again. "Feel my head. Am I hot? Am I getting hot?"

"Now, don't panic," said Jack. "You had some soup earlier and nothing happened. Allergies can wear off, you know?"

"It could take a while for the lemon juice to travel round my system." Trudy looked at her watch. "How long since bowl number one?"

"Will I phone for an ambulance?" asked Bridget, halfway to the pay phone. She had a raging paramedic fetish. (As well as a doctor fetish.) Those green uniforms with "paramedic" emblazoned across the back made her feel positively wanton. She had frequent fantasies about being strapped to a metal stretcher and lifted into a helicopter. In a raging storm, preferably. In the highlands of Scotland, if it could be arranged. And then, as she lay hovering between consciousness and unconsciousness, the gorgeous paramedic (with his high Celtic cheekbones) would loosen her clothing, and their eyes would meet briefly and . . .

"No, no. I'm not going to go into shock," gasped Trudy. "At least, I hope not. Quick, get me a pint of water. I might faint, though. Maybe I better get away from this stone floor before I keel over?" There was a scramble as Lily, Jack and Marie filled a pint glass apiece, and they gathered around Trudy and rubbed her back in sympathy as she drank all three.

"Is it not bad for you? To drink so much fluid in one go?" asked Jack.

"My father once drank sixteen pints of lager in an afternoon and he still won at darts," offered Bridget. And then she became very quiet and looked extremely embarrassed. "Only joking," she added in a small voice. "He's a teetotaler. Never touches the stuff."

"It feels like Alice in Wonderland, doesn't it?" said Daisy in a worried voice as they all waited for Trudy to collapse. "Is she going to get bigger and bigger, or smaller and smaller?"

"Come on upstairs with me, pet," said Lily to her beetroot-faced barmaid, "and lie down for a while. You've only had a teeny wee drop of lemon juice, and the soup was simmered for two hours anyway, and probably all the juice had evaporated by the time you ate it." She put her arm around Trudy's waist and guided her up the stairs. They went into Lily and Jack's bedroom and Trudy lowered herself gently onto the big brass bed.

"It's lovely in here," Trudy said, taking in the pale pink walls and the glass doorknobs on the bureau. "Did you decorate this room yourself, Mrs. Beaumont?"

"Yes, I did. I'm glad you like it. Now, would you like a cup of tea with some sugar in it for the shock? Or will I phone your mother? Or will I fetch a basin in case you need to be sick?"

"My parents live in Birmingham these days, Mrs. Beaumont. They're both theater nurses. They wouldn't be able to visit me at short notice."

"Trudy, you poor pet. Is there anything at all I can do to help?"

"I think I'll just have a little nap, now. If you don't mind, Mrs. Beaumont. I feel very woozy."

"That's fine," said Lily. "You sleep as long as you like." She puffed up some pillows and covered Trudy's shoulders with the satin eiderdown. Then she sat on the edge of the bed and talked gently to the trembling girl until she calmed down and felt sleepy. Within minutes Trudy was dead to the world. Lily stayed on in the room for fifteen minutes to make sure that Trudy didn't swell up and explode or develop green blisters on her eyes. Then she crept out and left the door slightly ajar. She wrote a big notice for the fridge door in red marker, saying *Trudy is allergic to lemons,* before going downstairs to tell the others that Trudy had pulled through. Privately Lily thought there was nothing at all wrong with Trudy, and that all she needed was some love and attention. But she decided to be a lot more careful in the kitchen, just in case.

LIAM BRADLEY ARRIVED later that afternoon and took up position in a booth near the door. His table was soon covered with loose pages of notes and five thick history books on the nineteenth century. He kept the door of the booth closed and he covered the pages with his arms when Lily came to take his order. She asked him if he was working on his second novel when she served him his usual pint and sandwich, and he told her that he was, but he wouldn't be drawn on the plot. It was top secret, he said. Lily had the most peculiar feeling that he was studying her face too closely when she was telling him about the new staffing arrangements. In particular he seemed fascinated with her eyes. But she dismissed the notion as ridiculous. What would he be interested in her for, she thought, when his own wife was both younger and sexier? She'd seen a picture of Betsy yawning once, in the newspaper. (At a book fair in Bangor.) Just to be on the safe side, though, she asked Jack to serve him for the rest of his visit, claiming she was busy counting mixers for the stock taking. Jack made three trips to Liam's booth that day but Liam wouldn't tell him anything about the new novel, either.

Bridget was kept busy showing Daisy and Marie how to make elaborate cocktails with crushed ice and chilled glasses. Daisy was given the important task of filling a food bag with ice cubes and smashing them up with a rolling pin. Then, Bridget demonstrated how to use the chrome shaker and how to pour with grace and poise. That was the whole point of cocktails, she told them. It wasn't the few drops of alcohol and the fruity flavor of the drink that was important. It was the idea of it, the glamour and the lifestyle choice of being a cocktail drinker, that mattered. Daisy was unimpressed but Marie nodded wisely and said Bridget was very clever.

They picked out four elegant-sounding drinks from Bridget's lengthy repertoire, and decided that would be enough for the Christmas program. Champagne cocktails were the first choice, followed by Sea Breezes made with cranberry juice, vodka and grape-

fruit juice. Also on the list were Peach Bellinis and Brandy Alexanders. They had a Sea
Breeze each to sample for taste and quality,
and then another one to use up the last of
the ingredients. Marie had two Peach Bellinis after that and she declared they were delicious. She said it was a dreadful pity
Michael Devaney had gone home because
she felt in the mood for a bit of romance. It
was the first time they'd heard her speak
above a whisper all day.

Jack and Lily were both delighted that
Bridget was as handy with the cocktail
shaker as she'd claimed because she was
costing them a fortune to keep. There was
hardly a scrap of food left in the kitchen.
She'd eaten all the jam, biscuits, pancakes,
cereal and chocolate in the cupboard. Lily
was thinking of adding a food supplement to
her rent.

Lily told the girls that there were several
Christmas parties lined up, mostly for the
students of the city, and that was why they
were having a crash course in cocktails that
day. Lily had made a few inquiries as to what
the other venues were charging and she had
slightly undercut them. They could only fit a
hundred people comfortably in the tavern at

any one time but some of the college depart-
ments were considering holding separate
events so that wasn't a problem.

Daisy and Marie were working well together behind the bar. The two of them
seemed to have bonded right away. Daisy
offered to give Marie a fashion makeover.
She was very handy with a sewing machine
and a bag of rags, she said. Today she was
wearing a long tube dress made of lime and
turquoise velvet patches. Marie, on the other
hand, dressed very simply in jeans and
T-shirts and didn't fancy being togged out
like a witch but she said she'd be happy to
hear some of Daisy's ideas. Say, after
Christmas when things were quieter.

At five that evening, Trudy reappeared
and apologized profusely for scaring the life
out of them all.

"That's all right," said Lily automatically.
"These things happen."

"I can't think why I didn't have a more severe reaction this time," said Trudy. "Usually I
have a temperature if I eat anything with
lemon juice in it. Maybe it was the parsnips
or the coriander that acted as an antidote?"

"That must be it," said Jack. "Thank God
for parsnips and coriander."

They told her about the cocktail lessons and the upcoming parties. Trudy made it clear that she couldn't serve any drink that required a slice of lemon in it. Lemons usually brought her out in a hot rash on her hands if she touched them, she said. So she was definitely off Peach Bellini duty. Lily said that was okay. Trudy could man the beer pumps instead. They couldn't all be stuck around the cocktail tray anyway, she added. There wouldn't be enough room. Then Lily and Jack went upstairs for a much-needed tea break.

"Now, let me get this straight. Bridget doesn't clean or cook," said Jack. "She spends half the night on the phone to a guy she claims is her ex-boyfriend. Note the word 'ex'! She eats more grub than a herd of elephants. Thank God she doesn't drink alcohol or we'd be ruined altogether."

"I know."

"Trudy can't go near lemons so she's off cocktail duty. Although we've seen no evidence of an allergic reaction, and I think the whole thing is in her head. And she doesn't seem to care for buttons, either, you mentioned?"

"Pearly buttons, mainly."

"Right. Marie is too shy to chat to the male customers. And Daisy's hair is falling out."

"What did you say?" asked Lily, filling the kettle under the tap.

"Haven't you noticed? There's long red hairs all over the floor downstairs."

"Oh, Jack. What'll happen if a customer finds a hair in their slice of pie?"

"We'll say to them, don't tell the others or they'll all want one!"

"What?"

"Hair. Hare. Rabbit. Rabbit pie? Lily, that joke went out with the ark."

"I'm getting too old for all this. What have I done?" She set the kettle on the stove and covered her face with her hands in a gesture of despair.

"I told you so. I told you so," he sang softly, pointing at his wife with both index fingers. "I told you there'd be something wrong with the lot of them. Available, as they were, at such short notice. I bet the job center was glad to be rid of them."

"Don't gloat, Jack, I'm warning you. I couldn't bear it."

"I'm only teasing. Come on, Lily. It's not so bad. You can't have staff without staffing problems. Haven't we always known that? They're nice girls despite the odd eccentricity. I like them."

"So do I, I suppose. Although sometimes I think I want to kill Bridget. She never remembers to leave us any milk for our breakfast. Honestly, last night I saw her heading to bed with a pint mug full of it!"

"Problem solved," said Jack, showing Lily a packet of soya milk he had hidden behind the vegetable rack. "Bridget will have to get up early in the morning to get the better of me."

"We'll keep going, then?" A fat tear rolled down Lily's cheek.

"Yes," he said. "Don't cry. We'll keep going." Downstairs, Trudy was fully recovered and enjoying the attention her allergy drama had created. The other girls remembered various medical horror stories from their childhoods and they had a great evening telling more and more outrageous tales to each other. Daisy had an aunt in Kent who got stung on the tongue by a bee and suffocated to death beside her own barbecue in the garden. When was that? the others asked. During Wimbledon, apparently. Daisy couldn't remember the exact year. The unfortunate aunt had been watching the television coverage through her patio doors and had been cheering for John McEnroe at the time.

Bridget had a cousin who once had hay fever so bad she had to be left in the bath overnight and covered with ice to bring her temperature down. Luckily this time there was a happy ending. The girl survived and went on to open her own hair salon in Sixmilecross.

"Another half a degree higher and my poor cousin would have died," said Bridget, with her eyes as wide as plates. "They had the priest in to give her the last rites and they had a big wooden crucifix that once belonged to some saint or other, rushed to the bathroom from County Cork. They held the crucifix on her forehead to help reduce the fever."

"You can't buy memories like that," said Daisy, sarcastically. "I bet the wretched creature still has nightmares about it."

Trudy seemed rather deflated by these hair-raising anecdotes. They made her own aversion to lemon juice seem very dull by comparison. She reminded them that she also had a button phobia. She couldn't stand within four feet of a button of any description without feeling queasy, she told them. And the other girls were very understanding.

"Pearly buttons in particular," added Trudy. "Pearly buttons make me heave."

"Don't worry," they said. "We won't wear anything with pearly buttons on it and you can stay behind the bar when it gets busy. Just in case the customers' clothes upset you." Trudy was delighted.

Marie, still slightly tipsy from the Peach Bellinis, confided that she fancied Michael Devaney like mad and that she was determined to tackle him (her words) on New Year's Eve. That was a huge relief to Daisy and Bridget, who were both planning to seduce spiky-haired David at the earliest opportunity. They were chattering away happily behind the bar when Lily told them the brothers had phoned to confirm they would be performing regularly at the tavern. Most nights over the Christmas period, probably. The girls were thrilled. Things were looking up.

When Bridget began bossing them around again during the late-evening shift, Daisy smiled at the others and winked conspiratorially.

"It's going to be great," said Daisy to her new friends Marie and Trudy at closing time as they waited inside the front door for the taxi. "Never worry about wee Bridget O'Malley and her mighty ego. If the three of us stick together we'll have a fantastic Christmas. I just know it."

6

SHAW STORIES
RIDES AGAIN

 PERRY SHAW WAS GIDDY with happiness. Liam Bradley had been on the phone for over an hour telling him about the plot of the new book.

"Aw, Limo. I mean, Liam. That's just fantastic news. I knew you could do it."

"I didn't know I could do it, Perry. It is not easy work, writing. Even though people think it is. There's nothing on earth as frightening as a blank computer screen."

"I never thought for one second it was easy, Liam. You're a genius," he soothed. And he gently touched the framed photograph on his desk of his twenty-two-year-old son who was a soldier in the British army. Perry could think of a few things more terrifying than a blank screen. But he remembered his golden rule: Never be honest with a writer.

"Anyway, the new book will be even better than *Bang, Bang*. I'm still undecided on the title, though," Liam went on.

"What about *Boom, Boom*? For continuity of style?"

"That sounds like two bombs going off. You haven't heard the ending yet."

"Is there an explosion? Or even better, two explosions?"

"Okay. Yes, there is. As it happens. The tavern gets blown sky-high at the end. Just when everything was sorted out and everybody is celebrating in the street outside. Someone tosses a lit cigarette near the door and whoosh! Up it goes!"

"Well, there you are! What causes it, by the way?"

"An undetected gas leak. Courtesy of the same company which unearths the bones of the first victim."

"And the second conflagration?"

"A car. Slinger's car is torched by Claudia."

"Isn't that fantastic, Liam? Isn't that very convenient? We'll call the novel *Boom, Boom,* then? While I'm selling it to the publishers?"

"Are you going to start taking bids already, Perry? Before I've even written it? Is that a wise thing to do?"

"Sure, Liam. If I don't start stirring up some interest immediately they'll just offer some other author a contract. And tell them to rip off your style. So don't worry. *Boom, Boom* sounds just right. Yes, indeed: another brilliant blend of mystery, comedy and soft porn, from the legendary Liam Bradley. The publishers will adore it."

"There's just one thing, Perry. You might not like it."

"Hit me," said Perry, hoping he wouldn't have to break his golden rule today of all days when financial salvation was so close.

"Well, I thought I would go for a surprise twist at the end?"

"I don't know if I like the sound of this, Liam."

"Okay. I'll tell you quickly. Slinger falls in love and fathers a child with the landlady of the tavern. Her husband sadly expires in the explosion, which is rather handy for our hero. No need for an untidy divorce case.

And Slinger settles down at last to the amazement of all the lads in the police station." Liam held his breath for Perry's reply. He wasn't surprised by what his agent said.

"No, no, no, Limo. I mean, Liam. No way! Absolutely not! Slinger simply can't fall in love. He must be free from emotional ties. That's the whole point of his character. He's a rolling stone."

"I don't want people to see Slinger as sad, being in his forties and alone. He's getting tired of rolling, Perry. He wants to gather a bit of moss."

"Well, he can't."

"But he's going to be thirty-eight years of age in *Boom, Boom.* He's going to have crow's-feet and hairy ears."

"So what?"

"Won't he be a little pathetic when he reaches forty and he's still living in a mess-strewn bachelor pad? With only his CD collection to keep him company at night? A man of thirty-eight doesn't look as hilarious with his trousers round his ankles as a younger lad does."

"Liam, I'm worried about you. Don't think, Liam. Just write. You work best when you don't think."

"But will Slinger still visit lap-dancing clubs when he's lonely for a woman's company? And tell his personal troubles to the falsely sympathetic bartender?"

"Of course he will."

"Before getting slaughtered drunk and throwing up in some old lady's prize flower bed on the way home? While she watches in disgust from behind the net curtains?"

"Yes. Oh yes! It's perfect! It's wonderfully immature. It's a fantasy, Liam. You know Slinger Magee is only a character in your book. He's not a real person. He's not you."

"I know that," Liam said uncomfortably. In reality, Slinger and Liam had a lot in common. They both thought that vomiting on other people's property was the funniest thing in the whole wide world.

"You grow up and be a big mature guy if you like, Liam. But Slinger is a hedonistic idiot and that's why millions of guys want to read about him. He has no responsibilities whatsoever. If he falls in love, all that will have to change. The magic will be gone. The sense of devil-may-care that the readers want. Come on, Liam. What do you say?"

"Okay. I'll do it," Liam agreed.

"That's my boy! Our hero can have one

crazy night of passion, but I want him gone from her bed before the sun comes up. Right?"

"Right," said Liam, thinking of Lily Beaumont's long dark hair spread across a linen pillowcase.

"Splendid. Now, when do you think you'll have a few chapters ready to show me?"

"Give me a month?" Liam sounded rather depressed.

"A month? Surely you'll have the entire book written in a month?"

"Perry! Are you insane?"

"Haven't you had four years to rest? Now, get cracking right away. I'm counting the days, Liam. And remember: don't go all arty on this. Plenty of smutty jokes, that's what we want. And I love the period costume idea. Put that in, won't you? I'll contact the main publishers right away and suggest something along those lines for the front cover. Slinger smoldering in a frilly shirt and the mysterious landlady just behind him in a tight satin corset?"

"Yeah, whatever. Thanks a lot. Bye, Perry." Liam sighed and wondered if he had any cigarettes left.

"Bye, Liam," Perry said brightly, and he hung up.

"You greedy hack," Liam said aloud in the empty kitchen, thinking of Perry's percentage.

"You talentless jerk," Perry sighed, alone in his London office, and thought of his precious son on active duty in the Middle East. "My boy is a better writer than you could ever be in your wildest dreams, Liam Bradley.

"We're going to retire on the back of *Boom, Boom,* as God is my witness," he told his wife over the phone that afternoon. "I'll raise my fee to twenty percent. I'll get more merchandise deals on the table and I'll get Limo on every TV show in the Western world to promote it. We'll make a fortune. Shaw Stories rides again!"

7

THE GREAT AUBERGINE
BRAIN WAVE

LILY AND JACK were enjoying an early night. It was midnight and they usually sat up until one o'clock in the morning but it was freezing, and anyway Bridget had fully commandeered the sitting room. Lily was afraid to even open the door and look inside in case Bridget had broken or damaged anything else. She'd recently found out about the lilac carpet being ruined and since the room was thirty feet long it was going to take all of the craft class profits to replace it. Lily was close to tears when she heard the estimate from the carpet showroom. And she was fed up with the state of the kitchen larder, too. It had never looked so empty and neglected. Bridget had even soaked a four-year-old salt-dough decoration in hot milk and eaten it thinking it was a stale bagel. She'd given herself killer cramps, which pleased Lily a little bit. But the murderous cramps didn't keep Bridget down for long. She'd eaten an entire jar of pickled onions for breakfast the next day as well as two packets of trifle sponge fingers.

So, Lily and Jack decided to go to bed early with a couple of mugs of hot chocolate and forget about their lodger for a while. The light outside the bedroom window had long-since faded to an indigo blanket. There was talk of snow on the evening forecast. Lily had piled three extra blankets on the bed and they were listening to a compilation CD of old 1980s tunes. "This Is the Day" by The The was softly echoing around the pink walls.

"I can't believe not a single one of our relatives has been in touch," said Jack suddenly as he sipped his chocolate. "You'd think they'd be curious about the proposed closure."

"Mmm. I wondered about that myself. There was a picture of the tavern on the news this afternoon. And I was raging when they said we'd been offered a quarter of a million pounds to sell it. How did the press find out?"

"Must be a leak in Halloran's camp," Jack offered.

"Or more blackmail tactics probably? Nobody will feel sorry for us now," sighed Lily. "Even though it's far more than we expected, I didn't want the details broadcast. Now the whole country will know our private business."

"I know. I think privacy has been made illegal nowadays."

"Maybe the thought of us being offered all that money for a place we inherited is just too much for our families to cope with? I can't believe it's been so long since we all got together. Ernest's funeral must be the last time I sat down for a meal with my own parents. You don't want to take the money and run? Do you, Jack?"

"I haven't thought about it, darling."

"Oh. You must have. Tell me," she said.

"Okay. I might have been tempted. A little

bit. We could certainly afford a detached house in a nice area. But we'd still need to work to pay the running costs. We'd have a lovely home but we'd be out of it all day long. Just like everybody else in the developed world. And then you have the starving millions with no homes at all to live in. It doesn't make any sense."

"That's what I've been saying for years," Lily agreed. "I knew you'd come round to my way of thinking eventually. We'd be no better off than we are now."

"So? What do you think?"

"We'll go ahead with the parties seeing as they're already booked and paid for," she said. "And we'll decide what to do at the end of February. Agreed?"

"Agreed." He drained his cup and snuggled down under the blankets. His strong arms went out and found Lily's neat waist under the warmth of the eiderdown. "Come here, you gorgeous thing." His warm fingers spread out across her back and began caressing her shoulder blades. She loved him to do that. But Lily wasn't in the mood for romance that night. She was worrying about Trudy and her various obsessions.

"Do you know something, Jack? I think Trudy has a little issue with hand washing," said Lily, still propped up against the pillows. "I noticed her hands were very rough and dry today."

"I saw that, too," he sighed as he withdrew his own hands. "I was going to say something to her about it but I thought I'd ask your advice first. You'd think the lemon allergy and the button thing was enough to be going on with."

"She told me at the interview that she was born in England and that her parents sold up and moved back there a couple of years ago. They made a big profit on their house, apparently, and wanted to downsize."

"Why didn't Trudy go with them?"

"They've only bought a tiny town-center apartment. There's no room for Trudy. Anyway, she still has a few months of her geography degree left to do. She's lodging with a couple of professors in Stranmillas but they're always out at some lecture or festival. And they don't believe in central heating."

"Oh dear," he said. "Do you think it could be because she's lonely? All these hang-ups?"

"I'm no expert on these things, darling.

She said she's always had them but they do seem to be getting worse. I might ask her if she'd like to move in with us for a while. There's plenty of room for another bed in there." She nodded down toward Bridget's room. "Massive, that room is. Far too big for one person, and Bridget is so small she could live in a matchbox."

"You've no chance! Ask Princess Bridget to share her sacred bedchamber? Oh Lily, you're a gag."

"It's worth a try. Bridget needs to learn how to cooperate. Plus, it's a mess in there. She's making herself far too cosy. She hung all her clothes on the curtain rail and it fell off the wall. Then she hung them on the picture rail and damaged the wallpaper."

"But I thought all this upheaval was only for a few weeks?"

"Trudy only needs a home in Belfast for a few weeks, Jack. She'll be finished college soon." Lily switched off the bedside lamps and lay down.

"Well, I'm staying out of it. It's your project. Now, where were we?" He held her hand in the darkness and began to delicately rub her shoulder.

"How can you still have the energy for this after the crowd of people we had in the bar tonight?" she whispered. "My feet are killing me. And don't make any noise! Bridget will hear us."

"She won't. She's snoring like a tractor." He pulled Lily toward him and began to un-button her pajama top. "I don't like this fab-ric," he teased. "It's as thick as a blanket. I think I'll bring out my own line of see-through pj's for women. Made of the finest lace? What do you think? Lily?"

"I think I'm going to paint the tavern aubergine!" cried Lily, and she sat up and switched on the lamps again.

"What's going on?" asked Jack, blinking rapidly and scratching his head. "And what kind of a color is *aubergine*?"

"It's a deep, dark shade of purplish-black. It's gorgeous. Look at this." She showed him a brochure from the DIY store that she had slipped under her pillow.

"But you always said white walls made the pub seem bigger."

"Yes, but see how well the gold acces-sories look against such a dark color?"

"Not as good as you look with those pj's off," he sulked. "Please?"

"In a minute. I need to think first."

"I can't do it in a minute. I'm a man of impulse, my love. Oh, never mind. I'm going to sleep. You artists are all crazy."

"Goodnight, darling. I'll be back soon." She grabbed her warm robe and slippers and hurried down the stairs. The bar was empty and dark except for the dying embers of the fire. Lily flicked on the bright overhead lights, which were hardly ever used, and looked at the room as if she had never seen it before. It was too long and plain, she decided. The walls, which were brilliant white only a few months ago, were now yellowing again and smudged with stains. A heavy blanket of cigarette smoke had turned the ceiling a nasty shade of brown, and the mirrors behind the bar were far too small. Lily thought the branded coasters everywhere looked messy and too masculine. She sighed and continued with her critical assessment. The lopsided stack of boxes of crisps and bar snacks in that corner was hardly the height of sophistication, either, and crisp sales were down anyway. Everyone said that crisps nowadays were far too hard: it was like eating razor blades. The stone floor and the mahogany booths and

glossy bar counter were lovely but the overall effect in the tavern was cold and cheerless. The old plastic Christmas tree they'd
assembled on the first day of the month was
leaning slightly to the left. It was only when
the fire was lit that the bar looked warm and
cosy. A total makeover was required.

"It's aubergine for this place, and I'll kill
anybody who tries to stop me," she said
aloud. She warmed her hands at the fire for
a few minutes before she went back to bed
and lay making plans in the darkness. Jack
was fast asleep, his long nose looking very
sculptural and noble in the moonlight. Lily
forgot all about Vincent Halloran's shopping
mall and almost shivered with happiness.
She wasn't even annoyed when Gerry Madden rang at four in the morning as usual. Or
when Bridget cracked the television screen
when she was rearranging the furniture in
her room early the following day.

"These things happen," Lily sighed like a
robot running low on batteries.

After breakfast Lily was hopping with impatience to get started on the decorating.
But it was Saturday and there was a class to
teach first. As she covered the tables in the

bar with sheets of newspaper, she told Jack that she was going out that afternoon to stock up for the great transformation. She was going to the DIY store for paint and mirrors and then to the art shop for Christmas decorations and a fancy hardback sketchbook for the visitors to sign.

"Sure," he said. "Do you want me to come with you?"

"I'd love you to," she replied. "But I want you to stay in and pay the young lad when he brings the new bed for Trudy."

"You've already phoned up and ordered one? It's only just gone nine."

"I left a message on the answer-phone a few minutes ago."

"And what about Bridget? Have you asked her about this?"

"Bridget owes me a favor. Several favors, to be honest. She's caused over a thousand pounds of damage already and she's only been here a few days. The carpet will be a real hassle to replace. And the china teapot was a family heirloom. Not to mention the television, which cost hundreds."

"And the roll-top bath," Jack said quickly, and bit his lip in fear.

"What?"

"She dyed a skirt black in the bath overnight and ruined the enamel. I was going to nip out to the shops myself and hide somewhere until you calmed down again."

"My lovely bath! Where is she? I never noticed a black stain."

"She's in her room, crying her eyes out. There's a bath towel over the stain. That's ruined, too."

"Is it . . . ?"

"One of our embroidered ones from Spain? Yes, I'm afraid so."

"Never mind crying her eyes out. I'll gouge them out with a spoon. She's ruined the other best towel already, mopping up spilled tea. I told her there were plenty of old towels in the hall cupboard. But did she use one of them? Oh no! Little Miss O'Malley has developed a taste for the finer things in life. You know what, Jack? I think I'll have to let her go. She's nothing but a liability."

"Lily, it's done now. Calm down. It was an accident. She had the dye in a basin and it leaked out through a hairline crack."

"But how could she do something so insane? Who puts black dye in someone else's antique bath? And why are you taking her side?"

"I'm not taking her side. She lives here."

"She doesn't live here, Jack. She's a lodger. It's not the same thing at all."

"Well, that's all academic. It's her bath, too."

"But it's an antique bath. You don't take risks like that with a period piece. Is she crazy or what?"

"Lily, to tell you the truth, I think Bridget is making up a lot of stuff to impress us. She probably isn't used to having nice things, and just doesn't know how to take care of them. I bet her mum doesn't even work in Marks. I asked her yesterday, what branch? She couldn't tell me and she got all flustered about it. There are a few drips of dye on the bathroom door as well, by the way. On the hall side."

"That's all we need! That shade of cream is discontinued now so we'll have to paint the hall doors again. I feel a bit dizzy, Jack."

"Sit down, for heaven's sake, woman. I'll get you another cup of tea. You've been overdoing it, getting stuff together for the wreath class."

"If you say I've been overdoing it once more, I'll divorce you."

"Will you really?"

"No." She wept into the sleeve of her mohair cardigan for a minute, and Jack sat down beside her and gave her a big hug.

"Shush, shush," he whispered. "We'll have the bath recoated. It will only cost a few hundred pounds."

"Oh Lord, don't talk about money. That's the profits from my second class gone, too. And I haven't even collected the fees yet."

Jack was about to say I told you so, again, but he didn't have the heart to. It was the main reason he didn't believe in having lots of people in his life: because lots of people automatically meant lots of problems.

"Why don't you bring Bridget a cup of tea and tell her it's okay about the bath?" Jack said cheerfully. "And you can get your own back by telling her about Trudy moving in today."

"Yes, I'll do that," said Lily, and she dried her eyes on a tea towel. She went up the stairs with a heavy heart, saw the dye stain on the bathroom door and took a series of deep breaths. The very thought of sanding down and repainting all the hall doors again was enough to bring on a heart attack. All those detailed Victorian panels to go around with the sanding block. And all because Bridget was so stubborn she had tried to dye an old skirt instead of just buying a new one. Outside Bridget's door, Lily blessed herself for courage. She knocked gently and turned the handle. Bridget was lying facedown in the single bed with her white curls peeping out from underneath the red blanket.

"Bridget," Lily began. "I need to have a word with you."

"I'm so, so, so sorry," Bridget wept, before Lily had a chance to speak. "I had no idea I would wreck the bath. I was only trying to look nice for the Christmas parties. I wanted to buy a new skirt but I couldn't afford one after I set aside my rent money."

"I'm not angry, Bridget. Honestly. I'm not. It was an accident. I know that."

"Really? I thought you'd batter me."

"Don't be daft," said Lily. "These things happen. However, there's something else I want to talk to you about."

The second bed was delivered at lunchtime just as the craft ladies were filing out with their fat, luscious wreaths. Lily bought another set of new bedding for it right away. When Trudy arrived at the tavern for work that afternoon, Lily invited her to stay, and she didn't need asking twice. She went straight back to the professors' house in a taxi to collect her clothes and her cassette player and her collection of herbal remedies. Bridget was seething with resentment at this gross invasion of her privacy but there wasn't a thing she could do about it. She was lucky the Beaumonts didn't throw her out on the street and sue her as well after all the expense she had caused them. And Lily had offered to reduce her rent to forty pounds a week because she had to share the room with Trudy. So Bridget had no option but to help Jack push the new bed into place and tidy up some of her laundry that lay on the sofa in a stale and jumbled heap.

The worst part was that she wouldn't be able to lie in bed talking to Gerry for half the night anymore. It was an intimate, almost loving, kind of ritual and she had come to enjoy it immensely. Gerry had given her a contact number in America and she was phoning him for a couple of hours each night. They'd chat about lots of things as Bridget lay in bed looking up at the painting of the angel over the fireplace, and imagining that the two wedding rings were for herself and Gerry. It was a much more satisfying relationship now that they had split up. They had finally learned to communicate. When sex was off the agenda it left nothing else to do except talk about the simple things in life.

It wasn't cheap, naturally, maintaining this transatlantic non-relationship. But then it was a very modern kind of love and Bridget was a modern girl. It was cheaper than Gerry using the hotel telephone, she told him, when he said she didn't have to call him every night. And besides, the phone bill wasn't due for a few weeks yet. She'd seen the most recent one in a kitchen drawer when she was looking for the ice-cream scoop. But now that Bridget had to share her accommodation with that mixed-up, painted-up head case Trudy Valentine, she would just have to go and sit in the tiny kitchen or the freezing bathroom to phone Gerry. While her roommate with the laughable eyebrows was tucked up in bed. And that would be the end of the midnight feasts as well. Bridget could hardly be seen wolfing down mountains of bacon sandwiches and gallons of tea with Trudy Goody looking on. It was ut-

terly depressing. Just when Bridget had
landed on her feet at last, Lily Beaumont had
to go and play the big softy.

Trudy was a tidy-freak on top of everything else and she had the whole room shipshape in no time. She produced an
over-the-door set of hooks and all her
clothes were neatly hung up within seconds.
The plates and cups that were festering on
the floor were collected and left to soak in a
basin of hot soapy water on the draining
board in the kitchen. She vacuumed up a
week's worth of toast crumbs and opened
the window to let in fresh air.

"There!" Trudy exclaimed when she was
finally finished. "Isn't this cosy?"

"Yeah, real cosy," muttered Bridget, dying
to throw herself on top of Trudy's perfectly
smooth duvet and wrinkle it. Bridget was
somehow offended by Trudy's endless re-
moval of dirt and grime. She suspected
Trudy had mild psychiatric problems and decided not to get too friendly with her. And
anyway as the single full-timer on the staff, it
was only right that Bridget should keep her
distance from the others.

"Come on," she scolded. "Enough of the
chambermaid routine. Let's get back to

work." And she gently pushed Trudy out the door.

"I'm on kitchen duty today," said Trudy brightly, and she skipped into the kitchen and reached for an apron off the back of the door.

"Watch out for the killer lemons, then," said Bridget spitefully.

Down in the bar, Lily was chatting to Barney and his friends in the end booth, and telling them about the aubergine paint she was going to buy. And they were all so interested, and warning her to make sure the walls were clean before she started painting. Dark colors did not disguise imperfections in a wall, Barney said. It was actually the opposite: they showed them up. Bridget sighed with boredom, and sighed again as the door of the tavern opened to admit about twenty students coming in to celebrate the end of a set of exams. Marie had just been dispatched upstairs to bake pies with Trudy, and Daisy was going shopping with Lily to help her choose new Christmas decorations for the pub. Jack was on the phone, arranging for the bath to be collected for recoating, and for a temporary plastic replacement to be installed. So it was up to poor old Bridget to serve the students. She reached for a stack of pint glasses and placed them out in a neat row below the pumps.

"Yes, what'll it be?" she asked them as they began counting out loose change on the counter. One guy asked her if he could pay for three pints of bitter with ten-pence pieces. Oh boy, Bridget moaned inwardly. Students!

At six, the writer Liam Bradley came in for a drink on his way home from the Linenhall Library. Because all of the booths and seats were full, he had no choice but to sit at the counter. He set his stack of books down and smiled at Bridget and she smiled back at him. Even though she was feeling absolutely fed up, her innate wealth-radar was alerted. Lily had already told her something about him: that he was a writer, a best-selling writer. And married, too. But that didn't bother Bridget. She quickly assessed Liam's appearance. Hair transplant. Very unnatural shade of black, she thought. That was the first thing she noticed about him. Having lived in America, she could spot transplants a mile off. His hips were too flat. His shoulders were a little too narrow but not bad. Height: medium. Eyes: gray but ordinary. His

clothes were expensive and a little preten-
tious. Stand-up collars on his shirt, con-
cealed buttons down the front. But his voice,
when he began talking, was sensuous and
deep. Bridget thought he was deliciously in-
triguing. And she sensed a kindred spirit in
Liam Bradley. He was like herself: he wanted
wealth but was intimidated by wealthy people. She decided to find out more about Liam
Bradley. See what made him tick. Before she
made up her mind if she wanted to seduce
him or not. It would give her a hobby to pass
the time with until Dr. Gerry Madden got his
commitment issues sorted out. And David
Devaney succumbed to either Bridget's
charms, or those of Daisy the beanpole.

8

PARTRIDGES
AND PEAR TREES

LILY AND JACK set to work at
closing time. They refused
Trudy's offer of help and sent
her to bed along with her reluctant roommate, Bridget.

"Thank you so much, Trudy,
but no. You must get your
sleep," said Lily, "because the
two of you will be opening up the tavern tomorrow on your own."

"Yes. We'll be unconscious in our beds,"
said Jack. "This will take us all night. I'm sure
of it."

"Okay, then. See you," agreed Trudy. Bridget had already bolted up the stairs, anxious to avoid being dragged into the painting session. She planned to get her full eight hours of beauty sleep and be looking her best for whenever Liam Bradley returned. David Devaney was still on the short list, of course, and he was miles better-looking than Liam, but Liam had more long-term investment potential. She must ask Lily if Liam's wife was pretty and if his marriage was a happy one. And there was always the chance that Gerry might call from New York. She was still hopeful he might propose before his thirtieth birthday. His fear of commitment might well be eclipsed by his fear of being left on the shelf. It was about time Bridget's romantic possibilities increased. She changed into her tank top and shorts in record time and was fast asleep before Trudy had even finished brushing her teeth.

With the two girls safely tucked up for the night, Lily prepared a pot of tea and some chicken and ham sandwiches for her and Jack. They both quickly changed into old jeans and worn shirts, and swiftly carried the leaning Christmas tree up to their bedroom. Lily was so excited about the decorating project that she didn't feel a bit tired. When the tavern walls were painted, she was going to assemble the three new artificial Christmas trees and decorate them with the gold-beaded pears and the gold-filigree partridges that she and Daisy had chosen in the art shop earlier in the day. She had hundreds of white fairy lights in her shopping bag and three handmade angels with golden robes, as well. She planned to place the biggest tree to the right-hand side of the chimney. One smaller tree was going beside the front door, and one was for in behind the bar. She had spent an absolute fortune on the decorations but she wasn't going to worry about that now. The DIY shop had delivered several large mirrors with ornate gold frames, and Jack was going to hang them up when the paint was dry.

She had contacted some journalists who reviewed pubs and restaurant food for their newspapers, and they accepted her invitation to visit the following evening, and she was determined to impress them. Everything was going to be absolutely perfect. They wolfed down their late supper and began the task at hand.

Jack moved all the furniture in the middle of the room as close together as he could and laid dustsheets over it, and also over the counter and the benches in the booths. Then he levered the lids off two large tins of paint with a screwdriver and took a few moments to grow accustomed to the richness of the shade, as Lily gasped with delight. She knew immediately that it was going to be wonderful and that they were going to change the atmosphere of the bar entirely, in one night, for the price of a couple of tins of emulsion paint. Jack wasn't so sure.

"Lily, are you sure this paint isn't slightly brown?"

"It is not brown at all. It just looks brown in this harsh overhead light."

"Well, maybe it'll be more purplish when it dries?" he said doubtfully.

"It's aubergine and it's going on these walls tonight." She dipped a cutting-in brush into the first tin and rushed over to the nearest wall. On the paint went with a firm swipe and they both held their breath. "It's beautiful, isn't it?" she said. "Quick, pour some paint into the tray and get going. I'll do the edges."

"Righto. Do you think we'll get away with two coats?"

"Oh, yeah. If not, we'll do a third one tomorrow night."

Jack loaded up the fluffy roller and quickly applied a layer of paint to the entire right-hand wall above the booths. It looked beautiful where it finished beside the soft red bricks of the fireplace. It was definitely very dark but they reminded themselves that when the Baroque mirrors were in place, the effect would be lifted dramatically. For over three hours they worked nonstop.

By four in the morning, however, they were both struggling to stay awake. Lily couldn't stop yawning and Jack's eyelids were twitching with fatigue. They heard the phone ringing upstairs just as they were conceding defeat. The walls were nowhere near finished. It was taking much longer to go all around the edges than they'd planned. When Jack went upstairs to make some coffee, Lily lay down on one of the benches to rest and fell asleep at once. Jack found her there when he returned with two steaming mugs of instant cappuccino five minutes later. She was in such a deep sleep that she didn't even feel the spare paintbrush sticking to her cheek. He smiled and set down the coffee mugs before gathering her up in his arms and carrying her gently to bed. He

switched off the lights with his elbow and decided not to worry about the half-painted
bar. They would finish it in the morning.
There was never a full house in the mornings. It would be okay. He would set the
alarm for eight and they would resume the
makeover. They both slept fully dressed, too
exhausted to even take their clothes off.

But when Jack opened his eyes again, it
was after five on Sunday evening. He lifted
the bedside clock and rattled it but it was still
working. They must have slept right through
the alarm. He kissed Lily softly on the cheek.
Her face was pink and flushed with warmth.

"Lily," he whispered. "Don't panic but
we've slept in. Lily?"

"What?" she mumbled. She was still
drowsy. "What time is it?"

"Five o'clock."

"That can't be right. We only went to bed
at four."

"No, silly. Brace yourself. It's five in the
evening. It's Sunday evening."

"What?" she cried, suddenly wide awake.
"It's Sunday evening already? Oh, Jack!
How did this happen?"

"I have no idea. We must have been worn

out. Listen. It's all quiet downstairs. I can't hear police sirens or anything. I think Bridget and Trudy must be doing okay on their own."

"Come on," she said, stumbling out of bed and heading for the stairs with her socks hanging off. "God only knows what's going on down there. Did we remember to cover up the paint tray? I bet Bridget has tripped over it and ruined the floor." Jack followed her down the stairs and they both hesitated for a moment before pulling open the door. What they saw left both of them utterly speechless.

Barney Cunningham was balancing on a plank between two stepladders, brushing bright white paint onto the embossed wallpaper on the ceiling. He was puffing away on his pipe and had covered the shoulders of his tweed jacket with a tea towel. Joey Fontaine was in behind the bar expertly painting all the hard-to-reach bits around the optics, and Marie was wiping away stray drips with a roll of kitchen paper. The bottles and glasses had been removed from the shelves and were stacked neatly on the counter. Francy Mac was applying emulsion with Jack's abandoned roller to the area around the door, and Trudy was peeling masking tape away from the finished areas. By the looks of things, they were well onto their second coat and were almost finished. The three trees were in the middle of the floor beside the tables and they were fully decorated, angels and all. The fairy lights were neatly threaded among the branches and the plugs were taped to the trunks, ready for action. Daisy was collecting up all the leftover packaging and stuffing it into bin bags. Trudy smiled at Lily and Jack as they came into the bar and tried to take it all in. The mirrors had been hung, although they hadn't heard the hammer knocking in any nails. Even the fire was lit and Bridget was sitting at the counter, polishing Lily's collection of glass bottles with an old cloth.

"Well, I never! Here they are at last, the two sleeping beauties," laughed Barney. He dropped the brush back into the tin and climbed down from the plank. "I think you'll find the ceiling well improved."

"Oh my God," Lily began.

"What do you think of all this?" asked Joey. "The elves have been in here tonight."

"And they're very thirsty," added Francy Mac, and he winked and nodded his head toward the pumps. They all laughed.

"Well, aren't you just sweethearts?" said Lily softly, bursting into tears. "A drink for everyone, Bridget, if you please. Whatever they want." The tavern had never looked more elegant. It would not be stretching it to say it was actually approaching sophisticated. Lily and Jack were both thrilled.

"It is aubergine," Jack said at last, and Lily hugged him.

They all helped with the finishing touches, moving the Christmas trees into place and folding up the dustsheets. There was a strong smell of paint in the air but Barney said the fire would draw it out in no time, as he folded up the ladders.

"I really enjoyed that," he said, as he returned the borrowed tea towel to Bridget. "It was just like the old days. A bit of life in the old dog, yet. Gin and tonic, please, young lady. If Mrs. Beaumont is paying."

"Ah yes, painting away merrily beside a real turf fire. We've had a great time," said Joey. "Mine's a whiskey and lemonade," he added. Bridget served both drinks and started a pint of stout for Francy Mac. He never changed his order, he said, no matter what the occasion.

"Who lit the fire?" asked Jack, feeling slightly territorial.

"I did," said Barney. "I hope you don't mind. I couldn't believe it when I came in this morning and the grate was empty. You should have had a notice on the front door to warn me." Everyone laughed again. Bridget began putting the bottles back in their little window alcoves. It was so beautiful in the tavern now that Lily was almost grief-stricken they hadn't done it up years ago. So much for her lifelong dedication to the space-enhancing properties of white paint. Color was the way forward, she decided. Modernity was history, so to speak.

"Thank goodness we had no customers," said Jack. "There would have been chaos in here this lunchtime."

"We closed the pub, Mr. Beaumont. Except to Barney and the boys here. Sorry. But there was no other way we could get the work finished," Trudy explained. "I phoned Marie and asked her to come in and help. Daisy, too."

"I thought you might have wanted to decorate the trees yourself, Mrs. B?" said Daisy quickly. "I hope you don't mind me doing it. Bridget wanted to surprise you."

"And that's just what you've done. They're heavenly and all the decorations are so well balanced. I couldn't have done better myself. Thank you, everyone."

They all said it was nothing but there was a fantastic mood of achievement in the room. Marie said she had a big pot of beef stew simmering upstairs and they were all more than ready for a plate of it. Fifteen minutes later, everyone was full and content.

"Well, isn't this fantastic?" sighed Lily. "I can relax now. There's nothing else to be done. Let's not bother with opening up for the evening crowd. We'll have a day off. I think we've earned it."

"Aren't you forgetting the pub-grub critics?" said Jack.

"Oh, damnit, that's right. They're coming at seven this evening. I'd better get busy," moaned Lily. "I'm making vegetarian wraps and a salmon pie. Will you help me, Marie?"

"Sure," said Marie. "I'd love to."

"I see a few people coming down the street," said Jack, looking out the window. "It looks like some of your craft ladies, Lily."

"Oh, isn't that nice?" said Lily. "They said they might call in today. Quick, open the door. But don't let anyone else in. I don't want the place too crowded for the press visit. I wonder what the craft group will think of the new look?"

"Let's switch on the fairy lights and see," said Francy Mac, and he plugged in the biggest tree.

"Oh, it's out of this world," said Daisy. "It's the prettiest tree of all time, Mrs. B. Really and truly." It was the best tree any of them had ever seen. The tiny white lights glittered against the dark walls, and the gold-colored decorations were very rich and precious-looking. They quickly powered up the smaller trees and were just putting the last of the glasses and bottles back on the shelves when the ladies filed in and stopped abruptly.

"Well, isn't this gorgeous. I see you've been busy," they said happily. "It's very swish now, isn't it? Oh yes! It's like Buckingham Palace." Barney, Joey and Francy Mac swelled up with pride. "Are you still serving soup and sandwiches?"

"Great to see you again, ladies." Lily beamed. "We've got beef stew today."

"There's just about enough left, if we use small bowls," whispered Lily to Marie as she slipped upstairs, forgetting entirely that she wasn't wearing any shoes.

That evening, on the dot of seven, a small party of journalists and photographers turned up and sat at the bar counter. They were all wearing ripped jeans, heavily patched denim jackets and scruffy suede boots. Obviously, the height of urban chic this year was the rugged look, Bridget decided, as she poured them complimentary drinks. Lily introduced herself and thanked them all personally for coming. The photographers took some enormously complicated cameras out of their bulky canvas shoulder bags and began taking light readings and lining up good shots.

"These pictures will be terrific," they said. "Love the wall color. And the Chrimbo trees. Nice."

"Thank you very much," said Lily, blushing. "We've just finished the painting. It's very good of you to come at such short notice. I thought you'd be all booked up with the bigger establishments at this time of year?"

"Well, we are, actually. But we like to cover several places each week, ideally. Different sizes and price ranges. Our editors will do the final choosing, though. It's not up to us who gets in the paper."

"I see," said Lily, with her fingers crossed

behind her back. The food was all ready and they even had some expensive napkins to go with it, with a picture of an old-fashioned Father Christmas on the front. "Shall I bring down the sample menu, now?"

"Yeah, that'd be great. Just a couple of questions, first? Why have you redecorated, just before the pub is demolished?" asked one very young girl reporter. Jack and Lily didn't think she was old enough to have left school yet. She switched on her tape recorder and set it on the counter. Jack fled upstairs and left Lily to conduct the interview on her own.

"Well," she faltered, "we just thought, why not? It's Christmas, after all. And the demolition is not confirmed, you know. And we might as well bow out in style, if and when that day comes."

When the interviews and the food-tasting were over, Lily asked them all to sign the visitors book, and gave them a Christmas pudding each to take home. There was a brief session of hand shaking on the doorstep and then they were gone.

Next morning, Jack was dispatched to buy the first editions. Lily was jittery with nervous energy, wondering if the editors had decided to be merciful. She fluttered around the kitchen, lifting jars and dishes and setting them down again, achieving nothing.

"Please, let this work out," she said out loud. They had almost as many customers as they could cope with already but Lily hoped the newspapers would help bolster support for their cause. Bridget and Trudy stayed in their beds, not wanting to be in the same room as Lily if the reviews were poor, or worse, nonexistent. Trudy buried her head in a textbook and Bridget wondered when would be a good time to tell Lily that she had had another little accident. She'd sat on a fountain pen and broken it, and the ink had bled onto the rose-patterned sofa.

Lily knew, when she heard Jack running up the stairs, that the news was good. The tavern had been included on the front page of both papers, probably because of the impending closure, they thought. He read the pub-grub reviews out to Lily as they sat in the kitchen drinking tea.

"First one... 'Bowing out in style: Beaumont's Tavern on Maple Street is one of Belfast's hidden treasures. Boasting a real turf fire and stylish Christmas decorations, my delicious salmon pie was barely marred by the discovery of a long red hair in the bottom of the dish.'"

"Oh no! Jack!"

"I thought you served the food? Not Daisy?"

"I did. But Daisy served the second round of drinks. It must have fallen in then." Lily covered her face with her hands. "What else? Any more bad news?"

"No. It's a terrific review apart from that one thing."

"I give up. No one will come to eat here, now."

"Wait! There's more... 'It has recently been announced that Maple Street may be demolished to make way for a new shopping center. I, for one, think that Beaumont's Tavern should be saved, as it has stood quietly and majestically in the center of Belfast for over two hundred years. . . .' That was decent of them." Jack showed the photographs to Lily. The tavern did look fabulous.

"Let's hope it's true that there's no such thing as bad publicity. What's the other paper say?" Lily asked in a weary voice.

"It says, 'The atmosphere was world-class and the vegetarian wraps were delicious but the menu was very limited overall.'"

"Can't argue with that. Let's see the picture. It's good."

"Yes, and they've printed our address and telephone number at the bottom."

"Do you think we might get any new bookings?" Immediately, the phone began to ring. Lily ran out to the hall to answer it. "If this is Gerry Madden, I'll scream my head off." She picked up the receiver. "Hello? Beaumont's, can I help you?" There was a pause, and then Lily said yes several times. Jack noticed that Lily's beautiful dark hair was full of aubergine paint splashes. He was thankful the journalists had not mentioned that in their articles. She hung up the phone and came back to the table, triumph plain on her face.

"Who was that?"

"It was a woman from America. New York, to be precise. Well, she's over here now, on a long holiday. Clare Prendergast is her name. She wants to hold a party here on Christmas Eve. For about seventy-five people, she reckons. I said yes."

"Great stuff. Well done, Lily. Food and all? Music?"

"Yes. She wants to hold a kind of belated wedding reception for herself and her husband. Peter, I think his name was. She says they had a very modest wedding three years ago in New York but now they want to invite all their Irish friends to a big party in Belfast, and they loved the tavern's decor in the newspaper picture. The Devaney brothers can play for an hour or so at the beginning of the evening. And here's the best bit . . ."

"What?"

"She said she would like some hits from the 1980s played if that's possible. So you can dig out all your old forty-fives and pretend you're a DJ!"

"Lily, I can't do that! With decks and stuff?"

"That doesn't matter. I told her we didn't have proper disco facilities. She said it would be so much more authentic to play genuine vinyl on an old record player and it doesn't matter if there are jumps and scratches. She sounds really nice."

"She sounds bonkers. Jumps and scratches! I suppose I could tape some songs onto cassettes and play those? But I'm not giving a running commentary."

"You pet. It'll be a lovely way to see in Christmas. Don't we love that era, ourselves? Oh Jack, I wish we'd done things like this years ago. Don't you?"

"Not really. I kind of liked it more when it was just you and I. Life was a lot more peaceful around here. But, I'm okay with it. It'll give us plenty to talk about later on, I suppose?"

Just then, Bridget came into the kitchen, looking extremely shame-faced. The small matter of the ink stain on the couch had been superseded by another disaster.

"What have you done this time?" asked Lily, her mood resolutely upbeat.

"Mrs. Beaumont, I'm sorry. I broke the bottle of Chanel. It just fell off the little shelf."

"That's okay, Bridget. These things happen." Lily was beginning to think she would have those words inscribed on her tombstone.

"I didn't touch the perfume, honestly," Bridget stammered. "I wasn't using it or anything. I must have bumped into the shelf when I was getting out of the bath." Jack and Lily exchanged glances. They knew that Bridget had surely been helping herself to a little bit of luxury, and now she'd added one of Lily's most treasured possessions to her long list of domestic casualties. That bottle of Chanel had been Jack's present to Lily on her last birthday. Bridget didn't know it but she was only saved from instant dismissal and eviction by the great news of Clare Prendergast's Christmas party.

"Is there anything I can do to make it up to you?" asked Bridget as she opened the bread bin and looked inside hopefully. There was a packet of fresh butter croissants nestling beside a granary loaf. Her round blue eyes lit up.

"That's okay, Bridget. As long as you re-place the perfume by the end of the week, we'll say no more about it," said Jack cheer-fully, and he winked at Lily and went to light the fire downstairs. Lily said nothing, and hurried into her room to make the bed. Brid-get was in shock as she heated up four croissants in the oven. She couldn't believe they were making her pay for the perfume. And it was a big bottle, too. Probably about one hundred pounds' worth. If she'd known they would ask her to replace it she'd have bought her own bottle in the first place. She preferred Clinique anyway.

"Good grief," she whispered to herself. "First, they shack me up with a button-phobic nutcase and now they have me shelling out for jumbo bottles of Chanel. And me only on minimum wages. I better stop phoning Gerry in New York or I'll be in the poorhouse this time next year."

The phone rang several times that Monday morning. Lily was never away from the half-moon table. By lunchtime her little notebook was full of party details and requests. She was careful not to agree to anything that was beyond her, but overall, she had managed to secure over two thousand pounds' worth of business. Then Clare P. (as they'd decided to call her for short) called back to say she had been telling her husband's family and friends about the party, and they'd had the idea of coming in fancy dress. Stars from the 1980s would be the theme: Adam Ant, Robert Smith, Steve Strange, Cyndi Lauper. Lily thought that was a brilliant idea, and said she would get the staff to dress up as well. They agreed on a simple menu of roast turkey wraps with salad and mixed canapés.

"And there's one more thing," said Clare. "If it isn't too much trouble? I'd like a wedding anniversary cake? Just one tier, I thought. With smooth white icing on the top and sides? Maybe we could have some fresh white roses as a decoration? Something very simple and understated. Can you help me?"

"I certainly can," said Lily. "I know just what you mean. Leave it with me. I'll bake the cake myself."

"Oh, you're a lifesaver," said Clare P. "I knew when I saw your lovely tavern in the newspaper that you were just the place for us. The others we looked at were far too big and cold. I can't wait to meet you. I'll call in later today with the deposit."

"That's fine. I'll be here all day," said Lily, and she hung up and smiled at her reflection in the hall mirror. She was soon sliding another fruitcake into her trusty stove. "I hope we survive this Christmas without falling apart," she said as she closed the oven door. "And that includes this poor stove!"

9

GERRY HAS A BREAKDOWN

 LIFE IN THE TAVERN was pretty hectic that week, with extra deliveries arriving day and night from the brewery, and boxes of cooking ingredients stacked around the flat upstairs. Lily arranged to have fresh meat for the stews delivered each morning from the butchers because there wasn't enough room in the fridge for it. Marie was a great help to Lily, and she said she enjoyed cooking and baking far more than serving drinks. She was really too shy to talk to the men, she admitted, but that was okay be-

cause her puff pastry was second to none. Trudy was terrific at pulling pints but she still couldn't face making cocktails. And of course, Bridget was sulking over the loss of her privacy, with many heaving sighs and comments on the lack of storage in the bedroom. Lily wondered what Bridget needed so much privacy for, but she hadn't the energy to ask.

Gerry Madden was phoning from New York every night, and Lily didn't know it but most of the time Bridget was calling him back. But she timed the calls and didn't stay on for more than fifteen minutes. Her ex-boyfriend was much more relaxed now than he used to be, she thought. He didn't always interrupt her to tell her she was wrong about things. Gerry thought the women in New York were far too outspoken and direct, and he longed for home and the more submissive females of the Emerald Isle. There was a very set way of conducting courtship in New York and he didn't like it. There were rules you had to follow and a definite etiquette to be observed. He much preferred the Irish way of meeting women: stoically avoiding any emotional conversation for months on end before eventually getting so drunk he lost all his inhibitions and fell into bed with the first pretty girl who would have him.

He told Bridget he would be home on the thirteenth of December and that he would be straight round to take her home to his apartment and make love to her all night. He hadn't looked at any other women in the Big Apple, he said.

"Promise, honey. Not a single one."

Bridget didn't believe him for a second and she wasn't sure she wanted Gerry's romantic attentions back anyway. She was very comfortable in Beaumont's and she loved her new bed and her purple silk curtains with the beaded tiebacks, and the little fridge in the kitchen that was groaning with Swiss cheese and Florida coleslaw and Italian olives and wafer-thin turkey slices. All she really wanted was to talk to Gerry and imagine that the angel in the painting was carrying two wedding rings to her. And pretend that Gerry was a kind and decent man who would always look after her, the way her tormented parents never had. She thought she might go back to him on the condition they get formally engaged and set the date for their wedding. But if she was honest with herself, the reality of life with Gerry could be quite bleak. He wore her out for days at a time with his declarations of love, and then she would tease him about marriage, and then he would flirt with other women and go on the drink. Bridget used to think she liked a bit of melodrama as much as the next woman but when she looked at Lily and Jack and saw how calm and deep their love was, she felt extremely confused. Maybe she had some commitment issues herself, always choosing to fall for the wrong man? Wasn't that what all women who were living with scoundrels were doing? Weren't they making a choice? It was self-destructive behavior. The magazines said that some women were simply more used to dysfunctional relationships because they had been brought up in one. Was that what had happened to her? Bridget wondered.

It was ten minutes to four on Friday morning and Bridget was wide awake. She looked across the room at Trudy's bed but Trudy was fast asleep. They'd moved their beds to opposite ends of the room and put the sofa in the middle as a kind of divider. Bridget had the telly on her side but Trudy didn't care. Trudy was a bookworm. She was always raving about some book or other. This week it was *Angela's Ashes* by Frank McCourt. Of course Trudy had read it before lots of times, but she said she always liked to read that book at Christmas because it made her so grateful to be alive. The thought of the poor children gathering lumps of dropped coal on the Dock Road on Christmas Day made her appreciate her own life a lot more. She told Bridget how the family had waited and waited for God and his angels to deliver them from the slums of Limerick but all God did was give fatal pneumonia to half the children. The tragic memoir made Trudy feel grateful she didn't have to go out looking for dropped coal, even if her own parents rarely had the time to phone from Birmingham and ask how she was getting on with her geography degree.

Bridget knew all about drunken fathers and empty larders already so she had no time for *Angela's Ashes*. The drink made men fools and women lonely. She knew that from bitter experience. That was why Bridget's mother eventually gave up moaning by the fire and joined her husband in the pub. She was tired of being alone so she said goodbye to her dreams of domestic bliss and became an alcoholic instead. With a rare flash of insight Bridget saw her own future mapped out before her. She'd marry Gerry when he got tired of running to his therapist. They'd have a couple of children together and furnish a nice house in South Belfast. And then he'd get bored with domesticity and start playing golf and drinking at the golf club, and she'd be left sitting at the fire like her mother before her. Well, she wasn't having that. She'd thought in the past that as long as she married a man with money she'd be secure. Even if she were unhappy a lot of the time she wouldn't be hungry and cold. But these last few days in Beaumont's had given Bridget a glimpse of married life the way it ought to be lived, and she wasn't sure she was prepared to wed for money anymore.

It was time to say goodbye to Gerry and look for another (more emotionally stable) man. And after Christmas she'd look for a new career as well. She was an excellent barmaid but she was tired of being around alcohol all the time. She might even go back to college and pass some exams, but whatever happened she knew her days as a barmaid were numbered.

"I declare to God above if he's listening,

that I will never be Gerry Madden's girlfriend ever again. As long as I live, I won't fall for his smooth talking. And that's final," she said. "Otherwise I'll be no better than my own poor mother." As if on cue, the phone began to ring in the hall. Trudy woke immediately and sat straight up in her bed.

"Not again," she moaned. "Will you pull the cord out of the wall, for heaven's sake? That man is pure crazy. Why does he never call you at a normal time?"

"Because he's not right in the head, like you so rightly pointed out," sighed Bridget. "And I can't answer the phone because I just made a sacred vow to get over him."

"Mr. and Mrs. Beaumont will be awake in a minute. Oh, Bridget."

"You go, Trudy, and tell him I'm out with a new man or something. I know! Tell him I've emigrated but you don't know where to."

"Bridget, I don't want to get drawn into this."

"Well, then, let the damn thing ring all night. He's never going to propose to me so I don't care. Tell him to play his head games with some other female." And she lay down again and pulled the red throw over her head. Trudy put her fingers in her ears and tried to block out the ringing by humming a rock tune. But it was no use. The sound was making her nerves jangle. She couldn't ignore it for another second. She leaped off her bed and raced to the telephone. She snatched it up and yelled down the line.

"What do you want?"

"Hello?" said Gerry. "Bridget? Is that you? What kept you?"

"This is Trudy Valentine. Bridget's new roommate," she spluttered. He didn't seem to have registered the rage in her voice yet.

"Oh, right. Will you put Bridget on the line, Trudy? I've come home early from the United States. Thanks, love."

"Love? Love? You listen to me," Trudy cried. "Bridget is tired of this carry-on and so are the Beaumonts and so am I. Just who do you think you are? It's the middle of the night! You're supposed to be a professional person, aren't you? Helping your patients and that sort of thing? Not keeping us mere mortals from our beds. Have you any idea what sleep deprivation can do to people?" Trudy paused for two seconds to gather her thoughts.

"Might I suggest you take some deep breaths at this point?" Gerry soothed. "You sound very agitated."

"I'd like to agitate you, you selfish moron. We're hardworking people here, you know. We're rushed off our feet, so we are, and you're nothing but a big spoiled baby. And Bridget says your mattress is full of fleas and you're never going to marry her and you're too materialistic and always drooling over stupid cars and she doesn't want to be your girlfriend anymore. Have you got that? Why don't you do us all a favor and go teetotal? You're an absolute disgrace to the National Health Service. You're round the twist. And so is your body clock!" And she slammed down the phone so hard she broke the receiver in two. Trudy picked up the two pieces and fitted them back together uselessly. "Oh dear. I didn't mean to do that," she told Lily, who had just come down the hall in her dressing gown.

"It's okay. I don't care," said Lily. The genuine Art Deco telephone had cost her one hundred and twenty-five pounds in an antique shop on Royal Avenue but at that moment she would have given five years of her life for one unbroken night's sleep. "These things happen. I was just about to put the telephone through the window and myself after it. These calls have been driving me and Jack out of our minds." She gathered up the cord, wrapped it around the broken telephone and dropped the whole thing into the wastepaper basket. "Good riddance. Come on," she said to Trudy. "Let's go and have some hot milk and toast." She put her arm around Trudy's shoulders and they went into the kitchen together.

Bridget lay astonished in her bed. Who'd have thought that poor old Trudy would have so much spirit in her? Trudy Valentine, who was scared stiff of harmless buttons, was like a cornered lioness when she didn't get her eight hours! Ho, ho! Then the smell of hot buttery toast made Bridget's mouth water and she reached for her tatty robe and made her way tentatively to the kitchen. Jack was awake, too, by this stage and the four of them sat beside the warmth of the stove, passing butter, jam and marmalade around the little table. They made an agreement to disconnect the telephone (a new one) every night from now on, and if some relative were taken ill they would just have to wait until the morning to be told the grim details.

Twenty minutes later, as they were setting their cups and plates into the sink, there was an almighty smash at the front of the building. They all froze.

"That sounded like breaking glass to me," whispered Jack. "Could it be vandals? Where's the baseball bat, Lily? Is it still in the hall cupboard?" There was a sudden roar outside. A man's voice was howling in pain. It ripped the silence apart like a chainsaw. They all jumped several inches off their seats. Trudy took her own pulse and Bridget froze with shock.

"That sounded very close," whispered Lily. "What the heck is going on?" There was another smash. "I think it's happening right outside. We've never had an attack before, Jack."

"My bedroom," cried Bridget, and she ran across the hall with her mug of tea clasped to her chest. Lying on her bed were two half-bricks and several large and jagged shards of broken glass. "Oh, no! My lovely bed." As she was standing there, numb with outrage, another piece of masonry came through the window and what was left of the glass pane dropped to the sill and shattered. Bridget peered out of the frame, trying to spot the culprit in the alley below. The others hovered by the door.

"Come away from there, for God's sake, Bridget, before you get brained," cried Trudy.

"Who'd be throwing bricks at this time of the night?" wondered Lily. "Was there a parade today?"

"Call the police, Lily," said Jack. "I'm going to sort this out."

"You are not!" his wife hissed. "There could be a whole gang of them."

"Who would do a thing like this? Unprovoked, too. We're a neutral pub." Jack was bewildered. "We have no flags up. Have you barred anyone recently?"

"No," wept Lily. "I have no idea who it could be."

"Well, I'm not paying thugs to stay away from here," Jack vowed.

"Wait! I think I know who it is. At least, I'm pretty sure. It must be Gerry Madden," Trudy said suddenly. "He's come home early from New York. I forgot to tell you."

"I might have known," wailed Bridget. "And you ate the face off him. He's not used to being spoken to like that."

"Oh dear," said Trudy. "I didn't mean for this to happen. I thought I'd scared him off for good. You said you never wanted to see him again. But it seems I've pushed him too far." Another stone came flying into the room just as Bridget moved out of harm's way. They could hear a man's voice shouting from outside.

"Bridget! Bridget, come out! We can't end it like this. I came home from America to be with you. They've suspended me from the hospital and it's all your fault."

"Ah, for pity," Bridget moaned, rubbing her tired eyes. "How is it my fault, you loser?" she shouted down to the alley.

"You broke my heart. I was inconsolable. I couldn't concentrate on the medical conference."

"Liar! Tell the truth, Gerry. You were hitting on other women. Weren't you?"

"I tried to chat to a few girls because I was lonely. It was just for the conversation, just for the company." He was almost in tears.

"I don't believe this." Bridget made a face at Lily and Jack to show them she was sorry for Gerry's behavior. Trudy was shaking her head with disapproval, which made Bridget even angrier than the broken window. "You were drunk, I suppose?" she called to the street below.

"A few harmless drinks, I had. Some gorilla got the wrong end of the stick and beat me up. Said I was eyeing up his girl." Gerry was speaking normally now.

"Serves you right."

"He was built like a Panzer tank, for God's sake. He was like a barn on legs. Jesus, I don't know what they feed Americans on when they're growing up. He nearly killed me, Bridget. He stood on my neck. But the hospital suspended me because of it. I was the one with the black eyes."

"Go away, Gerry. I'm not interested anymore. You need serious help. Why don't you get yourself some goddamn help?"

"I have nothing now, Bridget. Nothing but you." Yet another stone came sailing through the empty frame and struck the television screen, but that was already broken so nobody bothered saying anything.

"Leave me alone," Bridget said. "I'm doing fine on my own."

"You weren't saying that all those times you rang me," he shouted back. "You've rung me nearly every night since you left me."

"I thought you said Gerry called you?" Lily

accused. "Do you mean to say Jack and I are helping to fund this insanity? Bridget, answer me." But Bridget only dropped her gaze to the lilac carpet and her lips closed in so tight they disappeared.

"Right," said Jack. "This nonsense has gone on for long enough." He rolled up the sleeves of his dressing gown, threw on two odd shoes and went down the stairs like a whirlwind.

"Jack, don't hit him," gasped Lily as she followed him through the bar. "Not unless you're a lot bigger than he is."

"Give him the thumping of his life," said Bridget, tiptoeing across the broken glass to assess the damage to her clothes. The two girls went to the edge of the window to look out on Maple Street but all they could see were shadows and shapes in the darkness. After a minute they could hear scuffles and a bin falling over.

"I hope Jack flattens him," said Bridget. "This coat is ruined. Look at the size of that hole. I hate Gerry Madden. Take that!" She threw her mug of tea out the window and there was a cry of pain below.

"You're loving this," accused Trudy. "Mr. Beaumont could get arrested for assault.

You're nothing but a troublemaker, Bridget O'Malley."

"I am not. You don't know what you're talking about. I never asked Gerry to come here and cause a scene. Sure, I left him weeks ago."

"That was just an attention stunt. You're never off the phone to him. You're a tease."

"Leave me alone. Look at the state of my lovely bed." Bridget began to sob again. "He does love me, in his own way. He's just very emotionally damaged."

"Oh, please. He's a selfish toad and you're letting him get away with it."

"You ought to be on my side. Not his."

"Bridget, this isn't about taking sides. A relationship should be about two people who care about each other and respect each other no matter what anyone else thinks. It's not about convincing others that your love is real or not real. Why do you have to drag us into your fiasco of a love life?"

"Well, what about you? Miss Trudy-string-of-allergies-Valentine? Collapsing every five minutes with a lot of made-up phobias. There's nothing at all wrong with you. You're the one who's craving the attention. And you have the nerve to accuse me of the same thing."

"You take that back. It's bad enough being a phobic without being condemned for it by the likes of you. Every day is a struggle for me. It's exhausting."

"I will not take it back. Nothing happened over the lemon juice. You're faking the whole scene. No wonder you were available for work that day. What kind of a barmaid can't touch lemons? Good grief! Why don't you get over yourself?"

"Me? What about you! At least I wasn't sacked from my last job for making personal calls to psychics. And then blaming someone else into the bargain."

"I was not sacked."

"Oh yes you were. Don't deny it. I'm not an idiot, Bridget. You have no respect for other people or their belongings. Sure you have this place nearly destroyed." At that moment Lily came back inside.

"Break it up, girls. I'm going to the police station," she said. "Jack's been arrested for hitting Gerry. The two of them have been taken away already."

"Oh, now! That was quick," said Trudy.

"How did the cops get here so quickly? We never got round to calling them."

"There just happened to be a police car passing by."

"Typical. There's never any around when you need them. Is Gerry badly hurt?" Bridget wanted to know.

"No, Jack only punched him once but it looks worse than it is because he had two black eyes already. He can't even open one of them."

"A souvenir from New York, obviously," said Trudy quietly. "That man is dangerous."

"Do the police believe it was Jack who caused all the injuries?" asked Bridget.

"Yes," said Lily. "They're going to charge him with grievous bodily harm. And on top of all that, he was hit on the forehead with a mug full of hot tea. Who threw a mug out the window, for God's sake?"

"I'm sorry," said Bridget. "I was trying to hit Gerry. I'll go with you and tell them about the broken window. Gerry started it."

"I'll go, too," said Trudy. "To keep you both company."

"No, pet. You stay here and see if you can get a joiner to come and board up the window," said Lily, yawning. "A twenty-four-hour glazier would cost the earth."

"Please don't leave me here," whimpered Trudy. "I'm afraid of the dark and we're down at the end of an alleyway."

"Suffering Jesus," said Bridget. "Are you serious?"

"Yes," said Trudy. "I don't like to be alone at night."

"Is that the last phobia you have or are there any more I should know about?" asked Lily gently, putting her arms around the shivering body of Trudy Valentine.

"No. That's it," wept Trudy. "Honestly. Lemons and buttons, mainly. And dirty hands and the darkness. That's why I lodged with the professors, you see. I didn't want to be alone in digs at weekends when the other students went home. I didn't really mind the subzero temperatures they liked to live in, as long as they were there to keep me company."

"Listen," said Lily. "I'll go and be with Jack, and the two of you stay here and tidy up this mess as best you can. Okay?"

"Okay," said the girls, sobered by the situation they were all in. Trudy's short display of temper had vanished. Bridget was totally weary, and dying to go to sleep, but her lovely bed was covered in broken glass.

"That impossible man. Thank God I didn't stay with him," muttered Bridget, and she went to look for some newspapers to wrap the glass shards in. Trudy began lifting clothes out of the way and shaking splinters off the blanket.

Lily threw on some jeans and a warm coat, and called a taxi to take her to the police station. As she waited for the horn to sound at the end of the street, she packed an outfit for her husband to wear home from the cells. It was bad enough being arrested in the first place, but being arrested wearing a dressing gown soaked in tea, and wearing one blue trainer and one brown boot was bound to be absolutely excruciating for him. She knew the policemen on duty would be killing themselves laughing at her beloved husband. Bridget O'Malley had a lot to answer for.

When Lily came home along with a very subdued Jack five hours later, she told the girls that he had been let off with a caution. Jack headed straight into the shower and then went for a lie-down. Lily made tea in the kitchen and told the girls all the details.

Gerry had passed out in the station and had been taken to hospital for observation. For a while they feared that Jack's punch might have put Gerry in a coma, and poor Jack was inconsolable with worry. But luckily the doctor in the emergency room had spotted that Gerry was well over the safe limit of alcohol intake and had pumped his stomach for him. Gerry had been put on a drip and after a good sleep, the rogue psychiatrist was fine. When Gerry eventually woke up he was so glad to be alive he returned to the station to drop the assault charge. He told the duty sergeant that he was sincerely sorry for all the trouble he had caused and that he would not be bothering Bridget O'Malley or the Beaumonts anymore.

When he had slept off the worst of the trauma Jack emerged from the bedroom in a sober mood. He had a thin blue bruise on his forehead from where Bridget had hit him with her mug of scalding tea. But that was the least of his worries. He had a caution now. A police record. And he had been the butt of many jokes in the police station. Lily tried to convince him that the whole thing was Gerry Madden's fault, and that Bridget's ex-boyfriend was so irritating he would drive anybody to the brink. But Jack was disappointed with himself for losing control that night. He said he didn't want the incident mentioned ever again.

He also decided it was time he put his foot down concerning life in the tavern. He asked Lily to tell Bridget to get dressed in the mornings before wandering about the apartment, and that any further broken items were to be deducted from her wages. He said that Trudy must go to the doctor to get help with her phobias or he was going to let her go. He couldn't go on living with the atmosphere of anxiety that Trudy created. He stuck a calendar on the wall of the bedroom, with a big red circle drawn around the last day of February 2005. Whatever happened on that date, he said, whether the tavern was demolished or not, it would be the end of the line for Bridget and the other girls. He wanted things to go back to the way they were. Just the two of them in the living quarters. And the blissfully quiet life they were used to.

Lily, on the verge of collapse herself, had no choice but to agree with him.

10

BETSY GETS WHAT SHE ASKED FOR

 IT WAS LUNCHTIME on Saturday, the eleventh of December. Betsy Bradley crawled out of bed and almost broke her leg slipping on a tottering pile of glossy magazines that was strewn around the floor of the guest bed-room. She swore several times, lit a cigarette and sat on the edge of a small armchair, rubbing her sore ankle. The overflowing ashtray and the small army of old cups and saucers on the bedside table depressed her. She didn't like sleeping here. There was no wide-screen TV or huge ad-joining bathroom for a start. Only a compact

white-tiled shower unit in the tiny bathroom that she kept banging her elbows on. She missed her creature comforts almost as much as she resented her husband, and it was humiliating that he had banished her like this. He hadn't asked her to move out of their bed when he was working on his first book, come to think of it.

Liam was behaving very oddly these days. She thought Perry's recent phone calls had put him under a lot of stress. Liam had no interest in making love to her. Even when she'd taken pity on him and bought a cream lace basque and garters in a really expensive lingerie boutique on the Lisburn Road, and paraded around the townhouse in them the day before, he'd shown not a flicker of interest. In a rage of rejection she'd driven straight round to Richard Allen's riverside penthouse with the new lingerie on under her fake fur coat and he'd gone positively wild with passion. They were meeting again tonight and Betsy was rather looking forward to another amorous session on the sheep-skin rug beside Richard's gas fire. He had a nice Christmas tree as well, all decked out in red glass icicles and imitation shiny red apples; a very stylish scheme for a bachelor.

Liam wouldn't even bother getting a tree if he lived alone. Suddenly she became very angry with Liam. He was forcing her into having this silly affair where she was delighted by red glass icicles. Honestly, the lengths she'd had to go to, just to feel like a human being. Just to feel a man's warm skin against hers, and to hear a male voice whisper her name in the dark. Betsy marched down to the first floor and banged on Liam's door.

"I want to talk to you," she shouted.

"I'm sleeping," he mumbled. "Up all night, writing. Wake me in eight hours."

"No, now. I'm coming in." She turned the handle and burst into the room. Liam was lying in a disheveled heap in the middle of the four-poster bed. He was still wearing yesterday's clothes and was clearly suffering with a massive hangover. The remains of a fish supper lay scattered on the floor as well as several empty cans of beer, and there were pages of notes everywhere.

"I demand to know what is going on," she said.

"No. Go away. I'm tired."

"I will not go away. What have you written,

then? Show me!" She snatched up a few sheets of paper from Liam's bedside table and began to speed-read.

"No!" roared Liam. "That's private. It's not finished." He stumbled out of the bed, but Betsy was too quick for him. She bolted back to her own room and locked the door. Then she read the new chapters. She was not impressed by what she discovered. Slinger Magee had fallen in love with some dark-haired beauty in a Victorian blouse and he was giving up his immature and sexist ways forever. And doing everything he could think of to get this uptight woman to fall in love with him.

"Come out, you she-devil, and give me back my work. I'm giving you two minutes and then I'm going to break down the door," Liam yelled, and then groaned as his hangover reasserted itself. He didn't intend for anyone to read those pages, ever.

"Don't be pathetic. It's solid pine, you fool."

"I'm counting two minutes on my watch."

"His character is based on you, isn't it? Have you fallen in love with someone else?"

Still no sound came from the hall.

"You have. Haven't you? Is it the landlady

from that bar you go to, on Maple Street? Tell me, Liam. Because I'll find out eventually." Betsy had seen a picture of Lily and Jack in the *Newsletter,* and she thought Lily looked rather nice. A bit frumpish, and a horrible old-fashioned blouse. But still, nice. "Because if it is her, you've no chance. The husband is a stud. He's gorgeous-looking. I'd jump on him myself if he'd let me."

There was no answer.

"If you don't say to me, right now, 'I love you, Betsy Trotter, and I always will,' I'm leaving you. I mean it." Betsy bit her lip. Surely her husband would say the words even if he didn't mean them. He always had before. Their marriage had been built on denial since 1995, when Betsy had caught Liam in the empty first-class section of a 747 making love to a stewardess on a flight home from Ibiza.

Betsy waited for five whole minutes but there was only a dread-filled hush in the house. She read the chapters again and then decided to confront her husband a second time, but when she opened her door the top landing was deserted.

Liam was in the master bathroom having a shower. A puff of scalding-hot steam drifted out from underneath the connecting door. Betsy went to his personal computer in the study to see if she could print out some more of the story but he had removed the disk. She felt sick when she thought of all the times she had prostrated herself across her husband's designer glass, and very cold, desk. She was on fire with the shame of it. He had no respect for her anymore. Had he ever? He was bored with her. Betsy was afraid of losing him, then.

All the remaining papers on their bedroom floor were gone. She looked in his bedside cabinet but it was empty. His notebooks and all his reference books were also missing. The door of the bathroom was firmly locked. She twisted and pulled at the heavy glass doorknob but it was useless. She sat down on the four-poster to wait. After a while, the shower was switched off but then she heard him squirting shaving foam and rattling around in the cabinet's top drawer for a clean razor. Sighing, she found a carrier bag and collected up the empty beer cans and salty chip wrappers. She opened the window wide and tidied the bed. When Liam finally emerged from the bathroom half an hour later he was clean-smelling and neatly shaved and wearing fresh clothes. His briefcase was bulging with all the missing writing materials, neatly stacked and straining against the zipper. He tried to walk past her but she held onto his arm, pleading with him, her last scrap of dignity discarded.

"Liam, I want you to be honest with me. Are you having an affair? I know we've both had our flings in the past but if this is serious I have a right to know." She waved the loose pages in his face. "This woman in your story, she has the same sort of blouse that Lily Beaumont wore in the *Newsletter* article."

"I can't talk about this now, Betsy. I have to think about my book."

"Just say the word. One word is all I need, Liam. Is it over? Yes or no?"

He stopped pulling away from her and took a deep breath.

"Betsy, I'm sorry about this but I think it is time we were honest about our relationship. It's over. And it's been over for a long time. This open-marriage thing was just our way of denying the truth. We're not good together."

"It was your idea that we see other people. You said it was a grown-up way to live."

"I'm going to stay in a hotel for a few days and then we can put the house up for sale.

From the proceeds we can buy a place each in a slightly less prestigious area. We never belonged in this street anyway."

"Liam, no!"

"I'm sure Richard Allen will help you find a new property. We'll get divorced when I have time to sort out the details." He snatched the pages from Betsy's hand and stuffed them into his pocket.

"Goodbye," he said sadly.

Betsy was so shocked she could not make her mouth form any words. Liam stared at her tattooed lips and turned away in disgust. Why bother with the outline, he wondered, if you weren't going to fill it in with lipstick all the time? He went out into the hall and began to descend the stairs. Betsy willed herself into action. She leaned over the banister, now in floods of tears.

"Goodbye? Is that it? Is that all you can say to me? After we've notched up ten years of marriage? Why? Limo! I mean Liam. We've had our ups and downs but I still think it's a good marriage. Why are you leaving me? I want to know why." He looked at her and she was appalled at the sense of detachment she felt from him. He was not only bored with her. He had almost forgotten her already.

"Why? I'm leaving you because you don't know who W. B. Yeats is. Or should I say, was? And you dress like a tramp. And your hairstyle is too young for you. Will that do for starters?

"Your shepherd's pie is stodgy and you never remember to grill the mashed potato. You leave smears all over the kitchen appliances when you clean them. You're nothing but a gold-digging tart."

"You've had other lovers, you hypocrite!"

"You have the nerve to ask me to buy you a house in Dublin. So you can swan around playing tennis with the Irish gentry. No Malahide millionaire would be seen dead with either one of us, you stupid cow. We're Northerners. We don't belong anywhere else but in this godless no-man's-land of a dump."

"I'm bored, Liam. I have nothing to do all day."

"Why don't you get a job and buy your own damn house?"

"Because it's a full-time job putting up with a tedious creep like you!" she shouted. And then she burst into noisy tears.

Liam shook his head, dismissing her, and hurried down to the entrance hall, where he frantically collected his jacket, car keys and laptop computer.

The door banged shut and he was gone. She ran down to the hall and pressed her face to the glass in the side panel. In a daze she watched his black sports car speed out of the garage and down the avenue. Then she turned around and looked at the stairs going up and up, and at the delicate glass chandelier swinging slightly in the draught. There was a feeling of unreality about the house, she thought. Like when you went to the cinema in the middle of the day, and when you came out it was still daylight when you thought it would be dusk. She went to the kitchen and made some bacon sandwiches and a tall mug of cocoa for breakfast, still wearing her baby-doll pajamas. For the next three hours she went from room to room, packing all of Liam's possessions into bags and boxes, and stacking them in the garage ready to be collected. The last thing to be dumped in the cobwebbed gloom was Liam's author portrait.

Betsy went upstairs, ran a hot bath and got in. She lay there for a long time, thinking up lots of different ways to hurt her husband.

Was he famous enough for a kiss-and-tell story? she wondered. Would the media be interested in the fact that Liam Bradley based the character of his so-called maverick detective on his own pathetically adolescent sexuality? And then she cried her eyes out when she saw Liam's old razor lying on the windowsill in a small puddle of soapy water.

In a fourth-floor room in the Hilton Hotel, Liam plugged in his laptop and went on typing. He would deal with the fallout from his failed marriage later. When he had finished the book. He might hire a detective and have Betsy followed to get some evidence of her adultery. His most recent infidelity had been only in his dreams. She couldn't use the plot of his book against him because it was a work of fiction. In the meantime he had to get on with his writing. Maybe Perry would fly over from London soon and pick up the manuscript in person? He'd said he had a couple of interested parties lined up already. Was the first half nearly finished? The first twenty thousand words even?

Liam was working on two versions of *Boom, Boom.* One for Perry, and one for himself. In Liam's personal version, the death-wish detective was coming in from the cold, giving up casual sex and becoming a pillar of society who got great respect from everyone he met. Perry was cross with him for wasting time. He said it was madness to change Slinger in any way but Liam was a very stubborn writer, and said he had a feeling that the politically correct Slinger would prove very popular with the publishers.

"Look at all the playboy celebrities in Betsy's magazines," Liam had told his agent. "Boasting and bragging about getting a few dozy models into bed. Nobody's impressed with that malarkey anymore. It's only because they have a few bob in the bank that the girls will have anything to do with them. Aren't we all having sex, all the time?" (Well, Liam wasn't but that wasn't the point.) "What's the big deal about a couple of minutes of fornication? They're a laughingstock, all over the Western world. These Himbos! It's cringe-worthy. No, it's time for a change, and Slinger will be symbolic of that change. Women will love it. I'll reach a whole new readership. You'll see." Perry wasn't convinced but he said he would put out feelers, see what the publishers thought. And if they didn't like it, Liam would just have to accept it. They reached an uneasy compromise.

Perry began a round of business meetings with a summary of both books in his briefcase, and Liam booked the room in the Hilton for a month. He realized with a heavy heart that he would be living in a rented room over Christmas. But then he consoled himself with the thought that he wouldn't have to spend any more time with Betsy's boring relatives. He wouldn't have to eat Betsy's dried-up turkey dinners or buy her a romantic present or have sex with her while wearing a Santa hat.

He poured himself a gin and tonic from the minibar and ordered a plate of assorted sandwiches and a pot of coffee from room service. He told the hotel receptionist to withhold all his telephone calls. Only Perry Shaw was to be put through. And only after nine at night, he added. Liam knew that if he went at his new novels like a man possessed, he could write five thousand words a day. And he was going to finish them both by Christmas, even if it killed him. It was his tribute to Lily Beaumont. And when the books were finished, and Liam had a few months to himself before the PR marathon began, he was going to tell Lily Beaumont how he felt about her. He was going to tell her he loved her. Of course, it was doomed. In his heart he knew that it was doomed to end in a broken heart on his behalf, and probably a broken nose as well, when Jack found out. Jack didn't say much but the man was built like a brick wall. Yes, Liam was going to give the women of the world what they maintained they'd always wanted, and that was honesty. He was going to tell the truth for once in his life, and just let fate take its course. He'd already been honest with Betsy. He'd actually done her a favor, telling her those home truths about her gaudy appearance. Now she could tidy herself up and snare another man, someone as uncultured as herself. They'd be very happy together.

There was a knock at the door, twenty minutes later.

"Room service," said a husky voice. Liam dashed across the room, yanked open the door and grabbed the tray. He shoved a five-pound tip into the hand of the startled young man and closed the door in his face. Then he took off his watch, threw it across the carpet and began to type. He was going to write until he had five thousand words completed, and he wasn't even going to check the time until that happened.

11

DAVID AND THE WITCH

Friday, December 17

IT WAS LUNCHTIME. Daisy stood at the bar counter with her art folder, her portable sewing machine and a big bag of clothes on the floor beside her. She looked very shaken and there was masonry dust in her bright red hair.

"What happened to you?" asked Bridget. She was standing behind the bar with a tea towel slung over her left shoulder. Daisy thought Bridget looked ridiculous, as if she had worked in the tavern for years already.

"Would you believe it, the ceiling in my student house collapsed?" Daisy said, scratching a piece of plaster out of her collar. "I never heard of that happening before. Have you?"

"No. Was it terrible?" Bridget stifled a yawn.

"It was bloody loud. I'll say that much. We thought it was the Second Coming of Jesus. You could see the sky from the ground floor. It was totally freaky. And the dust was un-real." Daisy began to shiver gently. Bridget thought Daisy was in shock and she called for reinforcements.

"Yo! Daisy's house fell down," Bridget yelled up to the kitchen. "She's here now, shakin' like a leaf. Traumatized, she is!"

"I am not traumatized, Bridget. I'm just cold, that's all," Daisy snapped. Bridget O'Malley was hardly bigger than a flowerpot, but she could be a massive pain in the arse, thought Daisy crossly. She didn't want a drama made out of the whole thing, just somewhere else to live for a little while.

"What caused the collapse? Was it a gas leak? Are you hurt? Was anyone else hurt?" asked Lily, rushing downstairs. "Was it the heavy rain last night?"

"I think that's what it was, yeah," croaked Daisy, and her shivering intensified. "The roof was sagging anyway. It was a flat roof."

"A flat roof in a wet climate like this?" Lily shook her head. "Builders! Are they all crazy? Did you not have any inkling the house was dangerous?"

"No. The bathroom ceiling was dripping water all night but we thought it was nothing serious and just put a bucket underneath. Then, this morning at breakfast the lights flickered and went out. And the next thing there's this weird cracking noise in the rafters and the whole lot comes crashing down into the bedrooms."

"You could have been decapitated," gasped Bridget with fake horror in her voice, and she turned away to polish the optics. Daisy ignored her.

"There were clouds of dust everywhere. I was coughing. The other girls were coughing, too, and we couldn't open our eyes. We were in the kitchen at the time, eating some leftovers from a Chinese take-away, and we never got to finish the chicken balls."

"Give her a double brandy, Bridget, and stop laughing," scolded Lily, trying not to laugh herself. "Daisy and her friends could have been killed. Thank God you were on the ground floor at the time, Daisy."

"I know. Well, one of the girls was upstairs in bed when the roof came in."

"My God. What happened?" Lily said, genuinely shocked.

"Her boyfriend's back took the worst of it. They're both being treated for shock." Daisy shook her head sadly.

"I bet they are. Well, they can't say the earth didn't move for them," said Bridget with a wicked glint in her eye. And she served the double brandy and went running to the bathroom to have a good giggle to herself.

"Most of my artwork was ruined," moaned Daisy, rubbing her dusty eyes with her sleeve. "And I've nowhere else to go."

"Your parents?"

"Divorced. Remarried. New families to care for. No room for me."

"Couldn't they squeeze you in somehow?"

"Not easily. Anyway, they both live miles outside the city. I'd never be off the city bus. And they'd have me babysitting on a permanent basis."

"You can stay here, Daisy. Get that brandy down you," said Lily, and she took her mobile phone out of her pocket. She tapped in the number quickly. "Hello, is that the Perfect Pine store? Lily Beaumont, here. Is it too late to change my order? Oh, good. Could you bring me a set of bunk beds instead of a third single? I'd like English traditional pine, please. Although Mexican style will do, if you've no English pine left. Oh, you have? Lovely! Thanks a lot. I really appreciate it."

"What was all that about?" Daisy asked.

"I ordered another bed an hour ago, for Marie. Her parents were repossessed this afternoon, so she's homeless, too."

"That's awful. Poor Marie."

"I know."

"What happened?" asked Daisy, momentarily forgetting her own problems.

"Her parents were both laid off from a textiles factory six months back, when the contract went overseas. They're very depressed, which is hardly surprising." Lily held another glass to the brandy optic, and took a sip. "It must be a terrible thing to be homeless. Especially at this time of year."

"Yeah. That's the global economy for you," sighed Daisy. "God look down on them."

"Well, we must try to struggle on, I suppose. You and Marie will have to bunk up with Bridget and Trudy. And I do mean, literally bunk up. We're running out of space."

"I was hoping you'd say that. Thanks, Mrs. B. You're a brick. Where's Marie?"

"She's upstairs in the kitchen, making beef stew. Her poor parents are staying in a bed-and-breakfast in Rosetta for the time being."

"What will Bridget say about me staying in her room? We're not the closest of friends, Bridget and myself."

"She'll say nothing. The glazier has been here all day hammering and banging. Such a racket for a new window! And I've had to buy her new blankets for the bed. We couldn't take the risk of a stray splinter."

"I see."

"Go on up and have a sandwich and a rest, and we'll fit the bunks in when they come. We might have to rearrange the entire room, though." Lily went to serve some customers and Daisy trailed her belongings up the stairs. Bridget's face was like thunder when she saw Daisy stacking her things in a corner by the door.

"Not you as well? Holy sugar! It's going to

be like the bedroom of the seven dwarves in here tonight."

"Believe me, this wasn't planned," said Daisy. "I like having my own room. I'll be out of here just as soon as I can." And she went gingerly into the bathroom to have a shower, as Lily had suggested. It felt weird taking off her clothes in a strange bathroom and she was tempted to get dressed again and throw herself on her mother or father's mercy. But then, Daisy thought of all the chores they would ask her to do. So she stepped into the plastic bath and turned on the hot water. God knows she didn't want to share a bedroom with Bridget O'Malley but she didn't want to spend Christmas babysitting, either. At least here she was getting paid for her services.

Jack spent the entire afternoon assembling the bunk beds and Lily had to make yet another trip to the department store for bedding. They wondered what they would do with all the extra furniture when and if the girls moved out again but then they reminded themselves that excess furniture was the least of their worries. After much deliberation, they decided to place the two single beds on either side of the window with the chest of drawers in the middle. The bunk beds went to the left-hand side of the door and there was enough room on the right-hand side for the sofa, the TV and a small coffee table. Lily gave them the rug from her own bedroom, to make the sofa area more comfortable, and the girls tidied away their clothes as best they could, under beds and on Trudy's door hooks. Daisy chose the top bunk and Marie was happy with the bottom one. She said it reminded her of being a little girl again, and she laid her pajamas on the pillow. There was a school-dormitory air about the room when they were finished, and all the girls except Bridget were very happy with the new arrangements. There was even time for a quick cup of tea and a slice of apple pie before the catering for an emergency booking resumed in the kitchen. Bridget and Daisy worked all afternoon behind the bar, and at six, Marie and Trudy joined them, bearing many trays of delicious nibbles for the local rugby club's annual bash.

At seven, the Devaneys arrived in their squeaking leather trousers and took up their positions beside the chimney. Daisy wasn't in any way animated by David's arrival that evening, and Marie wasn't too excited by Michael's shy smile, either. They were both still in shock at losing their homes and tired with all the recent late nights they'd had in the tavern. Even when David dedicated the final set of the evening to the lovely bar-maids, they barely noticed. The boys were slightly deflated.

At ten-thirty, Liam Bradley called in for a spot of social contact. He was starting to talk to himself in the hotel room and thought he would take a short break and walk to Beau-mont's for a change of scene. He looked aw-ful, with dark purple shadows around his eyes, and he hadn't shaved for a few days. His mobile rang but he switched it off without answering it. Liam sat down in a dark corner at the end of the counter, away from the cen-ter of the party, and offered to buy Bridget a drink.

"I'll have a cola, thanks," she said, pulling off the top and drinking it by the neck. "What can I get you?"

"Double vodka and diet lemonade. I'm cel-ebrating," he told her.

Oh dear, thought Bridget. Now that he's bought me a bottle of fizz, he expects me to be his listening post.

"The new book?" she asked politely. "It's going well?"

"Indeed it is," laughed Liam. He sounded very drunk already. "It's the biggest pile of rubbish that ever graced a computer screen but it's going to make me rich. I tried to convince Perry that Slinger should be a nice guy but he wasn't having it. So it's business as usual, and big bucks here I come!"

"Congratulations," Bridget said, and yawned in his face. She served his drink and moved away from him. She was so tired by now she didn't care about observing the niceties anymore. All those late-night phone calls to Gerry Madden had finally caught up with her body clock. Bridget didn't know who Perry and Slinger were and she didn't care, either. Ever since she'd found out Liam Bradley had a sexy wife, she had lost all interest in him. Married men could be mean enough with money, she'd discovered. Divorced men could be even meaner. So that road was going nowhere. She'd been kidding herself to even think that it could work. Gerry Madden was already off her hit list. Now Liam Bradley was off it, too. Liam's neck blushed as red as Daisy's hair when he saw how bored Bridget was with him and his great book. She didn't ask him a single question about it. His male pride was badly dented. He held his hand up to attract her attention when she came to his end of the bar a few minutes later.

"Same again, love?"

"Surely." She thought the writer looked close to collapse but that wasn't her problem. If he fell off the stool, Jack could just shove the old bore in an ambulance. Men! And they think they're better than we are, Bridget thought sadly. She began to load empty glasses into a rack, aware that Liam's eyes were boring two holes into her back.

"Do you not bother with crime fiction much?" he asked her, when the other drinkers were busy clapping for the Devaney brothers. They had just completed a rather good session of U2 songs.

"Do you want me to be absolutely honest?" said Bridget, steadying herself on the counter. She was so tired she was near to fainting.

"Yes. Be totally honest," he slurred.

"I haven't read a book for years, crime fiction or otherwise. I'm not in the least bit cultured and I don't care who knows it," she said, looking straight into Liam's narrow gray eyes. "I'm twenty-five and I have my whole life ahead of me, and I'll have plenty of time for reading books when I'm in a rest home sixty years from now, with my knees under a tartan blanket."

Liam considered this information. "That's refreshingly honest. What's your name again?"

"Bridget O'Malley."

"Bridget O'Malley. What a cute name! That's like a cat's name in a Disney movie."

"Do you want another drink?" she sighed, looking at her watch.

"I just left my wife, Bridget O'Malley. What do you think of that?"

"That's too bad, Mr. Bradley."

"Yes. We had no children together, though. So it could be worse, I suppose?"

"I suppose," she sighed, and rolled her eyes. Why had she ever thought being a barmaid was a terrific way to meet men? By the time they got her length they'd been kicked up and down the soccer field of life, and were unraveling at the seams a bit. She wiped the counter in front of Liam with a clean cloth and slapped down a fresh coaster.

"Still. Chin up. Eh?" She almost laughed in

his face when she saw how shocked he was by her indifference. Liam had been drinking all afternoon, and he was almost too numb to feel insulted by the dreadful lack of respect shown to him by this young woman. Bridget wasn't bad-looking. He wouldn't turn down a fifteen-minute session with her. But compared to Lily Beaumont, she didn't have a chance.

"She was not a cultured lady, my wife," he said. And he burped loudly.

"Are you big on the culture yourself, Mr. Bradley?"

"No. I wouldn't know a good play from a bad one."

"Why should she, then?"

"She just should. She has nothing else to do all day. She should be reading books of highbrow poetry, and making me look good at parties." Liam closed his eyes for a minute to stop the room from spinning. But that only made it worse so he opened them again.

"You know what, Mr. Bradley?" said Bridget.

"Please call me Liam."

"Liam, maybe you're just not suited to married life? Don't worry about it. Lots of men aren't. My advice to you is this: hire a cleaner to do the housework, and forget about culture and all the rest of it. Good luck with the book, now." She moved away from Liam as he digested this information. Although he tried to engage her in further conversation, she avoided his eye and kept herself busy at the cocktail section. She wished the night would end so that she could make herself some tea and toast, and snuggle up under her new blankets. She would just have to try really hard not to notice the other beds in the room.

By eleven twenty-five, the Devaneys were packing up their guitars and there was a stampede to the counter for last orders. The noise level had reached a crescendo and there was still another half hour of tidying up to go. Bridget could hardly breathe through the fog of cigarette smoke even though the overhead fan was whizzing around at top speed. Her feet were killing her but she couldn't wear flat shoes or she wouldn't be able to see over the beer pumps. They were nearly out of cranberry juice and colored sugar and champagne.

"Out of the frying pan," she sighed again as yet another order for twenty Peach Bellinis came through, only one minute from closing time. So much for thinking this place would be a holiday camp. When one of the drunken rugby players lay on the counter and said he fancied her like crazy, Bridget merely rolled her eyes and ignored him. She was beginning to think it might be time to give up on men altogether and enter a convent. The angel on top of the smallest tree smiled down at her as if to say, This night is nearly over, you'll be okay.

Then, Liam Bradley passed out onto the slate floor of the bar and the rugby players cheered their heads off.

"That writer fellow looks like a bigger drinker than Dr. Gerry," Bridget told the angel sadly. And David Devaney had the hots for Daisy. Any fool could see that. He was looking at her all night. Even though she was as tall as a beanstalk and dressed like a witch from a kid's TV show.

"Oh God!" whispered Bridget, as Liam was carried outside. "What will become of me at all?" She gave Daisy such a look of disdain when she brought a tray of dirty glasses back to the counter after closing time that Daisy was visibly shocked.

Bridget didn't know it but Daisy was very close to the edge herself. She'd been looking forward to having her student digs all to herself this Christmas. She'd been planning lots of lazing around in front of the telly, ordering pizzas and wearing cucumber face masks. Now she'd have to help out in the tavern all day, every day. She was grateful, of course, and the food would be lovely, but her own house collapsing had brought it home to her how vulnerable she was. And that maybe a degree in theater design wasn't the best start in life? Would she ever have a little home of her own? she wondered. Or would she always be living out of a suitcase?

At the end of the night when all the customers had been ushered into the clammy, damp and sleety night, still singing at the top of their voices, Daisy sat down beside the fire and had a little fit of melancholy. Her large, green eyes were pools of sadness. Lily, Jack, Trudy and Marie were upstairs queuing for the bathroom as Bridget had beaten them to the hot water again. So Daisy had elected to turn off the lights downstairs. She decided to leave the Christmas tree on for a while, though, as she warmed her hands on the dying embers. Only the day before, she had fallen out with both her parents over this year's Christmas Day arrangements. Her father said he'd be very offended if she didn't spend the day with his family. And they could do with some help with the children, as his wife, Sheila, was working in the hotel for a few hours in the morning. And Daisy's mother said that it was the least she could do to spend the day with them because they'd only just moved into a new house and the walls needed three coats of paint. She seemed to think that Daisy would be only too happy to be painting walls over her Christmas holidays.

"Sure, aren't you an art student?" her mother had said brightly. "You can help me pick out a nice shade of beige for the sitting room. I've narrowed it down to four." Daisy just wanted them to say they loved her and that they were sorry for turning her life upside down when they decided to get divorced and remarried and have more children and take on stepchildren. She sighed and wondered how she would go about renting another room. She didn't want to outstay her welcome here. But none of her friends had a vacancy and she had nothing in the bank for a deposit on a one-bed flat. She wondered if the Beaumonts were going away for Christmas Day. She'd rather spend the day alone here than watch her parents being all lovey-dovey with their new partners. Although Daisy accepted divorce as a civil liberty, it was still hard to watch her birth family implode. And it was impossible to decide which parent to spend Christmas Day with. No matter which one she chose, the other would feel rejected. Last year, she'd spent Christmas morning with her father's family and the evening with her mother's. But even that was complicated because it felt like she was comparing the celebrations, with both sides asking what the others were doing. And now she had seven extra presents to buy for her stepsiblings, and no money to buy them with.

There was nothing for it but to ask if she could hang around here on Christmas Day. If the Beaumonts were going away for the day, they might let Daisy stay on in the pub and keep an eye on things. She twirled her red hair up into a bun and picked at some loose sequins on the hem of her short black skirt. Be positive, she reminded herself. It was great of Lily and Jack to take her in, and the room upstairs was cosy and homey even with four beds and a sofa in it. They'd made a little sitting room in one corner with the sofa and the television, and Marie was planning to hold a midnight feast soon. (Poor Marie, she was reverting to childhood pleasures, over the trauma of losing her home.) Daisy told herself to cheer up and just go with the flow. Something would turn up just when she least expected it.

Just then, there was a knock at the door. Daisy jumped. She went over to the window and peeped out but it was too dark to see anything.

"We're closed," she called out. "I'm sorry, now."

"It's David Devaney," said a man's voice. "I've lost my wallet. Could I just check if it's here? Before I go to the trouble of canceling all my cards?"

"Sure," she said, opening the door. "We'll have a look." After ten minutes of searching, Daisy found the wallet behind the turf basket.

"Aw, nice one," he said, hugely relieved. "I don't know how that happened." Daisy had a fair idea. There just wasn't room in David's back pocket for a five-pound note, let alone a wedge of leather an inch thick. She handed it over with a lopsided grin. With some considerable effort, he managed to slide the wallet back where it belonged. Daisy thought he looked gorgeous in the firelight, even if he dressed like a cabaret singer from 1970s California.

"Well, I suppose I'd better get some shut-eye. I missed college today," she said, covering a yawn with her hands. He looked curious. "Long story." She smiled. "Involving chicken balls and an awful lot of dust."

"Tell me," he said. "Unless you're too tired? Or maybe I could take you out for a meal sometime and you could tell me then?"

They stared at each other for a few moments before David tilted his head to one side and slowly leaned in for a kiss. Daisy was still considering whether she would kiss him back or not, even as his lips brushed against hers. Then, she decided to enjoy the moment. He was rather gorgeous, and she did fancy him. Bridget would be so jealous. And even though Daisy was sure it would be only a fleeting thing between them, before David moved on to his next gig, she allowed him to put his arms around her and hold her for a little while. After all, as Lily had said to the reporters, it was Christmas. . . .

12

BETSY'S BRIEF ENCOUNTER

Saturday, December 18

RICHARD ALLEN LAY DOWN on his comfortable black recliner and flicked through the pages of his address book. He wondered if he might invite that nice girl Sarah Jones out for dinner. They'd met at a house auction a few days earlier. Bit of a sad occasion, actually: a repossession job. Couple of factory workers by the name of Smith, going under. Sarah was a property developer from Belleek. She had mischievous brown eyes, and her family had plenty of money. He sighed with contentment, gazing into the flames of the fancy gas fire with white cones in it instead of coal pieces. The ornaments on the white tinsel Christmas tree twinkled and shimmered, and Richard was glad that he had the peace to enjoy such things. Not like his work colleagues, who were frantic with Christmas shopping for the children's presents.

There was a buzz from the intercom. He ignored it. Most likely it was only charity collectors or carol singers. But the buzzer rang again. And then a third time.

"Damn," he said, hauling his body over to the intercom. "Yes?"

"Richard. It's Betsy."

"Betsy Bradley?"

"Yes! How many Betsys do you know?"

"Come on up, Betsy," he said, reluctantly pressing the button.

"I just thought I'd surprise you," she said, gasping, when she had climbed the three flights of stairs to his level. Richard was disappointed. He'd been looking forward to watching an action movie on Sky TV and then nipping across the street to Kane's bar for last orders. He smiled weakly at Betsy as she tottered in across the wooden floor on very high heels, and dropped onto the sofa.

"To what do I owe this unexpected pleasure?" he said, forcing charm into his voice. Betsy passed him a bottle of good champagne from her shoulder bag and took off her fake-fur coat and woolly bobble hat. She was wearing a tiny denim skirt, shredded at the edges, and a skintight pink T-shirt with BABE written on it in white rhinestones. Her legs were newly tanned and she was sporting long blond hair extensions.

"Blimey! Betsy, are you trying to put Pamela Anderson out of business?"

"Oh, you flatterer!" she cried. "I've had a lovely day pampering myself, and I thought I would call over and let you see the results." She crossed her legs seductively, and rubbed her hands up and down her shiny shins to show off her glittery manicured nails. In spite of himself, Richard was aroused. Okay, she was vulgar and cheap-looking, but in a good way. He uncorked the champagne and brought two tall glasses from the kitchen.

"I just love your tree," cooed Betsy, as he handed her a glass. "Where did you buy the decorations?"

"Can't remember," he said, carefully pouring the champagne. An ex-girlfriend had chosen them for him some years ago but he couldn't remember her name so it was almost the truth.

"Well, they're very nice," she said. "Sit down." She patted the sofa. Richard sighed. He was going to have to get in better shape, such was the rampant extent of his love life. He didn't want to keel over with a heart attack when he was only in his forties. Betsy took a deep breath and smiled up at him. He noticed at once that she wasn't wearing a bra. She laughed when she saw his gaze dropping farther down, to her nut-brown thighs.

"I'm not wearing much down there, either," she giggled, and stood up slowly.

"Oh, is that right?" Richard downed his drink in one go and set his glass on the table. He slid a hand up the side of Betsy's skirt and found the thinnest of ribbon ties there. He pulled gently on one of the ribbons and a pink lace thong fell onto the wooden floor. They both looked at it for a moment. Here we go again, thought Richard, taking a deep breath.

"Shall I get undressed?" she asked, mock-shy.

"There's no need to, in these bits of clothes," he said slowly, and he pulled her down onto his knee.

"What about my heels? I might put them through the couch? They're as sharp as needles."

"Betsy Bradley, you're gonna kill me. You know I have a thing about spike heels," he moaned. But he gently flicked off her red shoes. There was no need to damage the furniture. They lay back on the sofa. He eased her skirt slightly upward, her T-shirt down off her shoulders, and forgot all about his movie. Betsy undid his buckle, pulled the belt right off and threw it across the room.

"Be rough with me, you tiger," she begged. She kissed him hard, covering his face with sticky pink lipstick. He pulled at Betsy's hair extensions in a calculated display of passion. She liked him to pretend he was going to hurt her, as long as he didn't actually do it.

"Careful," she warned, as a handful of the blond fibers came away in his hand. "This hairdo cost me an absolute mint, not to mention how long it took." He apologized at once, and the pace of their lovemaking slowed down a little. She wanted to kiss him for a while first but he was anxious to consummate her visit. She pushed his hands away from her hips. "Just a minute," she purred. Betsy thought she saw a trace of impatience creep across his face and she felt mildly cross with him. He could never wait, just like Liam. Trying to revive things, she slapped him hard across the face. Genuinely shocked, he held her hands tightly by the wrists and he rolled over, pinning her to the sofa.

"You're gonna be sorry you did that," he panted, and she laughed out loud and kissed him again.

"Wow," said Richard, gasping, when it was all over five minutes later. "That was great. I'm worn out."

"Thank you." She smiled. It was a bit disappointing, to be fair, that he had given her only five minutes of pleasure. After she'd spent an entire day preening and grooming for him.

"Are we celebrating anything in particular?" he asked, pouring them both another glass of champagne.

"Yes, we are," she said, after a dainty sip. "Liam and I have split up."

"Is that right?" Richard barely flinched, but

his body temperature dropped rapidly. "That was pretty sudden. What happened?"

"He's freaked out. Working on his new book day and night, and falling in love with one of the characters in it."

"Heavy stuff." Richard exhaled noisily. He'd never fallen in love with any woman, let alone one in a novel. "What are you going to do about it?"

"My brother Ted is going to sort him out. Ted's a lawyer."

Whoops, thought Richard. He'd forgotten about that. Poor old Liam!

"Maybe Liam is having a creative crisis of some kind?" he offered. "It'll pass."

"I don't care if it does pass. No man treats me like dirt and gets away with it."

"Fair enough." Richard finished his champagne and poured himself a whiskey from the silver tray on his coffee table. The table was made from the door of an Indian prison. He retrieved his belt and secured it with trembling hands. He was worried. He didn't want to be saddled with a scorned woman, having to listen to endless complaints about her evil ex-husband. Some females could keep the vat of bitterness boiling for years after a split. It was time to get rid of Betsy. He must get her to leave him. Engineer a split and convince her he was doing her a favor into the bargain.

"Maybe we should stop seeing each other for a while?" he began. "I wouldn't want you to lose out on your divorce settlement because of me. If Liam decides to sling a bit of mud in your direction?"

"Don't worry. There's no money in the bank. The house is all there is to fight over. And he's not getting that. Not unless he kills me first."

"I see." Richard began to panic. "Would you not try and make it up with Liam? I don't want you to be alone, Betsy."

"But I'm not alone. Am I?" she said quietly. And she kissed him on the cheek and pushed her almost-spherical breasts back under the rhinestone-encrusted cotton top.

"No," he whispered, and the whiskey burned a hole of indigestion in his throat.

"It's been great, coming here and forgetting about my troubles for a while. I don't know what I'd do without you, Mr. Allen. Let's see if we can beat five minutes, shall we?" she said. "I'm still in the party mood. Come on into the bedroom. I'm getting a cramp, kneeling here like this."

Richard suddenly lost both his composure and his sex drive. If they went into the bedroom, she might fall asleep afterward and end up spending the night.

"Betsy, let's get this straight? We're not a couple. You do realize that?"

"What do you mean, not a couple? We're lovers, aren't we? I know it isn't serious yet."

"Lovers, yes. But that's all. I'm not ready to settle down."

"You're forty-one, Richard. Get real! Unless you've discovered the secret of eternal life, I'd say you were cutting it a bit fine to be settling down at all."

"Forty-one is no age."

"You're old enough to be a grandfather."

"What are you talking about? I am not!"

"You are, too. Where I come from, if you're not a grandfather by your fortieth birthday, people assume you're a gay-boy."

"Don't talk rubbish. You're only as old as you feel, in this world."

"Oh, men! Such egos, you have!"

"Look, Betsy, I'm just being honest with you."

"That's what Liam said the day he left me. Then he called me a tramp."

"Yeah?" Richard was shocked, and secretly impressed, by Liam's rather direct approach with Betsy. He thought he might go out and buy Liam's first book.

"He said I showed him up at dinner parties. He wanted me to tell poems over the roast beef, or something." She rearranged her skirt and wiped some lipstick off her face with the back of her hand. Richard felt sick. What would happen if one of his friends spied them out together?

"Recite poetry," he corrected. "You recite poetry. You don't tell poems."

"Don't lecture me. Can you recite a poem? Can you? Go on, then, I'm waiting."

A horrible silence descended. The affair, which had ticked over quite happily for several years, suddenly lay down and died on the glossy floorboards.

"I never claimed to be Samuel Beckett," Richard sighed. You could take the woman out of the ghetto, he thought, but you couldn't take the ghetto out of the woman. He looked intently at his watch.

"Forget it," she snapped. "I know when I've been humped and dumped. I know when I'm not wanted."

"Come on, Betsy. You know it was just ships

passing in the night. You know the two of us were never going to have a white wedding."

"Yeah. But I thought you liked me a little bit more than this. I thought it was about more than just sex. Where did it go wrong, Rich? Don't you care about me at all? Talk to me, honey."

"Don't you have female friends for all that talking stuff?"

"No. I'm quite lonely, to tell you the truth."

"Maybe you need to get out more? Get a job of some description?"

"Maybe I will, Richard. Thanks for the advice," she said bitterly. So much for being a kept woman, she thought. Nowadays you had to be slim, attractive, on the pill, sexually experimental and independently wealthy for a decent man to want to sleep with you. And even then, it was nearly impossible to get your hooks into a bloke. She had done things with Liam in the past that made her feel quite sordid, and now it was all for nothing. He didn't want her. And Richard didn't want her.

Betsy shoved her knickers into her handbag and prepared to leave the building with a backside bare to the world.

"Goodbye, Richard," she said, putting on her coat and hat. "Don't bother to call me."

"Okay." He tried his best to look sorry, winking sadly at her.

Betsy paused at the door, sniffing softly. Richard thought she was trying to make him feel pity for her. He walked in the opposite direction, over to the French windows, and opened them wide. He stood on the balcony, breathing in the cold, fresh air. With her hand on the doorknob, she turned back to look at him for the last time.

"Goodbye," she said again.

"I'm sorry, Betsy," he replied. "There was nothing special between us. I'm only being honest with you. Would you prefer it if I told you lies?"

"Yes, actually," she said. "I would."

Back home in Marlborough Avenue, Betsy let herself in through the heavy front door and sat down on the bottom stair. There was a kind of peace, she realized, that came over a person when their whole life just upped and fell apart. Trying to hang her dreams of fame and fortune on Liam Bradley's writing career had been very tiring, these last ten years. She had put so much effort into massaging his fragile ego that she had lost sight of her own personality. And the ungrateful brute had dumped her like a half-eaten cheeseburger anyway. Richard Allen's rejection was merely the last straw.

Now, she was free. Her life was a clean sheet, a blank page. She must pull herself together and keep moving forward. And she decided that her bottle-blond-and-breast-implant persona had been a complete failure, too. Somehow, men saw her as less than human, these days. She was just a sexual target for them. The fake boobs weren't bringing her much happiness, anyway. She must book the operation to have them taken out before Liam stopped the joint account at the bank. Sighing, she pulled herself up to a standing position and went to look at herself in the hall mirror. Her eye makeup had gathered in dark smudges on her eyelids. Her face was dull and vacant-looking.

"Come on, girl," she told her reflection. "You can do better than this."

13

LIAM'S CHOICE

Sunday, December 19

THE DAYS HAD FLOWN BY.
Liam and Perry Shaw sat in the coffee
lounge of the Europa Hotel, half-hidden behind three potted palms and a grand piano.
The meeting was not going well. Liam was
feeling very trapped and agitated. He was
weak with the want of sleep. Perry was just
feeling weary. He'd flown over from London
that morning and he was tired and he had a
twinge of pain in his back from the cramped
airline seat. The two men poured tea and
buttered scones, delaying the moment of

conflict. Eventually, Perry coughed gently, and began.

"Now, Liam, why make this difficult on yourself? I've told you more than once that we're almost ready to sign the contracts. Several contracts, to be precise. And you've written the book the way we agreed, haven't you? The first draft, anyway?"

"Yes, I have. It's far too short as it stands. It'll have to be lengthened. But it just doesn't feel right."

"I appreciate that, and I did try it your way but no one wants the new, improved Slinger. No one cares about respect and loyalty, just a roaring good time. Not even for a smaller advance. So we're both agreed."

"Well, as long as the money is good. But I still don't like the title."

"Now, don't even go there, Liam. The publishers love the title. That used to be the catchphrase of Basil Brush, you know?"

"Wasn't he a hand puppet?"

"A hand puppet, yes. But he was an institution, Liam. A star: that's what he was."

"My novel has a hand puppet's catchphrase for a title."

"It's hilarious, I'm telling you. And because it's a gas explosion, it's not even Slinger's fault the whole street is wrecked at the end. Now, doesn't that make you happy?"

"I suppose so. But he's such a loser. Who would ever love him?"

"No, he isn't. He's a hero! The publishers loved the first few chapters, Liam. They just loved it. And there's interest from two major TV companies. That means we're going to get our second series!"

"But Slinger ends up alone again."

"Yes, but not by choice. The landlady's husband is blinded in the explosion, so she stays with him out of a sense of duty, and Slinger's heart is broken forever. So, he's not a loser. He's heartbroken. And the nod to *Jane Eyre* is great."

"What?"

"Her great love was blinded, too. Never mind."

"I still think the husband should have croaked it."

"No, he had to survive. I mean, the pub is blown to bits so your woman has enough to worry about."

"But Slinger's childless and alone, Perry. He should have fathered a child, at least."

"He's solving crimes. He's cleaning up the streets."

"Oh, who cares? I'm fed up with Slinger Magee and he's my creation. I'm just not happy with the whole thing." Liam ran his fingers through his hair and winced at the thought of all the interviews he would have to endure. Would he have the energy to tell all those lies? To attend all those launches?

"Right, Liam. Listen to me. I'll give it to you straight. I'm tired and I need to sort out this year's accounts. Are you going to sell the book the way the publisher wants it? Or are you not? Because I can't afford to waste several weeks negotiating deals for a book that won't be delivered. I need a positive answer in the next five minutes, Liam. If you can't give me one, our working relationship is hereby terminated."

"Are you threatening me, Perry? I thought we were friends."

"We are friends, Liam. I'm telling you the truth. Nobody will buy the book if Slinger goes soft and gets married. Or anything soppy like that."

"Well then, maybe we should forget about it?"

"Suit yourself. Where's that waiter? I need a drink."

"Perry, are you all right? You don't look too hot."

"I'm okay."

"Really?"

"No. I'm not okay. My son called me today. He won't be home for Christmas. They're moving to another base and he can't tell me where, and I can't communicate with him for the next three weeks."

"Jesus, Perry. Why didn't you say?"

"Because I don't want to talk about it, or even think about the danger he's in until he's back home again."

"Yeah, right, I can see where you're coming from. Is he okay, Perry? Is he coping all right, out there?"

"I don't know. He wouldn't tell me if he wasn't coping. What could I do about it? He knows I'd only worry myself sick. My wife is having trouble sleeping. She's up half the night wandering the house, blaming herself for letting him join the army when he was seventeen. It was what he wanted but we should have tried harder to talk him out of it."

"Oh, rough luck. I'm sorry, mate."

"I thought he would be home by now. I just want to drive out there and pick him up in the

car, the way I used to collect him from primary school."

"Perry, I had no idea you were feeling this
way."

"You're lucky you have no children, Liam.
I'll tell you that. There's no pain on earth like
the pain of not being able to save your own
child from danger. So you see, Liam, your
book deal means nothing to me at this moment. I'm only here to advise you on your
career."

"Of course. I understand totally. Why did
you fly over here today? You could have
phoned."

"I wanted to keep busy. If I take time off
work and just sit about the house, I'll go
mad." Perry went to the men's room to
splash cold water on his face, ordering another drink on the way. Liam sat alone by the
palm trees and knew what he had to do.
Compared with poor Perry's, his own troubles were slight.

"I'll keep the book the way you want," he
said, when his agent came back to the table.

"It doesn't matter to me, Liam. My percentage would have made me a lot more
comfortable in my retirement. But I'll survive

without you. I have twenty other authors, you know?" The gin and tonics arrived and they both looked out the window while the waiter tidied up the table and gave them fresh coasters.

"Perry, please. Tell them I'll have a completed draft ready by Christmas. A couple of scenes need a boost, near the end."

"Liam, honestly, I don't mind. Do it your own way and find another agent."

"Please, I mean it, Perry. If you can't sell my book with a romantic ending, nobody can. If you think Slinger Magee should end up comatose on the floor of a back-street bar, then so be it."

"Are you sure?"

"Yes."

"No going back?"

"No."

"Promise me?"

"Yes. Promise. I won't change my mind."

"Cheers, then, Limo. I mean, Liam. Here's to *Boom, Boom.*"

"Cheers, Perry."

14

FLU

Monday, December 20

LILY WOKE UP at seven, gasping for a drink of water. Her head was pounding, her throat was on fire and she had heavy dull pains in both legs. Even her eyes felt hot and uncomfortable. At first, she thought she had a severe hangover but then she realized she hadn't drunk much alcohol in months. There was only one possible explanation for how she was feeling, she thought with a sinking sensation. She had caught the dreaded flu. There was an epidemic of it in Belfast, they said on the news.

"Jack," she whispered. "Are you awake?" And she erupted into a fit of ticklish coughing that made her eyes run, and a hateful hot flush spread over her pretty, pale face.

"Yes, I'm awake," he said in a husky voice. "But I'm going to go back to sleep for half an hour and so should you. Then we'll wake up again and hopefully this flu we've got will be only a bad dream."

"Oh no. You, too? I feel awful, like my blood has been siphoned off and replaced with hot water. Are you dizzy? I'm dizzy. Oh, for heaven's sake! This week, of all weeks! There's a party every night from now till January the sixth."

"Except Christmas night."

"Yes, three points for observation, Jack. I was planning to sleep all through that day."

"I hope it's only a three-day thing, and not the dreaded three-week job I've heard about. Harry Frew's been out of action for a month, he told me on the phone yesterday. He's almost lost the use of his legs, he said, he's been in bed that long."

"Don't even joke about it. The first party is tonight," Lily groaned. "Well, this is a judgment on me for thinking I could change the world. I might have known everything would collapse in chaos." She coughed again and reached for a tissue to blow her nose. "It's too late to cancel. We'll just have to keep going, on our hands and knees if need be. I might be found dead of pneumonia behind that bar but I'm not giving up."

"Calm down, pet. I'll fetch you a hot lemon drink. We'll use the power of mind over matter. I read about it in the newspaper: people who think positively usually get better a lot sooner than complainers do." He gingerly sat on the edge of the bed and placed his feet on the carpet. Immediately his vision began to deteriorate. "Whoa! Black spots I have, dancing in front of my eyes. Aw, Lily, this is a bad flu all right."

"Don't move, pet. I'll get up. Black spots in front of my eyes is about the one symptom I haven't got. You lie down and have another hour's rest. I'll see if any of the girls are awake. Maybe they can make a start on the party preparations? That's what they're here for, after all."

"You're right. I'd almost forgotten they were supposed to be working here." He flopped back onto the pillows and groaned as his headache deepened. Lily padded next door in her cosy robe and slippers, and was amazed to see the four girls sitting up in bed watching breakfast TV and munching thick slices of toast and jam. The heady aroma of freshly ground coffee filled the room even though the window was open to let in fresh air. The room was surprisingly tidy despite housing four young women. Lily sensed Trudy's hand, in the neat stacks of possessions in every corner and in the freshly folded pile of clean laundry on the sofa.

"Mrs. B! Good morning! You look a bit ropy. Are you sick?" Daisy asked from the top bunk.

"Oh, girls, don't come near me. You might catch something. I feel terrible."

"Is it flu?" said Daisy. "There's a bad flu going round the Art College."

"Yes, I'm afraid it might be flu. Jack has it, too."

"You wore yourself out with the decorating," said Bridget wisely. "Painting walls is a lot more physically draining than it looks."

"How would you know?" muttered Daisy. "All you did was dust the bottles."

"At least I didn't bring germs back here from the Art College," said Bridget defensively.

"It's not my fault Mrs. B and Mr. B are sick. I haven't got the flu, so it can't have been me," Daisy cried, setting her cup on the little wooden ladder.

"Whatever the reason, I'm going to plough on," said Lily. Privately, she blamed the stress of paying for Bridget's one-woman Demolition Derby for making her and Jack ill. But they needed Bridget desperately and they couldn't let her go. She could turn those cocktails out at an amazing speed. "We are going to be incredibly busy over the next few days," Lily added.

"You stay in bed and we'll get the tavern open," said Daisy. "She threw off her blankets and climbed down from her bunk. "We'll all pitch in, won't we, girls?"

"Would you?" gasped Lily, beginning to cough again. "That would be so nice of you. I haven't felt this wretched in years."

"Not to worry," announced Bridget, taking charge. She wasn't having Daisy bossing her around, under any circumstances. "Trudy and Marie can bake the pies for lunch, and Daisy can clean and polish the bar."

"What will you do?" asked Daisy, her temper rising. She didn't object to doing the cleaning. It was far better than slaving over the cooking, actually. But still, she'd liked to have volunteered for mop and duster duty, rather than submit to Bridget's orders. Bridget still seemed to believe that she had some authority over the others, just because she was the only full-timer.

"I will start getting the cocktail ingredients ready. There's a big party at seven, in case you've not looked at the calendar. And there are dozens of new glasses to be unpacked from their boxes and put through the dishwasher. I've got to color the sugar for dipping the glasses. And there's a fire to light." She hopped out from under her pile of blankets and raced to the bathroom with her sponge and bath towel.

"Leave some hot water for the rest of us," the other girls chorused.

"Thanks, girls. We really appreciate this. Are you sure you know where everything is?" Lily fretted. "There's extra flour in the crockery cupboard, and rolls of tin foil in the cutlery drawer. About four pies should be enough, I think? Ten slices in each, and serve with the salads for lunches?"

"Yes, we know," said Trudy. A stack of poetry books slithered off her pillow and fell onto the carpet. Sighing, she gathered them up and stacked them neatly beside the bed. Her self-improvement campaign would just have to be put on hold for the day.

"Off you go, and stay in bed for a while. I'll bring you and Mr. Beaumont a cup of tea," said Marie, pulling on a fleecy jacket with teddy bears on it.

"Oh, lovely! Now, I think four pies should be sufficient," said Lily, still worried about the catering. "We surely won't have more than forty lunches each day, even with the recent publicity. If there's time, you might consider a mushroom and nut strudel for the vegetarians? I left the recipe on the notice board. It only takes fifteen minutes in the oven, apparently."

"Right, now off you go. We'll manage," said Daisy. "And if we have a domestic emergency, we know where you are."

"And we'll not set fire to any tea towels, this time," added Marie. "Now we know how hot the stove rail can get." They all smiled warmly at each other. Their confidence made Lily relax a little bit. She thanked them again, and told them to come to her the minute they needed help. They chased her out the door with many promises to fetch her if there was a disaster, and even more reassurances there wouldn't be.

Lily trailed back to bed and clambered in beneath the eiderdown. Jack put his arm around her and kissed her forehead.

"You're quite warm, you know. Maybe you have a temperature?" he said.

"I'm hot stuff. No, I'm okay, just about. Cross your fingers, darling. The lunatics are taking over the asylum. But they've given me their word they won't burn it down."

Lily and Jack lay in each other's arms for a while but then had to move apart as they felt hot and stuffy. Lily thought they should try to get up and dressed but the room was very cold. They decided to stay in bed. Trudy and Marie were soon frying onions, chopping steaks and rolling pastry in the kitchen, so they couldn't go in there and contaminate the pies. The bar would be chilly and the sitting room was full of beds. There was nowhere else to go and nothing else to do. As they fell asleep, side by side and holding hands, they could hear and smell the various preparations get under way with a surprisingly small amount of fuss. Bridget could be heard chinking glasses downstairs and

Lily only counted two smashes. Daisy soon had the whole place full of the scent of citrus furniture polish, and the hum of the vacuum cleaner was quite a soothing sound when someone else was using it.

At eleven o'clock, there was a gentle knock on their bedroom door and Trudy came in with a tray bearing tea, toast, scrambled eggs, a dish of marmalade and a couple of newspapers. There was also a selection of painkillers, two glasses of water and a box of mentholated tissues.

"Wakey, wakey," she trilled.

"I must be dreaming," said Lily, struggling to open her eyes. "Isn't this lovely? I thought you forgot about the tea."

"Oh, I was here twice before with it, but you were both unconscious. Sorry to wake you up this time," said Trudy. "And there's more," she added proudly, nodding toward the door. "They're decent, Marie. You can come in now." Marie came edging shyly into the pink bedroom, carrying a portable television she'd asked her father to drop by. She set it on the bureau and switched it on. She also plugged in the old Christmas tree. The room suddenly became much cosier as the tree cast its yellow, pink and orange shadows across the walls. On daytime TV a young woman was making Christmas stockings out of fluffy towels, curtain tassels and toy sleigh bells.

"I always like a bit of telly when I'm under the weather," Marie said, and hurried out again. "Got to keep an eye on the stove. Two pies down, two to go."

"Oh, this is great. I feel better already," Lily said and then reached for the painkillers as another wave of pressure attacked her brain. "Jack, the cavalry has brought food." She prodded him on the shoulder. Jack muttered his thanks from deep underneath the eiderdown. He felt quite shy with all these young girls running about the place. He was afraid to get dressed without locking the bedroom door in case one of them burst in and caught him in his shorts. Trudy left the tray on a chair beside the bed and went back to the kitchen, announcing that she was going to make the best mushroom and nut strudel that had ever been seen in the city of Belfast.

"I should say something clever at this point, regarding Belfast and nuts, but I haven't got the energy," said Jack, and Lily laughed even though it was sheer agony to do so. Lily and Jack sat up in bed and enjoyed their brunch. It was slightly surreal, hearing the girls do all the jobs they used to do. Especially the rasping scrape of the shovel on the hearth as Bridget removed the ashes from the fireplace. Jack had to restrain himself from going down to check that Bridget was not using too many lighters, or covering the tavern in cinders. At lunchtime, they could hear Barney, Joey and Francy Mac arriving downstairs, and after a while the familiar scent of Barney's tobacco came drifting up the staircase.

"I think I'll have a shower," Jack told Lily as the afternoon wore on. "See if the hot water helps my head feel any better. Maybe if I steam open my pores, some of the pain will escape, too."

"Maybe, but I doubt it. What a time to get sick."

"I was going to try out the new chip maker today."

"It's called a deep-fat fryer." She laughed again. "Ouch! And you'll do no such thing. You might get even worse if you don't rest."

"What about tonight's event?" he asked. It was a Christmas party for journalists from the *Irish Independent,* their friends and families. Lily had offered to make fat potato chips, wrapped up in paper cones, as one of the side dishes. She'd suggested making the cones out of pages from *The Mirror,* a rival newspaper.

"I've already told Marie all about it. She says she'll be only too happy to man the fryer when the time comes."

"And the rest of it? How will they manage?"

"Bridget has a system," explained Lily, "of making enough mix for twenty cocktails at the same time, and pouring it along a row of frosted glasses. It's quite a spectacle, I believe. And Daisy said she'd make a hundred cones out of the newspapers and line them with greaseproof paper, ready for the chips tonight. They can serve cold sausage rolls and chicken wraps with salad and coleslaw. And the desserts are already made. So we're fine. Jack?" But he had dozed off again, sitting up in the bed with a fork still in his hand.

At five, Daisy popped her head in to ask where the glue was kept. She handed Lily and Jack two small dishes of strudel with a drizzling of sauce made from port, redcurrant jelly and balsamic vinegar. They sat up to test the new dish and declared it delicious.

"This is fantastic, Daisy. It'll be fine served cold for the party tonight," said Lily.

"It's all gone, Mrs. B. That was the last bit."

"What do you mean?"

"Trudy made forty portions, and they all sold this lunchtime."

"What about the steak pies?"

"All gone, too. It's heaving down there. Human soup, it is. Bridget is serving pints at the speed of light. I have to admit, she's pretty good under pressure."

"So, did you run out of food, then?"

"No, we served open prawn sandwiches to the stragglers. We've lifted a fortune of money."

"Where is it?" said Jack at once.

"It's in the kitchen, in a bucket under the sink, Mr. B."

"Oh Daisy, that's not a very safe place to put money."

"We didn't know what else to do with it. There's no room in the till. Do you want more strudel made for the party? There's plenty of mushrooms and phyllo pastry left over."

"If Trudy has the energy, that would be fantastic," said Lily. "It looks very upmarket. Thank you."

"Yes, thank you," added Jack. "We're both

very grateful. Are you sure you're all okay?
Did you get some lunch, yourselves?"

"Yeah, we grabbed a bite. Must dash, or
Bridget will be on the warpath. See ya."

"What do you need glue for, by the way,
Daisy?" called Lily.

"For the paper cones." She popped her
head back in the room.

"I think sticky tape would be better. We
don't want to poison anyone. There's a new
roll beneath the bar." Lily blew her nose
loudly.

"Gotcha." Daisy winked.

"Will you be able to close up tonight?"
Jack asked. "Do you want me to come down
to eject the stubborn ones?"

"No, that's okay. We just found out Trudy's
got a black belt in karate. I'll get on with the
cones, then, Mrs. B?"

"Thanks, Daisy, you're an absolute trea-
sure," coughed Lily, stunned that Trudy
wasn't afraid of aggressive men when she
was terrified of pearly buttons. Lily and Jack
looked at each other and simply shrugged.
Every day that passed brought with it a surprise or a shock of some kind.

Lily and Jack decided to stash the bucket
of money in the wardrobe, and then spent

the rest of the evening listening to their favorite records from the 1980s, and making some compilation tapes on Jack's old stereo. By the time the first party of the season was drawing to a close with a riotous singsong and much cheering and clapping in the room below, they had settled on some iconic songs for Clare Prendergast's Christmas Eve celebration. "Sometimes," by Erasure. "The First Picture of You," by the Lotus Eaters. "Everyday I Write the Book," by Elvis Costello and the Attractions. "Don't Talk to Me About Love," by Altered Images.

"That fairly takes me back," said Jack, wiping a tear from his eye. "If my poor body wasn't in agony from top to toe, I'd take you in my arms right this minute and do things to you that decency prevented on that riverside bench in 1984."

15

THE WAITING ROOM

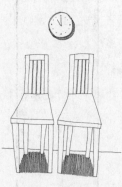

Tuesday, December 21

TRUDY HOVERED by the door of the waiting room, unsure what to do next. Every instinct in her soul was telling her to run back along the pale green corridor, down the stairs of polished black marble and out he revolving doors to safety. She could be home in minutes, curled up on her bed with *The Nation's Favourite Poems.* She was currently memorizing "Do Not Go Gentle into That Good Night," by Dylan Thomas

(1914–1953). She didn't need all this fuss and nonsense. It was Lily Beaumont who had talked her into phoning for an appointment, and to Trudy's great alarm, the receptionist had said there was a cancellation and could she come in at eleven? Unbeknownst to Trudy, her own doctor had called in a few favors to secure the precious appointment. He'd been trying to get her to come here for over two years.

But Trudy's phobias, or her little notions, as she liked to call them, were not really a problem. Everybody had something wrong, she reasoned. Some perfectly law-abiding women went shoplifting when they thought their husbands were having an affair. Some otherwise sane and normal men simply couldn't get on an airplane, even if they'd just won a luxury holiday. Trudy twirled her crocheted scarf around her neck, took it off, then put it on again.

"Excuse me, are you looking for the counseling rooms?" said a gentle voice behind her. She turned around and realized with a jolt that it was Gerry Madden. She recognized him straightaway from a picture in Bridget's photo album. The blond crew cut, the ice-blue eyes, the tanned skin and the expensive jacket. But of course, he didn't recognize Trudy.

"Yes, the counseling rooms. Indeed. But I'm not sure if I'm in the right place," said Trudy softly. "It's somewhere along this corridor. The receptionist told me the room number, but I forget. Will we just sit down and wait anyway?"

"We might as well. As far as I know, this is where the old counseling takes place, right enough. I, um, I shouldn't be here, really," he said. "Stress-related work thing, you know?"

"Same here," Trudy said. They both shook their heads in fake amusement. "These meddling doctors, always fussing and fretting over nothing. Aren't they a laugh?"

"I can't seem to settle the old head these days. It's silly," he told her. Keep talking, he told himself. Say anything at all to her. Anything to fill the excruciating silence that all waiting rooms were cursed with. They ought to have soothing music piped into this room, Gerry thought. Or better still, CDs of the comedian James Young. "No need for all this palaver. Waste of taxpayers' money. I'm only here to keep my doctor happy."

"Me, too. I don't believe in therapy," Trudy said, and they both turned bright red. "Therapy" was such a scary word, she thought. It implied mental illness, Victorian asylums with bars on the windows, screams in the night. "I have a few little phobias, that's all. Sure, who hasn't, in this day and age? I feel daft, to tell you the truth." She smiled at him. There were no other patients in the room. It was the last session before lunch.

They went in and sat down, carefully studying the dried-up posters on the walls. There was an old *Interiors* magazine lying on the coffee table, with a beautiful Christmas tree on the cover. The tree was decked out in strings of popcorn and cranberries. They both reached for it at the same time.

"Sorry," he said. "You have it. Gerry Madden is the name." They gingerly shook hands.

"I'm Marie Smith," Trudy lied. Well, she couldn't risk telling Gerry her real name. After all, she had shouted at him on the telephone and also said that he was round the twist.

"Pleased to meet you, Marie Smith." He smiled. Trudy was struck with how handsome he was in the flesh. Very alive, somehow. Those blue eyes of his were full of mischief. And his shoulders looked rather good in that tweed jacket. No wonder bossy

Bridget had put up with his heavy drinking and his marriage-avoidance for years. Trudy could well see the attraction of the man.

"I'm not really into interiors," she said, hoping to God the nurse would hurry up and take one of them into the inner sanctum. "You have it." She indicated the glossy publication. In the end, neither of them got to read the article on designer conservatories. The magazine lay untouched on the table, and Gerry prayed that none of his colleagues would come along and see him waiting for the nurse. It was an extremely humbling experience for him to be sitting on this side of the door. Even if he was only going to see a behavioral therapy nurse and not an actual psychiatrist. Relaxation techniques! Oh, the shame of it. His doctor and best friend, Toby Kerr, had recommended them, the day after Gerry had been suspended from his job. Gerry had little faith in the program, even though he'd been recommending relaxation techniques to his own patients for years.

They chatted for a few minutes about the weather, the possibility of snow on Christmas Day and whether reality TV shows were a bit of harmless fun or a shocking waste of time and resources. They both agreed that paying washed-up celebrities good money for eating a few grubs in the jungle was nothing compared to being an African orphan who had no choice but to eat grubs every miserable day of his or her life. Gerry said he was tempted to take a career break and go to Africa himself. Do some humanitarian work. He almost said he'd like to counsel severely traumatized people, but he stopped himself just in time. That would give his occupation away.

"Would they let you take time off work? I mean, what do you do for a living?" asked Trudy. Really, she shouldn't put him on the spot like this, but she couldn't help it. She was suddenly fascinated with Gerry Madden.

"I own a car showroom," he said at once. "The BMW garage in Finaghy." It was the answer he gave to all his potential girlfriends. For some reason, they felt uncomfortable being chatted up by a psychiatrist. They thought he might be able to see through their fake femme-fatale personas, or even manipulate them into bed using some secret parlor trick. Besides, high-performance cars were the only things he knew about, outside medicine.

"I see," Trudy replied calmly. His face betrayed not a hint of unease. He was a good liar. Bridget had already told them all about Gerry's fantasy career with BMW.

"And you? Where do *you* work?" He wanted to know where he could find her again. His heart was pumping with adrenaline. He wondered if he might be going bonkers, after all. He was just getting over that miniature firebrand Bridget O'Malley, and the bruises from her attack with the CD stand had barely faded from his arm when he started obsessing about Trudy Valentine, and what she might look like. He wouldn't recognize the girl if he saw her in the street. And yet because she had shouted so viciously at him down the phone, he had been shocked into giving up the drink. On a trial basis, at least. Five years of AA meetings hadn't been able to convince him he could live without the confidence and courage the drink had always given him. Of course, passing out in the cop shop had been fairly traumatic. Not to mention having his stomach pumped. He'd been beaten up by a New York bodybuilder, punched in the eye by Jack Beaumont, and he'd been suspended from the hospital. But it was Trudy Valentine, of all people, who had managed to reach his soul. He'd felt human for the first time, when Trudy bawled him out. He'd felt connected to the real world, not like he was just watching it on TV. Was it merely a coincidence? Or was there some spiritual connection going on between the two of them?

And as if that wasn't crazy enough, he now had feelings for this lovely girl with her dark brown eyes and long black hair. Weird penciled-on eyebrows, but he supposed the real ones would grow back eventually. Had he developed some rare complex? he asked himself. Some addiction to falling in love with any beautiful female he encountered? Maybe he should see a psychiatrist?

"I work in a meat factory in Dungannon," Trudy said in a steady voice. "I make steak and kidney pies all day long, with my little white hat on. It's a dream job." He smiled at her, unable to work out if she was joking or not. If she was joking, and he laughed, that would be a good icebreaker. But if she wasn't joking, he might offend her. So he smiled, in what he hoped was an ambiguous way. He fancied her like mad, but then he thought of Trudy Valentine and how she had possibly saved him from ruin. He thought he would go to the tavern and see Trudy for himself, and if

that didn't work out, he would go to Dungannon and look for this mysterious girl with her
twinkling dark eyes. And her little white hat.

"I hope you don't mind me asking," he said
then, "but could you give me some advice?
From the feminine perspective?"

"I will, if I can," she said. "Is it about catering?" She was beginning to warm to Gerry.
But she remembered how unstable he was
supposed to be, and tried desperately to
keep a polite distance.

"No, it's not about food. You see, there's
this girl I'd like to ask out on a date but
there's a problem."

"What is it?"

"Um, I used to date a friend of hers, you
see. Bit of a roller-coaster relationship by all
accounts, but that's another story. God
knows what my ex has told this new girl
about me. Anyway, I phoned the place where
my ex lives, rather late the odd night, and
this girl, the one I like now, got a bit peeved
off with me. If you follow?"

"Maybe a simple apology to both of them
would be enough?" suggested Trudy. Good
grief, she thought. How many women is this
guy involved with? For he couldn't be talking
about her? He couldn't be saying he wanted

to go on a date with her? Could he? He didn't even know what she looked like. Well, he did now. But he didn't know that he was presently talking to Trudy Valentine. Oh, brother! What a tangled web. . . .

"Maybe," Gerry sighed. "But in my experience, these things are never as straightforward as that." He bit his lip and looked at his watch. Surely a nurse would call one of them in at any moment? He couldn't wait to get this ridiculous session over with so that he could go and get plastered in a quiet pub somewhere. With a start, he realized that he couldn't get wasted anymore. If he didn't get his act together immediately, they'd have no choice but to sack him. And if he lost his job, he'd lose his apartment and his car and his lifestyle. In fact, he'd lose his entire identity. He'd have nothing to do all day except drink and feel sorry for himself, and go on drinking to fill the empty hours. And he didn't want to become a chronic alcoholic. Being a functioning alcoholic was bad enough. He wanted to get better again. He was just going to have to cooperate with the nurse, and talk to her about his anxiety symptoms.

That unfamiliar feeling of reality hit him again. He sat up straight in the chair. He was

Gerry Madden. He was an alcoholic. And he'd drifted into a pattern of heavy drinking because he had the personality of a charming rogue, but was trapped in the body of a shy man. Good God! It was so simple, really. The drink gave him the confidence to be the life and soul of every party. Good old Gerry, always game for a laugh. His student days were a haze of hilarious parties and boozy foreign holidays. Embarrassing photos of him on a bus shelter roof wearing a traffic cone on his head, on a hotel balcony in Paris minus his trousers, locked in a luggage cage at Heathrow airport. And by the time he got his degree, he was physically addicted. By then, it was easier to go on playing the part of the eternal bachelor than face the hard slog that drying out would have been. That was why he had stayed single all these years: because a wife would have been too hard to deceive. Of course, Bridget hadn't minded the way he'd carried on. But that was because her parents were hopeless cases altogether, and compared to them Gerry was a good catch. It had to stop. Toby told him he would damage his organs if he kept going. Well, Gerry knew that already.

But the way back to sobriety was long and

difficult. Every time he was annoyed or upset or anxious, he'd have to deal with life the hard way. Sober. Gerry pictured himself lying on the bench in the next room. Tensing and relaxing his toes, legs, arms, body and face. Taking deep breaths and listening to restful music on a cheap cassette player. And not just today, either. Six times at least, he had to attend to even be considered for reinstatement at the hospital.

Trudy watched him as he stared out the window. He really was very attractive. The bruises on his face were almost gone now, faded to a delicate lilac. Trudy thought he looked like a cowboy in a Western film, with his deep-set eyes and tanned skin.

"How did you get the bruises on your face?" she asked suddenly. He seemed shocked. A pink blush of embarrassment crept across his neck. He thought that made three hot flushes so far that day. Maybe it was the withdrawal symptoms kicking in early?

"Well, I made a bit of a show of myself one night, in an Irish bar in New York. I was only paying a young lady a compliment but her boyfriend took it the wrong way. I meant no harm. There was drink taken, needless to say. But I'm off the drink now." Why had he told her that? He'd as good as admitted he was a wino. Well, that was the end of any hopes of getting to know this gorgeous woman now. But he was amazed when she turned out to be very supportive.

"Well done," she said gently. "More power to you. It can't be easy."

"That's why I'm here, you know?" he found himself saying. "To learn how to relax without the jar."

"Well, good luck. I'm sure you'll succeed."

"Maybe. I want to succeed. . . . I'm fed up making daft mistakes."

"And I'm fed up worrying about being allergic to things all the time." Trudy smiled. There! She had shared something embarrassing with him, too. Now he needn't be sorry he had revealed a weakness in his character to her.

"Are you seeing anyone?" Gerry asked after a minute, encouraged by her friendliness.

"I beg your pardon?" Trudy shifted uncomfortably on the hard plastic seat. Well, Gerry Madden was some boy! Was he actually hitting on her, in the waiting room of the Department of Mental Health? That would be something interesting to tell their grandchildren. Stop it, she cried internally.

"I mean, have you got a boyfriend?" he added. "Just curious."

"Curiosity killed the cat," Trudy said quickly. She wasn't going to start dating Gerry, even if he was lovely-looking. She didn't want him smashing any more windows at Beaumont's Tavern.

"Sorry if I spoke out of turn," he said. "I was only asking." He looked genuinely sorry. "It's just I was wondering if your partner was supportive of your coming here, or if you felt it was better to go through counseling on your own?"

"Well, okay. I'm currently single, as it happens. I'm far too busy for a boyfriend." Christ, where was that nurse? Trudy was about ten seconds away from doing a runner.

"A lot of girls say that to me, nowadays," Gerry mused. "I've had no luck with the fairer sex, these last few years."

"You could have married Bridget," Trudy wanted to say. But then, she didn't blame him for not popping the question. Poor old Bridget could be very annoying and selfish sometimes. In spite of herself, Trudy wanted to know more about Gerry. Surely she couldn't be seriously attracted to him, herself?

"Tell me about this girl you were planning to ask out. The one you annoyed by calling late in the evening? What's so special about her?" she asked.

"She's honest," he replied at once.

"Lots of people are honest."

"She's brutally honest. I admire that in a woman."

Oh dear, thought Trudy. That's me blown out.

"I see," she said lamely.

"Yes. And she's gorgeous." Well, he hadn't a clue, but what the heck?

"What does she look like?" Trudy asked after a brief pause.

Gerry took a deep breath. But before he had a chance to reply, a door opened at the other end of the room and a nurse came out. Amen! Saved from having to tell yet another lie!

"Trudy Valentine?" the nurse said with a big smile. "I'm ready for you now."

"Oh, great," croaked Trudy, and stood up so fast her scarf got caught on the arm of the chair, and she pulled it out from the wall. Gerry looked at Trudy as if he'd been slapped across the face, but she only smiled apologetically at him and turned away. She followed the nurse into the first counseling suite, and Gerry was ushered into the sec-

ond one by a new nurse he hadn't seen before. That was a relief, anyway.

"So," the nurse said when the door had
closed behind them. "I'm Ann. Tell me a little
bit about yourself, Gerry."

Gerry began a sanitized version of his
adult life, while trying to recall what he had
said to Trudy in the waiting room. How many
lies had he told her? And why had she told
him she was called Marie Smith and that
she worked in a meat factory? Or was she
not the same Trudy Valentine he had spoken
to on the phone? Maybe she was the same
Trudy Valentine but she had given him the
wrong name today because she was just
embarrassed to be here? And did she really
work in Dungannon? Or was that a lie, too?
He was in such a confused state he had to
go through the relaxation tape three times
before he could manage to unfurl his toes or
relax his face muscles at all.

When he came out of the suite an hour
later, Trudy had already left. He looked for her
in the hospital canteen, and in the gift shop
and at the taxi stand but there was no sign of
her. He drove straight to Beaumont's Tavern
and parked at the end of the alley on double-
yellow lines. He debated with himself for

twenty minutes whether he should go in or
not. He might be tempted to buy a drink if he
did go in. And Bridget might shout at him. And
there was the small matter of his fight with
Jack Beaumont. But then, he was dying to
see Trudy Valentine again. At least, he should
check if the girl he'd met in the hospital was
the one who worked here. What would be the
worst thing that could happen? he wondered.
Jack might hit him? He could handle that.
Bridget might hit him. He could handle that,
too. Unless she hit him with something really
hard, like maybe a barstool? On the positive
side, Trudy Valentine (hopefully, the one he'd
met today) might agree to a date. She had
been very sympathetic.

Then again, Bridget might make life hard
for Trudy if they began seeing each other.
Bridget was not likely to forget Gerry's reluctance to marry her. He rang Toby for advice.

"Toby, mate. I'm outside a pub and this girl
I like works there, I think. Maybe she's behind the bar at this very moment. Should I go
in? What do you reckon?"

"Are you not over Bridget O'Malley? You
told me you were over her."

"I like a girl called Trudy Valentine, now.
But I'm worried she won't give me a chance

because I lied to her about my job. Mind you, she lied to me about her job. At least, I think she did. It's complicated."

"Where did you meet this Trudy?"

"Today, at the counseling. But I liked her. Ever since the night I smashed the window where they both work, and got their boss arrested for assault. I broke the window because I thought I still loved Bridget, but then after I had my stomach pumped I realized it was Trudy I liked."

"Oh my God." Toby moaned.

"I talked to Trudy on the phone that night, Toby, but I just met her today. It's too weird to explain it all now. We really connected, you know? She's beautiful, mate."

"Gerry, your life is unraveling. That tavern is bad news for you."

"It's okay. I dropped the charges against their boss, and I know Bridget is over me even if she doesn't, and I think Trudy likes me a little bit. Positive body language in the waiting room, I think."

"What about ethics?"

"We're both patients. So I'm not breaking any code of conduct."

"Gerry! Are you not more concerned about being suspended?"

"Hang on, I'm getting a parking ticket."

"Gerry! What am I going to do with you?"

"It's okay. I know the warden. The guy was a patient of mine last year. Persistent Wellington-boot fetish, he was quite a character. He's ripping up the ticket. He's gone. Cheers, pal."

"Look, Gerry. If I were you, I'd go straight home before anything else happens."

"You know me, Toby. I'm hopeless. I've no common sense. What should I do? Should I head in?"

"I think a recovering alcoholic should stay away from bars. And even further away from barmaids. I think you should complete your counseling program, destress completely and get your old job back."

"It's okay for you, Toby. You've got a lovely wife and five healthy children. You've got an unblemished career. Trudy Valentine could be the love of my life, and she could be standing in there now, waiting for me."

"And I've got a seventy-two-year-old man waiting for me, behind the screen. And he's naked from the waist down," Toby whispered.

"Ah, Toby. I thought you were happily married?"

"Very funny, Gerry."

"Sorry, mate. I'll call you tomorrow. Let you know what happens."

"Sure thing. Watch yourself, now."

Gerry snapped his phone off, slipped it into his pocket and got out of the car. He stood looking down the alley for half an hour, but he was too nervous and too sober to go in. He decided to come back later in the evening when there would be fewer shoppers around to witness him getting another beating. He'd buy a load of relaxation tapes in that new organic café on Botanic Avenue, and he'd practice some meditation and have a hot bath, too. If that lot didn't relax him, nothing would. He'd take all his remaining booze and pour it down the sink. And give his apartment a good clean, just in case he got lucky with Trudy Valentine. Full of hope, Gerry hopped back into his car and left.

It was dark when he returned, and the shadows on Maple Street were stretched and menacing. Gerry could hear carol singers beside the big Christmas tree at the City Hall, singing "Silent Night." There was a stall selling hot dogs beside the Ulster Bank, and another one selling tinsel and sports socks a little farther down. Royal Avenue was still full of shoppers, however, bumping into one another with their carrier bags and umbrellas. But nobody paid him any attention.

"I have nothing to lose and everything to gain," he told the metal dumpsters. Gerry took a deep breath and headed toward the brightly lit amber windows of the little pub he had always considered too quiet and dull for him. Halfway down, he heard his car alarm go off, and he turned around to see another traffic warden giving him a ticket. He resumed his walk of destiny toward the heavy, nail-studded door.

16

MICHAEL, MARIE AND A CANAPÉ PLATTER

Wednesday, December 22

LILY AND JACK were still feeling awful, despite a near-constant supply of orange juice and chicken soup from Marie and Trudy. But the Christmas parties were going brilliantly and they'd even had a phone call of thanks from the *Irish Independent* editor to say they'd all had a fabulous time. And that they were still laughing about the *Mirror* paper cones.

The kitchen stove was bearing up well even though pie production had doubled.

And Trudy's mushroom strudel was one of the most popular dishes on their menu. They'd got an excellent review for it in one of the dailies.

On the down side, some of the students from last night's party had pocketed a few of the beaded pears and filigree partridges from the main Christmas tree, but Daisy had prevented further theft by securing the rest onto the branches with fine wire. She was seething with rage that anyone could have dared to steal the beautiful decorations they had chosen so carefully. She'd forgotten that she had been known to pinch a few pencils and pens from stationery shops in her time, when money was in short supply.

Liam Bradley called in just before closing time every night, to keep in touch with the little people, as he put it. He was looking haggard and sleep-deprived, but he said his new book was going well. Nearly finished, in fact. He told Lily that his wife, Betsy, was divorcing him, and that he would soon be a free man.

Betsy was getting to keep the house and was no longer speaking to him. He'd agreed to sign away his rights to the marital home to get Betsy to give up a half-share in his future earnings. It gave Liam great satisfaction to reach a deal so quickly. That way Betsy's shark-faced brothers wouldn't get to humiliate him in the courts. They were quite depressed when they discovered they weren't going to get their pound of flesh from Betsy's oddball husband. Letting go of the house was a small price to pay to be rid of her. He had grown weary of traipsing up and down four flights of stairs, anyway. Next time, he would buy a bungalow.

Betsy had flown to London the day before to have the gel implants removed from her chest. She had dumped all Liam's stuff in the garage, and he'd collected it and put it into storage. He would go house hunting when he got the first check from Perry. In the meantime, he was squandering his remaining bank balance on room service sandwiches and the contents of the minibar. Perry told him the big advance from one of the publishers would be coming his way at the end of January so he wasn't too worried about his future welfare.

And he had resigned himself to the dreary ending of *Boom, Boom,* too. Slinger drunk again and lying facedown in the gutter. The tavern getting blown to smithereens. Mad

Claudia torching Slinger's new car. His one true love, the beautiful landlady, waving goodbye to him from the airport. She and her blinded husband were going to retire to a tiny farmhouse in rural France, like half of Britain wanted to do in real life, according to the newspapers.

The publishers wanted a summary of book three, now. But Perry said that was up to Liam. Either way, he was winding up the agency at the end of next summer and taking early retirement himself.

Yes, things were looking good for Liam. Betsy was sorted. *Boom, Boom* was almost finished. It was his obsession with Lily Beaumont that kept him awake at night now. He could not close his eyes without seeing images of Lily. Smiling at him, baking perfect pies for him, dressing up in long coats and beaded chokers. Quoting Philip Larkin at posh book launches. She'd be heavily pregnant with Liam's child. Sleeping peacefully beside him in their bed. He wondered what she saw in Jack. The man was civil enough but he was boring beyond belief. He was not good enough for Lily. That was the truth. Maybe she had low self-esteem?

Lily thought Liam was very depressed,

when he sat at the counter each night, star-
ing into space. She told him not to worry and
that he would soon find someone else to
share his life with. He was a great guy, and
wasn't he talented and famous and well re-
spected about the city? That seemed to do
the trick of cheering him up. He shook Lily's
hand once and even kissed it tenderly.

Relations between Bridget and Trudy
were still slightly frosty, since Gerry Madden
had come into the tavern and asked Trudy
out on a date. She'd said yes, to everyone's
amazement. And Bridget was devastated.
Well, she claimed to be devastated but Lily
thought she looked rather relieved. Lily and
Bridget had a heart-to-heart about love over
a plate of hazelnut meringues and chestnut
cream. And Bridget admitted that she had
grown weary of Gerry and their turbulent relationship. She wanted the kind of peaceful
love and mutual respect that Lily and Jack
shared.

"Where will I find a love like yours?" asked
Bridget. "And how will I know when I've
found it?"

"You'll know," said Lily. "There won't be
any doubt at all in your heart, when you
meet the right person."

Bridget ate sixteen of the mini hazelnut meringues to console herself over losing Gerry, leaving a big dent in the batch for that evening's party, and Marie had to make some more. She went into the kitchen to begin baking, and realized that they had run out of chestnut puree and plain chocolate for the filling. She asked Lily for permission to take some money from the bucket under the sink (they hadn't devised a better banking system yet) and went to the Tesco store next door. When she came back, she saw that the Devaney brothers had arrived for a lunchtime gig and that Michael was talking to Lily. They stopped the conversation abruptly when she went past, and Michael smiled at her and blushed furiously.

David Devaney was dating Daisy, and the two of them were sitting at the fire now, deep in conversation about stage wear. Daisy was trying to wean David off leather and onto more fashionable fabrics. Marie staggered up the stairs, suddenly tired. Even if she did fancy Michael Devaney a lot, there was precious little she could do about it. She was far too shy to flirt with him, and she had hours and hours of work still to do this evening, and over the coming days. She could hardly refuse the Beaumonts the extra shifts they needed her to work, when she was camped out in their sitting room. Trudy was stacking dirty dishes in the kitchen sink when Marie arrived back at base.

"How's it going, Trudy?" she asked quietly.

"I'm parched. Tesco was like a refugee camp. I've never seen such queues." Marie set the kettle onto the stove and sat down, waiting for the water to boil. She eased off her boots and slipped on a pair of comfy mules. Trudy finished dusting icing sugar over a batch of mincemeat and pear tarts and set them on a tray, ready to be carried downstairs for the lunchtime diners.

"Can you manage without me this afternoon?" Trudy asked lightly. "I've already stuffed the turkey for tonight and it needs to come out of the main oven at six o'clock."

"Sure. No problem."

"Oh, thanks, Marie. Only, it's the badminton club do, at seven. And they want a load of fancy stuff like crab spring rolls and pesto crostini, and it's going to take ages. And Gerry offered to take me to see a matinee at the cinema. He's due in the bar any moment and I don't want to keep him waiting."

"You go ahead, you deserve it. I'll have a

quick tea break, and then get on with the canapés."

"I love you, Marie," said Trudy. "I'll bring these tarts down to the bar on my way out."

Marie flopped down at the table with her cup of tea and thought of her parents and siblings, gone to spend Christmas with relatives in England. Their old home had been sold at auction to a young woman called Sarah Jones, who had already stripped out all Marie's father's home improvements such as the stone fireplace, and painted the entire place a cold and lifeless white. The patterned carpets and frilly curtains went into a skip and were replaced with beige sea-grass and wooden blinds. The orange pine cabinets in the kitchen were sold, and now white oak doors, a stainless-steel counter and ultra-bright spotlights were the order of the day. Marie had seen it all when she went round to collect the mail, and she had wept on seeing the glamorous house that had once been a cosy family home. It was up for sale again within seven days. The asking price was nearly forty thousand pounds higher than the auction reserve. Marie was shocked at the heartlessness of it all.

She wanted to cry now but she didn't

have time. The badminton party was only six hours away and she had a lot to do. She surveyed the table in front of her. Ten tins of crab meat, six packets of phyllo pastry, a twisted knob of root ginger, ten baguettes, six jars of pesto sauce, four red peppers, fresh basil and a large bottle of olive oil. There was a mountain of dishes to wash, and she still had to tidy herself up for the evening's festivities. She sighed gently. Downstairs, she could hear Michael and David Devaney begin a love song that her parents used to dance to, and she had to stifle a sob. "Careless Whisper," by George Michael, was a great favorite of theirs. Marie hoped the Devaney brothers didn't know any songs by the Smiths. One note of melancholy and she would be overwhelmed by grief. Just then, Lily came into the kitchen.

"Are you all right, pet?"

"Yeah. Just getting a bit sentimental. Pay me no attention."

"Are you sure? I don't want you working if you're upset. You know, you could have gone to England with your family."

"No, I wanted to stay here. Honestly. I'd only cry all through Christmas dinner, seeing my aunt Tracy showing off her fancy china plates and her ivory-handled cutlery. And my poor mum saying it's all lovely, as if there was nothing wrong. I couldn't bear it, even if Aunt Tracy does mean well."

"I understand. Well, the good news is that Michael Devaney has offered to give you a hand here when they finish the afternoon set."

"Oh, Mrs. Beaumont, that won't be necessary. I'll be fine on my own."

"No, really. He was very keen. I think he likes you, Marie."

"I'm not in the mood for romance. Tell him thanks but I don't need any help." Marie was absolutely terrified at the thought of spending several hours in close proximity to the gorgeous Michael in his tight leather trousers. She was an emotional powder keg these days. Finishing her college course and losing her childhood home in the same year had left her in such a state of limbo, she wasn't thinking straight.

"I know I said I wanted to get to know him better, Mrs. Beaumont. But that was when I was high on cocktails. You know I'd be hopeless in reality. Tell him not to come up, will you? Please?"

"Too late," Lily quipped. "I said we'd be very grateful for his help."

"Is Trudy in on this, by any chance?" Marie wanted to know. "She didn't say anything this morning, about going to the cinema with Gerry Madden."

"Oh, never mind about Trudy," said Lily, with a leap in her voice that told Marie it was a conspiracy to match her up with Michael. "Have you got your eye on someone else? I didn't think you were seeing anybody at the moment."

"You know rightly I'm not, Mrs. Beaumont."

"Please call me Lily."

"Lily, then. I'd be mortified if we were stuck in here together. There's hardly room to slice bread let alone show a musician how to make canapés."

"Oh, come on, Marie. He's a lovely fellow. I told him what a star you were, cooking away up here because I have the flu. And how brave you are to cope with your parents away for the holidays. He said he'd be delighted to help you out."

"Won't he need a rest before tonight's do?"

"No. He says he can play the guitar in his sleep. And he might as well hang around here and help out, as go home and watch television on his own. Sure, David is here day and night, talking to Daisy."

"All the same. Why would he help me? I'm not his girlfriend."

"Not yet."

"Lily! What have you done? Are you matchmaking?"

"Maybe I am. He likes you, Marie. He told me."

"Honestly? If he likes me, why can't he tell me himself?"

"Because he's terribly shy. And so are you. And I think you would make a lovely couple."

"I don't feel relaxed around boys, Lily. I never have. I'm hopeless in clubs."

"I'm not surprised. The noise of those places, with the music thumping and pounding loud enough to deafen, and you can't hear anyone speak. It's a shame you missed the disco era I grew up in. Jack and I used to go to this great little disco near the docks, where the floor tiles lit up and the walls were covered with glittery wallpaper. We loved dancing there. It's closed down now."

"Sounds lovely. You must have some great memories."

"We do. Now, I'm going back to bed, and I suggest you have a soak in the bath, and a good rest. And then you and Michael can make all these fancy canapés together, and make some nice memories of your own while you're at it."

"Lily! Stop it!"

"I won't leave this kitchen until you agree to let Michael help you. Otherwise, I'll have to help you myself, and I have a headache that would drive any sane person over the edge."

"Okay, okay. You win. I'll have a bath, then. If Bridget has left me any hot water."

"That's the girl," said Lily. "Just borrow anything you need from the rest of us. Meanwhile, I'll have a good snooze, and if I feel up to it, I'll help out at the party later. I can clear plates and glasses anyway, without causing too much damage. Jack says he's still crippled, so I doubt he'll be any use. Is that kettle boiled? I'll take us in a couple of mugs of cocoa. The girls are downstairs, so you should have plenty of peace. Off you go." She patted Marie on the back, and satisfied that she was helping to start one of the great love affairs of the twenty-first century, she measured out the cocoa powder into two of her favorite pottery mugs.

In the bathroom, Marie turned on the hot tap and squeezed in a small tube of rose-scented bath cream that she got free with a magazine. She clipped and painted her nails while the bath was filling, and slapped on a cucumber face mask. Soon, she was soaking away her sore feet and feeling human again. She didn't allow herself to think about what a fool she might make of herself over the smoked salmon bites. Hopefully, they'd be too busy boiling new potatoes and slicing baguettes and chopping spring onions to be embarrassed. And if she felt overwhelmed by Michael's presence, she could always nip down to the bar on some pretext. Maybe say she had to help Bridget for a while?

She dried her hair poker-straight and pinned it up with one of Lily's pretty clips. She borrowed one of Daisy's many black dresses, Bridget's plum-colored bolero cardigan and some of Trudy's chunky bracelets, and she was all ready for her date.

"Except it's not a date," she told the bathroom mirror. "He's only helping me to make canapés."

However, when Michael appeared at the top of the stairs that afternoon, there was a distinct feeling of romance in the air. Michael blushed as he said hi, and Marie nervously chattered nonstop as she showed him the magazine clippings that Lily had left for them on the notice board. He seemed bewildered by the amount of ingredients on the table. Marie realized that he was even more self-conscious than she was and she felt sorry for him. Sometimes, she thought that she was the only shy person in the world, and that every other girl and boy could swing naked from the chandeliers at a moment's notice. But the truth was that most people found life overwhelming at times. That's what Lily had told her, and Marie knew it was good advice.

"Thanks for helping me," she said gently. "I really appreciate this."

Michael was studying the recipes with a frown of concentration on his face, and when he pronounced "canapés," it was so wrong she burst out laughing. And he laughed, too.

"You might not be thanking me in a minute," he said. "Who would have thought you'd need all this stuff here, to make those tiny wee things in the pictures?"

"Don't worry," said Marie. "It's not nearly as complicated as you think."

Together they divided the ingredients up into three piles, one for each dish, and then washed their hands before donning striped aprons and getting down to work.

"If you slice, oil and bake the bread, I'll roast the peppers for the crostini," she suggested. "Then, we can put the lot into airtight containers for later. They're served cold."

"Sure thing," he said, and tossed his curly fringe out of his eyes. "Is cookery your thing?"

"What do you mean?"

"I mean, are you a catering student?"

"No, I'm a languages graduate, waiting for a cushy translation post in Brussels to come my way."

"Oh. That sounds impressive." He seemed suddenly shy again. Marie recognized the signs. He was afraid to ask her about her career hopes, in case he made another faux pas. She was just the same herself, always afraid of saying or doing the wrong thing.

"It's nothing, really," she told him. "I just pick up languages very easily. I don't even like translation that much. It's just something I was good at in college."

"David and me never made it to college,"

Michael said. "Failed all our exams because we were playing music too much."

"Never mind. As long as you're both making a living? And you're happy?"

"It's not been much of a living, so far. We need to record a song. That would raise our profile and get us on the radio. Then we could charge more for gigs. You know, David's thinking of entering us in a talent show in London next year?"

"Oh, wow! One of those ones they have on TV? Where people vote, and everything? With millions of viewers?"

"Yeah. He's dead keen on it. He thinks we have a good chance of winning."

"Fair play to you, Michael. I couldn't do that for a pension. Not for all the money in the world! I'd drop dead with nerves."

"I'll tell you a secret. I feel the same way. I don't want to do it."

"I take it David doesn't know that yet?"

"I don't know how to tell him."

"Oh."

"I don't even know how to tell him I hate these trousers."

"Oh, Michael. They're not so bad." She began to giggle. "They're very nice on you."

"They're utterly sad, Marie. I'm ashamed of them. And the white shirts, too. They're a full-on cringe. But David's always been the brain of the operation, you know? He's always looked after me. And he thinks he knows about fashion."

"I'll tell you a secret. Daisy is planning to get rid of the leather altogether. She thinks she'd like to redesign your wardrobe. According to Daisy, the pirate look is over, and it's time for a return to tailored suits in light shades."

"Yeah? Bring it on."

"But now, what will happen if you want to give up music?"

"Oh, I love music. I don't want to give it up. But I want to keep things small-scale. Just play in venues like this. Stay in Ireland, and only work three nights a week. Or maybe teach guitar?"

"You don't want to be a big star, then?"

"No way. It's a crazy life. We used to play support for a rock band in England. We went on the road with them for six months last year. We were living on a smelly tour bus. I hated it. Too much hanging around between gigs. One of the band members OD'd, and now he's in prison for arson."

"Point taken."

"What about you? What's your dream?"

"I'd like to have my own business someday. I'm getting kind of bored with languages."

"Yeah?"

"Yeah. I mean, I do love cooking and the atmosphere of a little place like this is perfect, but the late nights are tougher on me than I thought. I'm dog-tired. So I thought I might re-train as a restaurant-based pastry chef? Can't see my bank manager agreeing to lend me the cash, though." She yawned in his face, and then apologized for being so rude.

"Why don't you sit down for a minute?" he said quietly. "I'll finish these crabby things. What do I do?"

"Well, I've already added spring onions and grated ginger to the crab meat. Just put a spoonful of the mix on each strip of pastry and roll them up. Then, brush the rolls with melted butter, and they go in the oven for ten minutes."

"Sounds easy." He reached for a packet of pastry.

"I'll make some tea," she said. "I seem to be making tea every ten minutes, since I came here." She fixed her hair when a long tendril slipped out of the jade clip.

"You, um, you look lovely, Marie. I meant to say it earlier. You do look very nice."

"Thank you. So do you." As she stepped past him to fill the kettle he put his arm around her waist and suddenly they were kissing each other tentatively. She felt his curly fringe brush against her forehead and it was strangely exciting. He touched her hair with his free hand, and she could hear him inhaling the scent of Daisy's strawberry shampoo. His arms were hard and firm from playing the guitar, and although she felt ridiculous and giddy, she also felt like she had found something that had been lost. They kissed for twenty minutes, until Bridget came barging in looking for fresh cream; and they almost fell over they were so startled. There was nothing in this life quite as fabulous as a first kiss that was perfect, Marie thought. It was a precious experience that could never be repeated. She knew that she had just made one of her sweetest memories.

Later, as they sipped their tea and sampled some of the pretty canapés, Marie and Michael realized that they were both feeling strangely relaxed. They began to chat at a normal pace, and the silent pauses between them were not embarrassing at all. At six o'clock, Marie lifted the turkey out of the main oven, and when it had cooled slightly Michael neatly sliced it up for the silver platter that was to form the centerpiece of the buffet. When Lily struggled out of bed at a quarter to seven in a brave attempt to greet her guests, she found Marie and Michael laying their culinary creations out in neat rows on the rented platters, and talking away as if they were old friends.

That night, Lily told Jack that he had lost both bets. Michael and Marie did fancy each other after all, and the party food was ready on time.

However, Jack wasn't remotely worried about losing twenty pounds to Lily in a bet. He was suffering from acute stage fright at the thought of his upcoming stint as DJ Nostalgia, as Lily described him on the tickets that Clare Prendergast had had specially printed.

17

A KNOCK AT THE DOOR

Thursday, December 23

 IT WAS SUCH A SHOCK when it actually happened. Even though Bridget knew in her heart of hearts that it was bound to happen someday.

At nine in the morning, there was a knock at the door of the tavern on Maple Street. Lily was lying awake, feeling sorry for herself and her sore throat, so she was the one who went to answer it. She thought it might be the delivery of yet another fresh turkey from the butcher's. But when she opened the door, it wasn't the butcher's assistant she saw standing there. Two police officers were waiting, side by side, with solemn expressions on their faces. The cobblestones were covered with a layer of slippery frost, and the policemen looked half-frozen themselves.

"Oh my God, is this something to do with Trudy Valentine?" Lily gasped. "Has Gerry Madden harmed her in any way? Let me check if she's in her bed." She turned back into the bar with her pulse racing.

"Hang on a minute. Gerry who?" called the first officer. Lily noticed there were tiny particles of ice in his mustache.

"Madden. Gerry Madden. He's a bit un-stable. They're in counseling together. He smashed a window here. I knew I should have said something when he asked Trudy out, but he seemed very calm. We thought he was on the mend." Lily bit her nails with worry.

"And you are?" The second officer got his notebook out.

"I'm Lily Beaumont. I'm the landlady here. Is Trudy okay? Please tell me."

"I'm sorry but we aren't here about Trudy Valentine. This is to do with an employee of yours, Mrs. Beaumont. A woman called Bridget O'Malley. She's a barmaid here, I believe? The employment office gave us this address."

"Oh Lord, is that all? What has she broken, now? She's very accident-prone, you know." Lily was so relieved that she wanted to laugh, no matter what the cost of Bridget's latest disaster. And it was laughable that the policeman had called Bridget a woman. Even though she was twenty-five, Lily looked on Bridget as a small child.

"I'm afraid we have some very bad news for Bridget. Her parents have passed away. They died last night."

"What?" Lily's heart nearly stopped. "What do you mean? Her parents, did you say? Both of them have died? Both dead?"

"That's correct."

"When? How?"

"If you let me explain, I'll tell you how," said the second officer patiently.

"It's very cold out here, by the way," added the first policeman.

"Well, of course. Come in and I'll make some coffee. Come in," Lily said, and she opened the door wide, thankful that all the clearing up had been done the night before. The fire was still lit, just about, so she added some turf from the basket, and fetched a pot of scalding-hot coffee and some leftover pastries from the kitchen. Lily handed out plates and cups, and sugar and spoons. Poor Bridget, she thought. Lily was glad now that she hadn't read Bridget the riot act over her mishaps in the tavern. What would happen to Bridget and her three sisters now they were orphans?

The policemen sat down near the fire and placed their caps on the table. At once they looked more approachable. Lily relaxed. She always felt like she was going to be arrested when she was in the presence of uniformed officers. Even though she hadn't done anything wrong. They introduced themselves properly.

"I'm John Kelly," said the tall one with the mustache, "and this is Steven Butterworth. And thank you for the coffee, Mrs. Beaumont, it was very nice. Now, Mr. O'Malley was unfortunately knocked down and killed by a lorry last night on the Lisburn Road."

"Oh, the poor man," said Lily sadly.

"He was in a deeply inebriated state and

simply stumbled out in front of the vehicle," continued John. "It was an accident. There were several witnesses who saw what happened. The lorry driver was not to blame but he's in shock at the moment."

"I'm not surprised," she murmured.

"They have him sedated in the City Hospital."

Lily was deeply shocked. What a sad and lonely death for Bridget's father, she thought. How tragic for him to end his days on the cold, hard road! Killed by a stranger. And the lorry driver's life would never be the same again, either. Tragedy heaped upon tragedy.

"That's terrible," she said. "I knew Bridget's father was a bit of a drinker, but this is just terrible. Did he suffer at all? I hope he wasn't in any pain."

"We don't think he was conscious, after the impact. It was all over very quickly. He was dead when the ambulance arrived, which was less than three minutes later. The accident took place right outside the hospital."

"I see. But what about Mrs. O'Malley?" Lily was getting upset now, not for the dead man, but for Bridget herself. The poor child was still sleeping peacefully upstairs. Lily felt awful for all the names she had called Bridget, when she and Jack were alone together. Idiot, eejit, butterfingers, flake, floozy, sponger. And that she had been on the verge of firing her several times. It seemed that being accident-prone ran in the O'Malley family.

"We went round to the house last night to inform Mrs. O'Malley of the accident," said John Kelly. "And she collapsed on the doorstep."

"Took the news very badly," added Steven Butterworth. "We called an ambulance but she had a heart attack before it could reach her. She died in John's arms."

"Oh, my goodness, what a dreadful experience. I don't know what to say. How awful for you," Lily said.

"It happens more often than you'd think," said John Kelly gently.

"I couldn't do your job for anything." Lily poured more coffee and braced herself for what was coming next.

"Can you tell Bridget?" asked John. "I think it would be better if you told her. News like this should come from a friend."

"I'll try," she faltered. "I hope I can find the right words."

"Just take a moment, Mrs. Beaumont, to

prepare yourself. I know you can do it. We'll be outside in the car, waiting to give Bridget a lift to identify the bodies. There'll be a post-mortem but it's all quite straightforward."

"I see," said Lily.

"Yes. The accident was witnessed, and the dead woman had a registered heart condition and was severely malnourished," Steven Butterworth said, and put a whole fresh cream éclair into his mouth. He washed it down with half a cup of coffee, and smacked his lips. "Thanks for that, it was lovely."

Lily's head was swimming. She hadn't heard of anyone in this country being severely malnourished since the days of the potato famine. How could Bridget's family life be this awful? Bridget never spoke about her parents, and Lily assumed they simply had nothing in common. But if they were both hopeless cases, as the policemen seemed to believe, then her childhood must have been traumatic. And hungry, no doubt. No wonder she was always eating. Lily suddenly recalled how she had laughed her head off when Jack's secret stash of soya milk had been found and drunk by Bridget. The girl was a phenomenon in that she could consume so much food and yet remain so tiny.

Bridget hadn't been to visit her parents since she moved in above the tavern, and she hadn't phoned them, either. Now Lily knew it was because they didn't have a telephone. Bridget was obviously trying to ignore their living situation entirely. Now she would have to go through this nightmare ordeal at the mortuary. And arrange a double funeral, too. And tell her sisters.

"Please, you tell her," Lily asked. "I haven't known Bridget for long, you see? I'm very fond of her, of course, but honestly, I don't think I could tell her that her parents both departed this world in the very same night."

"Okay," sighed Constable Kelly. "I'll do it. Fetch her down here, please."

Lily went up the stairs and knocked softly on the door. There was no answer. She ran back downstairs again and said, "Before I wake her, are you quite sure they were Bridget's parents? How do you know for definite?"

"The O'Malleys are well known in the hospital, Mrs. Beaumont. They've been in to the emergency room on numerous occasions, with various injuries. Bridget's name is in the book as their next of kin."

Lily nodded and went back up to the sitting room. This time she did not knock but went straight in and stole over to one of the beds beside the window. Bridget was sleeping with a contented smile on her face. The new blue blanket was tucked right up underneath her chin. She didn't look old enough to arrange a funeral for her own parents. Lily thought it was one of the hardest things she'd ever had to do, just to have to wake Bridget up.

"Bridget? Bridget, wake up. Can you hear me?" Lily whispered. Bridget opened her big blue eyes and saw Lily's worried face hovering above her own.

"It's my mum and dad, isn't it?" she said after a second. "Which one?" When Lily did not answer, she sighed loudly. "It's both of them? I suppose they burned down the house? Fell asleep smoking cigarettes? I always knew they would burn it down someday." And then Lily knew that she would have to tell Bridget the bad news herself. She couldn't make the poor girl wait until she went downstairs and faced the policemen on her own.

"Oh, Bridget. You're right, it is your parents. God! Listen, there's no easy way to say this so I'll just say it. They have died, but it was an accident. Your father was knocked down on the road and your mother's heart gave out when they told her. There are two policemen downstairs and they have all the details. You might have to go with them to the hospital. But I'll go, too." Lily held her breath for Bridget's reaction. Bridget reached out a small hand from under the blankets and Lily held it tightly. "I'll be with you, every step of the way," she said.

"There's no need," Bridget whispered.

"Don't be silly."

"I'll go to the morgue by myself, Lily. I'll be okay."

"Bridget, you can't possibly go through that ordeal on your own."

"I've caused you enough trouble already. The carpet, the bath, the teapot, the window, the perfume, the sofa." The girl must be in shock, thought Lily, to be going on about teapots at a time like this. What was that she said about a sofa, though? Lily's gaze darted across to her lovely overstuffed chintz, and she noticed the small patch of ink on one of the arms. Oh well, she thought. Another one bites the dust. . . .

"Bridget, you're no trouble at all. Please

let me help you. You're in shock. Here, put on your robe and come downstairs for a cup of tea, or maybe a brandy to steady you?"

"I never drank in my life, Lily, and I won't start now."

"Sorry, Bridget. I wasn't thinking. Of course you don't drink."

"I've seen the results of it once too often."

"Yes, I'm sure you have. Come on, we'll get through this day together."

"I don't want you to see their faces, Lily. You don't know what it's been like. They look so old. Far older than they really are. And their home is awful. Like a scene from Charles Dickens." Bridget got out of bed and put on a long blue coat over her pajamas. Lily understood that Bridget's shabby robe was not fit to be seen by two officers of the law. She was amazed that Bridget could still be so proud, in the middle of her terrible loss. The two women went down the stairs together, after Lily told Jack what was going on.

Bridget was calm and quiet as they entered the bar. But when she saw John Kelly standing there with his cap under his arm, she finally crumbled and sobbed until her head was throbbing and her heart was sore. John put his arm around her, and patted her shoulder softly. He was well used to comforting the bereaved.

But it was not for her late parents that Bridget wept so bitterly. She had given up on them many years earlier. She cried for what she never had. She cried into John Kelly's shoulder, and as she wiped her nose on his blue shirt she felt a bolt of electricity dart between them. She wept because she had no money for the funeral, and because she was ashamed of her job and because she would be homeless again soon when the tavern was sold. She wept for her three sisters and all the Christmases they had spent hiding upstairs while their parents drank the dole money, and cursed various jolly celebrities singing cheery songs on the old television. (A donation from the Saint Vincent de Paul charity shop.) She wept because Gerry Madden had cast her aside like an old coat the minute he met Trudy Valentine. And even though she didn't love Gerry anymore, it had hurt like hell. She wept because she'd wished many times that Lily and Jack Beaumont were her real parents and she felt disloyal for wanting such a thing. Finally, she had no strength left with which to cry. John Kelly released her from his embrace, and asked Lily for fresh coffee.

"You'll feel better soon," he said kindly.

Constable Butterworth gave Lily some general advice about the funeral arrangements while John comforted Bridget, and told her again the events of the night before. They gave the women time to dress, and then the four of them set off in the police car. Jack and the other three girls sat quietly in the kitchen.

In the mortuary, the bodies beneath the white sheets were obviously those of two short, thin people. They were like children, lying there under the spotlights. Lily didn't look at the faces of Bridget's parents but she knew they were small and battered, and dried up by a lifetime of hard knocks. Bridget identified them both with a slight nod of her head, while Lily waited by the door, and Bridget cried again as the relevant papers were signed. Then John Kelly drove them to the O'Malley home in a neat terrace with Victorian streetlights and tiny front gardens. The priest was waiting by the front door, a gilt-edged missal in his hand. He was an old man, but very kind-looking. He attempted to put on a brave face for the occasion.

"I'm most sorry for your loss, Bridget," he said, and they shook hands formally. "God bless you and your sisters in England. I said a Mass for you this morning."

"Thank you, Father Damien," she said. "You were very good to them, always."

"That's all right, my dear. I prayed many times for them, that they would find the strength to get over their addiction. They were good people, in their hearts."

"I suppose they were," Bridget said, without much conviction. "This is my boss, Mrs. Lily Beaumont. And Constable Kelly, who has looked after me today."

"Hello, Father." Lily smiled. John only nodded, and stood back respectfully.

"Lovely to meet you, Mrs. Beaumont. Bridget's parents told me she was very happy to be working for you." Lily duly told Father Damien that Bridget was a joy to have about the place. She was quite moved to witness such kindness from the priest. She'd have thought the old man would have been weary of scenes of sadness such as this. But he seemed genuinely concerned for the O'Malley family. Bridget found a key in her handbag and unlocked the door.

"Brace yourselves," she warned, as they went inside. The little house was cold and damp and all the curtains were closed.

There was hardly any furniture in the sitting room, just two light armchairs and a spindly coffee table from the 1950s. The table was covered with empty spirits bottles, and a huge ashtray that turned out to be a charred and battered biscuit tin. Surprisingly, there was a full scuttle of coal beside the hearth, and some tartan blankets on the chairs.

"Well, at least they had some coal and blankets," observed Lily, desperate to fill the empty silence. "They must have been quite cosy here, in the evenings."

"The Saint V de P Society provided everything you see in this house," said Bridget softly. "Mum and Dad would have slept on the bare floorboards, left to their own devices. The neighbors brought them food from time to time, and a social worker saw the bills were paid before they got their hands on the welfare checks. They were hopeless, the two of them."

Father Damien closed his eyes and said a prayer. John Kelly unplugged the television and put a fire screen across the hearth. A small pile of coal was still smoldering in the grate.

"Should have done this last night," he muttered, and Bridget closed her eyes with shame.

Lily shivered. It was, indeed, like a scene from one of Dickens's novels. She expected to see Oliver Twist coming down the chimney at any moment. In this day and age, when the country had never been more prosperous, it was a real shock to the system. The kitchen was equally bleak. There was a blue plastic dish rack, some chipped cups and plates, a loaf of cheap bread and a small box of budget teabags. A bar of pink soap with gray lines in it lay on the windowsill. Four tins of vegetable soup stood on the counter, and Bridget said they would have come from the annual charity church hamper. Her parents would never buy tins of fancy carrot soup at eighty-four pence each. A saucepan with no lid was upside down on the counter. The vinyl on the floor was worn through to the concrete beneath. The larder was empty. So was the fridge. The back door was not even locked. The house felt derelict, as if nobody had lived in it for years. There were no Christmas decorations in the house, except for a small sprig of fresh holly on top of a picture of the Sacred Heart. One of the neighbors must have brought it, Bridget said.

The bedrooms were even worse: empty and cheerless, with pillows on the beds that were as flat as paper. The bedroom that Bridget and her sisters had once shared was small, cramped and full of dust. Bridget picked up a solitary rag doll from the windowsill, held it against her cheek for a couple of moments and set it down again. They went back down the stairs, shoes clattering loudly on the wooden steps.

"There's nothing here that I want to keep," Bridget announced. "I'll phone the council and tell them they can re-let this place. If they can find anybody willing to take it, it's so damp. They never turned the central heating on, never."

"I'll take care of the house details, Bridget. Don't worry yourself about it," said Father Damien. "Shall I arrange the wake for tomorrow evening? We can borrow some chairs and candlesticks from the parish hall."

"Could we just bring the coffins directly to the church, Father? And not have a wake in the house? I think that would be for the best. They had no real friends around here. Only charity workers, and people from the welfare office. And neighbors who felt sorry for them."

"They were well liked, Bridget. It's not true they had no friends. You mustn't think that about your parents. It wasn't their fault that their addiction made them unworldly."

Unworldly, thought Lily, stunned by the empty feeling in the little house. That's got to be the greatest euphemism of all time, she said to herself. This is third world stuff. She couldn't understand why the children hadn't been taken into care. Possibly, there weren't enough foster places at the time?

"It's what I want, Father. I want some dignity for them," said Bridget firmly. "I don't want my parents to be laid out here, in this cold house with no comfort in it. I want the coffins closed, too."

A wise decision, thought Lily. I don't blame you one bit.

"As you wish, Bridget. I'll speak to the mortuary staff and the undertakers." Father Damien resigned himself to Bridget's unorthodox instructions. He was not convinced it was a good thing that his parishioners were making up their own minds about funerals these days. Still, at least she didn't want football strips or pop songs in the church. He was glad he was an old man and would not live to see much more change.

"What about the funeral expenses?" said Lily, suddenly. She felt more than a little guilty. All her adult life, she'd sold alcohol to the public and barely considered the consequences. Now, seeing the meanness and poverty in the O'Malley home had opened her eyes. "Can we help toward the cost of the coffins?"

"No way, Lily," said Bridget. "You will not pay for anything. I won't let you."

"The authorities will take care of that side of things," said Father Damien abruptly. He was a staunch Irish nationalist who resented any handouts from the government across the water in England, but what could he do about it? Even basic funerals cost a lot of money these days. At least there were plenty of holly trees and evergreens around the Parochial House. He would ask his housekeeper to make up a couple of nice wreaths to go on the coffin lids. And they had enough candles in the sacristy, thank God. They would put on a decent enough show for the funeral on Christmas Day. He sighed, remembering that he would have to make alterations to his prepared sermon.

"In the midst of life, we are in death," he sighed. Bridget looked as if she might cry again, but she only breathed in sharply and thanked them all for their support.

"I mean it, Bridget," said Lily. "Could Jack and I pay for the flowers, even? It's the least we can do for them."

"You never knew them, Lily. You never met them."

"Please, Bridget. I want to do it. For your sisters' sake, at least?"

"Lily, I know you mean well. But an extravagant funeral just wouldn't suit my parents. It would be wrong. It would be a lie."

"Oh, Bridget." Lily looked around the chilly sitting room with cobwebs hanging off the light bulb. She would take to the drink herself if she had to live like this. "We should do something nice."

"The trappings of a funeral are unimportant, Mrs. Beaumont. I appreciate your gesture, but Bridget is correct. Mr. and Mrs. O'Malley were very unhappy in this life. Now they are with the Lord. They are at peace and they have no need of fancy flowers."

Lily felt suddenly sick. She thought of her own parents, sitting in their modest kitchen in the north of the city, listening to the morning news on the radio and lamenting the state of the world. They had no interests of their own at all, beyond the gossip at the factory where they worked. Her mother's hair was nothing more than gray and shapeless tufts by now. Lily had been sent a photograph of her parents at a family christening last year, by a distant relative who didn't know they were not close anymore. She thought of her father's rugged hands, smoking away his weekends in the rocking chair. Her mother and father had never left the country, never eaten a foreign meal. Her mother refused to believe that homosexuals existed, and thought fabric conditioner was a swindle. They still refused to speak to Jack. They would take the grudge of Lily's lost degree to their graves. Lily never visited them. She wondered if it was because she loved them too much, or hated them too much.

"As you wish," she said softly, and looked at her watch.

"Come on," said John Kelly, taking command of the situation. "I'll drive you both back to Maple Street. There's nothing else to be done here."

"Thank you," said Lily, halfway out the front door already. She was stiff with fatigue and dying for a hot bath. "That's very kind of you, Constable. Or is it Officer? I'm not sure what to call you."

"Call me John." He smiled.

"Would you like to have the picture of the Sacred Heart, at least?" Father Damien took it off the wall and offered it to Bridget. "I brought this picture back from Rome, for them. It was blessed by the Holy Father, himself." Bridget looked highly offended. For one awful moment, Lily thought Bridget was going to smash the picture over her knee, and she was horrified. But then, Bridget's face softened. She accepted the picture gracefully and went out to the police car without looking back. The front door was locked and Lily gave the key to Father Damien. They waved to him as they drove away.

"He was very nice," said Lily. "I thought he was a kind man."

"He was the only real friend we ever had," said Bridget. "He always managed to find us a turkey and some toys for Christmas. He begged things from every store in the city, and organized a food collection in the church each year. One time, we got a fresh pineapple. Ma said it was only for snobs and she threw it in the bin."

"It was good of you to accept the picture," said Lily. "Father Damien was pleased about that."

"He thinks he's helping to restore my faith. I didn't want to hurt his feelings," said Bridget. "But I gave up believing in God a long time ago."

Later that evening, it was decided that Bridget should take a few days off work. She didn't want to, saying she would rather be kept busy. But Lily phoned Bridget's doctor, and he convinced her to rest for a while, and to speak with her sisters about what had happened. By seven that evening, Bridget was back in bed, where she fell asleep almost at once. She slept right through the party that night and only woke up at four in the morning for a cup of coffee.

She wished that Gerry would call and chat with her, but he had promised Trudy he wouldn't phone again at an unsociable hour. Bridget looked over at Trudy in the next bed, and wondered how she had managed to tame the wild Gerry Madden. He hadn't missed one session with the nurse. He'd even told Trudy he was trying to get his bosses to lift the suspension. He'd met with them several times, and groveled for all he was worth. He had offered to work over Christmas, too. He was a changed man. Bridget couldn't understand it. She couldn't get her parents to give up alcohol and pay her more attention. And she couldn't make Gerry do it, either. She must be unlovable. That was the only answer.

When she crept out of the room to rustle up a nocturnal snack a few minutes later, she was feeling very sorry for herself. Luckily, the kitchen was piled high with good things to eat. She saw a cake tin with her name written on a piece of paper and taped on. Inside was a selection of sandwiches wrapped in tinfoil, a generous wedge of chocolate fudge cake and a thick slice of cooked chicken. A little note at the bottom of the tin said, "We love you, Bridget, from Lily, Jack, Trudy, Daisy and Marie." Bridget sat at the table, looking at the note for a long time. She drank three cups of coffee but the delicious food was left untouched.

18

Lily Changes Her Mind

Christmas Eve

Trudy, Daisy and Marie did their best to cheer Bridget up the next day. She was strangely calm, and they interpreted her solemn state as a bout of depression. They told her that her parents had gone to a better place, and that they were now at rest, and all the usual platitudes. They said they had booked her sisters into a local hotel, for when they flew over for the funeral. They had also arranged for a beautiful wreath of red roses to be sent to the church. Bridget looked at Lily with pursed lips, but Lily said that Jack had ordered the wreath before she had time to tell him not to, and now it was too late. Daisy volunteered the lend of her best black velvet hat for the funeral, Marie donated a smart black scarf and Trudy said she would style Bridget's hair into a pretty bun for the occasion. Bridget said little throughout the day. She simply looked thoughtful and subdued. She tidied the bedroom, did a small mountain of ironing and watched a Bette Davis movie on the television.

She put the picture of the Sacred Heart under her bed, then took it out again and polished the grimy glass with a new duster. The picture reminded her of Father Damien and he was a good man. She decided to keep it to remember him by. She stood the picture on the mantelpiece, and tried to say a prayer for her parents, but the words died on her lips. She realized she couldn't remember a single one.

At three, she begged Lily to allow her to help with the preparations for Clare Prendergast's party, and Lily reluctantly agreed. They were slightly behind with the catering, as the lunchtime rush had been busier than usual. Word was spreading about the tavern's imminent demise, and more and more people were popping in for a farewell visit. The visitors book rested on a little table beside the grandfather clock and there were seventy-nine pages full of signatures by Christmas Eve.

"I really think you should have a lie-down, though, Bridget. You'll be on your feet all day tomorrow," Lily said.

"Look. My sisters don't get here for another five hours. And until they do, I can still help with the party food. Please. I want to enjoy a bit of life and noise before the funeral."

"Okay, pet, if you're definitely sure? Marie and Trudy can advise you on what to do. And I'll go down and help Jack and Daisy."

It was getting very hot and flustered in the kitchen. When yet another turkey was lifted out of the oven, a blast of hot greasy air came with it and the temperature in the small room soared. The window was wide open but even the icy chill flowing in past the glass storage jars couldn't cool the pink faces of the two cooks. Despite that, they were uneasy about accepting help from a girl in mourning.

"If you don't let me do something, I'll just

go ahead on my own initiative," said Bridget. "I'm warning you." She took a sharp knife out of the drawer and demanded to be given something to chop up.

"Fair enough," said Marie. "You can do the chicken and olive terrine, if you insist."

"I do," replied Bridget. "Just tell me how."

"Well, chop one onion and three rashers and fry them in olive oil for five minutes. Add a splash of white wine. Dice five chicken fillets and add some chopped olives and parsley. Then, you have to line a tin with more rashers and put it all in."

"Hold your horses," said Bridget. "Let me get on with the first bit and then give me the next installment. Cocktails are a breeze compared to this cookery lark." She smiled for the first time that day, and for a couple of hours there was peace and harmony in the kitchen. Platters of well-garnished party food were covered with plastic film and laid along the hall floor.

Lily and Jack were rushed off their feet behind the bar. They were still suffering from the effects of the flu, but the bar was nice and cosy, and they were both wearing warm clothes. Luckily for the customers, their sniffles and sneezes had subsided. They still

had shivery chills and painful joints, but nobody noticed them hobbling slightly, as
everyone enjoyed the delightful decor and
the tasty food. Daisy was swiftly clearing
plates and glasses, and manning the dishwasher on a full-time basis. She was secretly overjoyed that Lily and Jack were up
and about again, since she was absolutely
worn out. She was planning to look for
something else after Christmas. And that
meant she would have to move out, too. But
she wouldn't mention that until the Christmas rush was over.

Lily told Jack she felt quite weak, but she
just couldn't miss Christmas Eve in the tavern, no matter how ill she was. It might well
be her last one ever in Maple Street. She
was filled with bittersweet feelings about the
tavern. It was Lily's home and her refuge, but
she still hadn't recovered from the shock of
seeing the O'Malley place, and she doubted
she ever would. She'd always believed she
was providing something of value to the city.
The tavern was a haven of peace and comfort in a fast-moving world. But she also
knew she had really loved this building because it meant that she and Jack could iso-
late themselves from other people. It was

their excuse for not spending time with their difficult families. It had protected them from the stresses of the workplace, from friends and acquaintances that might require some of their attention. They had been rather selfish, in a way.

Lily had made such a fuss about her precious roll-top bath when it was ruined with black dye. Bridget had accepted the news of her parents' death with more dignity. What a burden of disappointment her childhood must have been, for her to think such a tragedy was normal. And now, Father Damien, with his food hampers and his kind words, made Lily think. She thought she wanted to help other people, too. She could make a real difference in the world, even if it was only a small difference. And she was not afraid anymore. No matter what happened in the future, she knew that Jack would always love her, and she would always love him. If Vincent Halloran was able to destroy their livelihood with his ugly shopping mall, then so be it. The Beaumonts would survive. One thing was for sure: they would never end up like the wretched O'Malleys.

Jack knew there was something on Lily's mind and he asked her about it, as he was pulling three pints of stout for Barney Cunningham.

"I'll tell you later," she whispered. "But if we can't prevent the closure, we'll be okay. I realize that now."

"Am I hearing things?" he said quietly, carefully leveling off the head of foam on one of the glasses. "Are you giving up the fight? You want to sell?"

"I'm not giving up," she replied. "Just accepting the possibility that we may lose the battle." Jack was stunned. "And besides," she added, "I don't think I could go on working at this pace until I retire. I've never been so tired."

"Well, this is a turn-up for the books. But, darling, you said things would go back to the way they were when this was all over."

"I know I did, but I think I was being naive. Don't worry, sweetheart," she said. "I'm exhausted and feeling sorry for myself at the moment, so it could just be a notion of me. I'll tell you when I have something more specific than a vague jumble of emotions. Okay?"

"Okay, my love."

Lily smiled at Barney, and set his three

half-glasses of Guinness on the counter. He nodded innocently and winked his thanks, but he had heard every word. He carried the little tray back to the booth with a heavy heart.

"Let's enjoy these," he said, as Joey and Francy Mac reached out their hands for the drinks. "I've just heard Mrs. Beaumont saying she may not be able to save this place. Close the door, there."

Barney drew his pipe from the breast pocket of his tweed jacket, and the other two watched respectfully as he filled it with tobacco and struck a long match.

"They'll regret it, if they leave Maple Street," said Joey.

"Aye. They were made for this place," said Francy Mac. "Do you remember the time they first took over here?" But Francy Mac's reminiscence was suddenly interrupted when Jack opened the door of the booth. He set a silver platter of assorted party nibbles on the table, and three large glasses of brandy. The three men looked at the neat rows of glistening pastries and savory snacks with wide eyes.

"Compliments of the season, to three of

our best customers," Jack said, in the most jovial voice he could muster. He was feeling quite emotional. It was a mixture of pre-disco nerves and Lily's sudden change of heart about fighting to hold on to the business.

"How kind," said Barney.

"Very decent of you both," croaked Joey.

"Yes, indeed," added Francy Mac.

"We just wanted to thank you for your loyal custom over the years," said Jack. "It might be the last time we're all together on Maple Street. So, thanks again, and Merry Christmas!"

"Merry Christmas to you, too," they said quietly.

"Lily says you are very welcome to join us tomorrow for Christmas lunch. If you have no other plans, that is? We'll be sitting down to starters around three. By the way, there's a party starting at seven tonight, and it could be a bit noisy. I'm playing some records, God help me. I'm sorry to say it's a private affair."

"Don't worry about us, Jack. We'll just nip out when the music starts," Barney said. "Thanks very much for the dinner invitation. Much obliged. We'll be there. Won't we, lads?" Barney had no family, so Christmas was a lonely time of the year for him.

"We will, surely. Thanks a lot, Jack." Joey was quite overwhelmed. He usually spent the day alone. His two children had moved to Australia years before.

"Cheers, Jack," added Francy Mac. His three children lived in Scotland, but he hated traveling there on his own. He usually spent the day visiting his wife's grave. "You're a good man. And many thanks to your good lady wife." Then the door of the booth closed again and Jack was making his way back to the bar through the crowds. They could hear him shouting, "Ladies and gentlemen! Please note! Private party at seven o'clock tonight."

19

THE PARTY
OF THE YEAR

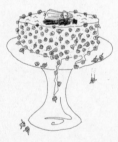

MARIE AND TRUDY were trying to keep an eye on the vanilla custard for the party buffet, as well as preparing the last of the various canapés and pastries. Bridget was icing gingerbread biscuits very badly, and Lily was counting out bottles of chilled champagne from the fridge. Daisy and Jack were downstairs clearing and cleaning the bar, ready for Clare Prendergast's fancy-dress party. In a moment, they would carry down all the food, and then they'd have about ten minutes to get changed into their party clothes.

"Thanks for doing those biscuits, Bridget. Although God knows what Father Damien will say if he comes to visit and sees you working," said Lily. "He'll think I'm a heartless slave driver."

"He'll think you're like a mother to me," said Bridget, quietly. "Because that's the truth." In the midst of the chaotic kitchen, they hugged each other.

"I never had a daughter of my own. I wasn't blessed with children," said Lily, wiping a tear from her eye. "I didn't mind because I was so happy with Jack. But having you girls here, these last few weeks, has made me see what I've missed. It's been wonderful, hearing young voices and seeing a bit of life about the place. Really, it has."

"Do you mean that?" asked Bridget, her face white with hope. Trudy and Marie looked shy, but happy, too.

"Yes, I do," said Lily. "I've loved having you here, it's been like having a real family. The extra work has been unbelievably difficult, but getting to know the four of you has been wonderful."

Bridget closed her eyes with happiness. She didn't feel quite so unlovable anymore. Then, the phone rang. Lily was glad of the distraction, because she thought she might cry, and there'd been too many tears in the tavern already this Christmas. The caller was a very excited lady asking about some cake or other, in a very high-pitched voice. Initially, Lily thought it was a nuisance call. But then, the jumbled words began to make sense. In a cold sweat, Lily knew it was Clare. And Clare wanted to know how the preparations were going. Lily almost had a heart attack when she realized she had forgotten to ice the anniversary cake.

"Everything is ready," she lied. "Come on over."

Lily came bolting into the kitchen to look for some packets of icing sugar on one of the kitchen shelves. She scrabbled around in desperation, finding nothing.

"Oh my God, I put them right here. Where are the packets of sugar? They're lost! They're not here. Oh, sweet Savior! Marie, get me some nuts and cherries. We'll improvise!"

"Lily, I've been meaning to tell you something," faltered Bridget. But Lily wasn't listening, as her panic mounted.

"Clare and her husband are staying in the Hilton, girls. They'll be here in half an hour, at the very most. They'd just ordered the taxi when Clare rang me. Oh, help. Help me do something to decorate this cake!"

"I iced the cake last night," admitted Bridget, in a small voice. "I couldn't sleep." Trudy, Marie and Lily froze. They looked at the gingerbread men with their wobbly smiles and too-big buttons.

"Where is it now?" asked Lily, her voice breaking with despair. "You didn't eat it as well, did you?"

"Of course not! I put it back on top of the cupboard there, in that big box." They all looked up at the spot Bridget was indicating. "I used ready-made marzipan, and mixed up the icing myself." Lily thought she might collapse with worry. Bridget was next to hopeless in the kitchen. And if the cake was ruined, there wasn't time to ice another. Or even buy a replacement. The shops were closing early because it was Christmas Eve. Bridget hopped up on a chair and carefully reached down the precious container. They all held their breath as the lid came off. The marzipan was slightly higher on one side, and the icing had been eased up into gentle peaks with a blunt knife. But because the icing was slightly too watery, the peaks had collapsed again into gentle waves, and some had dripped down onto the silver card base. The cake was studded with an entire packet of two hundred pink sugar-rose decorations. Lying down on the top, half-buried in the icing, was a tiny model of a married couple, which had come from Lily's own cake, long ago in Scotland. Jack had bought it and stuck it on a fruitcake from the supermarket; and they had eaten a slice each in bed, on their honeymoon.

"I found the bride-and-groom decoration in the sitting-room cabinet, when I was looking for a safety pin a few days ago," said Bridget. "The groom's left arm is missing, I know. But isn't he gorgeous, all the same?"

Trudy and Marie did not trust themselves to open their mouths. They could see that Lily's lovely cake was a disaster. But they weren't going to be the ones to tell Bridget that she had ruined the centerpiece of the party when Bridget's parents were still lying in two government-bought coffins on the other side of the city.

"Mind you, I put them on standing up. They must have fallen over during the night." Bridget tried to prick the miniature lovers out of the hardened icing with a fork. Lily stopped her just in time.

"Leave it, Bridget," she whimpered. "They're stuck fast." Lily wanted to strangle Bridget more, at that moment, than she ever had. She couldn't believe Bridget had used her precious wedding decoration. Bad enough that she had ruined the cake. But what would happen if Clare Prendergast wanted to keep the tiny bride and groom, after the cake was eaten? Lily treasured that little piece of plastic kitsch. It was the only keepsake she had left of her own wedding day. She cursed herself for not hiding it better. She should have dug a hole in the yard, ten feet deep, and filled it with her things before Bridget O'Malley moved in and turned everything upside down. Marie suddenly remembered she had to show Jack where the tablecloths were, and Trudy went to help spread them out over the counter. They squeezed out through the narrow door frame together and ran down the stairs. Bridget searched Lily's face for some reaction to her cake design. Lily held her breath and counted to ten.

"Do you know what?" said Lily, nodding her head. "It's fine. Absolutely fine." She was too tired to make a scene. If Clare wasn't happy with the cake then she could just throw away the bill. Lily Beaumont had finally reached the end of her tether.

"Thank goodness," said Bridget. "I was worried there for a minute. You all went a bit quiet on me. I mean, what other way is there to decorate wedding cakes?"

"I wasn't going to use any decorations, Bridget," said Lily tenderly. "I was going to smooth out the icing. And put real white roses on the top."

"Well, for pity's sake! That's nothing like what I did," cried Bridget. "I've messed up again, haven't I?"

"Not at all."

"Are you sure?" Bridget was still not convinced.

"She'll love it, I know she will." Lily was grim with determination. She only hoped that Clare wasn't easily upset. Trudy and Marie came back then, saying Jack had the tablecloths on the counter and they were to bring down the food. The two girls searched Lily's face for some reaction to the cake fiasco, but she only sighed and smiled weakly. They had a party to get through, and Lily didn't have the energy for any hysterics.

After several trips up and down the narrow stairs, everything was looking good. The fire was crackling away, most of the afternoon's cigarette smoke had cleared, and Jack was giving all the chairs a quick once-over with the mini-vacuum. Barney, Joey and Francy Mac said goodbye, and thanked Lily profusely for their unexpected dinner invitation.

"That's all right," she said, for the fifth time. "Sure, it will be lovely for us to have the company." And she saw them out onto the street. Back inside, it was almost time for the party to begin.

"If there's not much more to do here, can you girls get ready to serve?" said Lily, a heavy feeling of tiredness beginning to settle on her shoulders.

"Okay. I'm going to be Cyndi Lauper," gushed Daisy. "She had red hair, too."

"I'm going to be a female version of Adam, from Adam and the Ants," said Trudy.

"Haven't you been that for years?" said Bridget dryly, and they all laughed.

"And I'm going to be Kate Bush," said Marie. "Though not in anything too revealing. Her long skirt and wrap-over top phase, you know?"

"I wish I could go to the party," said Bridget sadly.

"We'd love you to be here," said Lily. "But

there's a taxi due at eight-thirty to take you to the airport, and your sisters need you to be strong for them." She slipped some rolled-up banknotes into Bridget's hand. "Here, take them out for a meal and talk about happy times."

"There weren't any," said Bridget simply.

"Make some up, then. Or ask them about their lives now. It's never too late to be happy," said Lily quietly. "And surely you don't want them to see you miserable? They had enough misery when they were growing up."

"You're right," said Bridget. "I'll do my best."

"That's the girl. Oh, and by the way, why don't you invite them over tomorrow for Christmas dinner?"

"Honestly?"

"Sure. It'll be no bother at all. After all the catering we've done recently. There's only the six of us, and Barney's crew."

"Thanks, Lily."

Lily set the wedding anniversary cake on a little table beside the main Christmas tree, and half-hid it behind a big sprawling garland she had made for the fireplace. The drips on the base were well covered by the fresh green foliage, and the two hundred

pink roses sparkled and shone like dia-
monds. They all surveyed the room.

"I think we've actually managed to pull it
off. Who'd have thought it?" laughed Lily.

"Thanks for last night, everyone," said
Bridget.

"For what?" they asked.

"For the note under the chocolate cake. It
was very nice of you."

"That's okay," said Jack. "Good luck for
this evening. Tell your sisters we're thinking
of them."

"I will." Bridget went upstairs to get ready.
After staying a minute or two to survey the
room, the other girls and Jack followed suit.

When Clare and Peter Prendergast arrived a few minutes later, they were thrilled
with what they saw. Lily let them in and explained that the rest of the staff had gone
upstairs to change. The late afternoon customers had drifted off and there was a sign
on the door that said, CLOSED FOR PRIVATE
PARTY. It was all very exciting. The Christmas
trees looked magnificent twinkling against
the aubergine richness of the walls. The fire
was glowing merrily with a bright orange
heart. The food was laid out on the counter,
which was now draped with gold-colored

cloths. There were gold napkins and a rustic wire basket full of red apples dipped in egg whites and sugar. Center stage was the cake that Bridget had decorated the night before. Everything about the cake was lop-sided, and Lily apologized and explained what had happened. But Clare and Peter laughed their heads off and posed behind it for lots of photographs. Clare had her hands on the cutting knife and Peter put his arms around her. They gave Lily a disposable camera and she took twenty pictures of them.

"Watch my fingers," Peter said, as Clare giggled and almost tripped over the leg of the table.

"This is a fantastic spread," said Clare, as she checked her back-combed hair in one of the gold mirrors. "I'm Madonna in the early years! Can you tell?"

"Yes. The lace hair band and all the cruci-fixes gave it away," said Lily, smiling.

"I usually obsess about my hair and makeup," explained Clare. "So tonight I thought I'd throw caution to the winds and come as a total mess."

"Don't listen to a word of it," said her ador-ing husband. "She was two hours in the hotel bathroom getting ready. She cut the arms off a perfectly good jacket as well." Peter was wearing a black leather coat and black jeans, which apparently meant he was the lead singer of the Stranglers.

"Peter doesn't do dressing up," said Clare. "Even for my special anniversary party. Would you believe he used to wear eyeliner?"

"I'm too unfit to outrun any thugs who might take against me, these days," he said shyly. There were footsteps on the stairs, and they turned to face the hall door.

"Meet DJ Nostalgia, aka my husband, Jack," said Lily, as Jack carried in the turkey, stuffing and cranberry sauce wraps and added them to the feast. He was wearing a gold lamé suit, which Daisy had found for him in a secondhand store. Apparently, some crazy man had once got married in it, and it had been hanging at the back of the shop ever since. "He'll be keeping you all glued to the dance floor."

"Oh my God," said Jack. "Don't give me a big buildup. I've never done this kind of thing before. Believe me, I'm a total novice."

"That's what they all say," said Clare, laughing until her eyes watered. She had never felt so happy and relaxed.

"This is just great, honestly," said Peter. "We're really pleased. The food looks wonderful. Let's kick off the celebrations with a few rounds of Red Witch, shall we? For old times' sake?" At that moment, Trudy and Marie came down the stairs in their finery and did a twirl for the general company. Marie's hair, now released from its ponytail, was a halo of mahogany spirals, and she had covered her face with softly shimmering glitter. She was wearing a white wrap-over top and a long gray flared skirt. She was a picture of elegance. Trudy had painted a white stripe across her nose, there were tiny plaits and feathers in her hair, and she wore knee-length trousers and a white lacy blouse. Clare took their picture and Jack slipped a background CD into the player. The party atmosphere leaped into life. Even before the guests arrived, they all knew it was going to be fantastic.

The girls looked briefly confused when they heard the Red Witch drinks order, but Lily showed them how to add blackcurrant cordial to a mix of lager and licorice-flavored spirit.

"Just very small measures, mind you," said Peter. "We used to drink pints of this stuff but if we attempted it nowadays we'd be ending the night in hospital."

"Blimey, you oldies know how to live," muttered Trudy, and there was another blast of laughter. Then Daisy came dancing into the room, her wrists dripping with bracelets. She was wearing several different colors of eye shadow, and her hair had been back-combed into a candy-floss cloud. She was wearing a red tulle skirt, a bright yellow vest and several studded belts.

"Aren't you getting changed, Daisy?" asked Jack with a wink, and the laughter flowed again.

"Technically, I should be in my bare feet but these tiles are awfully cold," she said. "So I'm keeping my boots on." They all glanced down at Daisy's sturdy leather boots. She had laced them up with yellow ribbons, as a compromise.

"Seriously, you should go on *Stars in Their Eyes.* You should be on the stage," said Clare.

"I'd love to be a pop star," said Daisy, dreamily. "Unfortunately, I can't sing a note and I can't dance, either."

"Don't let minor details like that stop you," trilled Clare, helping herself to a turkey and stuffing wrap. "Oh my word, these are absolutely gorgeous!" She lifted a side plate and began to fill it up with pretty nibbles. "I couldn't eat a thing at lunch I was so excited. I'm starving now. Hope you don't mind?"

"Eat away," said Lily. "It's your party." Jack, Trudy, Marie and Daisy took up their positions behind the bar. The Devaney brothers were next to arrive. Dressed in denim dungarees, flat caps and braces, they had come as Dexy's Midnight Runners. They were both very impressed by Daisy and Marie's sexy costumes. In fact, they thought it might be rather difficult to concentrate on the play list with such temptation in the room. They accepted Clare's invitation to sample the buffet before taking their guitars and going to sit beside the fire. As the CD came to an end they began a gentle version of "The Power of Love," by Frankie Goes to Hollywood. Everyone was visibly moved. Afterward, they decided to keep the love songs for the end of the night. Clare and Peter were looking at their watches, now. The guests were due any minute.

"I hope they haven't forgotten," said Clare. "Did we put the right date on the tickets?"

"Of course we did. They'll be getting

dressed up," soothed Peter. "Don't worry. Arrival times are more relaxed in Ireland." He popped the cork on a bottle of champagne and poured them all a glass. "Enjoy the peace, darling. It will be mad-crazy here in no time." David and Michael sang "Dignity" by Deacon Blue to calm the nerves of the happy couple. Jack turned the lights down and set the screen in front of the fire. He prayed the night would be a success. They all waited for any sign of life on Maple Street, and just before eight-thirty, they could hear the welcome sounds of happy chatter echoing down the alley. Then, the first of the guests arrived at the door and Jack ushered them in. The brothers sang a Madonna song, and Clare and Peter stole a quick kiss, martini glasses of Red Witch in their hands. The new arrivals greeted them warmly and presented them with gifts and cards.

"Oh gosh, I wasn't expecting presents," said Clare, hugging her old friends. "You shouldn't have, honestly."

"Nonsense," said one. "We missed the wedding in New York but we'll make up for it tonight." Then, there was another knock at the door and suddenly the tavern was full to the brim with delighted guests in fancy dress. Most of them had made a terrific effort to dress up in 1980s outfits for the occasion. The rest had never changed their style from the first time around. *Dynasty* shoulder pads, big hair, plastic jewelry, woolly leg warmers and even studded dog collars were everywhere. Clare produced a bag full of cameras and the flash bulbs were popping almost constantly. The turkey wraps disappeared within minutes, as did the rest of the party food. Daisy brought down the vanilla custard in a big pottery jug, and the infamous anniversary cake was quickly sliced up. With a serving of rich fruitcake and hot custard inside them, the guests were finally full up and ready to begin the dancing. Clare picked up the wedding-cake decoration and put it in a folded napkin in her handbag. When she got home to New York, she would wash off the icing and keep the tiny couple safe forever in a little glass box.

Lily saw Clare looking for the groom's missing arm underneath the garland, and had to bite her lip to stop herself from demanding the trinket back. Clare had earlier told Lily that fate had kept her and Peter apart for seventeen years. (They had met briefly in Belfast, as students, but then went their separate ways.) She said that Lily and Jack were very lucky, getting married when they were both so young. And it was true. Lily convinced herself that she would get over the loss of the decoration, in time.

"I'm sorry about the little arm," she told Clare. "It was already missing when we opened the box from the gift shop." It was the truth, although it had happened twenty years ago.

"Never mind. I loved the cake," Clare said kindly, and she snapped her handbag shut. Lily's heart skipped a beat with anguish, and she had to go and put some more turf on the fire as a distraction. Clare told the barmaids they looked fantastic when she went to the bar for a refill.

Lily nipped upstairs to change into her Sade-inspired outfit and have five minutes of rest. She needed to be alone for a moment. She was surprised to see Bridget still sitting at the kitchen table, her white ringlets making her pale face look even more ghostly. She had applied lots of blusher in an attempt to look cheerful, but the powder seemed to float in two round spots in front of her cheeks.

"Shouldn't you be on your way to the airport?" Lily asked gently, her rage at Bridget for ruining the cake ebbing away.

"The flight was delayed," said Bridget. "They rang from Heathrow to tell me. I re-booked the taxi for nine."

"Are you going to be okay, pet?" asked Lily, pouring them a small cup of tea each from the teapot. She added milk and took a sip. "Oh, I needed that. You don't know how tired you are until you sit down. Isn't that the truth?"

"They had such little lives," said Bridget sadly. "Such small, little lives. They just sat at home waiting for their dole checks and blaming other people for their misfortunes. I should have helped them more."

"Oh Bridget," sighed Lily. "You were only a child."

"Half the time they didn't eat enough, or Mum forgot to take her heart tablets. I should have done something."

"What could you have done?" Lily patted her arm. "Alcoholism is a terrible affliction. Didn't Father Damien say the neighbors kept an eye on them?"

"I walked out on my sisters, Lily. They were only kids at school when I left home. They cried their eyes out the day I packed a bag and moved in with some eejit of a boyfriend. I hardly knew him but he had a lovely clean flat."

"Bridget, don't torture yourself, please. You were only a kid yourself. What age were you when you moved out? Sixteen? They weren't your responsibility."

"But the guilt is killing me, Lily. It feels just as bad now as it did then. That's why I never kept in regular contact with my sisters."

"But they managed, didn't they? They got by?"

"I think Father Damien persuaded one of the neighbors to wash their school uniforms for them at the weekend. That poor man is a living saint."

"He is."

"I can't face them, Lily. I just can't face them. They probably hate me for bailing out like that. They could have been burned alive in their beds the way Mum and Dad carried on. Chain-smoking and falling asleep in the armchairs." Bridget cried a couple of silent tears. The fat drops rolled down her face, leaving white tracks through her blusher.

"They'll forgive you, Bridget. They'll understand."

"Even so. I can't forgive myself."

"Look, I'll come with you to the airport. This is too much for you to handle on your own." Lily stood up and yawned. "I'm too tired to serve at the party, and anyway, I'm sure they'll manage fine without me."

"Really?"

"Yeah, most of the food is gone and it's a self-service buffet anyway, and there's only ninety or so guests. There were a hundred and twenty people here last night. Jack and the girls will cope."

"I'd really appreciate it if you'd come with me," sniffed Bridget. "Thanks, Lily. Thanks for everything. I'm an awful bother to you. Don't think I don't know it."

"You are not a bother, Bridget. And you never were. You've helped me in ways you can't imagine. You took me out of myself and I'm very grateful to you. I was far too re-moved from everything. Sitting here like a bird in my nest all these years. Fussing over material things. Hoping nothing bad would happen to Jack."

"What do you mean?" Bridget asked.

"He was close to a bomb, once. He got over the shock but I never did."

"I know what you mean." The younger woman nodded her sympathy.

"So you see, you're not the only one with regrets. We should have traveled more, learned to drive, made more friends. Anyway, we're making up for lost time, now, aren't we? With four lodgers in the house."

"I thought you didn't like me," Bridget said in a small voice. "I thought you were only being kind when you said you did. Although I did appreciate your kindness."

"Silly!" Lily gave Bridget a hug. "I'm going to miss all four of you dreadfully when this is over. Just let me get changed into something smarter. I'll tell Jack I'm going out, and I'll be right with you. We'll pick up your sisters, go somewhere quiet and have a nice bite of supper."

"I am rather hungry, now you mention it. I didn't eat much since, well, you know . . ." Bridget looked at her watch. She looked smaller than ever in her new black suit. She'd decided to wear her funeral outfit tonight, in case her sisters thought she was not taking the death of their parents seriously enough.

"Honestly, you'll make it up with them, Bridget. I'm sure you'll be surprised at how much they've missed you. And at how well they're getting on in England."

"We'll see. Let's have another cup while we're waiting," said Bridget. She set her handbag and gloves on the sideboard and filled the teapot again.

Nobody noticed the two women slipping out the back door when the taxi depot rang to say the car was waiting at the end of the alley. Jack and the girls were serving cocktails and pints by the dozen, and the last of the food was rapidly disappearing. When each song came to an end, there was a huge round of applause. As the night wore on, Jack gave the Devaneys a break and played his old scratched forty-fives. His gold jacket was a great talking point, as the guests danced in the spaces between the tables. Jack almost enjoyed himself, and by the end of the night he was announcing the dedications with ease. But even though the party was a roaring success, Jack knew this was the one and only night of his entire life when he would be DJ Nostalgia. Clare had one too many glasses of Red Witch, and she had to sit down on the doorstep outside and wait until her head stopped spinning. But she wasn't disappointed about feeling unwell. In fact, she was quite pleased about it.

"It reminds me of the night I passed my

exams," she said, hiccuping loudly. "I got wasted drunk and fell asleep in a flower bed on the Lisburn Road. Thank God, my friends carried me home or I might be lying there yet!" Peter shook his head, and asked Daisy for a glass of water for his intoxicated wife.

"She's a very emotional person," he said, as he kissed Clare's forehead. There was a look of such devotion on his face that Daisy had to turn away.

20

ANYONE FOR GRAVY?

Christmas Day

LILY BLINKED AWAKE and heaved a loud sigh that the four girls could have heard in the room below, had they not been sleeping soundly. The bedside clock told her it was eleven in the morning. She turned to look at her husband. His long black eyelashes were flickering slightly. She knew he was on the verge of consciousness. She kissed him on the cheek.

"Merry Christmas, my darling," she whispered. "My DJ superstar!"

"Oh, stop! That was a one-off! Merry Christmas, sweetheart. A day off at last! Thanks be to God," he murmured. "I'm not getting out of bed all day."

"Haven't you forgotten something? We have a funeral mass to go to, and anyway we missed Midnight Mass because of Clare's party," his wife said gently. Jack groaned for about twenty seconds. He was so tired he would have given his beloved tavern away to a tinker for a few hours of peace and quiet. Then he reached for Lily's hand and held it, caressing her fingers softly. He realized sadly that their Christmas morning lovemaking tradition would have to be canceled also.

"It went clean out of my mind, the funeral," he said, turning to face Lily. "How could I forget a thing like that? And of course, we have guests coming to lunch as well."

"Exhaustion helps," Lily replied. "Don't worry about it. The party was fantastic last night, wasn't it?"

"Yeah, I think it was the best night we ever had in here. Right! Let's get up and get our funeral weeds on. The poor O'Malley girls!

What on earth will the priest say about them?"

"I'm sure he's had plenty of experience with difficult funerals. I said a prayer for them both last night as I was falling asleep. I didn't know whether to say God bless them both, or just good riddance. I was appalled for thinking that, Jack. But how could they have given themselves up to the drink so completely when they were blessed with those four lovely daughters?"

"The need for the drink was stronger, I suppose? Isn't it a miracle they weren't born with brain damage or something?" Jack was shaking his head in wonder.

"Bridget said her mother only got really bad after the children were all born. I suppose that's something to be thankful for?" Lily threw back the covers.

"Aren't we lucky that we didn't have a weakness for it, ourselves? They say it's an addiction you can be born with," Jack added.

"Maybe their mothers put whiskey in their bottles to make them sleep?" pondered Lily. "There must be a reason why they went mad for it like that."

"There you go again, looking for reasons. I told you, it's chaos out there, and we're only specks of dust in a cosmic hurricane." Jack shivered as he stood on the bare floorboards.

"Wow, did you come up with that line all by yourself?" she teased him.

"Yeah, I'm not just a pretty face." He threw on his jeans. "I could murder a cup of tea before I tidy myself up. God, it's really cold in here today. Is the window open?"

"No, pet. It's December! I'll wake the girls. The service is at twelve-thirty."

"Wait," said Jack. "Let me nip into the shower for two minutes first. I haven't had a hot shower since Bridget moved in here."

"Okay." Lily smiled. "I'll put the kettle on." Lily found her furry slippers. Jack preferred to go barefoot. He believed it kept him young. Slippers, scarves, caps and gloves were for old men, he said.

"What are we doing for lunch?" he asked, with his hand on the doorknob. "We don't usually leave home on Christmas Day. I take it there's no turkey roasting in the oven?"

"I'm going to cheat this year. I've got a turkey breast from the supermarket and I'm just going to slice it up and fry it on the pan. Everything else will be a cheat, too."

"How so?"

"Leftovers. I'm sorry, Jack, but I haven't the strength for another session in the kitchen. I've postponed the traditional feast."

"I think that's a fantastic idea, and I'll tell you what else I'd like to postpone. The party tomorrow night! Firm of builders, I didn't like them much."

"Jack, they'll sue us!"

"I'm only joking, although I think we all deserve to have tomorrow off. Right, give me two minutes and then you can rouse the sleeping beauties."

"By the way, Jack, we're giving out the presents just before lunch. I thought we would leave it till then as a mark of respect."

"Fine by me," he said, rather disappointed that he would have to wait another few hours to give Lily the fabulous silver necklace he had bought her. A moment later he came hurrying back into the bedroom to tell Lily that it had snowed during the night. They both went to the front window of the tavern to look out. Maple Street had been transformed into a strip of pristine white.

"I told you it was freezing," he said. "Don't these old buildings look fantastic with the snow collecting in all the architectural details?

There's a gargoyle on the roof across the street that you only notice when it snows."

"Quick," said Lily. "Get the camera and take some pictures of it all before it melts."

"It won't melt for a few hours yet. I can feel it in my bones," he said, hopping about on the cold floor. Jack thought it might be time to rethink his anti-slipper policy. As he was hunting for some warm socks in the bureau, Bridget slipped into the bathroom and bolted the door firmly behind her.

LIAM BRADLEY OPENED his eyes and tried to focus. His vision was badly impaired and there was a searing pain in the side of his head. It took him a few minutes to realize he was lying on the base of a broken wineglass. The sheets on the bed were soaked in spilled champagne, and there were two empty bottles standing on the bedside cabinet. He could hear a rustling noise but had no idea where it was coming from. He wondered what day it was, what time it was. His empty stomach rumbled in protest at his neglect of it.

"Get up, get up," he told himself. "Get up off this bed and order some food."

With a huge effort, he rolled over and forced himself into an upright position. The racing blood pressure in his head almost made him pass out. But then, he knew that drinking two bottles of champagne was never going to be a good idea. His mouth was so dry his tongue was stuck to the roof of his mouth. He staggered up on his feet and tottered into the bathroom. He held the ceramic light-pull in his hand for twenty seconds before pulling on it weakly.

"Here goes," he said. "Be brave, my old son."

He turned to face the mirror. No less than seven spotlights beamed down on him, showing every line, crease and wrinkle in his colorless face. The strong shadows made him look much worse than he really was. Those evil spotlights, he thought. Who designed them to be so unforgiving? At least he knew now what the rustling noise was. There was a check from Perry Shaw taped to his forehead. He must have done that himself although he had no memory of doing it. He peeled it off gently and read it again.

"Pay Mr. Liam Bradley five hundred thousand pounds only."

The events of the night before came back

to him in second-long flashes. He was attending a Christmas party in London. His new UK publisher had invited Liam and Perry to the celebrations, and Liam had drunk until he couldn't stand up. Free booze, the whole evening. He hadn't bothered with the food; he wanted to get pie-eyed instead. There was one particularly pretty waitress. Liam had asked her to spend the night with him. She'd slapped him across the face. Everyone saw. He'd thrown up in the Gents afterward with pure shock. He wasn't prepared for such hostility from a common serving girl. He'd gone around the room later, telling people he was an author from Belfast. But not to worry, he wasn't going to shoot anybody. He didn't have any stones in his pockets, he kept saying. Why had he done something as bizarre as that? He had no idea.

Thankfully Perry shoved him out into the street before the speeches began. It was raining heavily, and he'd walked up and down the streets of central London, feeling sorry for himself. Letting the rain soak into his clothes and his shoes. He'd had a fantasy he might be knocked down by a London bus and buried in Saint Paul's Cathedral.

Weren't there some famous writers in there in a crypt or under the floor? he wondered. Not too many from Belfast, though. He'd decided to go home. Somehow, he'd fallen into a taxi and made it to the right gate at the airport. He'd drunk some weak tea to settle his stomach and feigned sobriety long enough to board the plane. Once safely in his seat, he'd lain his head on a miniature pillow and slept soundly throughout the flight. The stewardess had had to shake him awake when the plane landed in his home city. He'd remembered, with a jolt, that it was the same stewardess he had slept with some years before, coming back from Ibiza. He'd smiled at her. She hadn't recognized him. When he'd walked down the steps onto the runway it was still raining like a monsoon.

Another taxi to the hotel; he didn't recall paying the driver. The room had been tidied up in his absence. There was a giant Christmas hamper sitting on the desk. A gift from Perry to celebrate the new deal, according to the gift tag. Liam had licensed the final draft directly to his agent, on the understanding that he would not have to promote it. It was three in the morning when he tore the cellophane off the hamper before fishing out the

champagne and continuing to drink. He remembered looking at his watch at twenty
minutes past four. After that, he must have
passed out.

He looked at his watch now. It was two
o'clock in the afternoon. On Christmas Day!
A day for happy families to be together, and
he had wasted the morning in a drunken
sleep. Slinger Magee would have been
proud of him. Liam laughed at his reflection
in the mirror.

"Well, you did it," he said. "Wrote the novel
in five weeks, ditched the wife, got out of that
blasted house in Marlborough before the
stairs wore me out. Sold said novel to Perry
Shaw for half a million. No promotion to do.
I'm a free man." He saluted his reflection. A
wave of nausea made him kneel down and
he thought he might be sick. But then he remembered he had spilled most of the champagne on the expensive eiderdown and he
was weak with relief. That was it, he remembered. He'd spilled the first bottle, almost all
of it. And so he'd opened the second one but
then he'd fallen asleep before he had time to
drink very much. Most of that bottle had also
soaked into the mattress. At some point during the night, he must have woken up for

long enough to set the bottles on the cabinet, but not his glass. He checked his face in the mirror. A deep indentation was still clearly visible across his cheekbone.

He had no idea how much alcohol he had consumed in the last twenty-four hours. He might have drunk himself to death. Or cut his jugular open with a shard of broken glass. Which would have been a very stupid act, given that he had made a fortune of money almost overnight. His clothes were damp and cold. He felt awful.

Perry had made him an offer he couldn't refuse as they said goodbye in the foyer of the hotel in London. Aware that Liam was ashamed of his second novel, and was unlikely to put much effort into the round of planned interviews and book signings, Perry had decided to buy sole rights to the manuscript and market it himself. He planned to tell the publishers and TV executives that Liam Bradley was in a private clinic being treated for alcohol-related stress and depression. Liam was to keep a low profile for six months. The resulting notoriety was bound to boost interest among the publishing industry. Perry knew for certain he would double his investment. If not treble it.

"Well, good luck to you, Perry Shaw," Liam gasped as another wave of nausea rose and fell. "You deserve it."

Liam peeled off his stale clothes and crawled into the shower, carefully rolling up the check first and sliding it into his right shoe. He sat there for half an hour, letting the hot water pound him into oblivion. He thought he might have fallen asleep for ten minutes but he couldn't be sure. Afterward, he felt marginally better. He brushed his teeth thoroughly and had a shave, wrapping his face in a hot towel first. This made him so relaxed that when he was finished he lay down on the floor beside the bed, still wrapped in a giant bath sheet. He reached for the telephone and dialed Reception. Wouldn't it be nice to live in a hotel forever? he thought, as he waited for someone to pick up at the other end.

"Hello? Hello, there. It's room four-oh-one, Liam Bradley. Yes, Merry Christmas to you, too. I was wondering, is the maid available today? I've spilled some champagne on the bed, I'm afraid. Sorry about that! Could I have some new sheets?"

"What about the mattress? Have you wet that, too?"

"Have I wet the mattress? Gosh, I have no idea. I'll check. It is rather wet. Sorry." The girl on the other end of the phone made a rude gesture at the receiver. Today of all days, when they were mad-busy with the festive lunch menu, that wino in 401 had to go and ruin his bed. She hoped for the maid's sake it was only champagne she would have to clean up. She paged a chambermaid and explained the situation. Then she came back on the line.

"I can have a new mattress brought to your suite and made up with fresh linen, sir. But I'm afraid it will show up on your bill."

"That's okay. Can I have some dinner brought to my room, also? Christmas dinner, and a pot of tea? I know I didn't book it yesterday but I'd be very grateful, miss, if you could work a little magic for me." He crossed his fingers. "I think I've caught a chill, you see, and I don't feel up to the dining room."

"I'll see what I can do, Mr. Bradley. I'm sure Chef will oblige but you may have to wait an hour or two. We're very busy at the moment."

"That's fine," Liam said. "Thank you very much. Maybe you could have the tea sent up in the meantime? And a spot of toast wouldn't go amiss." The girl hung up without speaking. The bloody nerve of some people, she thought. Caught a chill, my ass.

Liam lay down on the very edge of the bed and found a dry corner of duvet. He wondered how he would spend Perry's money as he waited for the tea to come.

BETSY BRADLEY, on the other hand, was full of purpose, and whizzing around her granite and steel kitchen like a whirlwind on fast-forward. No less than nine saucepans were resting on the industrial-size stove. Mashed potatoes with parsley and cream, plain mash for Ted, Brussels sprouts, carrots and parsnips together, carrots on their own for Ted's children, who were fussy eaters like their father, proper old-fashioned giblet gravy, cranberry sauce, bread sauce, vegetable soup. She peeked under the lids. The food was piping hot and smelled delicious. She'd been slaving since eight that morning, using only fresh ingredients and taking no shortcuts. The turkey was ready, covered with strips of crispy bacon, and packed with pork and apple stuffing. They said on the cookery shows that any stuffing should be cooked in a separate dish but Betsy had always loved hers soaked in the turkey juices, and it hadn't poisoned her yet. She checked the bottle of wine in the silver bucket; it was perfectly chilled.

"Ha!" she said out loud. "Who's a domestic goddess now! I think that Liam has been a jinx on me all these years. The dinner was never this good before. Now, what time is it? Hope my lot aren't late!"

Every room in the house had been decorated with white Christmas lights, fresh greenery, red and green silk baubles and red velvet ribbons. Even the banisters were draped in glistening branches from a posh shop in town. And she had hung miniature Santas made from tin cans on the big chandelier. Betsy had copied the ideas from an old issue of *Homes & Gardens.* It was all very vintage and tasteful.

She was dressed in neat cream trousers and a matching mohair sweater that covered up her modest post-op cleavage. Her hair was cut into a shoulder-length bob and dyed a glossy chestnut brown with honey highlights. The hairdresser had flicked the ends outward and Betsy thought she looked much more bubbly and animated than usual. Her

impossibly long fake nails had been con-
signed to the bin forever.

She had seventeen members of her ex-
tended family due for dinner in half an hour,
and she was hoping they wouldn't recognize
her. In the days since Liam had left her,
Betsy had become a new woman. She had
stopped being a slave to her looks, and had
started using her imagination. Her brothers
didn't know it yet but Betsy was about to give
them all a big Christmas surprise. She had
decided what she was going to do with the
rest of her life.

She was going to combine her hankering
for tennis with a spot of charity work. She
was going to open up a tennis club in
Belfast, employ some young people to help
her and give free lessons to underprivileged
children at weekends. Of course she had to
learn how to play better, herself, first. But
that was a mere detail. The main thing was,
she would get to meet lots of interesting,
wealthy, well-connected people, and she
would get lots of media attention because of
her charity work. There was bound to be a
nice plot of land somewhere that she could
afford with her house proceeds. She'd build

a dainty little clubhouse on it, and four tennis courts. She was going to sell this huge house while the market was still buoyant, and buy one of those chic little apartments on the other side of the avenue, and from there embark on her plan of world domination. Maybe, if her fortunes improved, she could move to Malahide someday, but this would be a good beginning. This time next year, she might be celebrating Christmas with actual, living, breathing celebrities. She'd be in all the glossy magazines then: "Ex-wife of Famous Author Helps Local Youngsters in Cross-community Tennis Project." She might win a *Tatler* magazine Woman of the Year award! A nice big lump of glass for the mantelpiece! She'd be the new best friend of Bono's wife! And if none of those things came to pass, well, at least she wouldn't be the sad, bewildered trollop that she'd become as Liam's wife.

She looked out the front window to see if her brothers Ted, Roy and Mark and their wives and children were here yet. They weren't, so she returned to her saucepans. The doorbell chimed as she was adding a knob of butter and some bacon crumbs to the sprouts. She flicked off the exhaust fan and went skipping to answer it. Eleven children swarmed in and ran up the stairs. They loved playing hide-and-seek in the bedrooms, trying to find the presents that otherwise wouldn't be handed out until after the main meal. She ushered in the six adults and closed the heavy door against the cold.

"Betsy, my God! You look fantastic," the women chorused. "What have you done to your hair? That style takes years off you."

"Thank you! The single life takes years off me," replied Betsy, laughing and patting her new hairstyle. "I've tidied myself up a little. Now I have the time."

"You're keeping fine, then?"

"God, yes. I've been liberated. You wouldn't believe how much work it was, looking after Liam. He was so untidy."

The women chuckled and made faces at their husbands. The men looked suitably chastened. But they were all delighted that Betsy was in such good humor. They'd been dreading this lunch, afraid that Betsy would be a sniveling wreck, threatening suicide in front of the kids. They had offered to hold the annual dinner at one of their own houses but Betsy was insistent that she would play the host, as usual.

"Liam never did lift a finger to help me on Christmas Day," she told Roy's wife as she helped the petite redhead out of her mink jacket. "Just sat about the kitchen, telling me not to put too much lard on the roast potatoes."

"Men!"

"I know. They eat like horses and then blame us for cooking the dinner. I thought I'd stab him the day he left me, but now I feel like I've been let out of prison."

"Good for you, Betsy. We're all taking your side, you know. We always thought he was a bit odd."

"You don't know the half of it, Muriel. Right, are we all ready?" She went to the bottom of the stairs and yelled, "Children, can you come and sit down now?" Then she turned back to the grown-ups, who were busy admiring the decorations. "I thought we'd stay in the kitchen this year. It's much warmer and we'll be closer to the fridge!"

"I can't wait to eat, Betsy. And the house looks fantastic." Ted patted his sister's arm and they smiled at each other.

"Thanks for all the advice, Ted," she whispered. "I might have lost everything in a court case. Liam really has flipped his lid."

"If he comes anywhere near you, Betsy, just call me and I'll have him arrested," soothed Ted. "Can't be too careful with these creative types. There's a fine line between genius and madness. I've always said it."

"I know, Ted. Now, let's eat!" Betsy had never looked happier or more relaxed. It was a miracle. "Now, just sit where you like, everybody, and I'll start serving right away. I have prawn salads for us and melon boats for the children, to begin with," she trilled. "Mark, you can carve the turkey this year; and Roy, would you open the sparkling wine? Lovely!"

The children all trooped empty-handed and complaining loudly into the huge kitchen, their mothers scolding them and telling them to behave themselves. Betsy opened the door again and took a quick glance down the avenue. There was no sign of Liam. She'd had a dream the night before that he turned up and begged for reconciliation. But clearly, he was not going to do that. And she didn't want him to. As long as she stayed with him, she'd never have the courage to be her own person.

She wondered how her family would react when she told them that she hadn't bought them any presents this year. Her nieces and nephews were spoiled rotten. And her brothers and sisters-in-law had everything money could buy. This year, Betsy had bought a herd of goats and a year's supply of schoolbooks for a village in Africa instead. She was going to give Ted a fun Christmas card she had found in the supermarket, with a picture of three goats on it. It was a wonderful idea, to help Africa for Christmas. And it only took her five minutes over the phone with a credit card. As a consolation, she had bought the children chocolate selection boxes and packets of coloring pencils.

She sighed and shut the front door. The wreath she had bought from the greengrocer's looked magnificent covered with a midnight frost that had not yet melted. The snow was getting heavier: large soft flakes that came swirling down from the sky, making you dizzy if you tried to follow the progress of one flake in particular. Betsy thought the street had never looked more beautiful. She was glad she would not be leaving Marlborough Avenue for a while. The downsizing had been Ted's idea. He'd told her not to make too many big changes in her life all at once. Betsy wondered what Liam was doing at that moment and if he was looking out onto the snow, too. Then she went back into the kitchen to join her family around the table.

BARNEY, JOEY AND FRANCY MAC stood at the end of Maple Street and caught their breath. They had met up by the gothic church beside Queen's University Student Union, and walked to the city center. This was the first year in over sixty years of friendship that they were spending Christmas Day together. They were all wearing their best clothes, and were clutching tins of shortbread biscuits and bottles of white wine.

"I feel a bit of a lemon, now," said Francy Mac. "I hope it isn't a real fancy do."

"Don't worry, I'm sure Lily and Jack wouldn't have invited us if it was going to be six forks each and all that malarkey." Joey straightened his tie.

"True," added Barney. "We'll just eat up, enjoy ourselves and go home early. So the young people can have a bit of a dance."

"And remember, all of us, to keep the stories of bare feet in church, and oranges in our Christmas stockings, to an absolute minimum," said Joey. "We don't want the lot of them in tears all day."

"Laughing at us, more like," said Barney wisely. "The youth of today think we make up all those stories. Did I ever tell you about the time I walked all the way to Donegal with only a raw onion in my pocket for lunch?"

"Save it for another day, old man. Righto, then. Let's go," said Francy Mac. "We're twenty minutes late already." An icy blast of air blew down the street and they shivered violently. Their light scarves and gloves were little use in such low temperatures. They hurried down the alley and were slightly surprised to find the door being opened by David Devaney.

"Hello and welcome," he said. "Mrs. Beaumont invited myself and my brother Michael to Christmas lunch as well. Wasn't that very nice of her?"

"She's a real lady," said Barney.

"The genuine article," said Joey.

"As long as you leave some turkey for us. I could eat a horse," added Francy Mac. And the other two men nudged him. They went in. The tavern was spotlessly tidy and the fire was flickering away, well stacked up with split logs.

"Hello there, and thanks for coming," called Lily, coming toward them. She was wearing a long purple dress and cardigan and had a white feather ornament in her hair. She looked a little tired and her nose was red and shiny, but she kissed and hugged each one in turn. "Now, let me introduce you to everybody. The Devaneys, you've met before. David, who is Daisy's young man! And Michael, who is with Marie! Over there at the bar is Gerry Madden. He's just begun walking out with Trudy. So you can see Cupid has been busy this Christmas!"

They nodded over to Gerry. He was sipping a glass of orange juice and looked very dapper in an expensive-looking white linen suit and green silk shirt. Lily hung up coats and the old men hurried over to the fire and began rubbing their hands. Jack poured them all a pint of stout.

"Bridget, you know, of course," continued Lily. "And these three lovely girls are her sisters, home from England for the funeral. We buried their parents this morning."

The old men nodded their sympathy to Bridget and her younger sisters. The four girls were like Russian dolls, all identical in appearance, and each one slightly smaller than the next. "Mary, Elizabeth and Teresa, meet Bernard, Joseph and Francis."

"Sorry for your trouble," said Barney.

"God rest their souls," said Joey.

"A sad time of the year to leave this earth but a good time to go to heaven," added Francy Mac. They all looked at him, astonished at his wise words. Bridget smiled weakly. She had no tears left.

"There was a terrific turnout in the cemetery, wasn't there, Bridget?" said Lily. Bridget nodded. "We weren't expecting many to go to the grave, it being Christmas Day."

"Yes," admitted Bridget. "They had a lot of friends, it seemed. People I never met before, or even knew about, came to pay their respects."

Bridget's sisters said nothing. They seemed a little bit distant. Lily supposed they must have found the entire experience quite surreal. She wished they weren't sitting down to lunch in the middle of a pub, and hoped the irony of the situation was lost on the young girls. And anyway, she kept telling herself, it doesn't look like a pub anymore: it looks like a country house dining room.

"Now, we're all here so let's eat," said Jack in a light voice. He had moved the tables into a neat row down the center of the room, and covered them with white cloths, extra-long white candles and little pyramids of juicy fresh oranges. Lily had scattered orange-foil-wrapped sweets along the entire length of the tables and placed her wonderful fruit-cake at the end. The slices of dried orange and shiny organza ribbon were the perfect decoration. Lily and Bridget had iced the cake the night before, after seeing Bridget's sisters safely into their hotel.

"Presents, first!" said Daisy, reaching for her handbag. She gave them all a pair of gloves that she had made out of scraps of felt from the Art College. Amazingly, they all fit perfectly. She had even stitched cute coin purses for Bridget's sisters.

Bridget gave small bottles of perfume to the women, and aftershave to the men. She hadn't been able to afford to replace Lily's gi-ant bottle of Chanel, but Lily didn't seem to mind at all. She thanked Bridget warmly for her gift and said she would keep the bottle always. Trudy had dainty boxes of Belgian chocolates to hand out, beautifully wrapped in red cellophane with purple raffia bows on the top. Marie gave jars of natural honey and bars of organic chocolate to everyone. Barney, Joey and Francy Mac distributed their tins of butter shortbread and bottles of wine. They were quite overcome to receive gifts themselves. They really hadn't expected such generosity.

Gerry Madden and the Devaney brothers had all bought designer costume jewelry for their girlfriends. They'd heard that was the ideal gift for a loved one, a few days earlier on breakfast television. And they were delighted with themselves when Trudy and Marie expressed great satisfaction with their gifts. Daisy went a little bit quiet when she opened her gift, but everyone assumed she was just lost for words. Lily adored her silver necklace with a crystal fairy pendant, and Jack tried on the warm jacket that Lily had bought for him.

Then it was time for Lily and Jack to give the staff their gifts. They waited excitedly for the girls to tear open the brightly colored wrapping paper. Bridget found a full-length extra-warm dressing gown, and a pair of pretty felt slippers, in her parcel. Daisy received a small CD player and a CD of party songs. (Her old cassette player had packed up two days before.) Trudy was thrilled with her elegant fabric-bound notebook and glass fountain pen; she said she was going to copy out her favorite poems into it as soon as she had time. Marie loved the rhinestone watch and earrings set she was given. She thought that Lily and Jack were trying to tell her, in a coded way, that it was time to come out of the shadows and start to shine a little. She gave them both a big hug.

Finally, they presented Bridget's sisters with crocheted woollen scarves in soft pastel colors. The girls were very touched by Lily's thoughtfulness. Barney was about to comment that all he ever found in his Christmas stocking, as a child, were oranges and walnuts. But he decided not to spoil the moment. It wasn't the fault of the young people that they were born a hundred years too late to know what it was like to be poor. And anyway, something about the guarded faces of the O'Malleys told him that they could tell a tale or two themselves about hard times.

They all found their places at the table, Gerry and Trudy sitting at one end with Daisy and David. Lily and Jack and the three old men sat in the middle. And Bridget, her sisters, Michael and Marie sat at the other end. Father Damien had been invited, too, but he always spent the day at the Salvation

Army hostel, helping to serve Christmas lunch. He said he liked to be seen to be busy on the Lord's birthday, but he promised to remember the O'Malleys in his prayers.

Lily said a short prayer now, before Jack served the carrot soup and wheaten bread. Marie lit the white candles, and Bridget buried her nose in a large white handkerchief.

"The table is beautiful, Lily," she sniffed. "You make housekeeping look so simple, but most people would never be able to do something like this. It's lovely."

"Isn't it also lovely to have all our friends round us, on this special day?" Lily said softly. "This past year has brought many changes to our lives. Some have been very sad. Some have been happy. Here's to the future, and to friendship." She held up her glass of wine.

"Here's to friendship," they all agreed. Then Jack went to fetch the main course before the mood of quiet optimism could begin to fade away. Lily went with him to carry the dishes of vegetables. When they came back, they told the little party that the old stove upstairs had finally paid the price for all its hard work.

"The door of the main oven just fell off in

my hands," said Jack. "I can't say I'm surprised. It's never been left to cool down, these last six weeks. Good job, the dinner was cooked." He set the platter of turkey down on the table and picked up a serving knife and fork.

"I don't suppose we'll find anyone to fix it right away," said Lily sadly. "At least you didn't get a nasty burn." She set a stack of heated plates and a dish of vegetables beside Jack, and Trudy went back up for the gravy and the tray of roast potatoes. "Mind your hands on that stove, pet," called Lily.

"What about the catering for tomorrow?" asked Marie. "There's a huge party on tomorrow night. And they've ordered tons of food. And Boxing Day is always busy for pub grub anyway."

"I'm tempted to cancel the booking," said Jack. "I didn't like the delegation that came to inspect the place. They actually asked me to show them the kitchen."

"Self-important bunch of suits," agreed Lily. "We should have said no."

"I'd love a day off, you know," murmured Daisy. "Let's all put our thinking hats on and see if we can come up with a good excuse."

"Sure, we don't need an excuse, if the

stove is broken," offered Bridget. "Just tell them there's been an emergency case of equipment failure."

"Daisy, Bridget! You can't mean that!" Marie exclaimed. "Lily, what about your good reputation? We've been doing so well lately, and all the media is behind us. We can't be seen to be out of our depth." They were all amazed at Marie's emotional outburst. She had changed quite a bit from the little mouse they had met on the first day.

"Look, you might as well know, girls . . ." Jack began.

"Jack, no!" Lily cried.

"Lily, it's no use, we have to tell them. Look, everyone, we really don't think we'll be able to save the tavern now, whatever happens." They all registered varying degrees of shock and disappointment. Jack immediately turned a deep red color. He had promised Lily he would not discuss this painful subject during the holidays. He didn't want to spoil Christmas Day but he couldn't bear to go on deceiving them all. The barmaids had been working so hard, putting in extra shifts. Even Daisy and Trudy, who were still students and had a lot of study and coursework to do.

"We can buy a cheap electric cooker to see us through to the end of February," explained Lily, giving her husband a reproachful look. "But after that, we may be forced out of business."

"Oh dear," said Barney.

"We weren't going to tell everyone yet, but it seems we are the only traders who want to stay. All the others have accepted Vincent Halloran's terms already."

"The traitors," whispered Barney. The shine of the day faltered a little for him.

"What will we do without our wee snug?" asked Joey sadly.

"There's always the old age home?" said Francy Mac. The other two old men exchanged horrified glances. "I was only joking," he added. "That place is God's waiting room. We're not ready for there, yet."

"Are you serious?" Barney said, looking at Jack. "Is it all official?"

"Yes, I'm afraid so," admitted Jack. "It was a really tough decision to have to make but we talked it over last night and we felt it was time to let go with dignity. We don't want to fall out with our neighbors. We won't tell Halloran yet, though."

"We'll make him wait till the very last day,"

added Lily. "It's the only satisfaction we'll get out of the whole thing."

"Well, that's a crying shame. The Halloran guy is only a gangster, I'm sure of it. There's no such thing as an honest rich man." Joey sounded very bitter. Bridget, Daisy and Trudy looked crestfallen but resigned. They were not planning to stay in the tavern forever. And neither was Marie but she still seemed genuinely shocked. She didn't want Lily and Jack to lose their home the way her own parents had.

"But things were going so well," she said. "Who cares about the other traders? We've been doing fantastic business. You said so yourself. I don't understand."

"I'm afraid that is exactly why we are giving up," said Jack. "We haven't had a day off or any time together since all this business with the shopping mall began."

"Indeed," added Lily. "We're exhausted and it's not been the same with so many people here every night. It's far too noisy. I've been turning down future bookings, in fact." She didn't add that most of the profits they had made so far would be used up in staff wages, and replacing various damaged household items such as the television and the sofa. Of course, a new carpet for the sitting room was off the agenda now, as was the repainting of the hall doors. But they had asked for an update on the phone bill, and the cost of twenty-nine long-distance calls to America was not cheap. Also, they were planning on giving the girls a generous bonus with their final pay packet.

"I guess we'll have to start looking for rooms, in the new year," said Marie, sadly. Lily and Jack nodded and apologized.

"It might be a good idea," Jack said gently. "Definitely by the end of February."

"What will you do, yourselves?" asked Gerry Madden, suddenly. It was the first time he had spoken to anyone else except Trudy all day.

"We haven't a clue," admitted Jack. "It will take us a while to adjust to the idea of moving but we expect we'll stay in the city somewhere."

"Come on, everyone, tuck in," chided Lily. "The food will be as cold as a tombstone." And then she could have kicked herself, as the O'Malley girls looked startled.

"I'll have a look at the stove for you," said

Barney, to fill the silence that followed Lily's tactless remark. "My mother used to have one and I was always fixing it."

"How kind," said Lily. "That would be great altogether if you could do anything. But have your dinner first, Barney."

"Ah, Barney is terrific with his hands, Mrs. Beaumont. He has hands on him for anything," said Francy Mac, sensing that the conversation was going to be an uphill struggle for the rest of the afternoon. He might have to dust down some of his old boyhood tales after all. Daisy played a Christmas CD that had come free with a Sunday newspaper to lift the atmosphere in the room when everyone began to eat. More white wine was poured. Gerry and the O'Malley sisters opted for sparkling water. For a few minutes the only sounds at the table were the softly sung hymns on the stereo, the occasional loud crack of a damp log on the fire and the gentle clatter of silver on china. Lily was pleased that she had managed to disguise the leftovers so well. A good rich gravy and nobody was any the wiser. In fact they were all very impressed that she had prepared so many different dishes.

"A fine meal, Mrs. Beaumont," said Barney, patting his lips with a napkin. "I've not eaten such a tasty meal since my dear wife, Susan, died, God rest her soul. She used to roast a goose every Christmas."

"I've never tasted a goose," said Lily quickly. She prayed Barney wasn't going to talk about his late wife. Any more talk of death and she was going to go loopy. "Aren't geese supposed to have a very strong flavor?"

"Not too strong, correctly cooked. Very nice fat, you get from a goose, excellent for frying."

"I must buy a goose next year," said Lily, glad that at least they were not talking about selling the tavern anymore. She knew the old men would be the hardest hit by the closure. The girls would move on. Three of them had found very likable boyfriends, and Bridget seemed to be bearing up well under her tragic circumstances. Bridget's sisters were, as Lily had predicted, very happy to be reunited with her. They had always felt she didn't want them when she'd left home. But once the recriminations and the hurt were aired and wept over, there had been hugs and kisses all around and promises to keep in touch this time. Lily didn't know if it was too late for them to become a close family again. Maybe the years apart had made a full reconciliation impossible. But at least they had made a good start.

"Oh, I forgot the cranberry sauce," said Lily, suddenly. "I always forget to serve the sauce until I'm half-finished my dinner. Isn't that very annoying?"

"I'll get it," said Jack, rising from his seat. He was worried that Lily was doing too much. She was yawning already. "Where is it?"

"Still in the microwave, in a big glass jug. Use oven gloves, darling, it'll be very hot, still." She handed the gloves to him.

"Please, allow me," said Bridget. She thought she might cry again and she didn't want to spoil the wonderful atmosphere Lily and everyone else had worked so hard to create. She took the oven gloves and hurried upstairs, planning to splash cold water on her face before she came back down again. She was the head of the O'Malley family now and she wanted her siblings to know they could rely on her. She had buried her bitter feelings toward her feckless parents for twenty-five years, and she didn't want them all to come pouring out now in front of these kind people. She darted into the bathroom and sat down on the fluffy bath mat for a moment. The twig hearts on the windowsill looked very pretty against the mottled glass. She would miss this little apartment, she realized, and not just because it was filled with lovely things. It had been more like a proper home to her than any of the other places she had lived in. The tears sprang to her eyes and there was nothing she could do to stop them. She would just collect her thoughts here for a moment, she decided, then wash her face and fetch the cranberry sauce.

Downstairs, the conversation staggered along on very wobbly legs. Jack tried to get the laughter going again by telling a funny story about a stolen turkey, two foreign bishops and a broken-down car. Suddenly, there was a loud knock at the door. Everyone jumped.

"Who on earth can that be?" said Lily. "Did we invite anybody else, Jack?"

"I didn't," he said, heading across the room. He peered out the side window, wary of burglars. Sometimes they just knocked on the front door and pushed their way in, he knew. It was terrible, the things they heard on the news.

"It's a policeman."

"Is it?" gasped Lily, her face suddenly turning pink.

"He's very tall," said Jack. "With a military-type mustache."

"It must be John. I mean, Constable John Kelly," said Lily in a jittery voice. "I wonder what he wants?"

"Better let him in and find out," said Jack, turning the large metal key.

"Anyone for gravy?" Lily piped up. She made a great fuss of pouring more hot gravy, walking twice around the table. She'd taken the liberty of telephoning John Kelly at the station to thank him for his kindness and had casually dropped into the conversation that Bridget had remarked, several times, what a nice man he was. Nothing as crass as telling him a bereaved girl had a notion of him. Nothing as direct as that! But Lily knew a woman in love when she saw one. She had also spotted the tender way John had looked at Bridget as they walked from room to room in that little house of cobwebs. And she had convinced herself that she wouldn't be committing a crime if she brought the two of them together.

"Well," said Jack, opening the door. "More

than likely he's come to see Bridget. What's delaying her, I wonder?"

"I'll see what it is," offered Daisy, and she went upstairs. The others laid down their knives and forks and turned to face the visitor.

"Good afternoon, everyone," John said quietly, stepping into the room. "I came by to ask Bridget how she was. Sorry, now! I didn't know you would still be eating."

"Why don't you sit down and have a bite of turkey, John?" asked Lily kindly. "I take it you're on a lunch break?"

"Um, yes, I am. I don't usually wear my uniform on my days off," he said, and tried to force a laugh.

"I bet he does," whispered Francy Mac to Joey. "I bet he goes to bed with every stitch on him. Even the hat." Joey gave Francy Mac a tiny shove to keep him quiet. Francy Mac had a grudge against policemen since the time he was told to remove his wheelbarrow full of pansies off the footpath outside his home. Apparently, his lovely floral display was causing a disruption during the school rush. You can never find a copper when you want one, thought Francy Mac. Where was this John Kelly last month when some thieving little rascal emptied my coal shed?

"Look, sit down and take the weight off your feet," urged Lily. "Everyone, save a bit of turkey for the cranberry sauce!"

WHEN BRIDGET HEARD that John Kelly was in the building, she went very quiet. She'd been drying her face in a fluffy warm towel when Daisy knocked smartly on the door and almost caused her to have a heart attack. She didn't think she would be disturbed, as there was a second bathroom downstairs. Daisy saw the oven gloves abandoned on the hall table and wondered what was going on.

"Are you all right in there?" she asked, leaning her face against the painted wood of the bathroom door. "We're waiting on the sauce, and like I said, you have a visitor. He's quite a looker." Although, he's way too tall for you, if he has romance on his mind, thought Daisy. She'd seen Lily getting flustered and knew at once she had been matchmaking again.

"I can't come out," said Bridget, after a moment.

"Why not?"

"Just."

"Are you ill?"

"I'm too tired for visitors, the funeral has

taken it out of me," Bridget said. "Tell him I've gone to bed. And tell the others I'm sorry, will you?"

"But your sisters are downstairs, Bridget. They'll be leaving soon. You can't stay hiding up here all day."

"Daisy, please. I'm exhausted. Can you cover for me?"

"Well, okay, but are you sure?"

"Yes."

"He looks pretty shy to me. He might not come back again?" But Bridget's confidence had deserted her. She was too used to dysfunctional men and doomed relationships and bizarre behavior. A nice man with a responsible job, turning up to speak to her like this, was not something she had ever encountered. It was bad enough trying to be civil in front of Gerry Madden (a man she had shared a bed with for over three years) and her own long-lost sisters, without trying to speak politely to John Kelly with an audience present. And if John had not come to see her because he liked her, but on some official errand, then it would be heart-wrenching anyway.

"Daisy, he hasn't come to ask me out on a date, you daft cow," she sighed, fishing for information. "Just because you're totally loved-up doesn't mean we all are."

"Remind me to tell you something about David Devaney later on tonight," whispered Daisy through the keyhole. "Now, just brace yourself and come out, will you? You can't stay in there forever. They want to knock the tavern down in March, don't you know. Or is this the start of some hard-core protest?"

"Oh God," Bridget whimpered. She wished she could throw half a dozen vodkas down her throat, to give her some confidence. But then she thought of Gerry, and her parents. That was the trouble with drink, she thought. The effects of it only lasted for a little while and then reality caught up with you again.

"What makes you think he likes me?" she tried again.

"Because he's got a massive bunch of flowers with him, but I didn't want to spoil the surprise." Daisy yawned, and wondered if she had any room left for dessert.

"Flowers?" said Bridget. Now that was interesting. . . . She took a deep breath and opened the door.

"Thanks for being patient, Daisy," she said. "My head's away with it, the day."

"That's the girl." Daisy smiled. "And by the way, I'm sorry for calling you a pint-size bitch. You're not a bitch, at all."

"Cheers," said Bridget. "And your love-heart trousers weren't a cry for help. Actually, I thought they were very nice." Smiling, they rejoined the company, and forgot about the cranberry sauce.

John was hovering beside the grandfather clock, trembling with nervous anticipation. He had declined Lily's invitation to join them for dinner. That could be very embarrassing indeed, if Bridget didn't want to see him again. He would just give Bridget the flowers and leave if he got a lukewarm reception. In any case, his lunch break was almost up. Bridget crossed the floor of the tavern as quickly as her tiny feet would allow. The others made a big show of eating but they were secretly straining to hear every word.

"Thank you so much for all your help," Bridget began, as John handed over the very large and expensive bouquet, rattling in its crisp cellophane wrapper. (He had bought it the night before and kept it in his locker in the police station.)

"These are really beautiful," she said,

looking at the bird-of-paradise flowers and the dark purple tulips. "You shouldn't have."

"That's okay. It's just, there was something I wanted to ask you."

"But surely there's nothing left to discuss? There was no will, no money, no bills left to pay except the electric. And Father Damien said he would sort that out for me." Bridget knew she was babbling but she also knew she was terrified of straightforward men.

"I haven't come about your parents," John said, his voice barely above a whisper. "I wondered if I might take you out to dinner, sometime?"

"Oh! My goodness! I wasn't expecting this!"

"I know it's very bad timing, but maybe when you're feeling a little better?"

"I don't know what to say," Bridget faltered. His businesslike manner was deeply intimidating but quite attractive as well.

"I lost my own parents to illness a few years ago so I think I know how you feel," John said kindly. "Leaves you a bit at sea, losing them both so close together."

"Yes," she said. "It certainly does."

"So what do you say?" he tried again. "Maybe in a few weeks? A month or so?"

"Yes." She smiled. "Leave me your number and I'll call you."

"That's great altogether." He gave her a slip of paper from his breast pocket. "Well, I'll be going, then. Cheerio, everyone! Merry Christmas."

They all turned to say goodbye to Bridget's admirer, standing beside her in the doorway. Him, six feet tall and wearing his policeman's uniform: Bridget looking smaller than ever in flat shoes and with her hair in a tight bun. They were quite the odd couple. Bridget closed the door behind John and sat down at the table in a daze. She hoped her sisters would not think she had been flirting with the man who had helped to organize the funeral of their parents. She'd thought he was going above and beyond the call of duty when she spied him sitting in the back pew during the funeral service. Bridget wasn't to know he sometimes went to the funerals of people he had met during the course of his work. She realized with a shock that John Kelly was the one good-looking man, apart from Jack Beaumont, she had never flirted with in her entire life.

Lily found a vase for the exotic flowers and then suggested they have some dessert. There was no need for the cran-berry sauce now. All the plates were empty, except Bridget's, and she was miles away. They began to stack plates and clear away the cutlery.

"Now, there's chocolate cake or lemon pie with fresh cream, or mince pies and ice cream, or pudding and custard," Lily reeled off. She longed for the sanctity of her bed-room, and to curl up with Jack and think of nothing but him. This emotional day was al-most over. Jack winked at her when he saw her smiling at him across the table. He could read her thoughts after so many years to-gether. And he was tired himself. He was be-ginning to feel his age for the first time. He was determined to cancel all business the following day and stay in bed with a box of chocolates and the remote control.

"I'm full up," Jack said, patting his stom-ach. "What's everyone else fancy?"

But Bridget's sisters were checking their watches, eager to be on their way to the air-port. They longed for their anonymous rented homes on the outskirts of London. Nothing exciting ever happened on the streets where they lived, and that was the way they liked it. They wanted to be part of the huge urban sprawl where nobody knew their parents had been chronic alcoholics, and no one asked them daily how their "poor parents" were keeping. The girls had worked hard to get on in life, finding training courses and then jobs in a large chain of hairdressing salons. Their flat, north of Ireland accents had faded gradually and been replaced by gentler London ones. At the graveside that morning, they had made a vow never to come back to Ireland again. They would keep in touch with Bridget but the next time they saw her it would be on their home ground in the genteel suburbs of Isleworth. They decided to pass on dessert, and gathered up their coats and handbags. They said they would like to spend a few minutes beside their parents' grave before the return flight that evening. By now, the grave would have been filled in and tidied up and they wanted to see it one more time. They shook everyone's hand warmly and Bridget hugged them all tightly, before they departed on foot for the taxi rank at the City Hall. She promised she would fly over to London to visit them after the tavern was closed down. Then, she went upstairs for a lie-down.

There was a feeling of emptiness in the room when the O'Malley sisters had left. Somehow, Lily knew that the Christmas pudding was not going to be enough to rescue the party. Barney, Joey and Francy Mac were looking tired, and they said they, too, would pass on dessert. They were full to the neck, said Francy Mac, and Joey shook his head. Lily felt sorry for them. They had probably been awake since dawn getting smartened up for the occasion. She suggested they all draw their chairs over to the fire and have a little rest before going home.

"Can I fix anyone a drink?" asked Jack, when everyone had refused more food.

"I wouldn't say no to a small whiskey and lemonade," suggested Lily, and there was a murmur of agreement from the assembled company. Jack stepped in behind the counter and reached down some highball glasses.

"David and Michael are going to London next year," said Daisy, as they sipped their drinks two minutes later. "They're going to sing in a talent competition on television. And I'm designing the costumes. Well, not costumes as such. Suits, really. But 'costumes' sounds better."

"Yeah, I reckon we have a good chance," said David. "Have you seen some of the losers on those shows in recent years? The producers are only having a laugh, I think. But the exposure will be unbelievable."

"Too right," said Daisy. "Millions and millions of viewers, they get. Absolutely millions." Marie held Michael's hand. His face had turned a sickly shade of gray.

"We're going to get new guitars, new songs, and Michael is going to get his hair cut. Aren't you, Michael?" teased David.

"Michael doesn't know if he's ready yet, for the glittery world of show business," Marie laughed gently. "Are you, Michael?"

"What's that?" said David. "He is surely, what are you talking about? We have it all planned."

"I think Michael would prefer to keep things the way they are," said Marie firmly. She had a steely glint in her eye that Lily, Jack and the other girls knew came from the alcohol she had consumed with her lunch. But Michael and David didn't know that. They all held their breath.

"Michael doesn't want to be a big star, David," Marie sighed. Obviously, the poor man needed things to be spelled out for him. David looked momentarily puzzled, then dismayed.

"Don't tell me you've changed your mind? Michael?"

"Marie is right," Michael said gently. "I told her a few days ago. I can't face the cameras and all that, David. I'm sorry."

"But that's nonsense, Michael. Just a bit of the old stage fright! You'll be all right on the night. Trust me."

"No, I won't. It's not just stage fright, David. I could get over that if I wanted a big career badly enough. I just don't want to be famous. I want to stay small, stay local. I want to be a pub singer at weekends and teach guitar during the week."

"Well, this is a nice thing to be told, on Christmas Day of all days," David said bitterly.

"Oh, don't start. You sound like Granny Devaney when someone told her Graham Norton was gay." Michael was mortified that his future was being discussed in front of other people. But then he was suddenly glad. If David wanted to slog his way up the glittery ladder of fame, taking on the lengthy touring, the nasty TV judges and the long list of record company demands, well, that was up to him. Michael just wanted an easy time and a quiet life. He didn't care about being rich. It was a relief to confess it all, at last.

"You don't mean that, you're just scared of the cameras. Now, listen to me. You can go to a hypnotherapist," David persisted. "I've heard of a man near Botanic Avenue who can do anything. What's his name again? Alan something . . ."

But Michael only kissed Marie's hand and smiled. "I haven't got the fame bug," he said. "You'll just have to win the contest and travel the world on your own, David. I'm staying right here."

"Trudy, talk some sense into this lad," pleaded Daisy, looking at her friend. Trudy was the wise one of the gang. That was obvious from all the poetry she read. But Trudy had enough drama going on in her own life and had no desire to get dragged into anyone else's problems. Besides, the nurse at the hospital had told her to avoid any unnecessary stress.

"Oh, count me out," said Trudy. "Gerry and me are going for a walk, actually." They collected their coats and set off, promising to be back soon. Daisy, David, Marie and Michael decided to go for a walk also. They could be heard discussing the talent show as they closed the door behind them. Lily and Jack were left sitting at the fireside with the three old men.

"A minute ago the room was full," said Barney.

"And now we're all alone," Joey sighed.

"That's life," added Francy Mac.

21

BRIDGET SAVES THE DAY

 THE FOLLOWING DAY, before Lily was awake, Jack slipped out of bed, took the telephone into the bathroom and locked the door firmly behind him. He dialed the out-of-hours contact number he had been given for the building contractors and waited an agonizing five seconds before the call was answered.

"Hello, Judy speaking. Can I help you?"

The woman on the other end of the line sounded tired and cross but Jack wasn't to know she had worked all day the day before and late into the evening, too. Vincent Halloran paid good wages but he had no respect for the usual nine-to-five business hours. Unsure of the success of his shopping mall project, he had been double-checking plans, costs and time scales all during Christmas Day to see if there was any way he could increase his offer to the stubborn Beaumonts. And that meant Judy had to be in the rented office in Belfast, too. A man as important as Vincent Halloran couldn't be expected to make his own coffee.

"Can I help you?" she said again, as Jack hesitated.

"Jack Beaumont, here," he began. "I'm afraid there's a problem about tonight's party, Judy."

"Oh, I'm sorry to hear that," she said. She waved across the office at Vincent. "There's a problem at the tavern, sir." He looked up from his desk.

"Yes," continued Jack. "The catering equipment has broken down."

"What, all of it? Can't you fix it?"

"No, I can't."

"Are you sure?" Now Vincent was coming over to her desk.

"It's a very old stove," Jack said firmly. There was no way he was backing down. He was having a day off or else he was going to collapse.

"Well, we don't mind if there's only cold food," Judy said quickly, with Vincent Halloran leaning over her. His face was like thunder. He had ordered this staff party for one reason and one reason only: as a way to meet the Beaumonts and talk to them, face-to-face. His repeated requests for an audience with them had been unsuccessful.

"Crisps and nuts, even?" she squeaked.

"I'm terribly sorry, but I've had to cancel," Jack said. "I'll return your deposit, of course."

"Wait! Surely we can still go ahead? I mean, you have a bar, right? You have drinks? We can bring our own food."

"Sorry," said Jack. "It's too late. I've let the staff go home for a few days."

"Well, I'm sure we can organize something? Everyone is going to be very disappointed," Judy begged, but it was too late. Jack Beaumont had hung up.

"What a rude man," she said to Vincent. "He just cut me off."

"Don't tell me the party's off?" boomed her boss.

"Okay, then, I'll write it down for you," she snapped.

"Get Beaumont back on the line right away and rescue the situation," he demanded.

"I'm going back to the hotel to lie down, Mr. Halloran." She yawned. "I can't keep my eyes open."

"You leave now and you're fired, Judy. Don't bother coming here in the morning, do you hear me?"

"Yeah, whatever," Judy replied. She stood up and put her cardigan around her shoulders. It was lucky for Vincent Halloran that she was a single woman with no husband at home to stand up for her, otherwise he wouldn't get away with this kind of treatment. Vincent fired Judy at least twice a day.

"I can't be bothered with a party now, anyway," she retorted. "I haven't the energy. You can notify the other guests, if you like." And she handed him a printout. They had invited everyone they knew in the north of Ireland.

"Judy, don't leave me. I'll give you a thousand pounds if you can set up a meeting." Vincent used his charm when all else failed.

"It's no use," she said. "The guy is plain bonkers. Like everybody else in this city, if you ask me."

"Please, Judy? There's millions riding on this."

"Not for me, there isn't." Judy wondered if she was the only twenty-seven-year-old woman in Ireland who was single, bored, working on Boxing Day and wearing a cardigan with horrible roses all over it that her grandmother had knitted for her.

"And I'm fed up in the hotel," she said. "I'm going to pack and go home to Dublin today."

"Two thousand pounds? Judy, I promise you, if you help me?"

"Will you put that in writing?" She slid a sheet of paper toward him.

"I will." He wrote it.

"Okay," she sighed, and sat down again.

"Keep trying, that's a good girl," Vincent Halloran told his loyal secretary. "And don't let slip it's our company that's building the mall. They'd never have taken the gig if they'd known." He marched back to his desk.

"Keep your wig on, I'm not stupid!"

Judy was very cross at being made to work during the holidays. She'd been looking forward to the party in the tavern, too. In such a small venue, she was bound to meet some new friends. Maybe even a new boyfriend: there was a bricklayer from Ligoniel she fancied like crazy.

"What about the party?" she said, as she dialed the number.

"It doesn't matter about the feckin' party," he roared across the office. "Book another party somewhere else, if you must. I don't care! But don't leave that desk until you get me Jack Beaumont on the line. Or you've set up a meeting. If he hasn't answered in another half hour, get yourself over there and break in."

"Yes, sir," she said crisply, hating him with every ounce of her strength. He was an obsessive bully. What kind of man would slyly book a Boxing Day party in a harmless little pub, and then throw the owners out on their ear a few weeks later?

LILY SMILED when she saw the tray of lovely things that Jack was carrying. She turned to look at her bedside clock but he had hidden it in the wardrobe.

"Don't even think about it," he warned. "Time is irrelevant today."

"But, the party?"

"It's canceled."

"How come?"

"They phoned just now," he lied. "Firm's gone bust."

"Oh dear."

"Not to worry," he said brightly. "Every cloud has a silver lining. Now, eat up. I found a packet of bacon stashed under the lettuce. Bridget must be losing her touch."

They both giggled as they munched their way through a stack of bacon sandwiches and sipped from enormous mugs of piping hot tea.

"Oh Jack, I'm ashamed to say I'm glad that firm went broke. My nerves are shredded and my back is frozen stiff," said Lily, stretching her arms. "Workers of the world unite."

"It's your lucky day, then," he teased, as he set the plates and cups on the floor. "Tense, nervous women are my specialty." He kissed Lily's neck passionately.

"That feels wonderful," she breathed, as he softly massaged her back.

"Now," he mused. "Shall I work my way up or down?"

"Surprise me," she whispered.

TRUDY FOUND A NOTE taped to Lily and Jack's attic stairway when she got up to make coffee. It said, "Do not disturb. We are having a day off. P.S. Tonight's party canceled. Jack B." Yippee, Trudy thought.

"Fancy that!" She hurried in to tell the others. Immediately, Marie and Daisy said they would phone the Devaney brothers and arrange a day out, but when they went to the telephone, the lead had been pulled out of the wall. There was another note on the hall table, which said, "Do not reconnect this line, under any circumstances. Jack B."

"Mmm," said Marie. "I think the strain is getting to our employers. I say we make ourselves scarce. Pronto."

"I'll give Gerry a shout on my mobile," said Trudy.

"Good idea," said Daisy, fetching hers to call David.

"Put me on to Michael when you've finished," said Marie. "I forgot to charge mine last night."

"What about you, Bridget? Are you going to call the long arm of the law?" Daisy teased, and they all laughed. "Ello, ello, ello!"

"I am not indeed going to call him, and my parents only buried." She sniffed. "What on earth would he think of me? I'm not a complete slut, you know."

"Sorry, Bridget," said Daisy. "I didn't mean it that way."

"That's okay," she relented. "I'll have a day in bed. It will be great to get the three of you out of my hair for a while. Have a nice time, whatever you do."

Bridget went into the kitchen and was just about to heat up the frying pan when she discovered it was already warm. And the kitchen had a lovely aroma wafting about it. She had a horrible feeling that Jack had found the bacon she'd hidden under a floppy head of lettuce the night before. She was extremely disappointed when her suspicions were confirmed.

"Damnit," she hissed, slamming the fridge door shut and flicking on the kettle. Oh well, she would just have a quick rummage in the containers. There was bound to be something nice. . . .

AN HOUR LATER, Lily and Jack lay half-asleep in each other's arms. Lily's very toes were tingling and all her aches and pains had been eased away.

"That beats cleaning and cooking," she sighed happily.

"It sure does," Jack murmured.

"I think I heard the girls go out a while ago," Lily told him. "What shall we do with this unexpected gift of peace and quiet?"

"Just lie here until lunchtime," he said. "And then I'm phoning for an Indian take-away. I never want to see another big cold bare slimy turkey as long as I live."

"Agreed. And if you hear any talk from me about saving the world, just lock me in the cellar until I calm down." She yawned. "I think I'll heat some water for a bath. I haven't had a good long soak in ages."

"I love you, Lily," he said softly.

"And I love you, Jack Beaumont," she replied. They began to kiss again. But they both jumped, and banged their front teeth together, when there was a sudden rap on the door.

"Lily? Lily, are you awake? Jack, are you in there?" asked an excited voice on the other side.

"Bridget? Is that you, Bridget?" Lily called, as Jack pretended to stab himself in the head. "We thought you all went out. Are you all right, pet?"

"Yes, I'm fine. But Lily, I've torn a big piece off the wallpaper."

"Bridget, honestly, it doesn't matter now,"

Lily sighed. "The whole lot might be landfill soon. We're having a lie-in."

"Trying to," added Jack helpfully.

"Yes, but there's something underneath the wallpaper," Bridget persisted.

"That'll be the wall," said Jack. "Is it hard and flat and made of bricks?"

"Oh, if you're not interested, I'll just go away," she said, suddenly cross. "There's no need to be sarcastic." They heard her stamping down the stairs and slamming the sitting room door behind her.

"What is it, Bridget?" Lily called, slapping Jack on the arm. He had no right to tease the poor girl, so soon after the funeral. "Bridget, come back," she yelled. The sitting room door opened again.

"It's a painting of a shoe," said Bridget, after a moment. "And it's been signed 'J. Lavery.' It looks like a lady's shoe to me, but God knows I'm no expert on old-fashioned clothes."

"Lavery?" said Lily. "Are you having me on? You better not be pulling my leg, I swear!" She leaped out of the bed and went running to the door, only remembering she was naked as she reached for the handle. Jack threw her robe across the room to her, and then looked for some clothes for himself. Maybe he should buy a robe, he thought, as Lily pelted into the hall, while he groped around for some jeans and a clean T-shirt in the wardrobe.

"We're coming," cried Lily. "What's going on?"

Bridget was hovering in the hall, unsure what to do.

"I was just shoving my bed back into place," Bridget explained. "I dropped a magazine down the side. Anyway, that bed is really heavy, so I gave it a good shove and it tore the paper right off."

"I'm with you so far," said Lily. "Show me." They went into the room, and Bridget pointed to the spot. There was indeed a painting of a woman's shoe peeping out from underneath several layers of paper and paint. And there was the signature, just as Bridget had described.

"Oh my God," gasped Lily. "J. Lavery! Could it be Sir John Lavery? If this is a genuine Impressionist masterpiece! I didn't know he painted murals. Oh my God!"

"I knew it was something special," said Bridget, smugly. "Is it an old poster, or what?"

"Bridget O'Malley, listen to me," said Lily, touching the painting gently with her index finger. It was painted directly onto the plaster, and it appeared to be the real thing. Lily was quite a fan of Lavery's work, and sometimes she even tried to dress like the elegant ladies in his beautiful paintings. "If this is what I think and hope and pray it is, then our wee tavern is going to be safe forever!"

"What do you think it is?"

"A mural."

"On this entire wall?"

"Maybe. Maybe on all four walls."

"But why is it papered over?"

"This world is full of mysteries, Bridget. Isn't that the truth?"

By the time Jack ran into the room three minutes later, Lily and Bridget were dancing round and round the room, singing for joy. Jack grasped the situation very quickly and pulled the bed right out for a better look.

"Let's get started on the stripping, shall we?" he said. "Where did we put the toolbox, Lily?"

"Oh, my darling man," laughed Lily. "We cannot touch this room. We'll have to get the experts in, properly qualified art restorers. If there is a mural under here, it will be extremely valuable."

"What if there isn't? What if it's just that one little bit there?" he said. "Sure, the paper came off handy enough. Let's have a go?"

"The wall is damp in this corner, Jack. That's why the paper came off so easily," Lily said.

"I thought it was a bit damp," said Bridget, rubbing her shoulders.

"But the rest of the room is dry as a bone. The wallpaper is stuck fast, and I've no idea what this paper is stuck on with, you see," added Lily. "We might ruin the entire thing if we pitch in with steam and scrapers. We've got to preserve it for the public."

"What do you mean? Will people want to see it?" said Bridget.

"Of course they will!" Lily exclaimed. "This is a fantastic discovery!"

"But what about us? Does this mean we get to keep the tavern, or not?" Jack wanted to know.

"Oh," said Lily, stopping her dance suddenly. "I haven't a clue."

As the two of them stood pondering this huge question, there was a knock at the front door. Bridget had sneaked off for a long soak in the bath, so there was no point in sending her to answer it. Lily peered out the front window. A well-built man in an expensive overcoat was standing there, along with a pretty girl in a rose-patterned cardigan. Vincent Halloran had lost his temper with the elusive Beaumonts and had finally arrived for a showdown.

"We've got visitors," Lily said. "And unless I'm very much mistaken, it's Vincent Halloran himself. And the young woman with him, she looks like his secretary."

"Will we let them in?" asked Jack. "I want to see the look on his face when I tell him all the money in the world couldn't buy this place now."

Two hours and four cups of coffee later, Lily and Jack and Vincent and Judy were still sitting by the fire in the tavern. Vincent was finding it hard to judge the mood of the situation. The Beaumonts were definitely very fond of this little place, and he could see why. It was cosy, warm and womblike with its low ceilings, dark walls and muffled acoustics. And of course, they were very excited about the fragment of mural upstairs. Vincent had been invited to view the painting with his own eyes, and he thought it did appear to be a genuine fragment of a much bigger mural. That dainty shoe might turn out to be part of an undiscovered artwork by Sir John Lavery. He had surprised Lily Beaumont with his knowledge of the Belfast-born painter: she'd taken Vincent Halloran for a hardened businessman who knew nothing about art.

He took some satisfaction in telling Lily that he knew Lavery was born around 1856, the son of an impoverished publican who drowned when John was only three.

"Lavery's mother died soon afterwards," he added, "and the child was sent to relatives in Scotland. He attended art college there before traveling extensively, and his career as a painter soared when he painted Queen Victoria in 1888."

And Lily was eager to tell Vincent what she knew, too: that the Anglo-Irish Treaty of 1921 had been drawn up and signed in Lavery's London home, 15 Cadogan Gardens, in South Kensington. And that, as a result of the treaty, Ireland was partitioned and then plunged into civil war.

They talked about the painter for quite a long time, until Judy was almost deranged with tiredness. She knew that Vincent was only humoring Lily. He liked art, but he liked getting his own way a lot more. He was finding some common ground, some connection with these people, before moving in for the main prize. He was like a wolf, really. She forced her face into an interested smile, wondering if Vincent would still give her the two thousand pounds. She'd go on a beach holiday in the Canary Islands with her friends. She'd buy a red bikini and get her hair cut in a new style.

Vincent thought the Beaumonts were far too attached to the tavern. It was almost a dependency thing, he decided. They had trouble imagining living and working outside of this little place. Vincent thought the two of them might be slightly institutionalized here on Maple Street. He knew he would have to tread carefully. The woman was an incurable art lover; there was definitely some potential here for negotiation. And Lily seemed to be the dominant one in the marriage. The husband would simply agree to whatever she wanted to do: Vincent would put money on that. He agreed that the Beaumonts needed time to consider their position and asked for more coffee.

Meanwhile Judy moved the Boxing Day

party to an Italian restaurant on the Malone Road, and was on the phone for half an hour, notifying the guests of the new venue. Her handsome bricklayer from Ligoniel was going to be there. She cheered up again.

At lunchtime, Barney, Joey and Francy Mac arrived and were soon safely installed in their favorite snug, pints of stout in front of them. The bar was closed to all other customers for the day. Bridget was sound asleep upstairs, and the three other girls were still out somewhere with their young men.

Trudy rang to say that she and Gerry were heading off to Donegal for the day, and they might even stay the night in a B&B. Then Daisy called to tell Lily that she and Marie were having lunch with the Devaney household.

"Have you seen the news?" Daisy added, before hanging up. "The tidal wave? Wasn't it awful? There's thousands dead." Jack switched on the radio at once, and they listened to the horrific details about the Asian tsunami. It had a very sobering effect on all of them. Homelessness was a global issue, Lily said suddenly, and Vincent sensed they were hardening their stance.

"Indeed it is," he agreed in a soft voice.

"And doesn't it just go to show you that life is very short? That you never know what is going to happen next? I suppose there's a lesson here for all of us: we should live life to the full, as if every day were going to be our last." Lily and Jack nodded their heads in agreement, but then Judy went and spoiled the mood with her rumbling stomach. Honestly, thought Vincent, that woman was the greediest person he had ever met. She was forever eating, drinking, chasing men and booking holidays.

"I'm starving," said Judy loudly. "Do you think I could have a sandwich or something, Mrs. Beaumont?" And then another hour was wasted as Lily made snacks and Jack prepared yet more pots of tea and coffee. Vincent gave Judy quite a look, but she ignored him and thought of her red bikini. She would resign as soon as she was back home in Dublin. She was bored with the building trade. Judy wanted to feel warm sand on her back and a bricklayer's warm arms around her waist.

"I won't lie to you, Mrs. Beaumont," Vincent said eventually, dabbing his lips with a napkin. "I could walk away from this deal. I'm a wealthy man, so I don't need the money.

But I've never lost a deal in my life, and I don't want to lose this one."

"And we've been very happy here for twenty years, and we don't see why we should have to move," said Jack.

"Especially to make way for a shopping mall. If it was a hospital or something useful, I could see your point," Lily added.

"Okay, I accept that," Vincent said, stifling a tiny yawn. It was time to put his trump card on the table. "But what if we can reach a compromise?"

"I can't see how we can do that," said Lily, momentarily puzzled.

"Well, you want to save the tavern from demolition, right? And I want to build this mall. Okay. What would you say if I built the mall around the tavern?"

"You mean, you'd cut a wedge out of the design?" Jack asked. "Only, I don't think I'd like to be right up against the side of it."

"No, I mean around the tavern, literally." Vincent began to sketch some ideas on a sheet of paper from Judy's notebook. "You see, if I lose four floors of offices in this corner here, and put a big glass wall along there, the tavern will be safe and sound from the elements for decades to come. My surveyor told me some time ago your roof badly needs replacing."

"You mean, the tavern will be inside the mall?" Lily was amazed.

"Yes, indeed. Protected by plate glass."

"Will we still own it?" asked Jack.

"No, I'll own it, but I'll pay to have the mural restored, and I'll run the place as a tourist attraction. Maybe serve tea and pastries downstairs during the day?"

"So, it wouldn't be a pub anymore?" Jack was confused.

"Not a working pub, no," said Vincent. "We couldn't allow people to go smoking cigarettes in it, or light a real fire. It would be far too dangerous. The whole place could burn down and take the mural with it."

"I never thought of that," said Lily gravely. "I wouldn't want to risk damaging the mural. Definitely not."

Vincent's heart twanged with excitement! He had their attention now. He was going to convince them to sell the tavern to him. He just knew it.

"What about the fireplace?" Jack wondered. "Say you were running a café in here? It wouldn't look right without a fire burning in the grate."

"We'll put in a black stovepipe electric heater, with fake coals glowing. It would cause far less pollution."

"Mmm," said Jack. "Maybe, but it wouldn't look nearly as nice as a real fire."

"I've seen some heaters that look extremely realistic," said Lily.

Vincent thought he could see them coming around to the idea of selling at last. It was time to risk everything on a make-or-break offer.

"Now, here is my assessment of the situation," he summarized, taking a deep breath. "You need a new roof. That'll set you back thousands. The mural will be costly to restore, also, and you may have to work with the relevant authorities. And they'll have your head turned with rules and regulations, believe me."

"Oh God, the rules and regulations!" Judy sighed. "It would drive you mad."

"There's the danger of fire damage to the painting to think of," Vincent continued. "And you currently use the room as a living space, which would make it difficult for art lovers to see the mural, if there really is one under all that wallpaper."

"That's all very true," admitted Lily, biting her lip.

"Now, I'll make sure the tavern and the mural are preserved intact, if you agree to sell to me today. I'll keep the tavern safe, and I'll put the mural behind glass, like the Mona Lisa. I'll increase my offer to one million pounds, and the two of you can go off on a nice holiday right away. When you come home you can buy another pub in a quieter spot, if that's what you want. What do you say?"

"I don't know," said Lily. "A million pounds. It's very tempting. I'll have to think about it."

"How will you get all these ideas by the planners?" asked Jack.

"Don't you worry about that," Vincent said. "That's my problem."

"Won't you be losing profit with the new design?" Lily pointed out. "You'll be losing out on office rental."

"Sure, but like I said, I've never lost a deal before. I have my reputation to think of. And besides, I like the idea. It reminds me of the glass pyramid at the Louvre in Paris: old and new coexisting in perfect harmony."

"I've always wanted to see Paris," Lily sighed. "We've never traveled. We don't even have passports."

"There you are, then!" Vincent said triumphantly. "You just sell the tavern to me now, apply for a couple of passports and off you go. Paris is very beautiful in the winter, so I'm told." Vincent had a second home in sunny Marbella. He didn't ever intend to find himself up the Eiffel Tower in a snowstorm.

"Oh, we couldn't possibly decide today," said Lily.

"We'll have to think about it for a while," said Jack.

"But I'm offering you a million pounds!" Vincent slapped the table with his big strong hands.

"Even so," Lily said.

"We would have to do some research," added Jack.

"Into what?" Vincent wanted to know.

"Where we would live when we come home from Paris, for one thing," said Lily. And Vincent knew that a great corner had been turned. He winked at Judy.

"Come on," he said to his secretary. "We'll be on our way now, and let these good people decide how they'd like to spend a million quid. It's been a pleasure talking to you, Mr. and Mrs. Beaumont."

"Likewise," Jack said. The two men shook hands, and the two women smiled at each other.

When Vincent and Judy had left, and Lily and Jack were whispering behind the bar, Barney lit his pipe and said, "You know what, boys? There's big changes a-coming to these parts. And I've been doing a little bit of thinking myself. Now, listen, what do you think of this idea?" Joey and Francy Mac pinned back their ears. Barney had been very quiet all afternoon, and they knew he meant business.

22

Slinger Magee
Rides Again

The rest of the parties went ahead without a hitch. Daisy, Trudy and Marie were told about the mural and the new offer from Vincent Halloran, but were sworn to secrecy on both counts. All four girls were quiet as they lay in bed each night, wondering what the future might bring.

Gerry asked Trudy to move in with him, but she surprised him by saying she was not ready to get serious with anyone yet. Of course, after that, he was determined to marry her. But Trudy told him that they both had a long way to go to overcome their various disorders, and they shouldn't complicate their fledgling romance in any way. Gerry told Trudy that she was selling herself short studying geography, and that she would make a terrific psychiatrist. Trudy only smiled and said that geography was a lot more straightforward.

Michael Devaney suggested that he and Marie go into business together someday. Maybe they should find jobs in the same café, restaurant or hotel first to gain some work experience, he added. Michael couldn't cook but he could sing and serve drinks. He thought Lily and Jack were great role models. And Marie amazed herself by saying she thought that was a lovely idea. They spent all their spare time looking through employment supplements in the newspapers.

David Devaney, on the other hand, just wanted to get Daisy's various patchwork dresses off her shoulders and see her red hair even more disheveled on a guesthouse pillow. He was always happiest with a woman when they were both horizontal and tipsy. Daisy knew that he had deliberately dropped his wallet behind the turf basket that night so he had an excuse to come back and kiss her. And she was a little bit cross that he had taken advantage of her affectionate nature when she was in a state of shock. But she forgave him because his romantic attentions were good for her ego. They'd had some enjoyable dates together, over the last few days, but always things ended with him twanging her bra strap suggestively through her dress, and she was getting fed up with it. Knowing Daisy's luck, the first time she slept with him the condom would snap off and she would get pregnant. With twins probably, for good measure. She remembered how her own parents were struggling to raise second families, and how they hadn't enough time or money to do anything nice. David was gorgeous, she thought, and she was delighted he was still determined to seduce her after dozens of rejections. But Daisy knew that the decent thing to do was finish with her new boyfriend. She had a lot of soul searching to do, and David had to conquer the world of show business. And she knew they'd never make it through the next twenty years together as smoothly as Lily and Jack.

Reluctantly, she told him they could not see each other anymore, on a bitingly cold day in January. They were sitting in the tavern one morning, quietly sipping cups of tea, when Daisy put her hand on his leather-clad knee and broke the bad news. He took it quite well. She said she'd always be fond of him, and she'd still like to change his wardrobe direction, but they could never be lovers. Then she went upstairs to get ready for work. David studied his face in one of the gold mirrors for twenty minutes after she had left the room. He looked even more handsome when he was heartbroken, he decided. That worry line above his right eye, that downcast gaze and the suggestion of a pout were very sexy. He looked a little bit like Elvis in the early days. He must remember this expression, he thought, and use it when he was singing a love song on the talent show.

Bridget was also having problems in the romance department. From time to time she fished John Kelly's phone number out of her pocket and told herself to call him right away, but of course she couldn't do it. She was still haunted by the events surrounding her parents' death, and afraid that John was just feeling sorry for her when he brought her those fabulous flowers and asked her out.

And she didn't like his job, either. She would worry about him far too much when he was on night duty down the Falls Road or the Shankhill. Bridget had no faith in the endurance of the human spirit. The first sign of trouble, she feared, and most people buckled under the strain. She had enough to do looking after herself. Never mind worry about John Kelly on the mean streets of Belfast after dark. And so John's phone number stayed in Bridget's pocket, becoming slightly more tattered and torn each day.

In her spare time, she wrote little cards and notes to her sisters in London, and signed them with lots of tiny kisses and love hearts.

LIAM BRADLEY WAS SETTLING in well to his comfortable suite in the hotel. The new mattress was much better than the old one, and a few expensive dinners had put the lining back on his stomach. The check for half a million pounds had cleared into his account, and he hadn't heard from Betsy or her interfering brothers since before Christmas. Perry Shaw was handling all the PR for *Boom, Boom,* and Liam hadn't been contacted for a single interview. His life had been looking quite sweet until he turned on the television one lunchtime, expecting to see a sentimental film of some kind, but instead getting the shock of his life. There was a picture of Lily and Jack Beaumont and the four nutty barmaids, taken at one of the Christmas parties. And there was some footage of Vincent Halloran, too, coming out of his Dublin office and waving at the cameras. Nobody could say if the great shopping mall project was going ahead yet: the Beaumonts had still not decided whether to sell. But the news station had discovered that Vincent Halloran was secretly hiring lots of extra workmen and booking up accommodation for them around Belfast. Every day, the newscaster said, the tavern on Maple Street was bombarded by local journalists and businessmen, all wanting to know what was happening. But the owners remained tight-lipped about their decision as the last few days to the deadline ticked away.

Liam felt restless and jittery as he paced backward and forward across the moss-green carpet in room 401. If the tavern were sold, where would the lovely Lily go? He might never see her again. Time was running out. He had emptied the minibar, so he tidied himself up and went down to the bar to think matters over. Several times after that, during the following days, he wandered across town to Maple Street, but he couldn't go in. He didn't just fancy Lily now, he realized with a heavy heart. He loved her. He had actually fallen in love with a woman for the first time in his life.

On the second-last day of February, Liam woke up in a grim mood of determination, and got dressed in his best suit and designer sunglasses. He drank until the hotel barman refused to serve him any more, and then fell into a taxi he'd kept waiting outside. The car dropped him off at the end of the cobblestones on Maple Street, and he went staggering down the alley to whatever fate had in store for him. He didn't know what he would say or do, as he pushed open the front door and went in. He was going to wing it, like Slinger Magee always did.

Unfortunately, Jack was the one standing behind the counter. Lily was upstairs, fretting in the kitchen. They were almost ready to call Vincent and tell him what they were going to do, and either way, it was going to be a very emotional time.

"Where is the lovely Lily today?" Liam

wanted to know, as he ordered a double vodka and Coke. His eyes were swimming in his head and his legs were shaking underneath him.

"I think you should have a coffee, mate," said Jack quietly, not wanting to embarrass the author in front of the other customers.

"I beg your pardon?"

"You heard me, Mr. Bradley. You've had enough to drink."

"Kindly serve what I ordered, there's a good man. I'll decide when I've had enough."

"No. Sorry now, sir. It's for your own good. You were carried out of here once before."

"Okay. Well, is Lily in the building? I wish to say goodbye to her. I'm leaving Belfast." Right, let's see what he does now, thought Liam. He can't refuse to let me say goodbye to Lily.

"I'll see if my wife is busy," said Jack. "Excuse me."

Liam waited for ten minutes until Lily came in through the hall door, closely followed by her watchdog husband. She seemed reluctant to speak to Liam, although he couldn't think why. He wanted to tell her that she had been the inspiration for his second novel, and that he was in love with her.

But he couldn't make his big speech with Jack standing there. He wished the landlord would go and change a barrel or something. The man had had Lily all to himself for years. It was time he set her free to become the muse of the world's best writer. World's best author, he corrected himself.

"You're leaving us, Mr. Bradley?" Lily said brightly, as Jack scowled in the background. "Going anywhere nice?" She offered to shake hands.

"Yes," he said softly. "I'm going to live in the Bahamas. You don't fancy running away with me, do you?" he whispered, as he held onto her hand and then kissed it.

"Oh, now," she said. "You're a proper caution! What would Jack say!"

"I mean it," he said. "I'm in love with you. Surely you knew that?"

"Mr. Bradley!"

"Please call me Liam."

"Pull yourself together, for heaven's sake, Liam. Why don't you stop drinking, eh? And you with such a great career, and all. Come on, now, settle your head."

"I mean it, Lily, I want you to come with me. I'm going to the Bahamas and buy a beach house there. Imagine you and me together, walking hand in hand along the shore." But Lily pulled her hand away from his trembling grasp and stepped briskly back.

"Jack," she said. "Mr. Bradley is leaving now."

"Lily, I love you."

But Jack was at his elbow and marching him toward the door.

"I love you, Lily!" Liam shouted out, and Jack gasped with shock.

"Go home, and have some dignity," Jack said roughly, as he pushed Liam out onto the cobbles. He was itching to punch him a few times, but then he remembered that Liam was very drunk indeed and probably didn't mean what he said. And also, Jack didn't want to end up in a police cell again. But then, Jack's long-dormant temper got the better of him, and he chanced one good swing at Liam Bradley's chin. Liam's sunglasses went flying as the blow reverberated up and down his spine. Jack shook his head sadly and went back inside, slamming the door behind him. Well, that was it, he thought. He was more than ready for a break from the hospitality industry now.

Liam, stunned and badly shaken, took a

few steps backward before tripping and falling heavily against one of the metal dumpsters. He cut his ear on a bolt, and ripped the back of his suit on a piece of glass. What a fiasco, he thought. He was only in the damn place a few seconds altogether. And now he was cut and bleeding, and Jack Beaumont hadn't even given him the satisfaction of beating him up properly. One single thump was all he could manage, and Jack hadn't even waited to see the other man go down. How humiliating! Liam lay on the ground for a few minutes, waiting for Lily to come out and apologize for her husband's behavior. And maybe kiss him better. Liam didn't wipe away the drips of blood that were running down his neck, hoping he would look much more masculine with a bleeding wound. But the front door of the pub remained closed.

Liam sighed heavily before pulling his mobile phone out of his pocket. Luckily, it was still working. He could phone the police and have Jack Beaumont arrested. He could phone the press and make a bit of a splash. But he couldn't be bothered with either option. He was lonely, he realized with a lurch of panic in his heart. He dialed Betsy's number in desperation. Betsy would come and collect him, he knew, and probably take him home to Marlborough Avenue for a while, and make him feel better. A farewell spot of kitchen-counter copulation might even be in the cards.

But when Betsy answered the phone, she only said, "I'm sorry, Liam, but I don't think it would be a good idea for us to see each other."

"Betsy, I'm hurt."

"What happened?" she sighed.

"Jack Beaumont hit me."

"So you were after his wife? I knew it."

"Come on, Betsy, I need a lift," he pleaded.

"Where's your car?"

"I'm pissed, for God's sake, woman. It's at the hotel."

"You may walk it, then," she said.

"Don't you want to see me?"

"No. I don't."

"Not even for a goodbye shag? For old times' sake," he quipped hopefully.

"Bog off, Limo," Betsy said, and she hung up.

23

THE STAR
OF THE SHOW

"EVERYBODY, STAND OVER THERE," said Lily, loading film into her camera. It was the last day of February 2005, the day when they would give Vincent Halloran their final answer. He was calling round in half an hour to hear the news, good or bad. The tavern was closed to the public for the occasion. Everyone was sure that Lily and Jack were going to sell but there was always a chance they would change their mind.

"I want to take a picture of everyone."

"You mean us, too?" asked Barney, peering out of the booth.

"Of course." She smiled at them.

"Oh now," muttered Joey, smoothing down his old jacket. "The shape of us."

"Speak for yourself," said Francy Mac, already on his feet.

"Good man, Francy," said Lily. So, Barney, Joey and Francy Mac lined up neatly on one side of the huge brick fireplace, and gave their best smiles for the camera. Daisy, Trudy, Bridget and Marie stood on the other side in a little huddle. Daisy did her best to look smaller, leaning in a bit, so she wouldn't be towering over the others. Bridget had her hands clasped tightly together, and Marie and Trudy had their arms around each other for moral support. Despite the long working hours and the constant tiredness, something special had happened in the tavern over the Christmas holidays. The nine people present had become a family of sorts, and even Francy Mac could feel the emotion fizzling in the air around them.

"Come on, the two of you," laughed Barney.

"We need the stars of the show," said Joey. For once, Francy Mac was lost for words.

Lily set the timer on the camera and then she and Jack took their places in the center. They stood in front of the dancing flames in the hearth and held hands.

"Say cheese!" said Jack, laughing. The flash bulb popped, and the moment was captured forever.

WHEN VINCENT HALLORAN came into the tavern, he knew that his magnificent plans would go ahead after all. There was a light feeling in the air: a shifting of atmosphere that told him his luck was in. Jack came out from behind the counter and shook his hand warmly. And Lily was smiling and laughing, and much more animated than last time. He wasn't to know that Lily's nerves were actually in tatters: she was scared stiff of moving out of the only home she had known all her adult life. But she did not want the twin responsibilities of caring for the Lavery mural and causing the other traders to lose their compensation money. And she was exhausted with all the catering and serving and domestic dramas. She kept telling herself that in a couple of months she would be enjoying herself in Paris, and she would have Jack all to herself again. And even that image made her uneasy because she had never been on a plane before.

"I hope the news is good," Vincent boomed. "Have you an answer for me? I can't wait any longer, I'm afraid. It's now or never."

"Well, then, yes," she said, in a breathless rush. "If the offer still stands, we are ready to accept."

"Excellent," he almost roared. "I knew you would! Fair play to you."

"It wasn't an easy decision," Lily added.

"I'm sure, I'm sure," Vincent agreed, his face beaming.

"And we haven't told anybody about you-know-what," whispered Lily, pointing at the ceiling. They had all agreed to keep the fragment of mural a secret, and let Vincent Halloran deal with the official fallout when the time came. As he had pointed out to them during the Boxing Day meeting, he had a lifetime of experience dealing with bureaucrats and bureaucracy. Bridget had been warned to be extra careful in the sitting room at all times, and they had moved her bed right into the middle of the room, where she would be less likely to damage the walls.

"Good, that's very good." Vincent was rubbing his hands together with joy, even though his wife had advised him not to do that because it made him look like a Dickensian pickpocket.

"In the end, that's what convinced us," Lily said. "It wasn't the money. It was the painting. We couldn't just leave something like that hidden away behind the wallpaper forever." Lily thought wistfully of the possibly great artwork waiting to be uncovered in her sitting room. She'd been so tempted, many times, to uncover it herself, but knew she must leave it to the experts. And that meant waiting until the mall was completed. They didn't want someone from the government poking their nose in and spoiling everything at this stage. Maybe taking over the tavern with a court order, and delaying work on the mural for several years until a satisfactory procedure had been worked out. When the time came to reveal it to the world, Lily and Jack were to say they had no idea it was ever there.

"Will we go upstairs and sign on the dotted line?" Vincent asked, eager to press ahead.

"Oh, it's a bit of a mess at the moment," said Lily. "What with the girls packing up their things and so on. We'll use this booth here by the clock, shall we?"

"Right you are," Vincent said. The three of them went in and sat down.

The old men and the barmaids exchanged looks of resignation. Somehow, they'd thought Lily would pull out of the agreement at the very last minute. But Lily had decided she loved her husband more than she loved the tavern. And Jack was looking forward to a rest.

"Now, you have put it in writing for us? That you'll preserve the tavern?" Jack asked quietly. "We must have assurances on that, or else we can't go through with this deal."

"Oh yes, I've had my best lawyers sorting it out. The mall will be built around this wee place, and it'll be very well protected during the construction. I wouldn't pull a dirty trick such as pretending the pub got leveled in an accident. Not after the money I paid for it, anyway. The new design has been approved already. They love it, in fact, at the Planning office. Here you are, now. I have the papers." He snapped open his briefcase and slid a fat document across the table toward them.

"Just sign there, and there, and there." He handed a new pen to Jack, and held his breath.

"Do it quickly, Jack, before I break down,"

whispered Lily. Jack printed his name out in a small, neat hand, and Lily signed hers with a curly flourish. Vincent immediately handed them the check, and they all shook hands a few times.

"Don't spend it all in the one shop," he advised, with a wink.

"Don't worry, we won't," said Lily.

"When do you think I can have the keys?" Vincent said.

"In two days, as soon as the check clears. No offense," said Jack.

"None taken, Mr. Beaumont. Just drop them into the Belfast office when you're ready. I'll send a couple of security boys round the minute you move out. To keep an eye on the place until we get the protective scaffolding up. Good luck to you, then. I'll see myself out."

"And you won't let the mural get damp, will you?" Lily said.

"No, I won't. I'll look after it, you have my word on that."

When he had gone, Lily and Jack hugged each other, and Lily allowed herself a few self-indulgent tears.

"Well, that's it," she said. "It's over."

"Yes. I suppose it is. I hope Great-uncle

Ernest forgives me for this," Jack sighed. "Do you think he's looking down on us?"

"Oh Jack, do you think we've done the right thing?" squeaked Lily with her hands up to her mouth. "I'm terrified. Maybe we should have stayed on?"

"Lily, we've been over all this. It was getting too much for us."

"But Barney and Joey and Francy Mac? And the girls?"

"Shush, now," he soothed. "Barney and chums won't be here forever. And sure, the girls were only here temporarily. One day, we'd have been on our own again, with a valuable artwork to look after, and we're not getting any younger."

"Yes, but what will we do if we miss the tavern? Or if Vincent has lied to us, and knocks the place down and then tells us it just fell apart or something?"

"He won't do that. He showed us the new design. He reckons it will look even better than the original idea. "

"What if he deliberately destroys the mural, in case the government tries to get involved?"

"Sweetheart, it's only a Lavery. Not a Picasso canvas, or a da Vinci fresco."

"Jack! How can you say that? Lavery was a wonderful painter."

"You know what I mean. If it isn't worth millions and millions, they'll be happy for Vincent to restore it and look after it."

"Are you sure?"

"Yes," he said, beginning to worry.

If Lily changed her mind now, he didn't know what he would do. It was hard enough for him to let the old place go, without Lily having a breakdown at the thought of leaving Maple Street. He tried a bit of emotional manipulation: he knew Lily had a lifelong devotion to the concept of angels.

"You know what?" he said, doing his best to appear inspired. "I think our guardian angel planned it this way."

"What?"

"Look at it this way, Lily. Great-uncle Ernest must have been inspired by angels to leave me this pub, in order to rescue the two of us in our hour of need. And now it's time for us to move on, and do other things with our lives. And that is why accident-prone Bridget found the mural, so the tavern would be saved from demolition. And so that Vincent Halloran would greatly increase his offer to us. The million quid was mostly to pay for our silence about the Lavery painting, of course. But the upshot is, we're financially secure for life. And if you hadn't been an art lover and recognized the signature on the wall, I would have ripped off all the paper and maybe destroyed the entire thing. So you see, everything came together like the pieces of a jigsaw."

"Mmm," Lily mused. "That's quite a complicated plan for an angel to come up with. Why didn't we just win the Lotto?"

"Because . . . because this way, we'll have to leave Maple Street to get the money! And this way, we'll get to do all the things we never had time to do before."

"Like visit Paris?" She was calming down.

"Yes, Paris. And Rome, New York, Venice, Sydney, Iceland, anywhere. We can live anywhere we like, when we've finished traveling. We can buy another pub near the seaside. Or just retire in a little apartment somewhere, do a spot of voluntary work, read books. Lily, we'll have the kind of life that everyone in the whole wide world dreams about having. We'll be free!"

"Yes, you're right," she said. "Come on, let's say our goodbyes to everyone. It's not fair to keep them hanging around."

24

HERE'S TO OLD FRIENDS

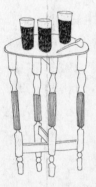 IT TOOK LIAM BRADLEY weeks to get over the shame of what had happened to him on Maple Street. That Jack Beaumont was nothing more than a knuckle-dragging caveman, he ranted to the bartender at his hotel. And Lily had turned out to be surprisingly cold, too. A real cold fish. Somehow, Liam had the idea she would be tearing her blouse off within seconds of him kissing her hand, caressing her own breasts and licking her own lips with desire. But his sweetest fantasy had come crashing to an ugly halt,

as he lay dazed on the cobblestones. Perhaps he was watching too many X-rated movies these days? he wondered. It seemed that all women were not nymphomaniac floozies after all.

Even daft old Betsy Trotter didn't want him anymore. Poor ignorant Betsy, who wouldn't know a book of poetry from a slap in the beak, had hung up the phone on him. She'd actually told him to bog off. It was unbelievable. And after her taking a luxury house off his hands, too, in the settlement. She could have spent one measly night with him, just to say thank you. Women could be a hard lot, he consoled himself. Liam decided he was better off without them. And that wasn't the end of the disappointment, either. It was only the beginning of it, in fact.

Liam Bradley went on a weeklong drinking binge in the middle of March, when he heard that Perry Shaw stood to make no less than four million pounds from the manuscript of *Boom, Boom.* And Perry didn't even have the decency to tell Liam the earth-shattering news himself. Oh no. Liam had to hear it secondhand from a bookseller on Royal Avenue: a lovely girl called Maria who worked as a buyer for one of the major bookstores. Her company had already placed a huge order for *Boom, Boom,* she told him when he went in to buy a newspaper, and just happened to bump into her beside the tills. Perry had sold the Slinger franchise to a string of filmmakers around the world.

Of course, Liam was straight on his mobile to Perry, but Perry's number had been changed, and nobody who knew Perry would tell him what the new number was. It seemed that Perry's days of being polite to Limo Bradley were over.

Liam lost track of two days completely, drowning his sorrows in anything and everything he could get his hands on. He was heard singing loudly to himself in his room at midnight by the other guests: "Anarchy in the UK," by the Sex Pistols. And the manager politely asked him to leave the hotel at the end of the week. Liam woke up in the bath on the day he moved out. The water was stone cold and there was a bloated ham sandwich floating in it. Slinger Magee would have been proud of such a sorry scene.

Then, as if things were not desperate enough, Perry Shaw became a national hero when he donated three million pounds of his *Boom, Boom* windfall to a benevolent fund for retired and injured soldiers. Oh, the injustice of it! The money that should have been Liam's to squander on expensive wine and cheap women went to buy false limbs for amputees and boring things like that. Perry did the rounds of the daytime sofas, and everyone in the country knew his name and saluted him. More money began to pour in from well-wishers, and Perry promised to set up a retirement home for widowed soldiers, a retraining center for the disabled and a comfortable and homely trauma-counseling suite as well. It was sickening. Liam's name was hardly mentioned.

A few days after that, Perry's beloved son lost half his foot in a shooting raid and was sent home to a tumultuous welcome. Mrs. Shaw came off the tranquilizers and the entire family circle gathered in London for a big celebration. Liam was not invited. It was the final insult.

Liam Bradley packed his bags and headed for the airport, to catch the first flight to somewhere warm that sold cheap liquor. He would sort out his emigration to the Bahamas when he had calmed down enough to fill out the forms. Belfast had lost its appeal for Liam altogether now, no matter what his fans would say about it. It had come to something when party-pooping wimps like Lily and Jack Beaumont and their idiot staff, and Betsy Trotter and her miserable money-grabbing relatives, were having a better time of it than was an author of Liam's caliber. He closed the little blind on his window as the plane took off, and asked the pretty hostess for a brandy and ginger, no ice.

BETSY TROTTER'S TENNIS CLUB was a great success. The bank manager lent the start-up money right away, when he found out she had a house to sell in the best part of town. Despite her selfish motives for setting it up in the first place, she found she enjoyed herself just as much as the other players did. She enrolled sixty-five paying pupils on the opening day in April, at the old rugby grounds on the Ormeau Road. And seventy-two non-paying children and teenagers as well. A couple of local papers turned up for the launch. Only minor papers, but it was a start. Her nieces and nephews decided not to bother going to the modest launch party, still sulking over the goats-for-Christmas affair. But Betsy didn't mind. The club was for ordinary people like herself: people who just wanted to improve their lives a little bit. She received a message of support from Sir Cliff Richard, and some signed rackets from several celebrity players, and she was beside herself with happiness. The start-up fees paid for her to hire a tennis coach, a nice-looking lad from Eastern Europe.

She became very fit as a result of all the extra exercise, and she found that concentrating on other people made her a much more content person. A few days after the tennis club opened, she received several letters from wealthy ex-wives across the country; they wanted to follow her example and set up their own projects. Betsy had to try very hard indeed to suppress that side of her personality that urged her to run to the hairdresser's and get her blond hair extensions back. Instead, she was completely professional about the entire matter, sending out business plans and cost estimations. By the time she was finally nominated for an award, she found such things didn't matter to her anymore. And when she heard on the grapevine that Richard Allen had proposed to some girl called Sarah Jones, she wasn't even a bit bothered.

*   *   *

AT THE END of the summer, demolition of the other buildings on Maple Street got under way but by then the tavern was tightly wrapped up in a protective shell of scaffolding and tarpaulin sheets. Lily and Jack's big brass bed was in storage, along with all their antique dishes and plates, but the stove was cleaned up and left where it was in the little kitchen. When the mall was completed and the tavern safely preserved inside, like an insect in amber, Vincent Halloran would reveal the long-lost Lavery mural to the general public, and reopen the tavern as a tourist attraction. He had already paid a couple of retired art restorers to uncover one wall, and they had discovered a beautiful collection of portraits of nineteenth-century drinkers, dancers, singers, servants, ladies and gentlemen painted right onto the plaster in beautiful shades of blue, gray and red. And then preserved in pristine condition because the owner's wife didn't like the work when it was finished and had it promptly papered over. Fortunately, her lack of good taste had been worth a fortune to Jack and Lily.

A series of cleverly positioned floodlights would shine down onto the tavern from the ceiling of the mall, and Vincent knew it would

win a string of design awards for its original-
ity. He felt he had done the right thing in al-
tering his designs for the mall, even though
he had lost most of his profits by doing so.
But then he landed a huge contract to build
more historically sympathetic shopping centers across Europe. He was so pleased he
decided to treat himself and his wife to a
weekend shopping trip in New York. Judy resigned, with her two-thousand-pound bonus
safely banked, and headed for the airport
with a jumbo bottle of sun cream, a trashy
paperback and a red bikini.

TRUDY AND GERRY completed their counseling program, and decided to carry out a year
of charity work before settling down to a long
engagement in Gerry's lovely apartment. If
they were still enjoying each other's company by then, of course. But they both had a
feeling they would be. Gerry got his old job
back in the hospital and Trudy finished her
geography degree, graduating with the high-
est honors. Which came in very handy in the
end, as they set off for Peru at the end of
June with nothing but two rucksacks and
one double sleeping bag. And a check for
ten thousand pounds that Lily and Jack had

given to Trudy as a going-away present. Trudy's parents were outraged that she didn't invite them to her graduation ceremony in the university, but she said what was the point in them flying over from Birmingham, when her old friends Lily and Jack were only up the road?

Her worries about buttons and dirty hands and the darkness faded away, too. And she realized with a surge of happiness as she sat on the plane with Gerry, that she had drunk a glass of lemonade with three slices of lemon in it at the graduation party, and never even noticed.

THE BEAUMONTS BOUGHT Betsy Trotter's townhouse in Marlborough Avenue, on their return from a dream holiday in Paris. They retrieved their beautiful brass bed from the storage depot, along with all their other things, and had great fun moving in.

The neighbors were delighted to see the back of Liam Bradley, and welcomed Lily and Jack into their social circle with a small tea party in the front garden of the house next door. Lily was having the time of her life making full use of Betsy's designer kitchen. Jack had taken up painting and was proving quite a talent, himself. Just before she left for Peru, Lily baked Trudy a celebration cake with a marzipan scroll on the top, and Jack put her picture in the *Belfast Telegraph* with a banner underneath reading, *Congratulations, Trudy!*

Then it was time to plan their next holiday. They decided to go to Australia. Lily said she would like a few weeks to rest before they set off for Sydney, and Jack said that was okay by him, and he bought another few tubes of paint and a big stack of canvases and brushes.

DAVID DEVANEY went to London on his own, to enter the talent competition, and got through to the final. He didn't win but he got a recording contract. The leather trousers were ditched by then, in favor of a lovely striped cream suit and matching tie that Daisy had picked out for him. They were still friends, and phoned each other every few weeks to catch up. Daisy bought a small cottage on Larkspur Avenue, using her ten thousand pounds from Lily as a deposit. She took in two other lodgers to pay the mortgage, and they were all the best of friends in no time.

* * *

MARIE AND MICHAEL found jobs on a cruise ship, and were allocated a pretty little cabin with two portholes. Marie worked as a pastry chef and Michael was a bartender. He could pick up his guitar and sing at a moment's notice, so that was a terrific bonus. And of course, Marie was multilingual, which was very handy considering the flocks of tourists they met each week. Marie had also received a fat check from the Beaumonts as a parting gift, and she gave it straightaway to her poor parents, who were going stir-crazy in the B&B in Rosetta. They used the money to rent a small chip shop with a flat above it in Portavogie, and Marie sent them postcards from all over the world. They pinned the cards to the walls of the chip shop and told all their customers how proud they were of their eldest daughter, Marie.

BRIDGET O'MALLEY went to visit her sisters in London and stayed on with them for a few months. She found a job working in a local bar, which she assured Lily was only temporary. She would find something better any day now, she told Lily, over the phone. And she was very grateful for the check, she kept saying. It was far too good of Lily, after all the damage Bridget had caused during her stint as head barmaid and cocktail waitress. She should be giving Lily ten grand, not the other way around, she said.

"Not at all," said Lily, with great gusto. Only for Bridget half-wrecking the tavern on Maple Street and finding the Lavery, they wouldn't have the money to give her in the first place. They were happy as could be in their beautiful townhouse with all their stuff out of storage, and the place was looking lovely. Jack could finally open his eyes fully without having them irritated by a fog of cigarette smoke, and he was slowly filling up the walls of the townhouse with his colorful paintings. They missed the old place, surely, but they could go and visit it when it was re-opened to the public as a Lavery-theme museum and café.

Lily asked Bridget if she had ever thought of giving John Kelly a call. And Bridget said no, she didn't think she was ready to take on another man yet, and probably John had forgotten her anyway.

"Well, you take care of yourself, now, pet, and call us anytime you fancy a chat. All right?" Lily said.

"All right. Love you," said Bridget.

"Love you, too," said Lily.

Jack knew by the expression on Lily's face when she put the phone down that her meddling days were not over yet. And he said she must do what she had to do, as long as she didn't involve him in her scheming. Lily duly got in touch with John Kelly and gave him Bridget's address in Isleworth. He got on the next plane, and picked up an engagement ring at the airport.

When Bridget saw him standing at the bar of the Irish pub where she worked, she burst into tears. She thought of her picture of the Sacred Heart, and of her lucky pebble, too. And wondered which of them had helped her to land this lovely man. And then John proposed, getting down on one knee on the dusty floorboards as the teatime customers applauded.

"You're crazy," she laughed, as she accepted his impulsive gesture.

"Not at all," he said. "I fell in love with you the first time I saw you, but it wasn't the right time to say anything."

"Is that really true?" she asked, tears streaming from her big blue eyes. "Or are you just being nice?"

"It's true," he said. "I told Steven Butterworth that very day I had fallen in love with you. Ask him if you don't believe me. He's going to be our best man, by the way."

"This is fabulous," she said. "But I insist on paying for the wedding. As it happens, I've just come into a bit of money. But I'd like it to be pretty low-key? Just my sisters and a few close friends?"

"Fantastic! That's just fine," he said. "We'll get married anyhow you like."

"I don't want to go back to Belfast, though."

"Okay, I'll move over here and join the London force. I love you, Bridget O'Malley. What else can I say?"

"You don't need to say anything else," she said. "I've been waiting to hear those words all my life."

And Barney? He continued to while away his days reading books and smoking his pipe beside the turf fire, but not in his old booth in the tavern. That had been Barney's big idea the day the pub was sold: he'd suggested the three old friends move in together. Sure, they'd spent most of their time sitting in Beaumont's anyway. And did it mat-

ter where they were, as long as they had a
bit of company?

Himself, Joey and Francy Mac left their little back-to-back houses in the heart of the
city and moved to a tiny village just outside
Bangor. Lily Beaumont had bought a
thatched cottage there with a view of the
ocean, and the three old men became her
tenants. It was a good investment, she said,
and they could have it for as long as they
needed it. It was a bit embarrassing, three
old guys living together, they thought, when
they moved in with their few bits and pieces.
But nobody in the locality bothered them;
and what was the point in soldiering on
alone in this world when you didn't have to?
And wasn't it lucky the cottage had three
bedrooms, they told the milkman, and also
the man who delivered the turf, and the post-
man, too. Just to make sure there were no
misunderstandings on that score.

Joey took up fishing, and Francy Mac
bought a springer spaniel pup to keep him
company on his rambles along the beach.
They took it in turns to make the dinner, and
Lily arranged for a local woman to come in
once a week with a can of polish and keep
things shipshape.

"Wasn't it lovely of Lily and Jack to remember us when they sold up and moved out of Maple Street?" said Barney one day as he looked out to sea from the sitting room window. "It's a grand thing to end your days with a view like this, amid good friends and with a decent landlord."

"Aye," agreed Joey. "It was, surely to God. I wonder who the eejit was that covered over the lovely painting in the first place?" Lily and Jack had let their dearest friends in on the big secret. "Although I suppose it kept the artwork from fading?"

"God rest their soul and I hope they're in heaven," said Barney. "Who's for a can of stout?" The other two nodded and he poured them one each. They had decided to become healthier, now that they were living in the country, and they had reduced their stout consumption drastically. But still, on summer evenings like this, when the seagulls were wheeling across the bay and there were a few sailboats bobbing on the waves, there was nothing sweeter than a sip of stout and an hour of gentle conversation by the fire.

"Here's to Lily and Jack," said Barney, raising his glass. "And their generosity."

"And here's to the tavern on Maple

Street," said Joey. "May she still be standing firm, long after we are gone."

"Indeed," added Francy Mac, patting the dog's head. "But I hope we don't kick the bucket for a good while yet." They all laughed at that. "Cheers!"